PRICKLY ROMANCE
BILLIONAIRE DADS BOOK 5

NIA ARTHURS

COPYRIGHT

This is a work of fiction. Similarities to real people, places or events are entirely coincidental.

PRICKLY ROMANCE
Copyright © 2022 Nia Arthurs
Written by Nia Arthurs
Edited by Jalulu Editing
Cover Design by GetCovers

PROLOGUE

SAZUKI

Blinding streaks of light blast through the windshield, spinning crazily as the car careens across the road.

In the driver's seat, Akira fights for control of the steering wheel.

A sickening crunch fills the air just as my entire body rattles.

The car falls still.

"Are you alright?" Akira asks, looking over her shoulder at me.

I nod.

Behind us, doors open and slam shut. Moments later, my protection team surrounds the car.

"I am fine," I say, calming them before they can ask.

"I did not expect a deer to come running across the road." Akira takes out her phone. "The car is damaged and you do not seem well. I will let Alistair know we cannot attend the gala."

I ease out of the car, ignoring my aching neck caused from whiplash. "I gave my word. I must be at the gala tonight."

Akira seems displeased, but she makes the call.

On the way to the event, I bend my fingers and release.

There is no pain.

Not even an ache.

But I am still on edge when I take the elevator and even as we walk closer to the banquet hall.

What would I have done if my hands were injured?

The sound of rich, decadent notes lures me from my thoughts. I stop in the middle of the hallway to listen. The player is not well-versed and yet there is something about the way they interpret the song. It is infused with feeling, a raw, unvarnished composition that's as arresting as it is unsettling.

"Sir?" My team is waiting for me.

I move into the banquet hall.

Inside, the beautifully dressed crowd is silent. All gazes are affixed to the woman on stage. She is small, dark, and pouring her heart out on the piano.

My piano.

As I watch her—eyes closed and face enraptured, my body recoils. It feels as though she is placing those hot, passionate fingers on my heart. I do not care for the way my pulse quivers. Nor do I care for the burn—a prickly sensation that reminds me I am more than the unfeeling man I have become.

My steps remain strong and sure as I storm to the front of the room along with my team.

At first, we are unnoticed. But it does not take long for a stir of whispers and startled eyes to catch sight of us.

I cross the stage.

My team forms a circle around me and the piano.

The woman's hands freeze on the black and white keys. She stares at me, fear written in the depths of her big brown eyes.

"W-who are you?"

I take a step toward her.

"What's going on?" Her eyes dart to my men. "Why are you up here?"

I still do not respond.

Panic crests her features. Face dainty and striking. Her fear twists something deep inside me. Brings all the shards of my broken heart to life.

But I do not want to feel.

And I resent her for being the one to kickstart what I thought was dead.

I plant one hand on the piano desk. The other, I set on the bench at her hip. She leans backward wearily. Her shaky retreat kicks up the hunter hidden in the depths of my soul. *Where do you think you can run, kitten?*

"Who gave you permission to touch my piano?" I ask aloud.

Her eyes get even bigger. I can see the anxiety flooding her. Drowning her.

Such innocence. Such naivety. A crushing force against my own jaded lens.

"They told me—"

"If you were going to force yourself somewhere you don't belong," I cut her off, "you should have at least put in more effort."

Her small shoulders heave and her eyes narrow. Anger slashes her brown mouth into a thin line.

I lean forward slightly. My fingertips brush over her hands. I am almost knocked back by the snap of energy that crackles from the touch.

This woman is dangerous. Fire.

I growl at her, needing to get her away from my piano. From me. Yet I cannot resist touching her.

Lifting her fingers, I warn, "Never place these hands on something they are not worthy enough to touch."

She snaps her hand back.

Rage radiates from her like heat waves that cling to the skin.

I motion to one of my men and they are quick to relocate the woman away from me. Even as the distance grows, the connection between us pulls and pulls.

I catch sight of her muttering curses at me before I pitch my eyes away.

Calmly, I take the seat in front of the piano.
She still lingers. Her scent. Her warmth.
A ghost in a T-shirt and jeans.
But I will not allow her to haunt me.

Uncontrollable feelings have wreaked their havoc on my life once before. I will not allow my heart—that has finally healed—to be destroyed twice.

CHAPTER 1
THE PIANO LESSON

DEJONAE

THERE ARE certain things you just don't do in life.

Like accompany your chai obsessed, supermodel best friend to sneak in a latte behind her husband's back.

Or drag her three-month old baby into a vicious middle school street fight.

Or immediately fall in love with a nine-year old ninja only to find out her dad is the devil himself.

But guess who did all three?

I lift a trembling finger as I stare down the man who single-handedly ruined one of the biggest nights of my life.

"You? *You're* her dad?" I croak.

"That is what I said," Ryotaro Sazuki responds in the world's most impatient tone.

If I could find a loose stone to throw at his face, I would.

Sazuki rips his gaze away from mine. Despite his gruff voice, his touch is gentle when he cradles his daughter's face.

I start making quick comparisons. Sazuki is tall and regal. Broad shoulders taper down to a lean waist. With his silky hair brushed back, his brown eyes and chiseled jawline reveal a chillingly sharp face. Even though he's dressed in a long-sleeved shirt and slacks, looking every bit the under-the-radar billionaire that he is, there's something cold and dangerous about him.

His daughter, on the other hand, is pure sunshine. Golden-brown skin, full, Cupid's bow lips, and long curly hair that reaches almost to her tail bone. The only hint of her mixed ancestry is in the shape and tilt of her stunning brown eyes.

This really is Sazuki's daughter.

I can't believe the Lord allowed this man to *procreate*.

Sazuki mutters something in Japanese and Niko seems to understand because she nods.

Turning slightly so the sun hits his formidable cheekbones, Sazuki grunts. "What happened here?"

My jaw drops at his rudeness.

Vanya pushes her stroller forward and sets a hand on my arm. "I got this."

She's way too calm. And I can only assume that being a new parent has given her inestimable patience.

"We were out for a stroll," Vanya begins, "and overheard some boys harassing someone in the alley. Dejonae ran off like Superwoman, and by the time I got here, the boys were on the ground and your daughter looked unharmed."

Baby Ollie starts cooing like she wants to give her eyewitness account.

Sazuki inhales a deep, measured breath. His nostrils flare and, with his eyes closed, he looks more intimidating than ever.

Sazuki's daughter glances up with a sheepish expression. She pokes her dad in the shoulder. Lips moving soundlessly, she signs, "How did you find me?"

"Akira." Sazuki scans her face. "You were supposed to meet her at the school gate."

Niko chews on her bottom lip and doesn't respond.

Abruptly, Sazuki turns to us. When his eyes meet mine, he frowns in distaste.

Glad to know the feeling is mutual, jerkface.

He dips his head, still looking annoyed. "Thank you."

"Deej did most of the rescuing." Vanya gives me a dazzling grin.

Sazuki seems unarmed by Vanya's smile, which is totally understandable. The plus-sized model is gorgeous. Vanya's been rocking fashionable clothes all through her pregnancy and that hasn't changed now that Ollie's joined us in the real world.

Today, she's wearing a flowing blue dress with a plunging neckline that shows off her cleavage. Her hair is slightly curled at the ends and brushes against her bare shoulders.

Sazuki finishes his little scan and then returns to scowling at me. "Thank you as well."

Wow. Growly much? "No need to thank me. I'm glad your daughter's okay." Bending slightly, I sign to Niko. "It was nice to meet you."

She grins, making her eyes collapse with happiness.

Sazuki's shock is hidden quickly. When he looks at me this time, it's with more than just disdain. He hesitates, mouth opening and closing before he comes to some kind of internal conclusion. Hands steady on Niko's shoulders, he steers his daughter away.

Niko stops him with a slight touch on his arm and I make note of how he leans down to watch her. One of my sister's biggest frustrations growing up was not being heard when she had something to say. I can tell that Sazuki and his daughter are close by how in-tune he is to her needs.

He's still a major douche-canoe.

But he's not a… horrible dad.

"I want her to come with me," Niko signs.

The scowl that crawls over Sazuki's face is ten times darker than before. "No."

Niko pushes out her bottom lip.

Vanya inches the baby stroller toward me and peers at the father-daughter duo. "What are they saying?"

"Niko wants one of us to go with them."

"Go where?"

"Don't know."

"And which one of us?"

"I'm not sure. She didn't specify."

Just then, Sazuki's sharp gaze swings to me and I swear, it's like he's *impaling* me with his eyes.

Vanya clears her throat. "I think I have an idea which one of us he *doesn't* want, but look... his daughter is pointing to you. I think she wants you, Deej."

"I'm not going anywhere with him."

"Why not? He's cute."

"Cute isn't the right word," I mutter. Sazuki's too sharp. Too angular. Too *intense.*

"You're right. Sexy is a better word, I think."

"Aren't you married?"

"What are you? The marriage police?" She snorts.

I scowl.

"Deej, I'm married. Not blind. And I'm not looking for me. I'm thinking of you. You and Sazuki can clear up whatever happened at the gala."

"I'm *never* forgiving him for what he did at the gala."

"What exactly did he do to you?" Vanya asks.

"Throwing me off his keyboard wasn't a big enough infraction for you?"

"I meant, what did he *say?*"

I shake my head. "All you need to know is that he's rude and obnoxious and not worth my time."

Niko's hands are still moving at warp speed. Sazuki watches intently.

"Did you know that Sazuki's daughter was deaf?" Vanya whispers while the two fight it out.

"I don't think anyone knew he *had* a daughter."

Vanya pulls the shade a little further over Baby Ollie, who's starting to fuss. "You know he comes from a line of super famous, super rich, super mysterious musicians, right?"

"I'm familiar with the Sazuki family," I respond dryly. Anyone with classical music training would have studied them at one point or another.

Vanya peers at Ollie. "I wonder if the reason Sazuki stayed out of the spotlight, maybe even the reason he's moving permanently to the US, has anything to do with his kid."

"It's none of our business either way." I bend over the stroller and coo, "Isn't that right, Ollie? Tell your nosy mama to butt out."

Vanya and Hadyn's three-month-old stops crying long enough to grant me a befuddled expression.

A sound of abject frustration comes from behind me. I check over my shoulder and see Niko pushing her dad my way. Sazuki's almost digging his feet into the sand to keep from coming over.

"I wonder why she wants you to go with her?" Vanya muses.

"Probably because I understand her."

"That simple?"

"Imagine how black travelers feel when they see another black tourist in a foreign country. It's like you know them and they know you even though you're strangers. The deaf community is kind of like that."

Vanya suddenly looks away. "Oh shoot. He's almost here. Act natural."

I roll my eyes.

Sazuki stops in front of us. He inhales a deep breath that fills his whole chest and then leaks out a resigned sigh.

"Are you busy?"

I keep my arms loose at my sides. "Yes."

"She's not. She's very un-busy." Vanya nudges me forward with her elbow.

I shoot a dark glare over my shoulder.

"*What are you doing?*" I hiss.

"Ollie's getting fussy. We'll head back home so I can put her down for a nap." Vanya juts her chin at Sazuki and Niko. Her long, dangling earrings brush against dark cheeks. "Go with them."

"What about chai?" I ask, knowing it's her weakness.

She hesitates but not for long. "We'll grab chai another time."

"I'm sorry." I frown at Sazuki because the last place I want to be is alone with him. Even if he comes with an adorable daughter. "I'm supposed to be Vanya's bodyguard. She gave birth a few months ago and she hasn't really recovered yet. I should make sure she gets home safely."

"That is fine with me," Sazuki says in his crisp accent. He tries to take his daughter's hand.

Niko pulls away, looks imploringly at me, and rubs a circle on her chest.

It's the sign for 'please'.

Must resist.

Must...

"Okay."

Niko jumps happily.

Vanya grins so wide I'm surprised her cheeks don't pop off her face.

"You'll pay for this," I whisper as I pass her by.

She winks and waves goodbye before she and Baby Ollie go traipsing in the opposite direction.

"What's your name?" Niko signs.

"Dejonae." I sign each letter slowly. "But you can call me Deej."

"Niko." She gestures.

"Pretty name," I answer with my mouth instead of my hands.

She beams, confirming her lip-reading aptitude.

We walk to Sazuki's fancy SUV. The thing is built like a tank. Sazuki opens the back door and gestures bluntly. His jaw is clenched and his eyes are on anything but me. The tension in his body suggests that he is not a fan of this plan.

You think I want to be here, you grumpasourus?

Although every bone in my body is telling me not to go anywhere with him, I climb in.

The car smells like him, minty and expensive. I'm surprised to find the passenger seat empty. The first time I met Sazuki, he had a small platoon of bodyguards following him around.

Niko scrambles in after me and locks the door. For a second, I have a mild panic attack.

What if this is their act?

What if they're a father-daughter team of con artists?

What if I'm their next victim?

Then I realize I'm being ridiculous. Sazuki is a billionaire with an incredible and extravagant family background. If he has to con poor college students for cash, then the entire world is doomed.

Niko slides into the seat right next to me. Her eyes are brilliant even though the light is dim thanks to the tinted windows.

"Where are we going?" I ask her, keeping my face turned to hers so she can read my lips easily.

She runs her fingers sideways, back and forth, as if there's a piano right in front of her.

I dance my fingers over imaginary keys. "Piano lessons? That's so cool."

Sazuki clears his throat. "Seatbelt, Niko."

She struggles with the belt and I lean over to clasp her in.

"Thank you," Niko signs.

"Welcome."

Sazuki starts the car before I've buckled up. I guess I know which one of our lives he values more.

Jerk.

"How do you know how to sign?" Sazuki growls at me.

I translate his question for Niko.

Her smile gets wider and she nods.

"My sister is deaf," I say out loud. "She's also a model." Well, an aspiring model. But being in the local Macy's catalogue totally counts in my books.

Sazuki makes a left turn. "Is that how you know Miss Beckford?"

"It's Mrs. Mulliez now and—" I realize I haven't translated his words for Niko and quickly rectify that. "Your dad asked me how I know my friend," I sign.

Sazuki glares at me. "She can see what I am saying."

"How?" My eyebrows pull tight. "She can't read your lips if you're driving and she's in the backseat."

I hear a *tap-tap* and drag my attention back to Niko. One sneakered foot is pointing to a screen that's embedded in the back of the chair. I hadn't noticed it when I slid into the car. The screen shows the lower half of Sazuki's face, starting at the bridge of his sharp nose, his small but full lips and ending at his chin.

"Whoa. Is that forwarding the feed in real time?"

"It is," Sazuki says.

Pulling out my phone to snap a picture so I can show Yaya later, I ask, "Who came up with that idea?"

"My dad," Niko signs.

It's too late to look unimpressed.

"Hm," I say, trying my best to reverse the ego-stroking.

Sazuki slows for a red light. His eyes meet mine in the rearview mirror. One corner of his lips hitches up in a ghost smile and...

Dimples.

Two of them.

My heart flails.

Dimples that big and cute do not belong on a man who looks like he could slay as the star of a samurai action movie.

I quickly glance away.

Get ahold of yourself, Dejonae.

My attention snags on Niko's comic book. I tug it from the middle of the chair. "What's this?"

She snatches it from me and hides it against her shirt.

Sazuki's half-grin fades, replaced with a parental look of censure. "Her favorite comic book."

"Let me guess." I tap my chin. "Echo?"

"What's Echo?"

"*Who's* Echo," I correct Sazuki. "She's a Marvel superhero."

"Superhero?" Niko signs.

"She's deaf and a great fighter." I frown, slightly perturbed by their confusion. "You don't know who Echo is?"

"No."

"But she's deaf."

"Am I supposed to know all the deaf superheroes?" Sazuki fires back.

"*I* do." I lift my chin proudly. "I searched them all up. It was important to me that my sister see how capable she can be."

"By introducing fictional characters to her?"

"You had better role models?"

"Chisato Minamimura. Ayumi Hamasaki." He pauses. "Even Beethoven."

"I actually recognize that one."

Niko giggles.

The ghost smile on Sazuki's face is fleeting. "We do not have to look to fictional creations for encouragement."

"I disagree. I don't think anyone should be limited by what's already been done. When we look at fictional characters, they aren't bound by physical rules or fear or even history. These heroes are the very essence of what someone can accomplish without limits."

"These 'heroes' are also not real," he insists.

"And Beethoven's dead. What's your point?"

"Yes, but he lived."

"And who's to say there's not a deaf crime-fighting ninja out there, kicking the butts of drug lords and kingpins? We don't know. Anything is possible."

Niko giggles and shyly slides the comic book over to me.

"*Last Game?*" I read the name on the cover. It's got a sketch of a couple holding hands. "This… wait, this looks like a romance."

Niko signs something I don't understand.

I scrunch my nose in confusion. "Can you say that again?"

She signs, "M-a-n-g-a."

"Manga?"

Her little head bob is both quick and adorable.

"I've told her to stop reading that trash," Sazuki mumbles.

Niko isn't even looking at the screen when she signs, "My dad calls it trash, but it's really good."

"You are not dating until you are married," Sazuki admonishes. "There is no need for such books."

I exchange a look with Niko.

The little girl rolls her eyes like she was raised by a black woman.

"Niko will return the book tomorrow." Sazuki lowers his head so both his eyes and mouth get caught on camera. "And you will apologize to Akira for making her worry."

Niko glances down, feeling the weight of her father's censure.

I decide not to take up for her in front of her dad. Anything I say probably won't help since Sazuki hates me anyway.

Instead, I slide the book back to Niko and sign, "Tell me all about your favorite stories. I'll check them out for you."

She brightens and bobs her head enthusiastically.

Sazuki watches me suspiciously through the rear-view mirror, but I smile innocently. This is between me and his daughter. What he doesn't know isn't going to hurt him.

* * *

"Hi, Niko!" An overly cheerful woman with big eyes, limp purple hair and a nose ring pops in front of us like an extra in a horror movie.

I launch back, yelping.

Niko's laughter peels out over the hollowed halls of Terrence Holler Music Academy.

It's a pretentious name for what is basically a rich people's after-school center.

Vaulted ceilings, chandeliers, and detailed wooden finishings remind me of an old church. The students are all wearing private school uniforms, complete with preppy skirts and sweater vests.

The adults look equally stuffy. My sneakers, crop top and high-

PRICKLY ROMANCE

waisted jeans are out of place amidst their sharp pencil skirts, pumps and panty hoses.

Who even wears panty hoses anymore?

Sazuki gives me a scolding look for yelling.

I curb the urge to stick my tongue out at him. He's lucky my parents raised me to be somewhat of a respectful member of society.

Purple Hair slants me a blank stare. "And you are?"

"She's my friend. Deej," Niko signs.

"I see." Purple Hair does not look impressed.

Sazuki wears his perpetually annoyed face when he says, "We apologize for the imposition. Niko insisted."

"I want her to stay," Niko signs.

Sazuki gestures to me. "I hope you do not mind if Miss Dajon—"

"It's Dee-jonae. Deej. Not Daj—"

"—If *this woman*," Sazuki cuts me off, "sits in on Niko's piano lessons."

Every muscle in my body tenses. *Did this man just cut me off?*

Niko grabs my arm and drags me down the hallway, saving Sazuki from—at minimum, a tongue lashing and at most, a swift kick in the groin.

We gain speed as we turn the bend. Niko's curly hair flairs behind her and, I can't lie, my inner child bursts out.

Musical instruments blare from every room. Violins, cellos and flutes. A cacophony of beautiful, musical chaos.

We skid to a stop in front of an empty room. The sounds bleed into silence. The room's got thick soundproof walls and lots of overhead lights. I inhale deeply, loving the scent of sheet music and instrument oil.

Niko shows off a grand piano. It looks exactly like the one Sazuki brought into the Belle's Beauty gala—the one he pushed my hand away from before he whispered in my ear and made everything inside me freeze.

"Is this yours?" I ask.

Niko grins, her head tilted and her eyes shining.

"Can you play?" I sign.

Niko takes the bench and pats the seat next to it.

When I start to move in, Purple Hair and Sazuki arrive.

"That's my seat!" Purple Hair blurts out before my butt can touch the cushion.

I freeze, mid-stoop.

"Sorry." Her puff of laughter lacks sincerity. Edging behind the music stool, she clasps her hands together. "The professional sits there. Not just anyone can teach, you know."

What is your problem?

"Right," I say coldly.

We exchange places. I stand behind Niko and her teacher, while Sazuki leans against the door and watches everything with his shrewd eyes.

"Niko," Purple Hair signs, "you remember what we did last week?"

Niko bounces her head.

"Let's begin."

The teacher sets the metronome on top of the piano desk. Leaning forward, she taps out the beat on Niko's leg while the little girl reads the music.

Niko plays expertly, hitting all the right notes. Unfortunately, she's a little behind the beat.

"No, no, no." Purple Hair shakes her head. "Niko, we've been over this. You need to *feel* the timing. *Feel* it."

Niko gives her a frustrated look.

"Let's go again."

Sazuki's phone rings while Niko and the teacher start from the top. He leaves the classroom to answer.

Free from his overwhelming presence, I start to relax.

Niko's light brown fingers sail across the keys. She's incredibly talented. There's a youthful, passionate expression to her music. She reminds me so much of my sister. Both of them are determined, talented, and capable of doing anything they set their minds to.

Niko hits a bad note. Her nose scrunch says she knows what she did wrong, but the teacher still points it out to her.

"You were supposed to go to A#," Purple Hair says with barely hidden annoyance.

Niko signs, "I know."

"She's probably nervous because I'm here," I say, trying to smooth it over.

"That is exactly why I don't allow visitors in class. She needs to focus and she can't play her best with an audience."

Keep quiet, Deej.

Don't start a fuss.

This isn't your place...

"She's going to have to play in front of an audience eventually," I argue.

Purple Hair swivels in her seat as if she'd been *waiting* for a chance to fight me. "Learning in front of an audience and performing in front of an audience are two different things."

"You have to start somewhere."

"Ma'am," Purple Hair speaks in her best, *I'm about to call your manager* tone, "if you can't remain calm and quiet during our session, I'm going to have to ask you to leave."

I scoff. Who exactly does she think she is?

Rather than let the tiger jump out of me, I glance at Niko and calm myself. After a deep breath, I respond in a similarly condescending manner.

"*Ma'am,* if you can't convey the point of your lesson without getting impatient and snappy at your student, maybe you should pursue a different line of work."

Red steals into her cheeks. Her eyebrows join in the center of her forehead. "Maybe you should learn to keep your mouth shut."

"What are you going to do if I don't?" I fire back.

Purple Hair half-rises from her chair.

Niko, sensing the tension in the air, turns too. Her beautiful eyes lock on my face. There's a wrinkle between her arched eyebrows and a tightness to her lips that signals discomfort.

She doesn't understand what's happening and we haven't been speaking slowly enough for her to read our lips.

A twinge of remorse hits my chest.

I shouldn't be starting fights in front of children.

Feeling slightly ashamed that I lost my temper, I bend to Niko's level. "It's okay, sweetie. Your teacher and I are just having a discussion about... Mozart."

Purple Hair flares her nostrils, but her voice is still that sickly-sweet tone. "Who exactly are you again?"

"I'm just a friend."

"Well, Miss *Friend*, are you a licensed music teacher?"

"No."

"And," her eyelashes flutter non-stop, "do you have a Bachelor's Degree in ASL?"

"No." I shuffle my feet.

"Then maybe you shouldn't speak on things you don't understand."

"Your methods are flawed. You shouldn't be so defensive when people point it out."

She gestures to Niko. "Since you're so full of advice, would you like to take my position?"

"I would actually."

Her eyes widen. She didn't expect me to agree.

Too bad.

I never back down from a challenge.

Ever.

I approach the piano. Purple Hair doesn't move out of the way at first and I have to wedge myself between her and Niko.

Niko shifts nervously. "I'm sorry I can't play it better," she signs.

"It's okay."

"Look, you're wasting our time—"

"Shush." I lift a hand at Purple Hair.

Her gasp of outrage barely penetrates my focus. While silence settles, I flip open my purse and search for the modified headphones I always carry around. Next, I pull out my phone.

"What are you doing?"

I ignore the question.

"Do you think she's going to hear anything on those headphones?"

I ignore that too.

"She's *deaf!*"

I sync the headphones with my cell and open the metronome app. The steady *tic-tic-tick* chants in my ear. *Good.*

Niko gives me an uncertain look when I slide the headphones over her ribs.

"Do you feel that?" I ask.

She pauses. Her eyes fall closed and I can sense the way she gets in-tuned to her body. After a few seconds, Niko nods.

"Good." I take her hand and set it on the piano. "Try again."

Niko plays with uncertainty. Purple Hair grins in delight when she falters. I pretend the aggravating woman isn't in the room and keep my hand on Niko's, coaching her through the music until she gets better at the timing.

"That's right." A smile inches over my face when she falls into the pocket of the rhythm. "Niko, that's perfect."

Niko's eyes light up and she gives me a hug. I wrap my arms around her back, squishing the headphones into her stomach by mistake.

She makes a pained grunt.

I wrench backward. "Sorry. Sorry."

She laughs and waves my apology off.

Plucking the headphones away, I turn to the teacher. "When one of our senses is impaired, we rely more heavily on the others. But what people often miss is that we also rely on our gut instincts. The spider-sense, if you will." I wave the headphones around. "You're tapping her leg to help her keep the time, but your timing is off."

"What?"

"You're playing a little ahead of the metronome."

Shame burns her cheeks red and she glances away.

"But even if you were directly on time, it can't replace *feeling*. Niko's got great instincts. Let her trust it."

Purple Hair huffs and opens her mouth to answer when a voice rumbles, "*Interesting.*"

We both turn around.

I'm shocked to see Sazuki standing in the doorway. He's watching me with hawk eyes.

I lick my suddenly dry lips. "How long have you been standing there?"

He stares me down, refusing to answer.

My cell phone chimes.

It's an alarm I set to remind me of my next class.

I jump to my feet. "I need to go."

Niko pouts.

"I have a graduation project I need to prepare for," I say apologetically to her. "But I'd love to hang out again."

Purple Hair gestures to the door. "Goodbye."

Jeez.

I stalk past Sazuki, but I'm not rude enough to leave without at least acknowledging him.

Careening to a stop, I tear off a piece of paper from the notebook in my bag and scribble on it. "This is my number if Niko wants to get in touch with me."

He takes the number without a word.

Okay then.

I smile at Niko once more, shoot another glare at Purple Hair—who returns it, and leave Sazuki behind.

It's strange, but I swear I feel his gaze burning into my back long after I'm gone.

CHAPTER 2
THE UNWANTED KEY

SAZUKI

"What am I watching?" Adam frowns at the cell phone that I stick in his face.

"Look at her."

"You brought me out here to boast about your new girlfriend?" He sounds annoyed.

I scowl.

He scowls harder and brings his coffee to his lips. "Spit it out, Sazuki."

"I think she is the missing link."

"Congratulations."

"Do you see it?"

"She's beautiful and she seems close to Niko." He yawns. "Why do you need my opinion before you date someone anyway? It's been years since your divorce. It's about time you moved on." He shakes his head and takes another big gulp of coffee.

I make a disapproving sound in my throat. "You misunderstand, Adam."

"About what? Her age? As long as she's legal, I don't have a problem with it."

"I'm not interested in dating her."

Adam gives me a disbelieving stare. "So you *don't* find her attractive?"

These Americans and their obsession with appearances.

"I am saying it is not the matter at hand."

He squints. "So you do find her attractive?"

I pause, choosing my words carefully. "Not the point."

"Hm." He leans back in his chair and stretches like a hibernating bear. "Why are you showing me a video of a college student teaching Niko to play piano?"

"Because of this." I play the video again, pausing at the part where Dejonae places the headphones on my daughter's stomach.

The sleep clears from Adam's eyes and he sits straight up in the chair. Mouth falling open, he whistles. "Did she just…"

"Use vibrations of the chest to improve Niko's timing? Yes." I tap my fingers on the café's smooth mahogany table, unable to restrain the nervous energy. "She modified her headphones to concentrate rhythmic energy. Somehow, the device was able to become a link between the music and the body."

"That's genius." He shakes his head. The wheels are turning rapidly in his brilliant mind. "How did she come up with that?"

"I believe this is the key we have been looking for."

He picks up the phone and starts the video over. This time, he studies it intently.

"Where did you find her?"

"In an alley." I pause. "But I first met her at the Belle's Beauty gala."

The phone almost drops out of his hands. "She's the girl who played your piano without asking?"

I nod.

"Will she want to work with you? I heard you laid into her pretty hard."

Rather than answer, I pick up the cup of tea that's still steaming and sip it. The matcha flavor hits my tongue, a mild version of the drink I enjoyed back in Japan.

Adam slides his elbow over the table and lowers his voice. "Be honest. Do you think you can get her to work with us?"

"I am certain of it."

He quirks a brow. "How certain?"

My eyes dart away from his. "About fifty percent."

"Not great odds."

"If all else fails, we can work around her. Reverse-engineer the idea."

"If she modified those headphones on her own, with no resources or access to our technology, imagine what she can do if she joins our team." Adam narrows his eyes. "Don't let your issue with her get in the way of business, Sazuki. There's a bigger picture here."

"I am aware," I growl. I have worked like a madman to get the foundation this far. I will not stand in the way of our mission.

His lips curl up in a smirk. "So you have a plan to convince the girl?"

"Ask nicely." I drum my fingers on the table again.

"And if that doesn't work?"

"Ask... less nicely." My tone is dry.

His smile gets bigger. "I'd love to be a fly on the wall when that conversation happens."

"Yes, well, knowing you, you'd build that fly and send the surveillance footage back to your horse farm."

He chuckles because he knows it is true.

Looking at him, one would never be able to tell that Adam is worth billions. Though he can afford to line his garage with Porches and Lamborghinis, Adam drives a pickup truck handed down by his grandfather. Today, he is dressed in a T-shirt with a hole in the sleeve and dusty boots.

"If all else fails, you can use your daughter to convince her," Adam says, pointing to the video where Niko is staring up at Dejonae in awe. "They seem to have a connection."

I frown. Niko is the reason I breathe, the reason I've left everything I know and love to live in a country that is not my own.

I would do anything for her.

But I refuse to use her for business.

"There is no need for that. Miss Williams will be mine. One way or another," I promise.

He peers at the video again. "I bet she'll give you a run for your money."

"I will take that bet."

"At five."

"Thousand?"

"Three more zeroes."

I chuckle. "You have money to waste?"

"I'd like to donate it to a worthy cause. Your foundation never looked for investors."

I steeple my hands. "We do not need outside money."

My personal accounts are enough to keep the foundation alive. In addition, the foundation is capable of creating its own revenue. I have everything in order.

"Money is still money, Sazuki. No sense turning your nose at it because it's coming from a country boy."

"It is not the money that makes me hesitate. It is the conditions that come with it. If you want to help, you can cut the strings."

"Scared?" Adam challenges.

I scoff. "I will acquire her cooperation in three days."

"I'm taking that deal."

We shake on it.

The door bursts open while we each lift our mugs. Adam straightens immediately, as if his body can sense his assistant's approach.

"Hide me," he whispers.

I shake my head.

We both glance away when Nova nears us. I've learned not to look her directly in the eyes when she is enraged. This way, I steer clear of most of the fire.

"You have a meeting in ten minutes," Nova says softly. Like *sobo*, my grandmother, she is quiet. Rarely ever raises her voice. Yet her flaring nostrils and the tense set of her lips communicates her wrath.

Adam slips out of the chair, arms raised. "I can explain."

"Oh?" Nova slaps a hand on her hip. Long braids slide over one shoulder as she stares frankly up at him. Her skin is dark, which makes the white of her eyes stand out even more. "Please do explain."

"Sazuki called me out of the house for an emergency meeting." Adam points.

I half-levitate out of my chair.

Such betrayal.

While Nova turns burning brown eyes on me, Adam steps behind his assistant and clasps both hands together pleadingly.

I grit my teeth and admit, "It is true. I did call him…"

"Mr. Sazuki," Nova gives me a prim smile, "I've been working with Adam for over six years. You don't have to cover for him."

I dip my chin. "Very well then. I won't."

Adam's eyes widen and he flings me an annoyed look.

I shrug and sip my tea, ready to enjoy the show.

Nova swivels on her heels. I have never seen her in anything flat, despite the fact that she is on her feet for hours thanks to Adam's hectic schedule.

"You were supposed to be in a suit and tie for our meeting with the Rodney investors. I told you repeatedly not to forget."

"I didn't forget." He shakes his head.

The tea is cold.

I lift my hand to order another.

Nova barrels toward Adam. Her head barely meets his shoulder, but one would not guess this by the way he shuffles back.

"Did you stay up all night working on that new invention when I *explicitly* reminded you to be in bed by nine-thirty?"

"Nova, my brain works on its own time," he explains. "Once I get an idea, I have to tinker with it—"

"Until four a.m.?" she hisses.

Fear flits into his eyes, but he hides it well and puffs out his chest. "If I choose to work on a project until four a.m. I can do as I damn please."

A waitress arrives and sets a cup of tea in front of me. I thank her with a nod, lift it and sip all without taking my eyes off the two in front of me.

"Is that so?" Giving Adam a scalding look, Nova fishes in the pocket of her dark red pantsuit, pulls out a cell phone and slams it on the table.

Adam's face drops immediately.

"I've failed my duties as your assistant," Nova says. "You no longer respect me or my opinions. Since it's clear you don't need me, I'll get out of your hair."

"Nova, don't be like that." Adam reaches for her.

Nova holds up her hand curtly and, with a frosty glare, yanks a lanyard from around her neck.

It gets caught in her braids.

She turns to me. "Mr. Sazuki?"

"Ah, yes." I set my tea down and gently pry the tail of the lanyard out of her coarse plaits.

Adam purses his lips. "Sazuki, don't entertain her."

Nova swipes the lanyard from my palm and smacks it on the table. "I'll hand in my official notice this evening. You are free to attend the Rodney meeting or spit in the face of the investors. I don't give a damn."

I retrieve my tea and blow on top of it. Quite tasty.

Adam grabs Nova's hand before she can storm away. While her face is to the door, a small smile flickers across her lips.

Adam does not see it. Though I believe that even if he did, he would not have understood it.

The push and pull between Adam and his assistant is a mystery to me. I would blame it on the looseness of American culture but, from what I have seen, westerners tend to be much more upfront in their romantic pursuits.

Adam and Nova have chosen the route of playing cat and mouse. I wonder if either of them will ever tire of the game.

"Put this back on." Adam turns Nova by the shoulders and slips the lanyard over her head.

She grabs his wrist. "What time should you be asleep before a big meeting?"

"Nine thirty," he answers dutifully.

"If this happens again…" She threatens.

"I'll get your severance package ready."

She scowls at him.

His lips twitch. "It won't happen again."

"Good." Nova arches an eyebrow. "Let's go. You're going to be late as is."

I catch Adam's eye and lift my tea in salute. He sighs heavily, looking both amused and resigned to his fate.

The man's inventions have become billion-dollar products. Right time. Right place. Right industry. It has been said that he keeps falling into money. But Nova is the one who manages that wealth, running his company like a well-oiled machine while he tinkers in his lab.

On some days, she acts more like his business partner than his assistant.

Other days still, she acts more like a wife than an assistant.

And, strangely enough, there are times when Adam seems to forget which she is as well.

"Sorry to cut your meeting short, Sazuki." Nova nods at me. "We have somewhere to be."

"Of course."

Adam gathers his baseball hat and smashes it backwards on his head. He looks like he belongs on a dusty road with a dog and a pickup truck rather than in a board meeting.

"Remember our deal, Sazuki," he says, placing a hundred on the table.

I nod.

"Oh," Nova turns back, "I saw Akira outside. Looked like she wanted to go in, but couldn't make herself do it." Nova arches an eyebrow. "Might want to see what that's about."

I look through the window and notice a black SUV parked outside. A woman is sitting in the driver's seat.

Akira.

She comes from a line of distant relatives who have been serving my family for generations.

How long has she been waiting there?

The bells above the door jangle, signaling that Nova and Adam have left. I slide out of my chair to follow them when my phone rings.

Ashanti.

A familiar mixture of guilt and weariness collide in my chest.

With a deep sigh, I answer the call.

As usual, I say nothing.

It takes only a few seconds before my ex-wife speaks. "Hi." Her voice is bright and smooth. Perfect for a singer.

"I was not expecting a call."

"Yeah, I just… figured I should check in." Ashanti clears her throat. "How are you?"

"Well." I leave it there.

"Niko told me she had an exciting day yesterday."

"Did she?"

"Yeah. She mentioned that she made a new friend. Someone who helped her with her piano lessons."

My lips tighten.

I wait.

"Niko really seemed to like her new friend," Ashanti adds.

I sigh heavily. What is she trying to figure out?

"Are you… dating her?"

There it is.

I feign ignorance. "Dating who?"

"Day-jon… Day… what was her name again?"

It's Dee-jonae. Not Day-jonae.

I keep that thought to myself.

Another passage of silence flows between us.

"We agreed that we would inform each other when we started seeing other people seriously."

Is this a scolding? "That agreement still stands."

"Then why didn't you tell me about her?"

I close my eyes and rub my temple. "There is nothing to tell."

"So you're not..."

"No." I frown. "Why does this concern you?"

"For Niko's sake, of course." She laughs nervously. "Our daughter's a very special little girl. I don't want her making new friends only to lose them without warning."

"I am raising Niko to be a strong, discerning person. She will not break so easily."

There's a shuffling on the other side of the line. "This is different. You should have seen her gushing, Ryo. I've never seen our daughter that excited about another woman before. It... it kind of made me jealous."

"You will always be Niko's mother."

"What if that's not enough? I'm always away lately. It feels like she's growing up without me."

"Niko is finally old enough to attend school without an interpreter and live her life with confidence. You should be free to do the same. Besides, we are taking good care of her."

I glance up and see that Akira has left the car. She is now standing outside it, staring at me through the café's glass window.

"I need to go." I am about to put the phone away when I hear Ashanti's voice.

"Ryo?"

I grit my teeth and place the phone back to my ear. "Yes?"

"You... you would tell me if anything is happening between you and that girl, right?"

"I will honor our agreement."

She sighs in relief.

I end the call and stuff the cell phone in my pocket. Leaving another hundred dollar bill on the table because I will not be outdone by Adam of all people, I leave the café and cross to the parking lot.

Akira straightens her stance when I draw near. Her dark hair is pulled back in a severe bun. Her black pantsuit clashes with her extremely pale skin. She's quite tall, almost as tall as me, and her height along with her stunning face draws the eyes of many American men.

The moment I stop in front of her, Akira bows at the waist.

"I should not have lost Niko yesterday." She keeps staring at my shoes.

"I received your letter of apology. And, like I told you yesterday, Niko managed to escape me many times."

"I followed you to America on your mother's request. My only job is to keep young Niko safe. I failed."

"There is a way you can make it up to me."

She straightens, a determined look in her eyes. "I will do it."

"This girl." I show her my phone screen.

Akira squints to make out Dejonae's face. "You are pursuing another foreign woman?"

"It is only for business."

She looks relieved.

"What would you have me do?" Akira asks.

"I want to know everything about Miss Williams. Her family. Her educational background. Her financial situation. Can you do it?"

Akira hesitates and then she dips her head.

"I would like a report by tomorrow morning."

"So quickly?"

"There is no time to waste." I raise my chin. "I must have this woman in my clutches before three days."

* * *

AKIRA DROPS off a folder at my residence at eleven p.m. that night.

There is a reason she is my mother's most trusted friend *and* the one who oversees Niko's safety.

"Do I want to know how you got your hands on this?" I ask, lifting the folder.

"You do not."

I nod. "Was there anything shocking?"

"Sadly, no."

I arch an eyebrow at her disappointed face.

"The American lives a quiet life. No prior arrests. No debt." Akira sinks into the chair across from my desk.

"No debt?" That sounds uncommon for the average college student in the US. "How did she afford her education?"

"She chose a college in her state and received a scholarship from the music department. She also worked a part-time job at a café in the area."

A music student. I scrub my chin. "What of her sister?"

I recall that Dejonae mentioned her sister was deaf.

Akira nods to the folder. I thumb to the back and locate another document. Attached to the summary sheet is a picture of a thick woman with dark skin and dreadlocks.

"The sister moves around a lot. She is rather free-spirited for someone who is deaf."

"Why can a deaf person not be free-spirited?" I challenge her.

Akira glances away. "I spoke out of turn."

A knock sounds at the door.

Niko enters wearing her *jinbei,* Japanese pajamas. The fabric is blue and cottony. Her arms dangle out of the wide sleeves.

"Do you need something?" I sign.

"I can't sleep."

I nod at Akira who quickly rises and takes her leave.

"Goodnight, Niko," Akira signs.

Niko waves to her.

I hold my daughter's hand and we see Akira out together. When she is gone, I drop to one knee and face Niko, my heart swelling with affection as I look into her sparkling eyes.

Lifting her hands, Niko runs her fingers over the air as if playing a piano.

"You should be in bed. You have school tomorrow."

She pushes out her bottom lip.

I laugh and give in as I always do. "Five minutes."

She holds up ten fingers.

"Seven minutes," I argue.

Niko's ten fingers wiggle in objection.

I arch an eyebrow. "Should I put you to bed immediately?"

She shakes her head and follows me to the grand piano in the center of our living room. Tonight, the moon is bright and it falls upon the piano, leaving a silver kiss atop the glossy surface.

I heft Niko into my arms and set her on my knee. Then, I take her hand and place it on the piano lid.

"Be careful," I tell her.

She nods as if to say *I know*.

Settling my arms on either side of her, I place my fingers on the keys. Softly, I pick out the melody of Beethoven's *Symphony No. 9*.

Niko recognizes the pattern and grins, causing her eyes to fall into one happy line.

"Easy," she signs.

I smile in response.

My daughter places her free hand on the keys and accompanies me. Together, we play in sync.

Her fingers dance over the chords with surprising dexterity. There is not a hint of hesitation or uncertainty in the way she approaches music. The notes are a comfort. A friend. She may not hear the way I do, but the way she experiences music is special.

Eventually, her eyes close and she plays without looking down at the keys.

I lift my hand, letting her take over the piece. Niko does not seem to notice that I have stopped.

I press a kiss to her forehead when the song ends. Waiting until she opens her eyes, I sign, "Time for bed."

After carrying Niko into her bedroom, I set her on the bed and pull up the covers to her chest. She wiggles her toes beneath the blanket.

"Goodnight," I sign.

Her hand shoots out of the blanket and latches onto the hem of my shirt. She tugs.

I look down at her, waiting.

"Will we see Deej again?" she signs.

I feel a sharp prick of concern. Like everyone in our family, Niko has a habit of keeping to herself. She rarely clings to one person. Even Akira, who has been watching over her since she was a baby, is treated with distance.

"Miss Williams is busy with her own life. She has no time to play with you," I tell her.

Niko's eyes flash with sadness. "But I like her."

"In life," I hesitate, "some people are only with you for a short time. Sometimes, you are not meant to be together always."

"Like you and mom?" she gestures.

I pin my lips together because the divorce has always been a difficult one to express to her.

"Yes, like me and your mother," I finally sign.

She frowns and then says aloud, "No."

My eyes widen when I hear her speak. Niko only sounds out her words when she's frustrated or upset.

My daughter pushes her hands into the mattress, sits up, and gestures, "*Sobo* says we make our own fate." A wrinkle forms between her eyebrows. She signs forcefully, "I want to play with Deej again."

I fold my arms over my chest.

My daughter stares me down, unwavering. It's a surprising and uncharacteristic show of stubbornness. I can only blame it on her encounter with Miss Williams.

Niko met Dejonae once and she's already a bad influence. She might turn my child into a rebel by the end of the month.

With a frown, I scold Niko, "End of discussion. Go to bed."

She pouts.

"I will not tell you twice," I add.

Niko makes a sound of frustration and flops backward.

* * *

I RETURN to my home office and sink wearily into my chair.

The files that Akira brought for me lay scattered on the desk. I dig my fingers into the photograph at the top of the pile and lift it.

Dejonae Williams.

Dark skin. Dark eyes.

A beautiful... headache.

Why is the key to my foundation's success trapped in *her* of all people? After the gala, I had hoped to never see her again. Yet our lives seem destined to become entangled.

"I will take what I need from her and she will disappear from both our lives," I declare to the silence. "Things will not be complicated."

Determined to stick with the plan, I draft an email.

To: *Dejonae Williams*
From: *Ryotaro Sazuki*
Subject: *Job Opportunity At The Sazuki Music Foundation*

Ms WILLIAMS,

FIRST IMPRESSIONS ASIDE, *I was very impressed by your ability to convey the principles of timing to my daughter, Niko, during today's lesson. I'd like to formally offer you a position at my foundation.*

Despite your lackluster background and incomplete musical degree, we will be offering you an impressive salary as well as an opportunity for a generous bonus.

Also note that, in the future, you will be reporting directly to me. I trust that you will keep any differences of opinions to yourself as we work together.

Your expected starting date is tomorrow. You can report to HR and let them know your school schedule so we can work within it.

I trust that you will do the smart thing and agree to these generous terms.

REGARDS,
Ryotaro Sazuki
Director of The Sazuki Music Foundation

I SEND the email and force myself to go to bed.
The next morning, I'm woken to a ping on my phone.
I snatch the device from my dresser.

TO: Ryotaro Sazuki
From: Dejonae Williams
Subject: Screw You

MR SAZUKI,

SINCE WE'RE TALKING *about first impressions, the one you left the night of the gala was also less than impressive. I found you rude and condescending. After a second meeting, that opinion hasn't changed.*

I RUB MY EYES, certain that I am reading wrong.
I sent a polite and professional email. Why would Miss Williams respond so rudely?
I shove the phone face-down into the bed.

After a few deep, intentional breaths, I lift it again, prodded by a mixture of curiosity and annoyance.

I'M oh-so-grateful that my 'lackluster background' and 'incomplete musical degree' managed to squeak past your sky-high expectations for an employee. What a benevolent boss you are.

Please note that no amount of money you could ever shove at me would make me accept a job at your foundation. I wouldn't work with you for a million dollars.

I LET OUT AN AGGRAVATED HUFF. The job market in the US is extremely competitive. To be offered such an impressive salary when she has not even completed her degree is unheard of.

There is more to the email.

I struggle to compose myself before finishing it.

LASTLY, *I do not plan to ever keep my opinions to myself. Just because I don't agree with everything that comes out of your mouth does not mean that my opinions are invalid.*

Your fear of hearing dissenting opinions is a mark of questionable character. I trust that you will reflect on yourself and what kind of employer you're being to the people who have no choice but to suffer at your company.

Lastly, thank you for trusting me to do the 'smart thing' , which I've decided is to stay the hell away from you.

REGARDS,
    Dejonae Williams
    Director of Kiss My Black Behind

. . .

I RE-READ HER LAST LINE.

Such insolence.

Such disrespect.

I have never in my life been spoken to that way, not in person and certainly not through an email.

Does she know who I am?

I bounce off the bed and pace my room.

Dejonae Williams is pure, unbridled defiance. But I have been able to tame far worse than she.

Grabbing my phone, I call Akira.

She answers on the first ring. "Ryotaro."

"Miss Williams requires more convincing." I look coldly through my bedroom window. "I would like to show her that no woman says no to me."

CHAPTER 3
CAGED SONG BIRD

DEJONAE

"Mama Moira's in town. Do you want to swing by the farmhouse after school?" Vanya's voice surges through my earbuds.

"Are you kidding?" I squeal. "I've been waiting ages for an invite."

She chuckles, but there's something off about it. "I'm glad you're interested," she says.

"What earned me the golden ticket?"

"No reason. It's just... been a while since I've met up with everyone."

"Is that why you want me there?" I swipe my ID card over the scanner and enter the library. "To take the heat off you?"

"No, of course not."

I stop in the middle of the Greek Theology aisle. "I have one condition."

"Name it."

"I want fry jacks."

"Can't guarantee that. Mama Moira cooks when she feels like it. Or when the kids beg. Which is often—*ah!*" The sound of something shattering erupts on her end of the line.

I gasp and turn back to the exits, ready to charge over to Vanya and Hadyn's place. "Are you okay, Van?"

"Damn it. I dropped something."

Baby Ollie starts bawling in the background.

"Babe, what happened?" Hadyn's voice leaks into my ear. *"Be careful. Let me clean that up."*

"Let me. I made the mess," Vanya insists.

"Baby, I got it. Why don't you wait in the living room? I'll calm Ollie and clean this up."

The worry in Hadyn's voice makes my heart tighten. As an aspiring songwriter, I'm sensitive to the way vocal tones convey feeling. Whatever's going on seems more urgent than Vanya stepping on broken glass.

"Is everything good over there?" I ask.

"Yes," Vanya says with a little more force than necessary.

"Like... in general?" I pass the memoir section of the library.

"In general? Life is different. I'm a new mom. My hormones are crazy and I don't know what I'm doing half the time." She laughs it off. "But what can I say? It's... yeah, motherhood is a lot, but it's great."

The sound of her breathing changes and I assume she's walking into another room.

"Enough about me," Vanya says. "What happened with you and Sazuki yesterday?"

My muscles tighten on impact. "Don't mention that man to me."

"Now *that* sounds like a story."

I stop in the music theory section and tuck my finger into the spine of a book. "He offered me a job, but in the most *Pride and Prejudice* way ever."

"*Pride and Prejudice?*"

"The book by Jane Austen."

"Not much of a reader," she answers.

"Blasphemy."

I find the reference text I'm searching for in the music aisle and tuck it into the crook of my arm. "I'll correct that later," I warn her. "But there's a part in the book where Mr. Darcy confesses his love to Elizabeth."

"Sazuki confessed his love to you?"

"No." I frown at the thought. "The point of the scene isn't that Darcy confessed. It's that he went on and on about how he loved Elizabeth 'against his better judgement'."

"Still not seeing the point."

I slap the book closed and the thud earns me a stinky look from the librarian.

"*Sorry,*" I mouth. In a quieter voice, I explain, "If you want something from someone, you say 'hey, I think you're great. Let's do something together'. You don't barge your way in, tell them how things are going to be and then emphasize that you're giving them a chance 'against your better judgement'. Who the hell is supposed to say yes to that?"

"I'm guessing Sazuki's job offer didn't lay on the flattery," Vanya says.

I slide my fingers down the book's table of contents until I find 'Beethoven's Hearing Loss'. Thumbing to the right page, I tell Vanya, "He made sure to outline how my lacking background and poor education meant that I don't deserve the position, but since he's the patron saint of goodness, he's giving me an opportunity."

"No." She laughs.

"He told me to start tomorrow. And *then*," my voice climbs, "he warned me that any 'differences of opinion' won't be tolerated in the office. All this before I've even accepted the job!"

"Sh!" The angry librarian scowls at me.

I place a finger to my lips and nod.

"Men." Vanya scoffs.

I roll my eyes and dig into my backpack. When I find my notebook, I lay it on the table.

"So what did you do?"

"I wrote him an equally professional email."

"Damn." She chuckles. "Is it weird that I want to see it?"

"I'll forward it to you later."

"Thanks."

"Babe, can we talk?" Hadyn says.

Vanya's voice gets tight. "I need to go, Deej. I'll see you at the farmhouse later."

I tap my headphones twice to end the call and chew on my bottom lip.

Is something going on with her and Hadyn?

I quickly trash the thought. Hadyn adores Vanya. The first time I saw them together, Hadyn was following her around, unable to take his eyes off her. Whatever's going on, I'm sure he'll get to the bottom of it.

I peruse the textbook and jot down notes for my graduation thesis until my phone vibrates on the table.

Class is starting in ten minutes.

Time to get a move on.

* * *

WHEN I LEAVE THE LIBRARY, I notice a fleet of black SUVs lined up near the quad. A woman climbs out and heads straight for me. She's tall and lean, pale as a vampire, and has her hair scraped back into a severe bun.

Whoever she is, I'm sure she has no business with me.

"Ms. Williams."

I jump when my name leaves her lips in a crisp accent.

"Me?"

"Mr. Sazuki would like to speak to you." She gestures to the car. It's impossible to see her eyes behind the dark shades she's wearing, but I can only assume that she's waiting expectantly for me to obey.

Oh hell no. I scowl at her. "Tell him I'm not here."

"He can see you," she says in a bland voice.

"By the time you get back to the car and report to him, I'll be gone." My smile is quick and cold. "Good day, ma'am."

I start to walk off, and she steps in front of me.

Annoyance sparks to life in my chest. "Tell Sazuki I said everything I needed to in the email. If he still doesn't understand, he can use Google translate."

The tall woman motions in my direction. On cue, the doors of all the SUVs burst open and a line of bodyguards climb out.

My eyes widen.

Before I can think to run, the guards surround me.

I get a flashback to that night at the Belle's Beauty gala when my piano performance was interrupted in the same manner. Only then, I was so scared and awestruck that I couldn't stand my ground when Sazuki entered the circle.

This time, I'm ready for him.

The chain of broad, suit-clad backs opens to admit Sazuki. His cold beauty takes my breath away. The man is as regal as he is sharp. He walks in calmly, like he's shooting a cologne ad and not doing what I'm pretty sure is kidnapping-adjacent.

I get into a fighting stance. "Touch me and you die."

Bold words, I know. I'm currently surrounded by a legion of beefy Asian bodybuilders in suits.

But I have nothing if not eternal optimism.

"Ms. Williams." Sazuki's eyes are cold. Everything about him is cold. Prickly. I'm starting to think I imagined the dimples he flashed yesterday.

"I don't know how you conducted business in Japan, but here in America, you can't force conversations by kidnapping innocent people."

"Kidnapping? We are simply having a little chat."

Is he joking? "You have twenty goons trapping me in place so I can't get to my next class. I'm sure that's breaking at least one law."

He shakes his head. "We are here to escort you to your class. While we walk, we can talk."

"What?" I screech.

He catches the eye of the pretty vampire. When the woman

nods, the guards shuffle forward. I search for a way to break out of the circle, but there are none. These guys are like human handcuffs.

Sazuki gestures for me to continue on the path.

I grit my teeth. I could stay here and fight with him, but I can't afford to be late. I've got Music 206 now, which is Ear Training Theory. Mr. Howell locks the classroom door precisely on the dot. It's my last semester and if I plan on graduating, I can't flunk my music electives.

"Your email seemed to indicate a misunderstanding between us. It appears you think I'm *asking* you to work with me. On the contrary, I am not."

His words are delivered so smoothly, so elegantly, that I almost miss the threat in them.

When it hits me, I stop walking.

The guards stop too.

Sazuki turns to me, his face impassive. "Name your price, Miss Williams. What I have is money. The only thing I do not have is time." He walks toward me. "And especially time to waste."

A hint of his cologne wafts through the air. *Why does such a terrible person smell so good?*

He arches an eyebrow, waiting for me to respond.

"Are you trying to insinuate that *my* time is less valuable than yours?" I spit. "Or that I'm so beneath you that I don't deserve the basic right of choice?"

"You do have a choice. The key is that *all* those choices lead to one place."

There has to be something wrong with him. No one is *born* this self-absorbed.

"What if I make the choice to slap you right now?" I lift a hand. "Where does that choice lead me?"

He doesn't bat an eyelash. "The probability that you will be able to hit me before one of my men stops you is quite low."

"I'll take my chances."

He steps so close to me that his Armani shoes kiss my dusty

sneakers. Lowering his face until it's almost on top of mine, he gives me a look of challenge.

I stare into his eyes and my insides do a somersault.

Standing in the middle of the circle, surrounded by his lavish display of power and wealth, it's hard to remain brave.

Sazuki lowers my arm until it swings loosely at my sides. Next, he lifts a hand and checks his watch.

"Your class begins in five minutes. You will be late if you dawdle."

"Is this how you got your first album released?" I walk angrily ahead to hide my sudden nerves. "You go around intimidating people to get what you want?"

"My first album was produced for a friend. And I do not usually work this hard to hear a yes." He slides a hand into his pocket. "Fortunately, I am willing to work hard to get what I want."

"Just say you're willing to play dirty. That would be more honest," I grumble.

We pass the concert hall and turn left. Sazuki studies me. "For someone so young, you're proving to be a handful."

"It's my way of thanking you for your tyranny."

There.

A flash of dimples craters both cheeks, but it's gone before I can blink.

We get to my building, but Sazuki doesn't stop walking.

"Where are you going?" I hiss.

We've been getting attention the entire way. Whispers have steadily increased since the quad. Plus I can see sneakers, socks and sandals gathering if I peer between the legs of the suits.

The entire campus is on alert. Which makes sense. It's not every day a fleet of SUVs take up all the parking spots and spit out beefy Asian men in suits.

And it's definitely not every day that those beefy guards blow through the quad like they're protecting a dignitary.

But I need this circus to be over.

Now.

It's one thing to be seen making a spectacle in the quad.

It's another thing entirely to walk into class with an annoying music prodigy and his not-so-subtle secret service.

I turn abruptly to Sazuki and stop him before he places one Armani-clad foot on the steps. "You've escorted me to my classroom. I've heard you out. That is way more than you deserve given your…" I glare at the suits, "tactics."

"I'm walking you to class, Miss Williams. That was the agreement."

"No, to have an *agreement*, you have to get both parties to say yes." I hold up a finger right under his nose. "Only one side okayed this. Therefore, there was no agreement."

He thinks it over and then nods. "A very good point."

"Great. Bye now. Let's not do this again." I breathe out, certain that Sazuki and his team will now disappear from my life as quickly as they'd arrived.

And I'm half right.

Sazuki waves at the tall woman and she gives a command in Japanese. Immediately, the suits line up and march back to the quad.

The woman draws close to Sazuki's side. I still can't see her eyes behind the sunglasses, but I can tell by her stance that she's looking around, ready to protect him.

"Why didn't you go with them?" I ask.

"I realized it would be distracting to have them follow us inside. I do not wish to surprise your teacher with twenty extra students. That would be impolite." He blinks steadily.

"And you don't think hijacking me on my way to class is impolite?" I screech.

His eyebrows knot as if he's genuinely thinking about it.

I throw my hands up. "Look, I don't care if you go or stay. Just keep away from… *gah!*"

My words are cut off when a crowd of students suddenly bombard us. They surge toward Sazuki, screaming his name, taking pictures, and hurling pens at him so he can give them an autograph.

"We should not have let the security go," the tall woman says to Sazuki while struggling to keep the kids away.

"Hey, watch it!" I fight the tide of people racing toward him.

One particularly hefty guy knocks into my shoulder. I lose my balance and fall backward.

Panicked, I reach out, desperately grabbing onto anything to try and keep me on my feet.

Warm, slender fingers wrap around my wrist. With a powerful tug, I switch directions and land straight against a wall of muscle covered in a thin white shirt.

Sazuki's scent fills my nose and I glance up slowly.

Our eyes lock.

His heartbeat quickens under my palm.

Mine clamors at an even faster pace.

I push him away and he sets me aside at the same time.

Sazuki brushes his shirt down and in a severe voice, he orders, "Stay behind me."

I want to argue, but I'd rather not be trampled.

Sazuki's protection team trot around the corner and flank us on both sides. The crowd gets considerably less rowdy, but the air is still charged with excitement.

To my surprise, Sazuki humors his fans. He signs his name over a hundred times, leans in for selfies, and flashes his dimples in front of cameras.

While *he's* having a good time, I'm late for class and getting angrier by the second.

When will this end?

The students all have something to say to Sazuki. Some express how much they love his family's music while others ask questions about his latest performance.

Sazuki takes his time, patiently answering everyone.

I'm sure he's doing it just to spite me.

By the time he's had enough and the protection team clears a path so we can enter the building, I'm steaming through my ears.

Sazuki checks his watch. "Good. You will only be a little late."

I level him a warning glare.

He pulls his lips in as if he's trying to hide a chuckle and that sends my temper through the roof.

"Is this funny to you? I'm super late and now the door will be locked—"

The classroom door bangs open in direct defiance of my statement.

"It *is* you!" My music professor, Mr. Howel, dances out of the classroom like a burlesque performer. One leg prances out first, followed by the other. His eyes are glazed with unbridled excitement. "Mr. Sazuki." He bends low at the waist, face to the ground. His bald spot reflects the light like a disco ball.

Why are they acting like he's the King of England?

"I'm honored." Mr. Howel is still speaking to the floor. He straightens and bows again. "Absolutely *honored* to have you join our class."

Sazuki arches both eyebrows smugly in my direction. If my professor and twenty bodyguards weren't watching, I'd probably smack him.

"Come in, come in," Mr. Howel offers.

The vampire woman slides close to Sazuki and whispers in his ear. He nods and then speaks to Mr. Howell. "Unfortunately, I have another appointment, but I will leave Dejonae in your care."

Mr. Howel looks so shocked that I could probably knock him over with a feather. "D-Dejonae? You two know each other?"

"No, we don't," I say.

"Yes, we do," Sazuki says. "She will be working closely with me."

"Over my dead body," I say under my breath.

Sazuki spares me an amused glance. Fixing his face into a stern expression, he says, "Take great care of her."

"Yes, of course. She's a promising student. Worthy of your support." Mr. Howel booms out a laugh.

My fingers curl into fists. I flash Sazuki another scowl.

His eyes sparkle and I realize that there's a sick, twisted part of him that actually enjoys seeing me squirm.

"Miss Williams." Sazuki gestures for me to go inside.

I turn with a huff and stalk into the lecture hall just as Professor Howel asks Sazuki, "When you have time, would you mind signing my album cover..."

I let the door slam shut behind me.

The moment I enter the classroom, I'm immediately surrounded. My eyes dart back and forth between all the eager faces. We're not a particularly friendly class and I've kept to myself while on campus, so all the staring is new.

And unwelcome.

I stumble to my seat, sinking in low.

A girl takes the chair next to me. She's got her hair dyed blue, but the color actually fits her peaches-and-cream complexion. Her eyes are a big, expressive brown and she smiles at me as I sink into my chair.

"That's enough breathing down her neck, you vultures. Give the girl some room."

A few students step back, but not far enough for my taste.

The girl grins at me. "Darlene, right?"

"Uh, no. It's Dejonae."

"Right. Right." She smacks her lips like we haven't been taking the same class all semester.

"I'm Taylor."

I nod and slip my ear buds in, hoping that'll deter Taylor and the others. My stomach's still burning from Sazuki's surprise visit today and I'm not really in the mood to talk to anyone.

"How do you know Sazuki?" Taylor asks.

"I don't."

"Come on. You expect us to believe that one of the most reclusive celebrities in the world just randomly decided to walk you to class?"

"I don't really care if you believe it or not. It's the truth."

The friendly facade drops and she gives me a frigid stare. "What kind of relationship do you have with Sazuki?"

I keep quiet.

She leans closer and whispers, "Are you his drug dealer?"

The cap on my temper pops and hot lava pours from my mouth. "What is that supposed to mean?"

"There's only a few reasons he'd be hanging around you. And it's not like you'd be his sugar baby." She scrunches her nose. "You don't look like Sazuki's type."

My jaw opens and closes. I don't know if I should be grateful that I don't 'look like a sugar baby'—whatever that means—or if I should be outraged that she doesn't consider me to be Sazuki's 'type'.

"Are you saying Sazuki wouldn't want me sexually because I'm black. Or that *since I'm black*, the only reason he would seek me out would be that I sell drugs?"

"This isn't a black or white thing, Deidra. I just want the truth."

"It's Dee-jon-ae!" I hiss. "And why the hell are you entitled to my business? You think saying you want the truth will make you seem less nosy and condescending? You think I'm so insecure that I'd jump at the chance to be friends with you because you now deem it appropriate to talk to me?"

She rolls her eyes. "Geez. You're totally overreacting."

"No, I'm expressing my emotions!" I want to throw my purse at her. "Don't minimize my feelings by calling me aggressive or loud or whatever other stereotype you can pull out of your ignorant brain. I'm responding appropriately. You were rude for insinuating that I'm Sazuki's drug dealer. You were rude for suggesting that I'm not attractive. And you're a hypocrite for acting friendly with me to try and squeeze out information on a celebrity. So you know what? Screw you." I flip her off because I don't have it in me to be politically correct today.

Snatching my bag off the floor, I storm down to the exits and smash the door open.

Has the entire world gone mad? Damn!

"Miss Williams." A mousy woman spots me in the hallway and motions to me. "The dean would like to speak to you."

I nearly groan. *What is this now?*

She turns sharply. "Follow me."

I let my bag slide down my shoulder and tip my head to the ceiling. I have a really bad feeling about this.

* * *

"Come in. Come in. Have a seat." The dean waves me forward. "Coffee? Soda? A little something to wet the throat?"

Ew. "No, I'm good."

He bobs his head. Dean Ferguson is a short, portly man—exactly what one would expect in the administration of academia: faded, brown jacket, balding head, wrinkles from years of breaking up catty, inter-department fights and meeting the needs of pushy parents.

"I checked and you don't have another lecture until this afternoon." He rounds his giant desk that's cluttered with files, binders, and family photographs. "I planned to ask Mr. Howel to let you out early because I just couldn't wait to speak to you. I'm glad we were able to nab you without issue."

"Can I ask what this is about?" I remain standing at the door.

He motions me forward. "Sit. Sit."

I dig my fingers into my backpack and approach the chair tentatively. It's one of those tall, wingback chairs that are more about looks than comfort. I squirm, trying to find a good position. After a few seconds, I give up and sit with my back ramrod straight.

The dean folds his hands together. "Dejonae, you have been an exemplary student during your three years with us. I understand that, on top of your scholarship, you also worked part time at a café near the university?"

"I did," I say warily.

"Exemplary. Truly. So many young people choose to blame their circumstances or their environment for their lack of productivity and bad choices. It is so inspirational to see someone like you take the opportunities given and make something of it."

Is that supposed to be a compliment? "What do you mean someone like me?"

"I just meant," his mouth opens and closes, "someone who receives financial aid." His cheeks turn blotchy. "Truly, Dejonae, I meant no disrespect."

He looks genuine and I realize I might be on edge thanks to Taylor's interrogation. I relax a bit. "You still haven't told me what this discussion is about."

"Right, well, I have very exciting news. The timeline for your graduation project has been tweaked. Rather than waiting until the end of the year to receive your credits, you may be awarded in early spring."

"Are you kidding? That's fantastic! But... how? I thought our final grades would be decided at the end-of-the-year concert? I've been researching my thesis for months." I think about my time in the library this morning. "I actually *just* settled on the direction of my report."

"You submitted a general thesis outline already, correct?" He flips on his glasses and shakes his mouse to wake up his hibernating computer.

"Yes. I chose the topic of music and the deaf community."

"I see that here." He whips off his glasses and a giant smile crosses his face. "Well, this is just perfect. Since your thesis is such an impactful one, we'd like to make a special provision for you."

"What kind of provision?" I break out into a sweat.

His ruddy cheeks gleam. "After much deliberation, the final grade for your end-of-year project will be decided by none other than..."

My heart starts racing. *Don't say it. Don't say it.*

"... Mr. Ryotaro Sazuki."

"I object!" I bounce out of my chair as if my legs are made of springs.

The dean looks around. "Miss Williams, this isn't a courtroom."

"Why is Sazuki deciding my grade?" I demand.

"He's a decorated musician, descended from a family of musical legends. There is no one more qualified than Sazuki. And, to make the deal even sweeter, Sazuki has agreed to let you work closely alongside him at his foundation. It would be a paid internship position."

I feel a clamp around my head and it just keeps squeezing and squeezing. So this was the real reason Sazuki came to my school. Cornering me on my way to class was just a torrid little bonus.

"Do you know how valuable it would be to your future career to have studied with a Sazuki? Doors will fly open for you, Miss Williams. You put the Sazuki name on your resume and you become unstoppable. This is a golden opportunity that any other student would die for."

"Then give it to them!"

The dean purses his lips. "Are you saying you will not accept the internship?"

"Yes. That." I point to him. "That's exactly what I'm saying."

He rubs his temple and sighs. "Well, this is unexpected."

"The best things in life are," I mumble.

The dean reaches for his glasses, slowly fixes it on his nose and looks at me. "I apologize, Miss Williams, but this path is non-negotiable. You either study under Mr. Sazuki or you will not be graduating this year."

My heart bursts like a balloon. "What?"

"Naturally, your scholarship will be revoked due to failure to meet your academic minimum and the penalty fee will be double that of the scholarship."

"Failure to meet... you'd be the one blocking me from meeting it!"

"That is one way to look at it."

"You're *threatening* me with my own education. Do you know how twisted that is?"

"Perhaps, but…"

I curl my fingers into fists. "What did he promise you? Money? A new school wing?"

"Mr. Sazuki will introduce us to the International Music Board. It's a highly exclusive membership group that will allow us to raise our music accreditation. We'll be able to offer a Masters or Doctorate degree in music. It's a very prestigious opportunity."

"But you have to sacrifice *me* to get it."

"I wouldn't think of it as a sacrifice." He taps his fingers together. "Miss Williams, I would not have agreed if I didn't think it would be a win for everyone involved. There is no downside to working with Mr. Sazuki."

"That's not your decision to make," I snap.

"Either way, it's been made. These are your choices."

Sazuki's words from earlier echo back to me. *'You do have a choice, but all those choices lead to one place.'*

I'm trapped. If I go home without a degree, everything I worked so hard for will be for nothing. All the long hours of practicing the piano, the late nights studying, the extra shifts at the café to pay my bills, it'll all go down the drain.

"Fine," I spit out harshly.

The dean brightens. "You're making the best choice, Miss Williams. Truly."

"But I want it in writing that the school is the one who came up with this idea. And I'd like an opportunity to participate in the showcase if my agreement with Mr. Sazuki falls apart."

"I can do that."

When I leave the dean's office, I stick my face into my backpack and scream my head off.

Normally, I can go weeks or months without getting angry. There's not a lot that ruffles my feathers. I grew up with a sister who never let her limitations stop her from doing what she wanted. Yaya taught me not to take myself too seriously and to roll with the punches. But this punch is determined to keep me on the ground.

I leave the admin building and try my best to forget that Sazuki exists. Unfortunately, word has spread around the school and random people keep approaching me.

By the time I'm finished with my last class, I'm eager to get to Sunny and Darrel Hastings' farmhouse and pretend today never happened.

I pick up a box of chocolates at a grocery store and then catch a taxi to the farmhouse. My mother taught me to never visit someone's house empty-handed, but I'm a poor college student so chocolates are the best I can do.

With a deep breath, I knock on the door.

Footsteps patter.

The door flies open.

Niko launches herself at me and wraps her arms around my waist. I'm shocked to see her and hug her back enthusiastically.

"Pretty girl." I run a hand down her long, curly hair. "What are you doing here?"

Prickles of awareness run over my skin.

I glance up and fall into a pair of sharp brown eyes.

Sazuki.

CHAPTER 4
NO INTERPRETATION

SAZUKI

"Slow down, Niko, or you might choke. Here, drink this."

I slide a glass of freshly squeezed juice over to her. Niko grabs the mug and takes a sip. Shyly, she glances at me and I nod my assurance.

Her shoulders hike to her ears and she looks around self-consciously. Tiny fingers sink below the table where she is, undoubtedly, gripping the edge of her skirt.

The food called 'fry jack' had distracted her so that she forgot to be nervous. Now, I see the uncertainty steal into her eyes again and it makes my heart pinch. Perhaps it had not been wise to let her accompany me.

"Do you like it?" A small woman with two grey plaits hanging down her shoulders asks. She's wearing a loose cotton blouse with an embroidered hem and a colorful red skirt.

Niko bobs her head.

"Thank you," I answer for my daughter. "It is very good."

"Your daughter's beautiful," another woman says to me. She's tall with long black hair. She and the elder have similar facial features and the same reddish-brown complexions. "You must be very proud."

"I am," I say simply.

Cheers erupt in the living room. I observe the group of three children who are scattered on the ground playing a card game. Niko notices them too. Longing enters my daughters eyes, but she chews on her bottom lip and stays seated.

"Would you like to join them?" I sign.

She shakes her head vehemently.

"Sorry about that." Holland Alistair stalks into the kitchen. He takes the seat beside me. "There was a small emergency at Belle's Beauty, so I had to take the call."

"Anything I can help with?" I ask.

He waves away my offer. "Ezekiel has it handled. Promoting him to manager was one of the best decisions I ever made." His eyes skate across the table and land on a woman with dark skin and curly hair. "Apart from marrying my wife."

Alistair's wife laughs brightly.

"Stop undressing my best friend with your eyes, you creep. There are children around," the woman with long hair scolds.

One of the children leaves the living room and trods past the dinner table. He gives Niko a curious look, which she quickly pretends not to notice. The boy adjusts his circular glasses and carries on.

On the way back from the kitchen, he grips a glass of water and stops at the table. "Mom, I think someone's outside."

"I wonder if Vanya's finally arrived," his mother answers.

"I haven't seen her and Baby Ollie in *ages*," the elder moans.

"Who is it, Sunny?" Alistair's wife asks.

Sunny checks a monitor in the kitchen. "She looks familiar. Wait... isn't that? I think it's Vanya's friend."

My ears perk up.

"Vanya's friend? The one who performed at the gala?" Alistair's eyes widen. He shoots me a panicked look.

I don't know what he is imagining and I don't care either.

Tapping Niko on the shoulder, I sign, "Dejonae is here."

The dark cloud that had been hovering over my daughter disappears. A brilliant smile charges across her face and it's almost blinding.

Niko hops out of her seat and makes a mad dash for the door.

Every head swings to her.

Even the children in the living room stop their game to stare.

My daughter does not notice. She throws the screen door open and wraps her arms around a very shocked Dejonae.

I watch for any hint of disdain to cross the college student's face. After all, Dejonae must be aware of my agreement with the school by now. If there is so much as a whiff of anger or hatred in her response to Niko—or any sense that she may take out her frustrations on my daughter—I will whisk Niko away immediately.

But Dejonae shows no signs of annoyance.

Her face lights up and she grabs my daughter back, holding her as if she plans to swallow Niko into her body.

I stare at them, my gut churning.

Niko trusts this woman.

How? When? Why?

Because of one encounter in an alley?

The connection between Dejonae and my daughter seems to be getting stronger at every meeting. Niko so rarely opens up to people. Now that she has, I cannot let her joy end in disappointment.

As if she can sense my fierce inspection, Dejonae glances up.

There is a stark difference between her reaction to Niko and her reaction to me. With me, anger gathers like storm clouds, spitting thunder from her expressive brown eyes.

Niko tugs on Dejonae's hand, breaking our stare.

My daughter points to the table where the fry jacks are gathered in baskets. "Have you tried that?"

"Not yet." Dejonae motions to her mouth three times. "But I'll probably eat a lot."

Niko giggles.

"Hi, everyone." Dejonae keeps her eyes trained away from me as she nears the table. "I'm Dejonae. Vanya's friend. Thank you for the invitation."

"Welcome. Welcome. The more the merrier." The elder waddles around the table with a swish of her thick, embroidered skirt. "Vanya told us you were coming."

"Speaking of," Sunny checks her phone, "where is Vanya?"

"She's not with me," Dejonae says.

"She and Hadyn were supposed to have arrived already." Sunny chews her bottom lip.

Alistair's wife looks up worriedly. "Dawn and Max said they were running late. Maybe Vanya sent a message saying the same?"

While Sunny and Kenya check their phones, Dejonae's eyes flick to me. *What are you doing here?*

I jut my chin at her. *Can't I be here?*

She scowls.

"I'll give her a call," Sunny says.

"And I'll give our new guest the grand introduction." Alistair's wife glides around the table. "Hi, I'm Kenya. We didn't get to meet formally that night. Everything was so chaotic. But I wanted to thank you for helping us out of a tight spot."

"You're welcome." Dejonae casts me a dark look. "And I don't blame you for how *chaotic* things became. It wasn't your fault."

I arch an eyebrow.

She stares daggers at me.

If she is expecting remorse, she will not get any. I can still see that moment at the gala like it happened yesterday. Music pouring into the hallway. The doors opening. A young woman, head bowed on the stage, her heart bleeding all over my piano as she played a raw, emotional version of Brahms.

She was a stranger touching my keys.

Touching my art.

Touching me.

Did anyone expect me to smile and applaud her in that moment? Would anyone welcome such a private and personal invasion?

"Okay then." Kenya flashes an awkward smile. "Let me introduce the rest of the gang." She points to her husband who is seated around the table smearing jam on a fry jack. "That's my husband, Alistair. You met him."

"I did. Hi." Dejonae waves with her free hand.

Niko, cutely, waves along.

"The cooking genius responsible for all of these tasty Belizean dishes," Kenya juts a finger at the crowded table, "is Mama Moira. She has a habit of adopting grown adults and turning them Mayan at heart no matter what race or culture they are, so don't be shocked if she sews you a cute embroidered outfit and you end up loving it more than your other clothes."

"Noted," Dejonae says with an easy laugh.

Niko watches Dejonae laughing and smiles too. I expect Dejonae to ignore my daughter, as so many tend to do. But she drops to one knee and signs out a summary of everything Kenya said.

Kenya waits patiently until she's finished.

When Dejonae rises again, Alistair's wife looks at her with fresh eyes. "You know sign language?"

"My sister is deaf," Dejonae signs.

"Oh." There's a moment of pause as everyone soaks in that information.

I have learned that people live in their own worlds, locked into their own bubbles, and until that bubble is popped, they go about believing everyone is exactly like them.

"You should bring your sister the next time she's in town." The elder breaks the silence first.

"It'll be a while before my sister comes home. She's busy with work."

"What does she do?"

"She's a model."

Happy wrinkles gather around Mama Moira's eyes. "How lovely. Another model in the family. Well, whenever she drops in, we'd love to have her."

"Come on. Let me introduce you to the children before another war breaks out." Alistair's wife gestures with dark fingers. "Competitions get loud and rowdy around here. I'd suggest you prepare yourself before they drag you into a game."

"I'm pretty competitive myself," Dejonae says.

Niko skips happily beside her.

I hear chair legs scrape the ground and feel Alistair sitting closer to me. When I turn, I find his eyes boring into mine.

"Is there still a problem between you and Dejonae?" he asks.

I reach for a fry jack to keep from having to answer immediately. The pastry is golden and smooth like the top of milk bread, but the inside is puffy.

"If I'd known she was coming to the house, I wouldn't have invited you for dinner," Alistair adds.

"To protect me or to protect her?"

He mulls it over. "That depends on who would do the most damage to the other."

"A wise response."

"I'm always on top of my game when I'm facing off with you, Sazuki." He tilts his fry jack toward me.

My eyes dart to Dejonae. She is sitting among the children. Niko is beside her, so close that her thigh is on top of Dejonae's.

Dejonae is signing out an introduction for my daughter.

"Why are you doing that with your hands?" A little girl with dark hair, pale skin and big brown eyes looks on in awe.

"Belle, don't be rude," an older boy with thick hair and sullen eyes scolds.

Belle frowns. "Why?"

"It's okay," Dejonae says. "It's not rude to ask a question."

"Sazuki, would you like to discuss business on the balcony?" Alistair offers.

"Just a moment." My daughter can get overwhelmed around strangers. I want to be close enough to jump in if there are any issues.

Dejonae nudges my daughter when Niko tries to retreat from

the conversation. Smiling kindly, she tells Niko, "Go ahead. It's nothing to be ashamed of."

"I'm deaf," Niko gestures with a hesitant frown.

A beat of silence passes as the children struggle to understand. The boy with the glasses speaks first.

"Cool!"

Cool? I freeze in shock.

Niko smiles and relaxes into Dejonae's chest. I have never seen my daughter so confident and at ease in front of strangers before.

"Niko has a good relationship with Dejonae," Alistair observes.

I keep my eyes on them, still alert. "Miss Williams knows sign language and Niko finds that reassuring."

"Speaking of sign language, Kenya's already talking about signing us up for classes." His expression remains stone-cold, but his eyes soften. "I'll sign Belle up for it too. It would be good for her to know more than one language."

"That is very kind of you."

He arches an eyebrow. "I'm glad you're here, Sazuki, but I'm guessing you didn't accept my invitation just so we could talk about sign language."

"No." I turn fully to Alistair. "I want your coding expertise. More precisely, your patterning algorithm."

He rubs his chin. "You're entering the coding space?"

"No. It's—"

Dejonae's laughter rings out, temporarily distracting me.

I glance into the living room again.

The children are on the floor playing cards. Niko is still tucked against Dejonae's side.

"What does deaf mean?" Belle asks, setting down a yellow card into a pile.

"It means she can't hear," the boy with the glasses says smartly.

"Then how can she play with us?"

Dejonae grins. "She can play just like you can." Turning to my daughter, she signs, "Play this card, Niko."

Niko sets down her card.

Dejonae screams. "UNO!"

Niko signs, "One."

My lips twitch. When I return my attention to Alistair, he's looking at me.

"Were you saying something?" I ask. "My apologies. Can you repeat it?"

"No need to apologize. I'm hyper-aware of where Belle is at all times too." He pauses. "I'm also hyper-aware of Kenya."

A self-conscious wave crashes into me.

I tug my collar away from my neck and pretend not to have heard. "My team and I are working on a sound wave prototype. Unfortunately, we hit a road block a few weeks ago. I believe the answer is in the programming."

"Who's your engineer?"

"Adam Harrison."

"Brilliant guy," Alistair says.

"Indeed, but programming is not his forte."

"So you want me to help you design the coding for this gadget?"

"Precisely."

"I'd like to, Sazuki, but I'm not sure I can handle the demand on my time." Alistair stares into the distance. "Between Fine Industries, Belle's Beauty and my family, I'm booked out."

"If it is too much strain on your schedule, we can license your technology. I will hire someone to take over the research."

He inhales deeply.

While Alistair thinks it over, I focus on Dejonae again. She is helping to clear up the UNO cards.

"Okay, guys," she says. "Since Niko and I are the new kids today, we'd like to propose the next game."

"What game?" Belle asks.

Dejonae's eyes sparkle. "Gestures."

"I'm in," the boy with dark hair says.

"Me too." The boy with glasses raises an arm.

"Don't start without me!" a new voice cries.

The screen door bangs open and a little girl with light brown skin and hazel eyes rushes in.

She sends a distracted wave toward the table. "Hey, Mama Moira!"

"Hi, Beth!" the elder returns.

Beth makes a running leap and drops to her knees, smoothly sliding across the hardwood floors. She gains speed and barely manages to stop before she crashes into the older boy.

He extends a hand and steadies her.

"Thanks, Mikey," Beth says.

"Don't call me that," the older boy grumbles.

"What took you so long?" the one with the glasses asks.

"Mom and dad had a meeting at Stinton Auto." Beth rolls her eyes. "They took *for-ever*." The newcomer whips her head around and notices Dejonae and Niko. "Hey."

"Hi." Dejonae grins.

"She's deaf!" Belle points at Niko.

"Cool," Beth says, nodding as if impressed.

Niko smiles tentatively at her.

"For this game, I'll be the points keeper," Dejonae says. "Everyone knows how to play Gestures, right?"

The children nod.

"I'll add a new rule. Anyone who uses sign language correctly will get two extra points."

"Oh, it's on," Beth says.

The two boys nod and lean forward as if they're ready to run a race.

Dejonae chose Gestures intentionally. The realization hits me right between the eyes. In other games, Niko would be at a disadvantage. By choosing Gestures, Dejonae did not simply even the playing field.

She gave Niko the upper hand.

I can't explain why I feel a sudden shiver.

"Okay," Alistair says.

I startle and face him with guilty eyes.

His lips are tense when he nods. "I'll make the time. I've heard about what your foundation plans to do for the deaf community. I think this is an important project and I want to be a part of it. I'll talk to Kenya and work out a schedule that she's comfortable with. I'd like to work hard and fast so the program is completed as soon as possible."

"That sounds like a deal." I shake his hand.

The door opens, admitting another couple. Right behind them is a man. The three send their greetings to the children who are so engrossed in the game that they barely acknowledge them.

Dejonae is the only one who turns and dips her head, shooting out a quick introduction.

"Vanya isn't picking up," Sunny says, emerging from the kitchen. She glides to the man who just entered and gives him a peck on the lips. "Hi, honey."

"Sorry I'm late. The therapy session went longer than expected. Did you say something about Vanya and Hadyn?"

The elder jumps to her feet. "Darrel, I brought *soursap* juice for you to try. It's in the fridge."

"Thanks, Mama Moira," Darrel grins.

The new couple notice me and lift their hands in welcome.

Alistair gestures to them. "This is Max and Dawn Stinton. Dawn is our resident mechanic. If you ever have car trouble, give her a call. There's never been a vehicle she can't fix."

Max Stinton smirks as he takes off his suit jacket. "That should be your motto, Dawn. *There's never been a car she can't fix*."

"I want royalties if you use my catchphrase," Alistair says with a straight face.

Their easy camaraderie makes me feel strangely alone. My whole life, I set my identity in my family, but I never quite fit in.

The nail that sticks out is struck.

I learned to work together for the greater good, following the path set before me. But eventually, my heart wavered and I fell off the path. It cost me the family's respect and approval.

Seeing this gathering, I wonder if all families are so severe.

And I wonder if some families are stronger even when they aren't connected by blood.

* * *

It is with an uncanny eagerness that I send Niko off to school the next morning.

She signs 'I love you' as usual.

I remind her not to run from her music lessons and then return the gesture.

After waving to Akira, my daughter slips out of the car and heads into the school building. The private school has its own on-staff interpreter, which was one of the reasons I chose to enroll her there.

"She seems eager to go to school this morning," Akira says, glancing at me from the rear-view mirror. "As eager as you are to go to work."

I pretend to scroll through the news on my phone. "Holland Alistair invited me to a gathering yesterday. I took Niko along and she made friends with the children. They all promised to sit with her at lunch." I pause. "Except the little one. I believe she is in a different grade."

"Niko made friends so easily?"

I nod.

"Can they sign?"

"Not that I am aware of."

"Then how does she plan to communicate?"

I think about how Dejonae helped Niko get over her shyness while simultaneously allowing the other children to see my daughter as just another peer. After that first game of *Gestures*, Niko opened up completely and Beth, especially, seemed to take to her.

"They will find a way."

Akira's hands tighten on the steering wheel. "You do not seem concerned."

"Is there something to worry about?"

"Children can be cruel. Especially to someone who is different."

"My daughter is strong. And I believe that her new friends will be good for her."

"Are they… of Miss Williams' complexion?"

I slant her a warning glare. "They come from respectable, wealthy families and two-parent households. They seem smart, driven, and well-spoken. Most of all, they were very kind. Their skin tones have nothing to do with their ability to keep my daughter company, so I do not understand the question."

Akira keeps quiet.

On most occasions, I would let her opinion pass. Akira grew up in Japan with very little exposure to other cultures. While in America, she suffered an incident which proved the stereotypes about Americans in general and black people in particular to be true.

Her comments have never crossed the line, so I choose not to fight with her. I know her loyalty to me and to Niko is unchanging. But this time, I feel compelled to discuss the topic.

Leaning forward, I ask, "Why did you assume that their complexion would have any bearing on their character?"

"You may choose to believe that it doesn't, but I know differently."

"You cannot judge an entire race because of a few bad encounters," I inform her sternly.

"Forgive me, Ryotaro, but I am feeling particularly protective of young Niko." She pauses. "I identified the boys who were harassing her in the street. Would it interest you to know that two of the four were black?"

I stiffen. A few days ago, I tasked Akira with finding the bullies that Vanya and Dejonae described. It had been easy enough to convince the shop owners to give up their security feed, but identifying the children had proven more difficult.

"Who are they?" I growl.

Keeping her eyes on the road, she lifts her tablet from the passenger seat and hands it to me.

I accept the device and turn it on.

There are four pictures of twelve-year-old boys. As Akira stated, two of them have dark skin, one is white and the other is racially ambiguous.

Akira flashes me a knowing look. "Now that you have seen it, would you still like to lecture me?"

"Akira."

"Am I not allowed to judge them on their actions?" Her voice trembles. "Am I not allowed to be outraged by their behavior?"

I grit my teeth. "Of course you are allowed to be angry—as am I—but painting an entire race with your bad opinion is not only unfair, it is extremely hurtful to Niko. My daughter is both black and Japanese. She cannot deny one or the other. To speak badly of an entire race is to speak badly of my daughter and her mother. This is unacceptable."

"Ryotaro."

"I cannot control your thoughts, but I ask you to guard your words."

Akira dips her head, still tense. "I will try."

I tap my fingers on the tablet screen, thinking about my next move.

"What would you have me do about the bullies?" Akira's eyes glint with revenge.

"Niko already dealt with the bullies. There is no need to go after them."

"Are you saying we will do nothing?" She sounds disappointed.

"I did not say that." Turning off the tablet, I set it aside. "How long will it take to find the names, addresses, and backgrounds of the children's parents?"

"Not long. If they attend Niko's school, they are likely wealthy and in the public eye." She slows the car in front of the music foundation. "What do you plan to do with the parents?"

I cut her a sharp look.

Akira laughs softly when it dawns on her. "I feared you had gone soft."

"This is why you should never doubt me."

A satisfied smile on her red lips, she nods. "I will get their addresses right away."

I look at my watch.

Dejonae should be in her first class now. It will be another two hours until she arrives.

Unbuckling my seatbelt, I gesture for Akira to follow me into the office. "We will get it done within two hours. I have a very important appointment today and I do not want to be late."

* * *

AMERICAN PARENTS ARE SO USED to being coddled that it takes little effort to get my point across. One particularly disgruntled mother tried to throw salt at me but, otherwise, I emerged from my visits unscathed.

Akira drives me back to the foundation where I call Adam, get an update on his work and finalize plans to show Dejonae the lab later today.

When there is a knock on my door, I give a distracted, "Come in."

A loud creak fills the air as the door widens.

I hear her before I see her.

Quick-paced footsteps. A heavy sigh. The scrape of a watch against jeans.

The air carries a hint of cinnamon.

I look up and fall into Dejonae Williams' stormy brown eyes hidden beneath hunkering brows. It is our fourth meeting and yet she remains just as adversarial today as she did the night of the gala.

She is surprisingly stubborn for someone so young.

And people rarely surprise me.

Miss Williams remains at the door as if she wishes to leave as much space between us as possible. Her T-shirt is short and shows off a strip of her toned stomach. Her jeans are tight around her legs.

A large clip holds most of her thick, honey-tinged curls at the base of her head. There is no makeup on her face, not even lipstick, and yet she looks fresh-faced and glowing.

The perks of being young.

I lean back in my chair, letting it swing just a little.

A glimmer of disdain lives within her obsidian gaze. *Will the kitten strike with her claws today?*

"Miss Williams."

"Mr. Sazuki." Her full lips round the syllables in a crisp, hateful manner. She possesses a unique ability to turn my name into an expletive.

I glance at my watch.

She huffs in annoyance. "I'm on time."

She is.

Yet another surprise.

I gesture to the overstuffed chairs. Like my home, I prefer my office to be well-lit and free of clutter.

Miss Williams hesitates, watching me suspiciously.

I quirk a brow. "Move quickly, Miss Williams. As I mentioned before, I have no time to waste."

"And yet you have no problems wasting mine."

I lean my elbows on the desk and steeple my fingers. "It seems you have something to say."

"I do." She marches to my table and smacks her hands down next to my laptop. Leaning in, she says firmly, "I'd like to make myself clear. I do not want to be here, and I do not appreciate the methods you took to *get* me here. You don't like your time wasted and I don't like to be disrespected, so let's try not to piss each other off by doing what the other explicitly stated they dislike. Hm?"

I hold her stare, keeping perfectly still.

She maintains eye contact and refuses to back down.

My lips twitch. Perhaps I was wrong to call her a kitten. Miss Williams is a tiger—claws out, teeth bared, ready to bite.

"Do we have an understanding, Mr. Sazuki?" she insists.

My eyes slide down her beautiful face to her lips, which are pursed in aggravation, yet still manage to look full and inviting.

The air thickens between us as I continue to study her mouth.

Dark in tone, almost maroon.

Soft.

How sweet would they be?

I get a sudden and unwanted urge to scrape my teeth against her bottom lip.

Ignoring the shifting in my pants, I stare her down. Miss Williams' stormy expression clears away as the silence stretches. People who wish to fight need an adversary. When none is presented, they quickly realize their own folly.

Her face morphs from unwavering to uncertain.

She's shaken so easily.

I blame it on her youth.

Or maybe her lack of real world experience.

According to her file, Miss Williams was raised by two loving and protective parents. They kept her close to home and provided everything she could need. She has not been taught how cold, how *ruthless*, the world can be as yet.

It seems I've been given the task to teach her.

A beat passes.

Two.

Her mouth softens. She withdraws from the table.

This retreat should not be so enjoyable. I do not wish to break Miss Williams, but I am interested to see how much of her fire I can withstand before I burn.

"Whether you like it or not, Miss Williams," I rise from the desk and approach her, "you and I will be working very closely together until your graduation."

"I'd rather report to someone else."

"Not possible." I stop directly in front of her.

"I don't like you," she states heatedly.

I lean close to her ear. "Is this any way to speak to the man who holds your future in his hands?"

Her eyes turn hot again and she slices me with a glare.

I walk past her to hide my amusement. "Come with me. We will start with a tour."

She hardly seems enthused to follow me outside, but she bites down on her bottom lip and keeps a few paces behind.

The receptionist jumps to her feet when I leave my office.

"Mr. Sazuki, would you like me to…"

"It is okay, Yumi. I will lead Miss Williams' tour."

She dips her head and returns to her station.

I gesture to the cubicles upstairs. "This is the administration department. Since we rent out the concert hall, a small team is responsible for event scheduling, keeping accounts, and coordinating with the city."

"Is the concert hall right downstairs?" Dejonae asks, sounding slightly intrigued.

I glance over my shoulder. "I will show you."

She follows me into the elevator and stays all the way on the other side. Despite the distance, I am keenly aware of her. The way she worries her bottom lip. The way she grips her purse. The way she tries hard not to look at me.

Her perfume rides the air, filling my stomach with a strange, tumultuous feeling.

I am glad when the doors open and I can stumble out.

Dejonae disembarks more slowly, her eyes darting all around the hallway. "There are so many signs."

"To make the venue more accessible." I sweep my arm to the right. "The concert hall is right up those stairs. The practice rooms are to the left."

A man exits a practice room and walks in our direction. He stops when he sees me and a shocked look crosses his face. I assume he is another fan and prepare myself for the usual exclamations, questions and requests for pictures.

But when we get closer, I realize his eyes are not on me.

"Dejonae?" The man gasps.

Miss Williams stops in her tracks. Her body tenses. "Jordan?"

"Do you know him?" I ask, feeling strangely possessive.

"Do *you* know him?" she whispers back.

I notice the badge on his shirt and remember that we'd recently hired an on-staff sign language interpreter.

Looking down at Dejonae, I say, "He is the newest member of our staff."

She looks back up at me and hisses, "He's my ex-boyfriend."

CHAPTER 5
THE MONSTER HOUSE

DEJONAE

"WHAT ARE YOU DOING HERE?" Jordan pins me with shocked blue eyes.

"Ummm..." I'm being held against my will by my sexy Asian boss-hole? I'm waiting for another sighting of Sazuki's rare but beautiful dimples? I'm counting down the days until graduation?

"I'm working," I say lamely.

But it's not enough for Jordan because he juts a pale finger at the floor. "Working here?"

I nod to Sazuki. "Working with him."

My ex's eyes jump to Sazuki and he straightens like an arrow. "Mr. Sazuki."

"You are?"

"Jordan Harrison, sir. I'm the new ASL interpreter."

"Welcome to The Sazuki Foundation."

"Thank you, sir."

They shake hands.

"Uh," Jordan's face starts turning red, "you've got a... strong grip... sir."

Sazuki releases Jordan's hand with a chilly nod.

I wrap my arms around my middle.

Deep breaths, Deej.

Both of the men in front of me deserve a swift kick in the groin. For different reasons, obviously.

Why the heck is Jordan here? Sazuki is already raising my blood pressure. I'm *not* in the mood to deal with my ex today.

I glance around the dark hallway. Is this some kind of haunted house? Everywhere I turn, there's a monster popping out to haunt me.

"I haven't taken the tour yet. If you don't mind, I'd love to join you." Jordan edges up to me.

Barely restraining my eye roll, I inch away from him.

Sazuki glances between the two of us. His expression looks more severe than ever when he nods and storms down the hallway.

"How have you been, Deej?" Jordan asks. He's trying to be quiet, but his voice is too loud and it bounces against the wooden walls.

I clamp my mouth shut.

"Deej?"

My eyes narrow into annoyed slits.

"You look amazing." Jordan tries again.

I'm sure Sazuki can hear everything he's saying and that makes this moment ten times more annoying.

I walk ahead of my ex.

Jordan doesn't get the hint and quickens his pace to keep up with me. "I've been trying to call you."

"I've been trying to ignore you."

"Don't be like that, Deej."

"Be like what?" I hiss.

"I hated the way we left things."

"You didn't seem to hate where your *thing* was when I caught you sending pictures of it to your ex-girlfriend."

He blushes. "I've been meaning to talk to you about that. What happened back then was a misunderstanding."

I walk faster.

So does he. "Even though you were out of pocket for throwing my cell phone in a blender after we broke up, I totally understand why you did it and I forgive you."

My eyes zip to Sazuki's back. He's wearing a sharp navy blue jacket over rigid shoulders. His trousers are impeccably tailored to long legs. Brown loafers complete the outfit. Despite how put-together he looks, there's an extra sharpness to the swing of his arms. Like a bright and shining sword that can cut with a swipe.

"Now is not the time, Jordan," I grumble.

"Does that mean you'll grab coffee with me later and we can talk?" he asks hopefully.

"No," I snap. His persistence used to be one of the qualities I loved about him. Now I just find it annoying.

"Deej, I miss you…"

"Ehem." Sazuki cuts Jordan short. Eyes hard, he gestures to a classroom around the bended hallway.

I walk in first. The other men join me, but I'm barely paying them any attention. My eyes are too busy soaking in the luxurious music room, complete with soundproof walls, white carpets, and a sound booth.

Guitars hang on one wall. They're designed to look like they're floating and it makes an incredible effect. A drum set is encased in see-through glass panels. Sheet music and microphone stands cluster in a group like gossiping friends.

"Whoa. Are we allowed to walk in here?" I whisper. It's so expensive-looking that I'm afraid my dirty sneakers will stain the carpet.

"Go in," Sazuki encourages me.

I take a hesitant step.

"We're calling this one the Mozart Suite. It is one of fifteen rooms."

"F-fifteen?" My eyes whip to his. "One-five?"

His dimples make a quick appearance before they disappear behind his firm expression. "At night, the rooms can be rented out for classes, recording sessions, or band practices for traveling musicians and celebrities. During the day and in the evenings, they will be used for teaching."

I take a deep breath, loving the smell of soundproofing foam. When I tip my chin up, I'm stunned to see that the soundproofing goes up to the walls. The entire ceiling is covered in expensive padding with custom, built-in lights.

"This must have cost a fortune," I mutter, turning in a slow circle.

"It did," he says matter-of-factly. "But it was important to me that we get it done quickly and well."

I jump a little when I realize that Sazuki is closer to me than I expected. His sharp eyes linger on my face and I feel a strange tension crawling in the air between us. It's more than just the usual 'I want to stab your heart out' energy. It's something stickier. Something that stretches and moves like taffy.

My fingers quiver when his eyes drop to my lips. Heat washes over me and I curl my fingers against my jeans to keep from glancing away.

Jordan walks between us, cutting off our eye contact. He turns his nose up at the lavish room. "Isn't this all a little unnecessary? They're just kids. They don't need all the bells and whistles to have a good time."

"Your opinion is noted." Sazuki slants Jordan a hard look. "Come this way."

I follow Sazuki into a corner of the room. He presses a button and a mechanical whir fills the air. I squeak when the wall starts to spin.

"Be careful," Sazuki says. He grips my wrist and tugs me backward, out of the way of the jutting platform. At the brush of his hand, my heartbeat skitters.

We both release our grip at the same time.

I focus on what the spinning wall revealed. It's a raised stage. Orange, red, and yellow pallets cover the entirety of it.

"What are these?" I ask, pushing my fingers into the material.

Sazuki opens his mouth. "It's—"

"It's a sound floor," Jordan rushes to fill in.

Sazuki gives him another cold look.

My ex shuts up.

I wish I had that superpower.

"It's a vibrating wooden platform that allows hearing-impaired students to get a better sense of the music. When they stand on it, they can synchronize without having to rely on visual cues."

"That's amazing." I'm genuinely excited. "Accessibility is always such an after-thought in community spaces like concerts or conferences. I love seeing it be prioritized like this."

His eyes soften.

"May I?" I gesture to the stage.

He nods.

I take off my shoes and jump on the platform. It's sturdy.

"Let me join you," Jordan says, already starting to worm off his sneakers.

Sazuki holds out a hand, barring Jordan from taking a step.

My ex gives him a befuddled look.

"Have you reported to HR?"

"No."

"Then your tour ends here. You can look around after you've filed the necessary paperwork."

"But…" Jordan slants me a pitiful look.

Sazuki clenches his jaw, daring Jordan to defy him.

Jordan gives up on arguing and pleads, "Deej, come find me later. Let's grab lunch together."

"Let's not," I say stiffly.

"Deej…"

Sazuki takes a small, threatening step forward. Jordan hurries out of the room, watching me with his puppy-dog eyes until he's through the door.

Though he's gone, his presence leaves behind a headache. I can't believe my ex is working here at the foundation. I'm hoping his duties as an ASL interpreter keep him far, *far* away from me.

In the silence, my eyes catch on Sazuki's. He folds his arms over his chest. "Would you like me to call him back?"

"Don't you dare." I hop off the stage.

Sazuki studies me.

I feel his inspection like a flame on my skin. "What?"

"Is your boyfriend working here truly a coincidence?"

I scowl. "He's not my boyfriend. He gave up that position months ago."

"He seems interested in reprising the role."

"He can be interested in whatever he wants to be. It doesn't mean I have to entertain him."

Sazuki looks pleased. "How did you two meet?"

"Why should I tell you that?"

"Inter-office dating is not allowed."

I snort. "You don't have to worry about us getting back together." I cross the room to the wall with the hanging guitars. "I don't give cheaters second chances, so it's never going to happen. Ever."

Pushing up on my toes, I try to snatch the neck of the guitar. It's about a hundred inches off the ground. My hands miss by a mile.

Frustrated, I turn around. "You should really drop these guitars lower. How do you expect children to..."

The rest of my words get clogged in my throat when Sazuki brushes against me. He leans forward and I duck my head like a turtle retreating into its shell. As tall as he is, he easily plucks the guitar from the hook and offers it to me.

My eyes widen. Every thought in my head vanishes.

He's so close.

And he smells *so* good.

I gather my wits and take a deep breath before saying, "What are you doing?"

His eyes meet mine. "The point is to keep the expensive instruments out of children's reach."

"On behalf of all short-stacks, I object. Your design should have accounted for adults who are vertically challenged."

His lips curl up and he smiles.

Dimples.

Two of them.

They sink all the way into his cheeks.

Oh, Lord. My heart can't stop flailing.

Sazuki arches a brow. "Are you going to hold it?"

"Hold what?" I blurt, my throat tightening.

"The guitar."

"Oh."

His smirk gets a little wider.

Struggling to breathe, I grip the guitar tightly and hurry to the stage. What was that? Why is Sazuki making me feel tingly inside?

Am I insane?

He's bossy and annoying and way, *way* older than me.

I slide the strap of the guitar over my neck and catch all my runaway thoughts, shoving them into a box marked 'do not enter'.

Sazuki stands back and observes me. "You know how to play?"

"Not as well as I know piano." I give him a dirty look. "Although you would say that I don't play that well either."

He glances aside. At least he's human enough to look sheepish. "I may have... overdone it at the gala."

"You think?"

His eyes narrow at me. "But you should not make a habit of touching other people's pianos."

"I'm sorry," I offer sincerely. "I didn't realize you hadn't given your permission for me to use your piano. If I knew you had a problem with it, I wouldn't have played."

He grunts.

I wait for him to return the apology.

He arches a brow. "Is there something else?"

"You don't have anything more to say to me about the gala?"

"I said I might have overdone it."

"Is that how you apologize in Japan? No 'I'm sorry' or 'I was wrong'. Just an 'I may have overdone it' and a scolding about how the other person is to blame?"

"We generally apologize with our actions. Or with a meal."

"Well, that's a lot less direct."

"Being direct is impolite." He smirks. "You Americans say exactly what crosses your mind whether it is wise or not."

"Should I start generalizing you Asians? Or is it only us Americans who are allowed to be the butt of jokes?"

His playful smile lingers a little longer. "Fair is fair."

"You're giving me a pass?" I say in mock astonishment.

He gestures for me to give it a go.

I shake my head because I know better than to fall into that trap. "I'll be the mature one for a change and avoid any cheap shots about Asian stereotypes." My eyes slide down his body unconsciously. "I bet you'd just shatter all those assumptions anyway."

"Exactly *which* stereotype are you referring to, Miss Williams?" The way his tongue rolls over my name is ripe with sultry suggestion.

Heat surges through my stomach. "Not the one you're thinking."

"How do you know what I am thinking?"

My legs are trembling and the guitar is suddenly a heavy burden around my shoulders. With Sazuki staring at me like that, I lose my edge. There's a frightening pull building between us, and I wonder if this is what it was like for Eve when she caught sight of the apple.

Rather than answer, I strum a chord on the guitar and close my eyes, focusing on the vibration at my feet. It's subtle but clear.

"Not bad," I murmur.

"It was designed by my engineer friend Adam. He made many improvements in all the rooms."

"Each of the rooms are built for accessibility?"

"Accessibility was our main concern when designing the rooms. The Sazuki Foundation will mainly serve deaf and hearing impaired students. The use of projectors and holographic screens are Adam's special touch, but our goal is to have plenty of visual cues as well as multiple contact points and translators in case a student needs to speak to someone."

My mouth falls slightly open. "You're kidding."

"Did you agree to work here without doing your research?"

I scowl at him. "There was no agreement, remember?"

"Beside the point." He offers his hand to help me off the stage.

I remember the electricity I felt between us earlier and jump off on my own, gripping the guitar so it doesn't swing wildly.

He gives me a knowing look. "The Sazuki Foundation was created for students like Niko who have very few options. It took me a long time to find a music school in the US that catered to students who are fully deaf. And even though classes were available at the private music school, the monthly tuition is not accessible to the average family. I wanted a place where deaf people of all ages and walks of life could enjoy, create and learn music in an environment made for them."

"What's the price of a class?" I ask, thinking that maybe Yaya would be interested in a few lessons when she returns home.

"It's free."

I try not to expose my shock, but I can't keep it in. "Completely?"

"The mission of the foundation is to offer music to every deaf child who wants to engage with it. Making classes free would provide the lowest barrier of entry."

I look beyond him to the fancy room, fighting back tears.

His frigid expression holds a touch of concern. "Miss Williams?"

"I..." Emotions make my voice waver.

A handkerchief appears in front of me. I'm stunned that people still carry those around.

"Here." Sazuki offers.

"I'm okay." I try to hide my face from him.

He takes my hand and slips the cloth between my fingers. His touch is comforting and I'm surprised by the urge I have to hold on and give his hand a squeeze.

"My sister started losing her hearing when she was three and I've watched her fight to fit into a world that refused to make room for her." I struggle to keep my voice from breaking. "I'm... I'm sure this place is going to change many lives."

"This is the intention."

My eyes dagger him. "You should have led with that. Maybe I wouldn't have had to be dragged here kicking and screaming."

"Perhaps. But what would have been the fun in that?"

I let out a stunned laugh.

He smiles back at me.

A loud sound shatters the moment.

It's his ringing phone.

Sazuki glances down and a dark look cloaks his face. The change in his demeanor is quick. A slight raise of his chin. A tightening of his posture.

He adjusts his blazer with hooded eyes. Gone is the subtly playful smile. The dimples have been put back on their leashes.

"The tour is over for now," he mutters. "You will need a pass and security clearance from HR. Wait for me at your desk."

"What am I supposed to do until you come back?" I call to him.

"Homework."

I'm rendered speechless.

He strides past me, a storm of steely fire. But he stops and flings a single, knife-like brown eye over his shoulder.

"Also, you will not be able to have lunch with anyone. You'll be working through noon."

His words are firm enough to jar me awake and remind me...

I really hate this man.

* * *

THE HR PEOPLE are nice enough, despite being a little frosty when I show up. They take me to a desk just outside Mr. Sazuki's office.

No one says much to me, although a lot of whispers erupt when I leave the room. It's clear the admin don't understand why I've gotten my position or what I'm supposed to be doing there.

Honestly, I'm not sure either. Sazuki worked so hard to get me inside his foundation, but he hasn't made it clear what my role is.

Teacher? Guinea pig? Consultant?

Now that I know the mission is to help deaf children learn music, I'm excited to get started. It sucks that I'm being benched.

I check my watch, bored out of my mind.

What if this is Sazuki's revenge? Chaining me to a desk, wasting my time while I wait on the sidelines?

The bastard.

Steady footsteps prompt me to lift my head. The vampire lady who'd been on campus with Sazuki yesterday saunters toward me. She's staring right into my soul. Without her sunglasses hiding her eyes, I can see the disapproval all over her. The closer she gets, the more her lips vanish into a thin line until there's nothing but a red slit above her chin.

I shoot to my feet. "If you're looking for Mr. Sazuki, he's not back yet."

"I'm well aware of Sazuki's whereabouts," she snaps.

Harsh. Okay, so... we're not going to be best friends any time soon.

"Can I help you with something?" I ask tensely.

She gives me a cold look and then nods with barely hidden frustration. "What would you like to eat for lunch?"

"I'm sorry?"

"Lunch." She emphasizes the word in her strong accent. "What would you like to eat?"

"Uh..." I blink rapidly.

Her voice climbs as if *I'm* the one who's wasting her time by being puzzled. "I am in charge of Mr. Sazuki's lunch and he expressed that I should get you both something today."

"He did?" My voice climbs. Somehow, that's more unbelievable than the fact that this entire foundation offers deaf students lessons for free.

The woman taps her foot.

I clear my throat. "I'll get my own lunch. Thank you."

She waves a hand. "Very well."

I want to dismiss her, but I've seen how close she is to Niko. She seems to genuinely care about both Sazuki and his daughter. For Niko's sake, I'd prefer to get along with her.

"Hey," I stick my hand out when she starts to turn away, "I'm Dejonae Williams."

She looks at my fingers like they're tiny worms that can bite her. With clear reluctance, she takes the hand I offer. "Akira."

"No last name?"

"You would not be able to pronounce it."

Well then. "Niko said you were the one who taught her how to fight."

She stares at me with an angry face and says nothing.

I lick my lips. "I get the impression that you've done a lot for her."

"Of course. I am Niko's family. Those ties cannot be broken."

I don't miss the stress on *family*, as if she thinks that I can't care about Niko because I'm not related to her.

"Of course. Family and friends are what make life special."

"Do you consider yourself family? A friend?" She arches a brow like a bull dog about to attack.

It's easy to tell that Akira is not my biggest fan, and that she's extremely protective of Niko and Sazuki. I don't blame her for wanting to keep them safe, since she seems to be their bodyguard, driver and personal security all rolled up into one. But what I don't understand is why she hates me. It's not like I played *her* piano at the Belle's Beauty gala that night.

Akira takes a step toward my desk, her expression menacing. "Let me make one thing clear. Many like you have tried and failed to trap Sazuki with your games. They have learned the hard way that he is not a man to be trifled with. Whatever your schemes are, do not think that worming your way into Niko's heart will draw you closer to her father. Sazuki has seen through every last one of you and this time is no different."

My temper ignites. *What the hell?* "I have no interest in dating Sazuki. Whether you believe I'm a gold digger or not is none of my business. You can think of me what you will." I step forward until I'm nose-to-nose, well, more like nose-to-chin, with her. "But you will *not* accuse me of using Niko to get to anything. She is precious and important to me and I will fight anyone who argues otherwise."

Akira opens her mouth to answer—only to fall silent as Jordan's voice intrudes from the doorway.

"Is everything okay here?"

Glaring goes back and forth between me and the lady vampire.

"Everything is fine," Akira finally says. She whips around, almost lashing me in the face with her silky black ponytail.

While she storms off, my gaze staggers on Jordan.

"It's lunch. I thought we could check out a diner nearby and talk."

"I have nothing to say to you." I take my seat, pull up a bunch of binders and flip through them.

Jordan approaches my desk. "Deej, *please.* You cleared out of my apartment, blocked me on social media and refused to speak to me for months."

"Did you really expect us to have a peaceful breakup after I caught you sexting your ex-girlfriend?"

"I told you. I can explain."

"And I told you," I huff, "I'm not interested in an explanation."

"Deej, I know you're upset, but we can't keep this cold war up. We have to work together every day. How productive are we going to be if we can't at least have a pleasant working relationship?"

I drag my gaze away from him, hating that he has a point.

"One lunch. Once we clear the air, I won't bother you anymore."

I check my watch. "You have twenty minutes."

"Lunch is an hour."

"I'm not eating anything with you. You have twenty minutes to talk. Downstairs. In the little café on the first floor. Take it or leave it."

"I'll take it," he says eagerly.

Already regretting this, I turn off my computer, grab my purse and follow him to the elevator.

* * *

"So... the reason I had those pictures of Annaliese on my phone, um..."

Jordan rubs the back of his neck and looks out toward the street. The café is just a few paces from the foundation's lobby. The see-through panels that make up the walls invite lots of sunshine. Two baristas man the counter. Three tables are scattered around along with a few fake plants.

I sip my coffee which Jordan insisted on getting for me before we sat down. "You've repeated the same line three times already."

"Deej," he suddenly pounces on my hand, "I don't understand why we have to keep going back to the past. What happened... happened. We should be adults about this."

"Being an 'adult' means having a discussion about how your needs aren't being met and you've started to look elsewhere. It means breaking up because you realize you're still in love with someone else. That's what being an adult means, Jordan."

"I know I messed up."

"If you know then why are we having this conversation?"

"Because you're upset about it."

The headache from earlier comes back and it's even worse. "Why would I not be upset about my boyfriend sending and receiving sexy photos from another woman?"

"Honestly," he throws his hands up, "I did it for you."

I almost spit out my coffee. "Come again?"

"See, I knew you were going to do that." His brows merge

together. "This is why men aren't honest, Deej. You women don't want to hear the truth."

I curl my fingers into fists. "And what is this truth that women can't handle?"

"Every man has the urge to cheat. Every. Man. It's inside you as a male to want variety." He taps his chest like a proud peacock. As if he expects a medal for being total scum. "I had to go and make sure that I wouldn't destroy what I had with you."

"Rather than breaking up with me and doing all the dirty texting and sleeping around that you wanted, you did *me* a favor by cheating inside our relationship?"

I'm impressed at his ability to deliver that circular logic with a straight face.

"I needed to get it out of my system." Jordan leans forward, his eyes imploring me to understand him. "But once I got back with Annaliese, I realized that she wasn't you. She could never be you. And now I'm more sure than ever that I love you and no one else. Now, I'm ready to settle down. Have a family like we always spoke about."

I snort and look away from him. If he keeps talking, I'm going to splash him in the face with steaming hot coffee and then I'll have to fork out thousands in hospital bills.

"I know I hurt you, Deej. But I wouldn't have been able to hurt you if you didn't love me. And I know there's some part of you that still feels the same way."

"No, actually, there isn't."

"I don't believe you." He licks his lips. "We had great times together."

"Jordan," I set my coffee down, "I didn't agree to this conversation to give you hope that we can get back together."

He scrunches his nose. "Then why did you come?"

"Do you realize that you haven't *once* said you're sorry?"

His eyelashes flutter in shock.

I tap one finger firmly on the table. "You yelled at me for destroying your cell phone—which I would do again by the way—

and then you got angry at me for 'snooping' through your stuff. You conveniently ignored what I'd *found* on your cell phone and went on and on about how there should be trust in a relationship. Trust. As if you hadn't broken my trust by screwing your ex."

"We never screwed," Jordan says quickly.

"I don't believe you."

"It's the honest truth, Deej. All we did was text a bit."

"And share intimate pictures?"

Red creeps up his face and stains his neck. "You were busy with school and it felt like we were getting distant—"

I'm the fool for entertaining this conversation.

I grab my purse and jump to my feet.

Jordan stops me by clamping his fingers around my wrist. "Wait. Wait. You're right." He bows his head. "I'm sorry. I shouldn't have messed with Annaliese. I shouldn't have picked up any of her phone calls or met her at the park…"

"You *met* her?" My eyes widen.

He realizes he let that information slip and blinks rapidly. "Only so she could return some of the things I'd left at her place. That's all."

My nostrils flare. "Get your hands off me, Jordan."

He holds on. "I love you, Deej. I can't live without you. Every time I turned around, I kept hoping you were behind me, but you weren't. Now that we've met again like this, I feel like it's the universe trying to tell us something."

"If the 'universe' wants me to get back with a cheater, then it probably needs a spanking. Now let me go." I pry at his fingers, trying to rip his hand off. But it's like I'm wearing human shackles.

"*Miss Williams.*" A voice that cracks like thunder echoes through the cafeteria.

A chill runs down my spine when I see Sazuki stepping into the lobby. He makes a tall, intimidating figure standing with his hands tucked into his slacks and his eyes burning into me. Behind him, the afternoon sunlight brushes a halo of flames around his body. It makes his watch gleam and his skin look deep and tan.

Sazuki says nothing else, but when his eyes drop to the hand Jordan has around me, my ex releases me at once.

I'm not surprised.

Sazuki radiates absolute power.

Emperor of his territory, looking out over all that he owns.

I can't explain why it makes me angry rather than grateful.

Why it sends my temperature spiking in my veins.

Maybe it's because I'm within that territory and, by default, I'm also at his mercy. Whether he wants to destroy me or save me, it's all within his hands.

Jordan rises to his feet. "We'll continue this later, Deej."

We will not.

My ex gives Sazuki a wide berth as he heads through the sliding glass doors. I'm left sitting at the table, feeling like a mouse in the presence of a dragon.

That annoys me too.

I'm not afraid of this man.

No matter how dangerous he is.

How dangerous he makes me feel.

His innate power makes me want to prove myself. Prove that he might own everything, but he doesn't own me.

I don't wait for him to call me over. I cross the giant lobby, diving headfirst into the thick energy that settles between our bodies.

"I told you to wait at your desk," Sazuki growls.

"And I decided I wouldn't do that." I arch an eyebrow at him. "It's lunch, Mr. Sazuki. My personal time. And I can do what I want within this hour."

He steps a little closer to me, his gaze intensifying. "Are you trying to test me, Miss Williams?"

My chest rises and falls with every enraged breath. My heart thuds so hard it nearly drowns out the music pouring through the café speakers.

I stare up at him, refusing to back down. It doesn't take me long to see the flash of annoyance in his gaze.

Rather than scare me, it energizes me. Anger is an emotion I can understand. One I can feed off of. He can't hide behind a stern face. Quick flashes of dimples. Dry, cold words. The more I can get him to react, the more in control I'll feel.

From now on, that's my plan.

I'll show the big, brooding dragon that he should never corner a mouse.

CHAPTER 6
LAB RAT IN LOVE

SAZUKI

"This place is incredible." Miss Williams gawks at the machines in Adam's 'shed'—a vastly inaccurate label for his large, expensive, and eerie laboratory.

"Thank you." Adam smiles at her.

Dejonae smiles back.

I grunt in distaste.

Miss Williams did not speak a word to me on the ride to Adam's estate. Now that we are no longer alone, she seems full of conversation.

Her footsteps halt in front of a robot arm. "You design robots?"

"I don't 'design' them per say." Adam draws closer to her and places both hands on his hips. Gifting the arm with an admiring eye, he explains, "I put things together. Consider me like a toy builder. Except my toys are complicated and expensive."

Dejonae laughs as if Adam just delivered the world's funniest joke.

Adam sticks out his chest, preening.

I stomp forward. "Enough chatter. Tell her why she's here."

Dejonae slants me a scolding look.

I return a frosty glare of my own.

"Dejonae, let me introduce you to…" Adam walks further into the lab and clicks a button. A light flickers on and he makes a sweeping gesture with his arm. "MTB."

"That's a very uncomfortable-looking headband," Dejonae says.

"It's not a headband. It's a highly sensitive sound engine receiver for deaf musicians."

Her eyebrows wrinkle.

Adam's hands flutter the way they do when he is excited and is forcing himself to slow down. "Think of the MTB as a Bluetooth device. It transmits 'sounds' via vibrations to the listener's head. Different types of vibrations allow for distinguished 'sounds'. In that way, someone who's deaf can *hear* music."

"Ah." She blinks rapidly.

"Do you understand?" I ask.

"Of course. I understand everything." Dejonae waves me off.

"You can ask questions," Adam offers.

"What does MTB stand for?"

"Music to The Bone." Adam looks at me and grins.

"He came up with the name."

"I figured." She smiles.

In spite of my frustration with her defiance in the lobby, I fight back a smile of my own.

"The reason we reached out to you," Adam waves his arms at the device, "is because of your modified headphones."

"My headphones?" She looks startled. "It isn't as fancy as your headband."

Adam assures her, "Maybe so, but the principle behind it reveals an understanding of vibrational resonance and timing. See, we've done a tentative test of the device, but something has been missing. We've seen that users still miss the right beats and get lost in the tempo."

"You think I can help."

"Sazuki saw you do it."

She turns to face me, her eyes picking me apart.

"That day with Niko." My voice is sober.

"Is that why you created this? For your daughter?"

"We didn't exactly create it from scratch." Adam lifts the MTB. "The technology to 'hear' vibrations already existed. It has for many years. In fact, you can say that a regular sound system can have the same effect on a larger scale."

"How so?" Dejonae looks genuinely curious.

Adam traces a triangle in the air. "A speaker is made of amplifying cones. These cones push air around it, creating pressure waves that convey sound."

A wrinkle appears between her eyebrows. "Okay."

"When the speakers push out vibrations—"

"Adam, stop." I lift a hand.

He goes quiet.

I motion to Dejonae. "She does not understand."

"Yes, I do," she says rebelliously.

I narrow my eyes.

Her mouth twists with defensiveness. "Quiz me."

"This is not a classroom, Miss Williams."

"You're doubting my ability to learn and comprehend information. Give me a chance to prove that you're wrong."

"I'm rarely wrong."

A spark of challenge rises in her gaze.

I shake my head. "Adam, explain it again and slow down for Miss Williams. Use smaller words so she can understand you."

Adam arches both eyebrows as if he does not wish to get in the middle of this fight.

Miss Williams storms in front of me, her shoulders taut and her jaw clenching. "I *said* I understood."

"Then show me." I fold my arms over my chest.

"Fine." Her slender hands suddenly cup mine, sliding down to my wrist and leaving a path of fire on my skin.

Electricity.

In the music room, I felt it.

But it's stronger this time.

I snatch my hand away. "What are you doing?"

Adam gives me a puzzled look and I realize I sounded too harsh. But Dejonae does not react in fear. She doggedly pursues me, wrestling my much larger hand between her palms.

"Scared?" She smirks.

I frown at her, fighting to keep my control. My body has a real, visceral reaction to Dejonae's touch. It's hot and intense, spreading from first contact until it singes every inch of me.

Rather than scared, I would say that she rattles me.

And I do not appreciate it.

Laughing softly, Dejonae guides my arm up to her face and sets the tips of my fingers on her neck.

Her skin is smooth.

Soft to the touch.

Temptation.

"The difference between noise and music is vibrations. In its simplest form, music is pleasant vibrations. Noise is bad vibrations." She arches an eyebrow at me. "Just like a person can give someone else good or bad vibes, music can convey feelings that are real and true. It's not superstition. It's nature. It's energy. It was humanity's means to survive against big, bad predators like you."

I scowl at her.

She shifts my hand so it skims lower down her throat, stopping just above her flickering pulse.

Her eyes gleam with confidence.

"Vocal folds produce sound when air passes through them and they vibrate. The vibration is what produces the sound wave of my voice."

She is too close to me.

Her mouth is full and taunting.

Unwanted heat, plus something visceral and forbidden, twists inside me. I do not know what to make of it, or *her*.

Perhaps I should not try to unravel that thread.

I step back, but Dejonae steps closer.

"Am I wrong, *professor?*" she whispers.

"You have a simplified understanding of the mechanics," I grumble. "Do not get cocky, Miss Williams."

"I'm not the one who's suffering from an over-inflated ego."

I start moving and I do not stop until I am right in front of her. "Would you like a gold star?"

"I'd like you to admit that I know what I'm talking about."

"You know a little," I concede grumpily.

"What a fancy way of admitting you're wrong."

I grunt.

How easily she unnerves me.

Her hand is still on my wrist.

Mine is still around her throat.

I could so easily grip her neck and squeeze. Hear her whimper my name.

A flash of heat climbs my spine.

I could break her.

But she has no fear.

Her thumb, unconsciously, scrapes against my wrist as we stare at one another.

I cannot walk away first. Breaking her grip would be admitting that she affects me.

And I will not have that.

"Guys?" Adam says hesitantly.

I had forgotten he was there.

Dejonae takes a step back as if she'd forgotten too.

We both breathe in deeply.

Adam's eyes dart between me and the feisty college student.

"You're right, Dejonae. Speakers are, in essence, patterned off of our vocal box. In order for the sound to be clear, the vocal folds have to vibrate together, symmetrically. If it's off by even a centimeter, the voice might be soft or hoarse. Engineers studied those principles and applied them to the modern sound system."

Dejonae gives me a cheeky grin. "Then they fine-tuned it so speakers could become portable."

"Exactly." Adam nods in approval. "You know your music history."

"A college class would not have given you such in-depth knowledge on vibrations. Have you done research of your own?"

She nods. "When my sister decided to be a model, she had a hard time walking to the beat. You know that most modeling shows have music, right?"

I did not.

Her brown eyes rise to mine as she continues, "Yaya could strut like Vanya Beckford on the runway, but if she couldn't 'feel' the music, she'd move out of time or mess up her cues. It was frustrating for her and I hated seeing her come back home in tears after getting kicked out of another modeling class."

"Is that when you found your headphone solution?" Adam inquires.

"I read about the different methods of siphoning vibrations and using energy to 'hear' music, but a lot of the devices out there were expensive or didn't suit her specific needs."

Adam makes a sympathetic sound in his throat.

My heart pricks in my chest. "It angers me when I hear that resources are inaccessible to those who need it. The Sazuki Foundation will, hopefully, address this." I jut my chin at the MTB prototype. "And this is the beginning of our mission."

"Once tweaked," Adam says, "the MTB will translate vibrations with more accuracy than any other device out there."

"I'm happy to help. What do you need me to do first?"

"You can start by handing over your headphones. We'll send you a research contract. Once you agree to the terms, you can send us the blueprints and all your research."

Dejonae fishes the headphones out of her purse and offers it willingly. "I'll email you the rest."

Adam sets the modified headphones on the table. "Next, I'd like you to check out our MTB. With your knowledge of vibrational resonance, you might be able to tackle some of the problems we've been facing. We'll start with creating the scenario," Adam explains. "And then we'll—" His phone buzzes. He hurries to grab it out of his pocket. "That's Nova. Excuse me."

Dejonae and I remain alone in the lab.

She cocks her head, looking at me awkwardly. I wonder what that uncertain expression on her face means.

And then I wonder why I am curious.

Since Niko's mother, I have never allowed a woman to take up space in my mind. Niko and the Sazuki Foundation have been my only focus for years.

"Do you know how to operate the MTB?" Dejonae asks.

"I do."

She arches a brow, waiting.

I hesitate.

Not because I have no experience with the MTB.

On the contrary, I was the first to test it.

I am hesitant because Dejonae Williams is beginning to annoy me in ways I wish she wouldn't. Like a common cold clawing at the throat, I feel the stirrings of something I would rather avoid.

Reluctantly, I approach the desk. Adam's workstation is cluttered with a sauder iron, goggles, nuts, bolts, screws and various pieces of sawed-off metal. I reach past the stacks of calculators to the ear plugs he keeps in a jar.

"To create the scenario, we need to plug your ears to give the effect of being deaf."

"You test the MTB on hearing people?" She sounds surprised.

"I do not wish to give anyone hope until we know for certain that the technology can work." I pluck two of the plugs and hand them to her.

She cringes. "I'm not… great with things in my ears."

"You use ear buds." I remember her tapping them when I walked her to class.

"But they don't… penetrate, you know?"

My blood turns molten at the images her words convey. Miss

Williams. In my bed. Sweat on her skin. Mouth open, moaning, as I curve her neck, face down. Eyes on our connected bodies.

Inappropriate thoughts.

I brush them away and fight to keep my composure.

"The ear plugs will not pen—go further than they have to. It will not be too uncomfortable."

She still looks squeamish.

"Would you like me to do it for you?" I offer.

She lowers her lashes, hiding her brown eyes from view. "Be gentle."

The heat in my veins becomes a terrible blaze. I should stop to drink a cup of water and cool down, but I walk to Dejonae instead.

"Wait," her gorgeous mouth trembles, pursing into a flat maroon line. "L-let me. I'll do it."

I offer the plugs to her.

She takes a deep breath and, with the expression of one about to saw her own limbs off, slips the first plug into her ear.

By the time she is done, her breath is labored and her curls are sticking to the sweat on her cheeks.

"I don't think I can do this," she pants.

"You have one more."

"Here." She stabs the ear plug at me. "You do it."

How strange to see her confidence falter. Every time we meet, she has been strong and outspoken. To think that a little ear plug would shake her like this...

"Hold still." I steady her shoulders.

She squeezes her eyes shut.

I brush a loose curl behind her ear to keep it out of my way. It springs right back, as defiant as the woman it adorns.

"Is it done yet?"

"Not quite," I say, focusing on the curl. "Turn around."

"What?"

"Turn around," I speak forcefully.

With her eyes still closed, she gives me her back. I set the ear plug in the pocket of my blazer and gather my hands at Dejonae's neck.

The moment she feels me taking out her butterfly clip, she whirls around. "What are you doing?"

"Fixing your hair."

"I'll do it."

I brush her hand aside. "Stay still."

"Don't you know you should never touch a black woman's hair without permission?"

"In this moment, you are a test subject, not a black woman." I press the wings of her butterfly clip and watch her honey-tinged curls spring free. They fall against my knuckles, kissing my hands softly. "And your curls are in the way."

"They do what they want."

"Like their owner."

She twists her head around to give me a dirty look.

I gently fix her head so she is staring away from me.

"Do you know what you're doing?" she complains.

"I have done Niko's hair many times."

The mention of Niko makes her shoulders relax. "How often do you do Niko's hair?"

"Almost every morning, except when I take her to a black hair salon to install braids." I rake my fingers over Dejonae's temple and into her scalp.

She moans softly and then slaps a hand over her mouth.

But it is too late.

My body burns with the memory of her soft moan and I know it will barge into my mind tonight as I ready for bed.

Making quick work of her hair, I fix all the stray tendrils into a clip and slide the ear plug in.

Dejonae turns to me the moment I am done and touches her ear tentatively.

"Can you hear me?" I ask.

She focuses on my mouth and yells, "What?"

I laugh under my breath and lean toward her. "Can. You. Hear. Me."

She pushes up on the tips of her toes, her lips an inch away from mine. "I can't hear you!"

This close, I cannot help but confront the truth of her beauty. Her brown eyes are obsidian marbles set in an exquisitely symmetrical face. Her dark skin, which seemed to drown in sunlight and gold outside, still appears a rich and flawless ebony beneath the lab's artificial white lights.

Stunning.

In the moment, I do something completely out of character.

I press my thumb to her bottom lip and swipe.

Her eyes widen.

She drops flat on her feet, staring at me as if she's been stunned by a thousand camera flashes.

"You are shouting," I sign.

Her eyelashes flutter and she seems to buy my explanation.

Still looking flustered, Miss Williams signs back, "What should I do now?"

Adam returns to the lab. "Sorry about that. Are you ready to put the MTB on?"

"She is." I gesture to her. "Adam, you take over from here."

"I'd rather man the computer."

"I will observe the results," I insist.

Then I step back.

Away from the woman who has proven herself to be impossible, irritating, loudly opinionated, and frustratingly stubborn.

You forgot 'gorgeous'.

My thoughts have taken a mind of their own. It annoys me to no end. Though I wish to despise her, I find myself—instead—intrigued by her dangerous mixture of innocence and sultry sensuality.

Dejonae looks at me with her big, enchanting eyes.

I turn my back. For her sake—and for mine—I need to keep a distance from her.

*　*　*

"I just left Adam's lab," I say on the ride back to the foundation. My phone is pressed against my ear, my tablet is on my knee and a document is open in front of me. "The programming we need is not as rigorous as I expected."

Dejonae is quiet beside me. She has not said much since Akira brought the car around. At the moment, she is staring through the window, looking out at the gleaming skyscrapers.

"I've never thought to apply our algorithm to vibrational patterns and music. I'm excited to roll my sleeves up and get working on the code," Alistair says through the phone.

"As are we. We would like to open the foundation to a beta group of students in the next week and roll out our first testing of the MTB two weeks later."

"Not a lot of time to perfect it," Alistair notes.

"Which is why we do not plan to officially announce the Sazuki Foundation to the media until after three months. It will give our team enough time to work out any issues."

I hear a slight groan. When I glance across the car, I notice Dejonae's expression shift in pain.

"I'm impressed by what you and Adam have done with the MTB. The specs are amazing. Maybe you missed your calling as an engineer, Sazuki."

"I did the easy part. I told Adam what I wanted and he made the impossible a reality." In the corner of my eye, I notice Dejonae sling an arm around her stomach. "Alistair, I will be in touch." I end the call and frown at Dejonae. "Are you unwell?"

"I'll be fine once I eat something." She digs her hand into her stomach, her lips wrenched in pain.

"You should have had lunch," I say sternly.

"I would have. But *someone* dragged me away to the lab before I could order something."

Guilt pangs a tortured rhythm inside me. When I saw her with her ex-boyfriend, I let my irrational thoughts take over. It did not occur to me to check if she had eaten already before I whisked her to Adam's lab.

"You should have spoken up earlier," I grumble.

She slants me a death glare. "How comforting you are."

I know better than to laugh when she is in pain. Pulling my lips in to hide my amusement, I ask, "Do you like sushi?"

"I *love* sushi. But I don't know if I can handle that after skipping breakfast and lunch."

"We will get you some soup. It will be lighter on your stomach." I tap the front seat to get Akira's attention. "Take us to Miko San."

Akira dips her chin, but her eyes are cold when they meet mine in the mirror. I ignore the look and lift my laptop bag. Fishing around until I locate a chocolate bar, I hand it over.

"You keep Snickers in your bag?" She gives me a starry look.

I smile. "It keeps Niko quiet when I am unexpectedly caught up in a meeting."

"So basically you're calling me a cranky child," Dejonae says teasingly, unwrapping the chocolate.

"If the shoe fits."

Soft laughter flows from her lips. "You fed me, so I'll forgive you for that."

My chest feels lighter as I watch her laugh. I realize I enjoy this expression just as much as I do her stormy scowls.

My phone rings.

I am glued to the device for the rest of the drive to Miko San.

Once we arrive at the restaurant, I leave the car.

Akira does as well. She observes me with disapproving eyes. "You do not have time for this, Ryotaro."

"Niko's school will be out in an hour." I check my watch. "I will take Miss Williams back to her university and pick up Niko after the final bell."

Akira shakes her head. "It is better if I take you back to the foundation and you let her eat here by herself."

Her suggestion irritates me. I glance over my shoulder to where Dejonae is waiting for me on the curb side.

Akira's voice is low with warning. "You do not need to cross any more lines with her."

"I have not had lunch either. Besides, it is not wrong for me to eat with a colleague."

Akira's eyes turn icy.

I jut my chin at the road. "Drive carefully."

She huffs when she rolls her window up and leaves.

Dejonae stares at the SUV that is becoming smaller in the distance. "She won't join us?"

"She will return to the foundation and wait for me there."

"Why didn't you invite her to stay? What if she hasn't eaten lunch yet?" Dejonae cranes her neck as if she would invite Akira back.

I'm stunned by her kindness, but I hide it well. "She *has* eaten. She takes her lunch an hour earlier to accompany me."

"Good to know not everyone is a machine like you, Sazuki." Her lips quirk, letting me know she is only teasing.

I slant her an amused look. "Come inside before you faint."

"Yes, please."

I open the door for her and greet the hostess who calls me by name. She seems surprised that I brought someone other than Niko and Akira with me, but makes no comments.

We settle around a table. Dejonae peruses the menu distractedly. Her eyes keep darting around the room. There are no windows and very few lights, adding to a semi-dark atmosphere. The tables are low on the ground and the chairs have no backing. Cushions, flattened by years of use, keep customers from sitting on hard wooden surfaces.

"This place looks legit," Dejonae says.

"Legit?" I repeat the word more awkwardly.

"I usually eat at the sushi bar or the buffet restaurant around my apartment. And neither of those places look or smell like this."

"This is the smell of history. The restaurant has been operating for generations. The taste of the food does not change even when ownership passes hands. Miko San is as close to authentic as I could find in the city."

"So it's kind of like your secret place?" She grins.

"Perhaps."

Dejonae bobs her head, her eyes sparkling. She is a lot more relaxed when the promise of food is evident. I make note of it.

The waitress arrives and welcomes us with a dip of her head and a smile.

"What will you have?" she asks in English.

Dejonae nervously shoves the menus at me. "You order."

I smile at yet another display of uncertainty. Why do I find her shyness so endearing?

After ordering two bowls of miso soup and rice, I hand the menus back to the waitress. She dips her head again and shuffles into the kitchen.

Dejonae closes her eyes. "The music is really good."

I take a moment to listen to the soft instrumental and realize that it is my grandparent's song.

Curious, I peer at her. "What do you like about it?"

"It's hard to put into words." Eyes still closed, she lifts her hands and runs her fingers as if playing an invisible piano. "There's something haunting about it. It gets into your head and it kind of… expands. But it doesn't push anything away. The bigger it gets, the more it ties everything together." Her eyes open and she winces. "That made no sense, did it?"

"It made sense to me," I murmur.

"Really?"

I slide chopsticks from the bucket in the middle of the table and hand one over to her. "This song is my family's."

"No." Her jaw drops. "Why didn't I recognize it?"

"Most people would not be able to recognize it by the sound alone. We have no wish to be famous."

"Yeah, what's up with that?" She breaks her chopsticks apart cleanly. "Most bands would be touring the world, hitting every concert hall and television interview they can. It's so weird that your family chooses not to step into the spotlight."

"The music speaks for itself and this is all we need." I shake my head. "The world has become so consumed with material things, flashy music, vapid connections that the things that lack substance seem to rise to the top simply because they're louder or flashier. There is honor in stepping back and letting our work make the difference."

She purses her lips. I am learning that this expression indicates her disagreement with a thought. "I don't think flashy music is 'vapid' or lacking substance. Not every emotion has to be complex. Sometimes, there's power in simplicity. Everyone can understand what it's like to get their heart broken. Everyone can remember the happiness of summer. The simpler it is, the more people can relate to it. That's important too. In my mind, music is supposed to bring people together. If we just use it to show how superior we are to the 'vapid, flashy, material-obsessed' people, then that just makes us snobs."

I tilt my head. "An interesting take."

"You're talking to a future professional songwriter," she says. "From what I've studied, your family is the exception, not the rule."

"My family had a concentrated sound and the determination to work hard."

"And the millions of singers around the world don't?"

I lean back.

"Your family was unique enough to catch the eye of a huge movie producer. Your copyright lawyers are renowned for keeping your work safe. You made a killing by forging your own path and sticking to traditional music, but not everyone can afford an IP lawyer to hunt down the counterfeits. And not everyone can break out into the Sazuki family level of success by going against the grain."

I watch her intently.

She licks her lips, her eyes darting to the side. "What?"

"You are very passionate about this."

"Because it matters to me."

I realize that I enjoy hearing her speak her mind. She has a clear point of view and a fervent way of expressing it.

Our food arrives. Steam pours from the miso soup and fried tofu. The rice is delivered in an iron pot.

Dejonae's eyes widen. "Are we supposed to eat all of this?"

"You eat what you can handle." I take my empty bowl, scoop rice into it and slide it over to her.

After sharing out my own food, I bring my hands together. "*Itadakimasu.*"

"Amen." She squeezes her eyes shut.

I chuckle.

One eye pops open. "Why are you laughing? Didn't you say grace?"

"Not in the Western sense." I stir the noodles in my soup. "It is a way of showing gratitude for the food."

"Oh." Her mouth forms a perfect circle.

"Go ahead and eat." I gesture to her.

She hesitantly picks up her chopsticks. When she takes her first bite, her eyes brighten. "Whoa. This is insane."

I smile, enjoying her delight. The more time I spend with her, the more I appreciate her candidness. Miss Williams does not hide her feelings, whether they are anger, fear, indecision, or happiness. I find her transparency refreshing.

We eat quietly for a while and, for the first time in a long time, I realize I want to break the silence during a meal.

I set my chopsticks down. "What made you decide to become a songwriter?"

"Me?" She chokes on the food still in her mouth.

I pour her a glass of water and hand it over.

She takes it, her fingers brushing mine. Dejonae does not seem to notice, as occupied as she is with regaining her breath.

"I," she coughs cutely, "was into music from a young age, but I didn't have the discipline to learn notes. I wanted to be a DJ. I figured it would be easier to blend two ready-made songs together than try to create my own."

"That seems like a fair assessment."

She smiles. "After my sister started going deaf, our lives changed completely, but what I didn't expect to change was the way people interacted with us. Suddenly, my sister was being bullied. Kids made fun of her right to her face thinking she couldn't understand because she couldn't hear."

"And you decided to kill them with music?"

"Something like that." She laughs. "I broke someone's nose and got suspended from school. My dad sat me down on the porch swings and told me that I could beat a thousand people and not change one person's mind or I could change a thousand minds with one song."

"Wise words. However, it's a little optimistic for a child to be so influential."

"Hey!" She wads a napkin and throws it at me.

It sinks to the table harmlessly.

I smile. "Your father is a musician too?"

"Only an admirer. His dad was the musician. A saxophone player in underground jazz clubs."

"Exciting." I lean forward, eager for more. "Did you follow your father's advice?"

"I did. I wrote a song for the summer talent show and dedicated it to my sister. It was about how strong she was and, simultaneously, how awful bullies are. I made sure to include all the awful things people had done to her in the song and I used their names too."

"Name and shame. Very effective. You were not dragged off the stage?"

"The complete opposite. I got a standing ovation."

"The song was that good?" I arch an eyebrow, impressed.

She snorts. "Oh, no, it was horrible. I'm pretty sure I stole the chords from *I Will Survive*'s bridge section. And I was cramming rhymes like a baby ramming a circle building block into a square hole."

I laugh quietly.

She chuckles too, her eyes sparkling. "But in my defense, it was impossible to find a good word that rhymed with Xander."

"Handler? Wrangler? For something particularly American… Star-Spangled Banner?"

She scrunches her nose. "You made that look easy."

"It is easy."

"In my defense, I was young and angry. What mattered was that I got the point across. After the talent show, people started protecting my sister when they saw someone messing with her. I practically saved the day."

"I did not realize I was eating lunch with a hero."

"I don't do it for the glory, but if you're really impressed, you can pay for lunch."

"Did you think I wouldn't?"

She smiles pensively. "We're not exactly… friends."

"A boss can pay for his employee's meal," I say. "They do not have to be friends."

"True."

The air gets tense again as she watches me, looking for something.

I glance down. "Are you finished?"

"Yeah. Just about."

"I will get the bill." I leave the table, rubbing my bottom lip with my thumb.

Dejonae Williams becomes more intriguing as time goes by. Keeping my distance may prove to be more of a challenge than I thought.

I pay for the meal and, as I wait for my receipt, dip into my pocket for my cell phone. When I don't find it, I pat around my clothes.

Still no phone.

I start to panic.

Where did I leave it?

At that moment, I recall that I took the phone out and set it on the table while speaking to Dejonae.

I must have left it there.

After receiving the receipt, I march back to the table. Dejonae's eyes meet mine. Her stare is so frigid that it sends a warning signal through my body.

"Your phone is ringing." She lifts the device up to me.

On the screen, shining in big, bright letters are the words…

Niko's Mother.

CHAPTER 7
MIDNIGHT INVITATION

DEJONAE

"I saw Sazuki drop you off again. You still expect us to believe there's nothing going on between you two?" Taylor plops her bag in the seat next to mine.

Today, her hair is dyed red at the ends. Her eye makeup is more dramatic with wings at the tips and heavy mascara.

"I don't recall inviting you to sit beside me," I grumble.

"Free country," she says with a smirk. Kicking up her feet on the chair in front of her, she settles in.

"Fine." I get up and gather my books. "I'll move."

"Don't be like that, Donna."

"It's Dee-jon-ae," I bite out.

"Right. That's what I said."

With a roll of my eyes, I snap my backpack across my shoulder and storm to another row. Everyone in the lecture hall watches me like I'm some kind of animal in a zoo.

I grit my teeth. How do celebrities live like this? I've been semi-famous for less than forty-eight hours and I'm already sick of it.

Thankfully, Taylor doesn't follow me to my new seat. The rest of the class seems content to stare and whisper from a distance.

PRICKLY ROMANCE

I set my headphones over my ears to tune them out and then I text Yaya.

Dejonae: When are you coming home for a visit? I need you.

Then I text Hadyn.

Dejonae: Is everything okay with Vanya? She hasn't been replying to my texts.

The door springs open and Mr. Howel enters briskly.

"Hello, class," he says with a frown. His eyes flit to me and he zooms in. "Miss Williams."

"Sir." I sit up straight, thinking he's going to scold me for being on my phone.

"How are you today? Feeling well?"

"Uh… I'm okay."

His face shifts and he laughs loudly. "Wonderful. *Wonderful!*" He sets his books on the edge of the piano. "Mr. Sazuki didn't… say anything about me, did he? He's supposed to let me know when we can meet for a performance session."

I squirm. "No, he didn't say anything."

"No problem at all. Let him know that I'm available any time." Howel makes a telephone gesture and clicks his tongue. "When his schedule allows, of course."

I sink into my seat as the lesson begins.

Everyone is staring and whispering all over again.

Why the *hell* did Sazuki have to show up at my school and make such a big splash? Now I'm marked for life.

My phone buzzes.

Yaya: I don't think I'll be able to come home, Didi.

Yaya: Is something wrong?

Where do I begin?

My cheating ex-boyfriend is now my co-worker.

My best friend has fallen off the face of the planet.

And my grumpy boss is…

Less grumpy than I expected.

Just the thought of Sazuki makes my heart speed up. If I close my eyes, I can see him. Standing in that sharp, princely way of his, legs longer than a tree, eyes boring into me with dangerous intensity.

When he gathered my hair in Adam Harrison's lab, I had the unbearable urge to ask him to never stop touching me. To keep running his fingers through my hair, down my arms and anywhere else he wanted.

Dangerous thoughts.

Even more dangerous?

The connection I felt in the restaurant. I haven't had that kind of chemistry with anyone. Ever. The fact that it's with *Sazuki* of all people is unbelievably irritating.

Especially when I think about the phone call.

Niko's mother.

His wife.

Or ex-wife.

Whatever the relationship is, she's still in his life. Still in Niko's life.

I'm the intruder.

I don't know what I was thinking. That we could be more than just boss and employee? That we could be friends?

Ridiculous.

Sazuki is so powerful, so larger than life, that he briefly eclipsed reality. But the cold, hard truth is starting to pierce through the haze.

The connection between us is only in my head.

Sazuki doesn't care about me. He doesn't care about anything but his daughter.

He's bossy.

Grouchy.

Reticent.

He barely sees me as worthy enough to touch his piano. To him, I'm just a flighty, naive, strong-willed college student he can push around at his convenience.

Well, screw him.

I'll do my job, earn my credits for graduation and try to find a way to keep in touch with Niko while forgetting her dad exists.

My phone buzzes during the lecture.

Hadyn: Van's not feeling too well right now. I've got an idea to cheer her up, but I'll need your help.

Me: Anything.

Hadyn: I'll discuss the details soon.

I turn the phone face-down, lost in my thoughts.

Hadyn's been taking care of Vanya since they were kids. Although he's never stated it outright, I pieced together that she's his first love.

I wonder if Sazuki's wife was *his* first love.

Was it love at first sight?

Was she his first everything?

At the direction of my thoughts, I sit up straight and shake my head.

Do not think about Sazuki or his wife.

"Miss Williams?" Mr. Howel stops in the middle of his lecture. "Would you like to ask a question?"

"Uh, what? No, sorry."

He gives me an accommodating smile. "No problem. You just let me know if there's something you don't understand."

I duck my head while he continues droning on.

After class, Taylor and her friends walk past me.

"How does it feel to become the teacher's pet overnight?"

I give her a withering stare. "Do you take your bullying lessons from Regina George? Come up with something original, Taylor."

She laughs. "Funny."

"I wasn't trying to be," I murmur, gathering my books.

She leans forward. "How did you do it?"

"Do what?"

"Get Sazuki's attention."

I try hard not to roll my eyes.

"You said it wasn't drugs or sex. So what was it?"

"Bad karma?"

She gives me a funny look.

I sigh. "Taylor, I'd gladly trade places with you. Why don't you go talk to the dean and work out your own internship? Let me know how it goes."

She scoffs and storms out of the class.

Screw her.

And her little posse too.

I'm at the end of my patience when I leave the lecture hall. My fingers dig into my books like I'm choking someone's neck.

Sazuki.

This is all his fault. My life was perfectly normal before he swooped in with his sharp cheekbones, dark eyes and sexy accent. He trapped me in his world, dropped a giant spotlight over my head and left me to pick up the pieces.

Now everyone sees him when they look at me.

It would be fine…

If I wasn't trying to forget about him.

Eyes follow me down the path.

Students stare and point.

How long until things go back to normal and people like Taylor stay the hell out of my face?

I near the quad. Late evening sunshine bakes my head. The clouds are puffy and tinged with orange blushes. In the distance, I hear music. Low quality. Grainy. Like the kind that plays from old video recorders.

A little girl sings, *'You shouldn't be a bully like Xander. Because bullies don't go to heaven!'*

I freeze.

That's the song I wrote for the talent show.

"Yaya?" I gasp.

Without thought, I fly across the quad and round the bend. There, on the sidewalk, is my sister holding up a boombox.

Her hair is long and straight with cute bangs cut bluntly over her forehead. Her skin is dark and so flawless it looks like God carefully poured a bucket of dusky brown paint over her before she was born.

Her eyes are big and expressive, her nose short and round, and her lips are fuller than mine.

The modeling world is *crazy* for ignoring her.

Yaya sees me and starts dancing off-beat to the music. Students pass her by, giving her weird looks. She grins at each of them and sets her eyes back on me.

"Yaya!" I squeal in happiness, crossing the distance between us at warp speed. When I get close, I attack her in a giant hug. The boom box nearly crashes out of her hands.

My sister lets me squeeze her to death before nudging me away.

I step back just an inch.

She sets the speaker down, still blasting music, and hugs me back properly.

We sway until I hear a man clear his throat.

"Excuse me, you girls shouldn't be playing loud music. This is a school campus, not the neighborhood barbecue."

I turn around.

The man's eyes widen. "Are you Dejonae Williams?"

"That's me." I brush my hair out of my face.

He motions to me and Yaya. "Sorry. Go ahead and enjoy your music."

"It's okay. I'll take it off."

I could have lived without his 'neighborhood barbecue' comment, but we are, technically, in the wrong.

"No need." He smooths a pasty hand over his sweater vest and lets out a nervous laugh. "I'm Professor Wayne, by the way. I teach Classical Russian Music History."

"Oh." I saw that class at the start of the semester, but it sounded tedious so I didn't sign up for it.

He steps back. "I have a class now, but I'd love to chat some time."

"With me?"

"And Sazuki."

My lips drop flat.

He retreats, his eyes still on me. "If you, by chance, have an opportunity to speak to Sazuki, would you mention me. I—whoa." He almost stumbles into a skater who's wheeling past. He recovers quickly, though a flush spreads up his neck. "I'd love to do a collaboration if possible."

"I'm not that close to Sazuki," I say.

"That's alright. Just mention it to him. That'll be enough."

"What was that about?" Yaya signs when the teacher bumbles away.

"Later," I say. Leaning over, I take off the boombox.

Growing up, Yaya loved blasting her favorite songs. Because she could only 'feel' the music, having the volume turned up helped her experience the changing rhythms.

I wonder how much easier her life would have been if Sazuki and Adam's technology had been available to her.

Should I ask Sazuki to save one of the prototypes for me?

Would he think I'm annoying for asking?

No more thinking about Sazuki. Off limits, remember?

My sister slings an arm around my neck. With one hand, she signs, "What's running through your pretty head?"

"Thoughts of you," I gesture.

She lifts her chin as if to say '*makes sense*'.

Yaya has confidence in spades. It helps that she is, genuinely, one of the most beautiful women in the world. She's tall, curvy, athletic and fearless. I know she's going to make it big one day.

"Does dad know you're here?" I sign.

She gestures, "I thought we could visit him together."

"He's going to freak."

She drags a finger down her eye to her cheek. "Mom will cry."

I snort. "She totally will."

"I'm here to get you first," she signs. "They'll be less dramatic."

I laugh.

Yaya slings her arm around my waist and hugs me to her. She smells like cocoa butter and sunshine.

I tuck my head against hers. After all the crap that's been going on, seeing Yaya is the absolute *best* thing that could have happened to me.

Yaya bounces me with her hip and signs, "Let's catch a taxi and go home."

* * *

WE WERE WRONG.

Dad is the one who cries.

Mom, shockingly, manages to keep her composure when Yaya jumps from behind me and signs, 'Surprise!'

I stand back and watch my parents hug Yaya, knowing how much it means to have her home.

"What are you doing, Deej? Get over here." Mom hooks an arm around my neck and drags me into the family huddle.

For a woman who's an inch shy of five feet, she's surprisingly strong.

I wrap one arm around my mother's slim waist and another around my father's happy paunch. They squeeze me in turn and we all take a collective breath together.

After dad releases me, he swipes under his eye. "It feels good to have both my girls home."

"I haven't been gone that long," Yaya signs.

Dad gestures, "You never call."

Yaya moves her dominant hand back and forth. "I'm busy."

"Even if you're busy, you should still remember to call."

"Don't scold her, Darius. She just got home." Mom gives dad a little shove.

Yaya rolls her eyes, but a grin plays across her lips.

Mom wipes dark hands against her jeans. "Are you girls hungry? Let me make you something to eat."

"I'm starving," Yaya signs. She throws herself backward into the couch and extends one long, muscle-bound leg.

My sister used to run track in high school and the muscle definition remained long after she quit.

"I'm not hungry." I follow mom into the kitchen to get some water. "I had a late lunch."

"What did you have for lunch?" mom asks, eyeing me over her shoulder as she reaches for something in the cupboard.

"Miso soup."

"Is that Nigerian?"

"It's Japanese," I mutter.

"I thought the only Japanese food you could stomach was sushi."

"Apparently not. The soup I had today was incredible."

"We should all try it out." Mom's smile lights up her face. "Wouldn't that be nice?"

I nod absently.

Dad stalks into the kitchen a hand on his stomach. His chubby cheeks bunch under his eyes when he sees me. "Hey, sugar, what's the latest with you?"

"Everything's the same."

"What about that café you were working at? Are you still there?"

"The shop went bankrupt," I say.

"Have you managed to find a new job?" Mom sets a loaf of bread and a jar of mayonnaise on the counter.

"Sort of. It's only a temporary thing. I'll probably be job-hunting again after graduation."

"Don't bother with that. Come back to work for me. I still haven't found a secretary as good as you." Dad walks over to me and kisses my temple.

"You mean you haven't found another secretary who will work for free."

"What are you talking about? I paid you by keeping a roof over your head and food in your stomach." He booms out a laugh.

"Exactly. Do you know how many labor laws you broke?"

Mom sets a cutting board on the counter and poises a knife over sandwich meat. "Ignore him. Your father's plan is to do all he can to get you girls home."

Yaya's footsteps make us all turn.

"Why did the party move into the kitchen without me?" she signs.

Mom sets the knife down. "Your father is on Dejonae's case again."

Yaya tilts her head and gives dad a warning look.

He throws up his hands as if to say *'I'm innocent'*.

"Deej is going to be a famous songwriter," Yaya signs. "Don't get in her way."

"Thank you." I toss her a knowing grin.

"I got your back," she gestures.

"Have you worked on any new songs lately?" mom asks.

I shake my head. "I've been too busy with school and looking for a job, but now that I'm working again, I'll get back to it."

"How about you, Yaya?" Dad signs. "Any new gigs after that Macy's catalogue?"

She scrunches her nose. "Not yet."

"It'll pick up," I sign.

She gives me a grateful smile.

Mom slides a finished sandwich over to Yaya. Then she turns her pretty brown eyes on me.

Everyone says we get our good looks from her. Mom is one of those classic beauties with finely arching eyebrows, sultry brown eyes, and perfect, Cupid's bow lips. Dad used to joke that she was drunk when she fell for him.

"Sweetie, are you sure you don't want something?" mom insists.

"I'm okay."

Dad opens a pack of chips and sets it on the counter between us. I nab one because I'm my father's daughter and I can't say no to cheese-dusted goodness.

Yaya fishes in her pocket and slides her phone over to me. I peer over the counter and nearly choke when I see a picture of me and Vanya.

It's from the day I met Niko in the alley.

Vanya's wearing her fancy blue dress and I look like a bum in my old sneakers, T-shirt and jeans.

"Have some water, sugar." Dad cracks a can of root beer, his version of 'water' and shoves it at me.

I gulp it down, cringing when the acid burns the back of my throat.

Yaya gives me an excited look. "You're still hanging out with Vanya Beckford?"

"We meet every now and then."

"When are you going to introduce me?" She touches the tip of her lips with a finger and drags it down. "I want to ask her some questions."

I cringe. "Now isn't really a good time."

"Why?"

"She just had a new baby," I sign. "And something seems to be going on with her."

Mom collapses into a bar stool. "Who? Vanya Beckford?"

I nod.

"That poor girl. People just won't leave her alone."

"What do you mean?"

"There was another article about her yesterday."

Both Yaya and I tense up.

"What did it say?" Dad eats his chips casually.

"They say she's getting rid of her baby weight too quickly. They even have scientific evidence saying she should be weighing a lot more after giving birth." Mom gestures, "People think she's extreme dieting."

Yaya's expression turns stormy. Her hands move at warp speed. "People always have things to say when they know nothing about someone. Why can't they leave her alone?"

"Exactly!" I hiss.

"If being a celebrity means having people care so much about my weight, then I'm good." Dad pats his belly. "I'd want these idiots to come and judge *me*. I'd tell them all about themselves."

"Vanya can't argue with them," I sign. "Or it'll hurt her business."

Yaya chews thoughtfully. "Maybe now isn't a good time to introduce me to her."

"I'll talk to her. I know she wants to meet you," I sign. "She just hasn't had the time."

Satisfied, my sister returns her attention to the sandwich and takes a big chomp. She normally eats a ton when she comes home.

Mom signs, "Deej, is your new job with Vanya Beckford?"

"No, I'm working for the Sazukis."

"Sazuki?" Dad pops another chip into his mouth. "Why does that name sound so familiar?"

Yaya signs, "Isn't that a car?"

"You're thinking *Suzuki*. These are the *Sa-zukis*. They're a super famous family who've been making traditional music for decades."

"I've never heard of them," she signs.

"And you probably never will. They live in the shadows, but they've sold more albums than all the biggest pop stars combined. And they did it without touring or going on television."

"Maybe it's money laundering?" Yaya signs.

"Are they part of the mafia?" Dad adds.

"No, they're not." My eyebrows crash together. "They're incredibly talented and shrewd business people."

Mom tilts her head. "Sazuki. He's a musician, right?"

"Pianist." I run my fingers over invisible piano keys.

"Wasn't there an article about how snobby he is? I read that he keeps to himself and doesn't talk to anyone 'beneath' him."

"Typical rich people," Yaya signs.

"Selfish." Dad tsks. "They have all that money and they don't do anything to help the less fortunate."

"That's not true." My voice climbs. "Sazuki built an entire

foundation to give back to the deaf community. And I'm betting there's a lot more he's done that no one knows about because he hasn't broadcasted it." My shoulders go rigid. "Weren't we just talking about how damaging gossip is? Why are we doing it to him?"

Mom's jaw falls open softly.

Dad's chip drops out of his mouth.

Yaya looks amused. She signs, "What's with you?"

"I just think it's unfair to judge people when you don't know them. That's all," I mutter sheepishly.

My family continues to slant me weird looks. I grab a handful of chips and stuff it into my mouth to keep from talking.

Dad wisely changes the subject and there is no more mention of Sazuki or his foundation until later that night when Yaya sneaks into my bedroom.

"You're still afraid of the dark?" I sign after rolling over and putting on the lamp.

She stands in the doorway and sticks her tongue out at me.

When we were little, Yaya would often come running into my room after a bad dream. *'I can't hear if a monster's coming,'* she would say. I promised to let her know if I heard any monsters.

"Some traditions should stay alive," she signs.

I laugh softly.

Yaya's changed into an oversized *Beethoven's Nightmare* graphic T-shirt. Her hair's wrapped in a cheetah-print silk bonnet. Silver moonlight caresses her prominent cheekbones.

She climbs into the bed. I scoot over to make room for her and prop pillows against the headboard so I can sit up.

"Is there something between you and your boss?" she signs.

"Something like what?" I ask out loud.

She makes a gesture that, to anyone who didn't understand sign language, would look suggestive.

Heat blazes in my cheeks. I repeat the gesture and then signal an 'x'. "It's not like that."

"Then why did you get so worked up?"

"Because it's the truth."

She slants me a disbelieving look.

I arrange my feet so I'm sitting cross-legged. "Because I know the truth."

"Why do you care so much about *his* truth?" she challenges.

"It's not about him. It's about his daughter," I gesture. "Sazuki's daughter is deaf. That's how we connected."

My sister raises both eyebrows.

"He invested millions to create a space for his daughter to learn and produce music. Rather than keep that space to himself, he's sharing it with the city. For free. Not only that, but there's this device…" My hands drop when I remember the NDA I signed. "My point is, he might be arrogant, rude, and obnoxious," I think about the lengths he went to get me to work with him, "but he's not *too* bad underneath it all."

"You like him," my sister signs.

"No, I don't."

"Why deny it?"

"I'm not denying anything."

She smirks. "Does he like you too?"

"Drop the 'too'. And to answer your question, he hates me."

"Why?" she signs.

"The first time we met, I was playing his super expensive piano without his permission. He thought I lacked 'honor' and made it clear what he thought of me."

"So? First impressions aren't everything."

"They are when the second impression is even worse," I sign.

"Why don't you give him a chance? Is it because he has a child? Are you afraid of becoming a stepmother?"

"Of course not." I sit straight up. "I love Niko. She's the smartest, sweetest, most intelligent little girl I've ever met. I'm half-certain that she's cooler than me."

Yaya's eyes sparkle. "I want to meet her."

I purse my lips. "Not going to happen."

"You said she was deaf, right?" Yaya wiggles her eyebrows as she signs, "What's wrong with two deaf girls hanging out and having fun?"

"She's Sazuki's daughter."

"So?"

"So he's not going to just… let her hang out with us."

"It doesn't hurt to ask."

I fold my arms over my chest. "No."

"Are you afraid he's going to find out you like him if you call him first?" Yaya gestures.

"I don't like him," I stress. "This has nothing to do with that."

"So call," she insists.

"I can't just pick up the phone and call him up. He's my boss."

She tilts her head, clearly not buying it.

"It's almost midnight, Yaya. That would be inappropriate."

"Ask him tomorrow then," she signs.

I scowl.

Yaya rolls across my body and fishes for my phone.

I yelp when her weight almost smothers me. "Ah! What are you doing?"

She grabs my phone and, with an evil smile, scrolls through my contacts.

My eyes widen. I try to wrestle her for the phone but years of running track and lifting weights means she's much stronger than I am.

My sister easily pins me down with her legs.

I struggle beneath her. "Don't you dare, Yaya."

The phone starts ringing.

I twist my head around to pin her with a dark look.

"Hang. Up," I sign.

She smirks and then drops her attention back to the phone.

The light turns green.

Yaya shoves the device at me.

"Miss Williams?" Sazuki sounds annoyed already.

I grimace.

Yaya pushes the phone at my mouth.

"Miss Williams," Sazuki repeats sternly, "why did you call me this late at night?"

I gesture frantically for Yaya to hang up.

She shakes her head.

Sazuki is going to kill me tomorrow.

"Uh, hi. Sorry to bother you. I'm calling because my sister and I are… we wanted to invite Niko to…"

Invite her *to do what?*

I give Yaya a desperate look.

"Bowling," Yaya signs.

"We're going bowling tomorrow night, and I was wondering if Niko would be interested in joining us."

There's a long silence on Sazuki's end.

He's going to reject me.

Humiliation makes my skin feel like it's on fire.

He thinks I'm an idiot.

A minute passes.

Did he hang up?

"It's okay if you're not interested," I say, trying to check if he's still there. "Yaya has this thing about making friends with every deaf person she meets. It was really her idea…"

Am I throwing my baby sister under the bus?

Yes.

Yes I am.

And shamelessly too.

Yaya scrunches her nose at me.

"I think Niko would enjoy that," Sazuki says finally. "As long as Akira can accompany her—"

"Of course. Yeah. Akira's more than welcome."

"*Ask him to come too,*" a robotic voice chimes.

Horror fills me like a swirling tsunami when I look back and see my sister.

With her phone out.

Using her evil text-to-speech app.

"Was that your sister?" Sazuki asks, sounding amused.

"Yes, she's…" I push Yaya off me and smack her phone away. It lands at the foot of the bed. "She's very friendly."

"Tell her I said hello."

My eyes bug. "What?"

"Did you tell her?"

"Why do you want to tell my sister hello?" I screech.

"It is called being polite, Miss Williams."

"You? Polite?"

He chuckles and the sound rolls over me in waves.

"I am the definition of cordiality."

I snort. "That hasn't been my experience."

"Your definition of politeness is clearly flawed then. I have no recollection of you being cordial either."

"Well, I'm not nice to *you*," I allow. "But in all fairness, you were rude to me first, so I think that's only right."

Yaya signs, "What is he saying?"

"He says hello," I speak and sign at the same time.

Her grin nearly splits her face in half.

"She said hello back," I translate as I watch my sisters hands. "And that I'm—" My heart stops. "Yaya, I'm not saying that."

"Saying what?" Sazuki asks.

"Nothing." I smack my sister's shoulder. "Sorry to take up so much of your time, Mr. Sazuki. I'll see you tomorrow."

"Goodnight, Miss Williams."

"Goodnight." I slam the 'end' button and toss the phone face-down on the bed.

My sister cackles loudly and clutches her stomach.

I glare at her. "Really? You wanted me to tell him I'm single?" I emphasize the gesture for 'single'. "He's married."

"Says who?" Yaya signs.

"Where do you think Niko comes from?" I argue. "Thin air?"

She signs, "They could be divorced."

"And they could be together or it could be complicated or they could have an open relationship. Whatever it is, it's none of my business."

"If you really don't care, then why not ask him?"

"Ask him yourself," I counter.

"I'm not the one who likes him," she signs.

"For the last time, I do *not* like him." My voice shakes and I'm glad, for once, that my sister can't hear it. "Sazuki's not my type. Even if he was, I can't stand him. He's rude and bossy and a know-it-all. Not to mention he's grumpier than the Grinch."

"You care too much. It's all over your face," she gestures.

"I don't care at all."

"Admit you have feelings for him," Yaya insists.

"I'm not admitting that."

"Then admit you want to…" She makes a circle and thrusts her finger through it.

I grab her hands and shove them down. "You better not do that in front of Niko tomorrow. If she starts signing about sex, her dad is going to kill me."

"*Killing is excessive.*"

I freeze.

Yaya blinks innocently.

Chills run down my spine.

Please tell me that's a ghost.

"*And in all fairness, Miss Williams, I believe the Grinch would out-grump me any day.*"

Oh, crud.

The voice is coming from my phone.

I inch forward and face the cell phone like it's a possessed doll in a rocking chair.

Yaya watches me intently.

I'm trying my best not to throw up, but I don't think I'll be able to hold it in. Moving so slowly anyone would think I'd turned geriatric, I reach for the cell and turn it over.

"Ah!" I gasp when I see what's on it.

The screen is completely green.

The little timer at the top is faithfully adding up the seconds.

I didn't hang up.

Yaya sees the screen. Her eyes widen when she realizes what it means.

"What are you going to do?" she gestures.

"I don't know!" I flail.

"Do something!"

I toss the phone at her. "You do something."

She throws it back.

"Miss Williams?"

I cover my mouth to make sure Sazuki can't hear my harried breath and smack the 'end' button. Then I smack it again, making sure the phone cuts off this time.

My sister gives me a terrified look.

I stare into her eyes. My insides are twisting and folding into themselves.

Please let this be a horrible dream. I'll wake up tomorrow and none of this was real.

But Yaya's hand on mine and the concern in her brown eyes is all the evidence I need.

Sazuki heard everything.

CHAPTER 8
DO NOT CROSS

SAZUKI

I scan the office the moment I walk in. The receptionist jumps to her feet and dips her head in greeting.

I wave a hand to her, a silent indication to relax.

My eyes land on Dejonae's desk. Apart from a computer and a small succulent, there are no personal effects cluttering the space. The chair is empty.

"Has she not arrived yet?" My voice climbs in surprise.

The receptionist sees where my eyes are pointed and straightens. "Miss Williams called HR. Apparently, she has an important group project today. She may not be able to come in."

I fold my arms over my chest, my gaze hardening. *So, the kitten is trying to run away from me?*

"Please contact Miss Williams and let her know that she will not be graduating if she misses a day of work."

The receptionist gives me a wide-eyed look. "Uh, yes, Mr. Sazuki."

Satisfied that my order will be carried out swiftly, I march into my office and settle in my chair. From my perch, I can see Dejonae's desk through the blinds.

Do not think you can get away so easily, kitten.

With a smirk, I open a document.

An hour later, the document is still blank.

Perhaps it is because I keep glancing up and checking Dejonae's desk every few seconds.

Why isn't she here yet?

Will she really not show after the threat about her graduation? How far does she want to test me?

Tension spreads across my brow. I call my receptionist. "What did Miss Williams say when you contacted her?"

"I don't believe I should repeat those words, sir."

I lean back in my chair, both amused and angry. I do enjoy a challenge, but I don't welcome it now. Dejonae's absence is a distraction and, with such limited time before the first students arrive, I cannot afford to waste a single second.

"Wait a minute, Mr. Sazuki. I just heard the elevator."

My heartbeat increases in speed. I lean forward.

"She has arrived."

"Thank you." I hang up and poise my hands over the keyboard to appear busy.

A minute later, a brush of pink flits past my blinds. Every inch of me turns toward Dejonae as she walks in. Her hair is piled up in a bun. Rather than her usual shirt and jeans, she is wearing a dress and red lipstick.

Stomping around to her desk, Dejonae jerks out the chair and plunks into it. Her eyes shoot to my window. When she sees me watching, her entire body stiffens. She stares back at me, dumbstruck.

I smooth a hand over my tie and rise.

She whirls her chair around and hunches over the computer keyboard as if the monitor can hide her. I feel her panicking with every step I take in her direction.

"You are late," I say, stopping in front of her desk.

"I'm aware of the time."

Such insolence. "Did you and your sister spend the night making more calls?"

Dejonae backs away from me like I am a cobra preparing to strike. "I don't know what you're talking about."

"I sincerely doubt that you are as clueless as you appear."

She returns my smirk with a mocking smile of her own. "Mr. Sazuki, you made your threats and now I'm here. What was so urgent that you had to hold my graduation hostage?"

"Have you logged into the foundation's portal yet?"

Her eyebrows hunker together.

I round the desk. "You should have received the schedule by now. From now on, you will need to be informed of all events. Things change very quickly from day-to-day."

"Why are you coming around?" Her voice trembles.

Rather than answer, I bend over her computer and set my arms on either side of her. Her smell is a tantalizing mixture of flowers and cinnamon.

I inhale deeply before speaking. "You did not answer my question."

"What question?"

"Did your sister make any more calls after me?" I wake the computer with a flick of my fingers.

Her eyes lock on mine, burrowing into my soul. She purses her lips. "No."

I am stunned by the relief I feel. What does it matter if Dejonae called another man at midnight? Why do I care if she and her sister discuss prospects other than me?

"By the way, why didn't you tell me you were listening?" She scowls.

"You seemed so deep in conversation. I didn't dare interrupt you."

"You should have hung up at least. That was a private conversation."

"So I am to blame?" My lips twitch.

"I didn't say that." She rolls her eyes. "I just don't understand why you listened in. You were practically spying on us!"

"Spying would mean that I intentionally left some kind of device in your room to overhear you. I did not." I slide my fingers across the track pad. "You are the one who called me. I did not force you to keep the phone on."

"You shouldn't have heard us," she says again. "That conversation wasn't for you."

"There is no going back, Miss Williams."

Her eyebrows form a deep V. "You are insufferable."

I blink, turn and study her. "You are inestimably bold for someone who was caught badmouthing the boss."

She makes an exasperated sound. "Fine. I did discuss you last night with my sister in the privacy of my own home, but it's not that serious. So can you forget it ever happened?"

"The perpetrator is not the one who should be making demands," I point out.

"We both know you have better things to do than worry about employee gossip. Perhaps you could start scratching things off your 'evil billionaire to-do list'."

My chest boils with amusement. I don a thoughtful expression and rub my chin. "Is 'Evil Billionaire' better or worse than 'Rude, Know-it-all Grinch?'"

Her eyelashes flutter. If she were of a lighter complexion, red would be staining her cheeks.

I type her name into the company's log system. "News of my divorce is readily available if you look. This is not a secret."

She holds her breath when I turn my face to hers. I am close enough to see the moles on her skin. Close enough to brush my lips against her own.

"You hung up before I was ready, Miss Williams," I inform her. "Since I am not your type, I was waiting to hear what was."

Her nostrils flare.

I hit enter and straighten.

The tension between us is too thick. Like a child with a lighter, it is only a matter of time before it catches a curtain or a gas tank and explodes.

I slide a hand into my pocket and saunter around the desk, needing that space between us. Dejonae clears her throat, not quite meeting my eyes.

"I've given you access to the company portal. Prepare to accompany me downstairs in an hour. I will introduce you to the teaching staff."

I turn away.

She shoots to her feet. Her chair skitters back. "Mr. Sazuki."

I face her calmly.

Her eyes crash into mine with a surprising amount of boldness. "I'm sorry. I shouldn't have talked about you or your relationship with my sister. From now on, I'll keep my work and my personal life separate. I'll make sure my sister does too. For Niko's sake, I don't want any misunderstandings."

My smile melts when I absorb her words.

I feel the wall she is building between us.

No, it is more fragile than that.

A line in the sand.

A boundary.

"No apology necessary, Miss Williams. I assure you, there is nothing to misunderstand." My voice is hard. "Niko enjoys your company and I have no problem with her continuing to spend time with you."

Dejonae glances away.

I turn stiffly and march back to my office, slamming the door a little too hard behind me.

* * *

D<small>EJONAE RISES</small> when I stalk out of my office an hour later. Without a sideways glance at her, I keep moving toward the elevator.

She is smart enough to follow me.

The receptionist pounces to her feet when I turn the bend.

"Is everyone downstairs?" I growl.

"One person is late, Mr. Sazuki."

Not slowing my stride, I shake my head. "We will start without them."

I stab the button on the elevator.

I would like to believe that I am a man of principle. The world turns, not because of the dreamers, but because of those who are not afraid to dive into something until they understand every inch of how it works. Only when we understand something, can we deviate and face the consequences of trying something new.

I know myself well.

My values. My principles. My worldview.

I have never lost my equilibrium because of a woman.

Not even with Niko's mother.

And I would like to pretend that Miss Williams' subtle rebuff this morning did not bruise more than just my ego.

I cannot.

She steps into the elevator with me, keeping her distance as always. She is standing at the opposite end as if she fears that I will devour her if she comes even halfway close to me.

And with how unravelled I feel, I just might.

Her perfume fills the space, trapping me in her scent.

The tightness of her dress is annoying. It shows too much of her shape. The flare of her hips. The cinch of her waist. The length of her slim legs.

The very sight of her gives me heart palpitations.

It's upsetting.

Distracting when I cannot afford to lose focus.

The Sazuki Foundation is the work of my legacy. I wish to help not just the deaf children in this city but, those across the world. With the MTB in its infancy and the music school yet to prove itself, I need balance more than ever.

I vow to myself that I will no longer entertain thoughts around Miss Williams, not unless they are strictly business related.

The elevator doors slide apart.

I storm off first and Dejonae is right behind me. Her heels click against the tiles.

Why did she dress up today? After our conversation, I am certain it was not for me.

Was it for her ex?

I shove the door of the conference room. It bangs open a bit harder than necessary. Dejonae slips in behind me. The door crashes shut, leaving a shot of silence in its wake.

Seven people occupy the seats around the table. The blue-eyed Caucasian at the helm is the one that sets my teeth on edge. His eyes flick around me and settle on Dejonae. He drinks her in like a dying man crawling toward a desert oasis.

It seems I am not alone in my admiration of Miss Williams' outfit today.

I stalk forward and arch an eyebrow at the interpreter. "You are in my seat."

"Am I?" Eyes still on Dejonae, he clumsily rises and clamors to where she is standing.

"Aren't you going to sit?" I bark.

The room goes still.

I feel Dejonae's eyes boring into me.

Time seems to slow as they both walk to the table. Dejonae takes the chair beside her ex-boyfriend. She sits with her back rigid, chin up, glaring at me through eyes that are ringed with thick lashes and mascara.

I lose my train of thought when I look at her.

Even though she is clearly angry with me, even when I'm inexplicably frustrated with her, the connection between us is not losing steam.

"Each of you were chosen," I rip my eyes away from Dejonae, "because of your background in music and ASL. But this does not mean that you are equipped to teach deaf students. It only means you have the potential to do so."

Dejonae folds her arms over her chest and glances away.

"Working with local schools and private academies, we have gathered a group of fifteen young children to be our first students. Think of the next few weeks as a beta program. Not only to test if students respond well to this environment but to test whether you have what it takes to teach."

People shift around in discomfort.

Dejonae is the only one who doesn't.

We lock eyes. She narrows hers in return.

I can feel the anger rolling off her body. It is there in the tension of her brow and the pursed lips that draw in like a flower when touched.

Did I call her a kitten this morning? I was wrong. She is out for blood. And I have a strong suspicion that I will be feeling her sharp claws the moment we are alone.

Why am I anticipating that?

Returning my focus to the very important task, I lace my fingers together. "I know many of you are accustomed to teaching your way, but your methods might not be best suited for your students. Which is why," I gesture to Dejonae, "you will each be training with her."

Dejonae's eyes pop open and she sucks in a breath.

"Miss Williams will be responsible for analyzing your ability to convey the lessons of rhythm and tempo, which are, for a deaf student, more challenging to grasp than simply playing the right notes."

"Mr. Sazuki."

I lift a hand to stop her. "Any questions?"

"I have one," Dejonae insists.

"Ask me privately." My voice cracks like a whip in the room.

"I would rather we talk about it now before you make any more unexpected announcements."

Her nostrils flare. Warning screams from her vibrant brown eyes.

My pants tighten.

I hate that her defiance—that magic flame inside her that never backs down from confrontation—ignites my blood.

A tentative knock breaks our stare-down.

A woman with purple hair and pale skin steps into the room. "Sorry I'm late," she whispers, shuffling in while holding her head down and gripping a leather purse. "Sorry."

"Miss Cottingham." I check my watch.

"I know." She cringes. "My car broke down and I had to wait for the tow truck…" Her gaze catches on Dejonae and she stops moving.

Dejonae looks equally surprised.

I gesture to the newcomer. "Miss Cottingham is my daughter's instructor. She worked previously at the Terrence Hall Music Academy. She will be a head trainer as well, second only to Miss Williams."

"Second?" Miss Cottingham gawks.

I slant her a sharp look. "Is that a problem?"

"N-no." She licks her lips.

I motion to the table. "Have a seat."

She takes the chair opposite Dejonae. The women give each other wary looks.

"As instructors, you will usher in the first phase of the foundation. In the second phase, we will introduce a learning tool to make lessons easier for our students. Miss Williams is assisting in the process of fine-tuning it." I nod to her.

She seems shocked by the acknowledgement.

"Keep in mind that we are here to serve, to inspire, and to protect. How we perform in this first phase will directly impact the success of The Sazuki Foundation." My eyes drift to Dejonae. "You are all an important piece. If you take your duties lightly, I will consider it as your way of asking to be released from your post."

Her lips fall into a thin line.

"That is all for today. You will receive your schedules and information packets on your first students from HR. If you have any questions, you can direct them to my secretary. That will be all for today."

Chairs scrape against the ground as the instructors leave the room.

I stay behind, keenly aware of Dejonae and her ex who are sitting closely together.

"We were cut off yesterday," he says, looking down at her, "but I'm hoping we can continue that thread of conversation later."

Dejonae slants him an annoyed look. "Not right now, Jordan."

"Sure. I'm willing to go at your pace, Deej. I'll do whatever I can to win your trust back."

His voice curdles my blood. I fight the instinct to kick him out of my sight.

But on what grounds?

Because I don't like his history with Dejonae? Because his intense pursuit of her annoys me?

He was hired for his skills, and I will not allow my… connection with Miss Williams to get in the foundation's path to success.

I tuck my binder under my arm and prepare to leave.

"Mr. Sazuki." Dejonae's voice is sharp and heated. "Can I speak to you for a moment?"

"Only if you can keep it to a moment, Miss Williams. You have a training session with the first instructor in," I check my watch, "five minutes."

"This won't take long," she bites out through gritted teeth.

Jordan glances between us. I jut my chin at the door.

He blinks rapidly. "Deej, I'll check you later."

Once he leaves and closes the door behind him, Dejonae stalks up to me. Gone is the sheepish woman who could barely look me in the eyes when I teased her about last night's call. In its place is the tigress who lives just below the surface.

Dejonae throws me a furious look. "What the hell was that?"

"What are you referring to?"

"We did not discuss me training other instructors."

"Did you not read your contract? It was listed specifically in the terms."

She scrunches her nose. "Who would read that many pages?"

I can't help a short snort of laughter. "In the future, Miss Williams, you should be careful of what you sign."

"Forget the contract. I can't teach other instructors."

"Why not?"

"Why not?" Her eyes bug. "Because that's way above my paygrade."

I arch both eyebrows. "You believe you are incapable?"

"I'm younger than all of them."

I step closer to her. "Is that the problem? Are you concerned about age?"

She looks away from me sharply, clearing her throat. "I'm not confident enough."

Her honesty surprises me.

Rather than tease her, I keep my voice steady. "After meeting Niko for less than an hour, you were able to convey to her a lesson that the teacher who had been working with her for months failed to convey. You have an instinctive gift for understanding what a student needs and relaying the principle with clarity. You have the patience to look beyond the limitations and find a solution. These are all traits that have nothing to do with your age and everything to do with your abilities."

As understanding dawns in her eyes, I feel a sense of pride. She should be made aware of her talents. Not everyone can work in a field this demanding and maintain their sense of empathy and compassion.

"You care for people," I say softly. "You make them feel comfortable and confident in your presence, which makes them believe that they can accomplish the task at hand. This is important for all students, but especially for students who may have been told that their disability will keep them from accomplishing their dreams."

She pulls her lips into her mouth, but that cannot stop the pleased smile from crawling over her face. "I didn't see it like that."

I want to touch her cheek and let her smile unfurl in all its sunny glory. It is the hardest thing to keep my hands at my sides instead.

"You will not be working alone. Miss Cottingham has a background in Special Education. What you lack in textbook knowledge, she can make up for. And I will be here." I look down at her. "I do not expect you to shoulder this alone."

"Do you really think I can do this?" she asks hesitantly. And then her eyes flash with a self-conscious spark.

The vulnerability is gone.

Mistrust eases back into her expression.

That transparency of hers is both a blessing and a curse. It allows me to read every thought in her head and, currently, she is beginning to remember who I am to her.

The tyrant.

The grouch.

The enemy.

"Are you sure this isn't you trying to set me up to fail?" She frowns.

I arch an eyebrow. "Do you think I have time to waste?"

She gives me another suspicious look, but with a strained smile this time.

"Dejonae." I set my hand on her shoulder. Her mouth taunts me with its slight tremble. "Outside of my daughter, this foundation means everything to me. I want to see it succeed and I am doing everything in my power to create something that will have a lasting impact on deaf musicians. I would not jeopardize that mission." My eyes harden. "For anything."

"I believe you."

My heartbeat picks up speed.

I'm overwhelmed by the urge to kiss her.

And it forces me to drop my arm.

"But, let's get one thing straight." Dejonae surprises me by moving closer and jutting a finger into my face. "You do *not* speak to me like that *ever again*. I don't care how angry or frustrated you are. Secondly, if you make decisions for me without consulting me again, I don't care who's watching, I will let you have it in front of everyone."

My lips twitch as I watch her flaring nostrils and tightening mouth. So small, so dainty, yet this formidable woman has steel in her veins, doesn't she?

"Do I make myself clear, Mr. Sazuki?"

I tilt my head. This close, with her eyes flaming and her body brushing mine, she's tempting me beyond what I can bear.

"We will see."

Her eyes darken in silent challenge. "I need more than that."

Heat travels from my chest to my pants. The way she looks at me, as if she would genuinely try to smack me into submission, is invigorating.

I'm stumped by the duality.

There are times when she is softer than a feather. Full of uncertainty and self-doubt.

A kitten.

And then there are times when the claws come out.

I ease back with a thoughtful look. "I will try."

She opens her mouth.

I hold up a hand. "That is all you are going to get."

Her hot eyes flash at me. Anger. Frustration.

Desire.

I see it pass through her, lingering in spite of her wish to cover it with her fury.

She is too transparent.

Her blessing.

Her downfall.

My stomach churns and I force myself to step away. Miss Dejonae might be unable to hide her attraction to me, but she has made herself clear.

I am nothing but her boss and the father of the child she has taken to.

She wants nothing more than that.

And I want… the same.

Dejonae stomps to the door without looking back. I am left in the silence of the music room, a pulse throbbing in my veins as I watch her hips sway back and forth.

Dejonae Williams is a problem, and I am not only referring to her sass.

So why is it so difficult to get her out of my head?

* * *

I LEAVE the office and pass Dejonae's empty desk. She has not been upstairs since the meeting this morning. It is alarming that I know her schedule in intimate detail and look for her even when I know she will not be there.

Akira meets me in the lobby. She is dressed all in black as usual, her hair scraped away from her face and her expression severe.

"I heard Niko will have her piano lessons here," she says.

"You heard right."

"With her old teacher?"

I arch an eyebrow. "Yes, Miss Cottingham needs only to tweak a few things, but she is a good teacher for Niko."

"I am surprised to hear you say that."

I slide dark glasses over my face.

Akira falls into step beside me as we walk outside. "I thought you would push Niko into Miss Williams' class."

"Miss Williams has school to attend." Although today's group assignment was an excuse to avoid me, I know there will be such distractions in the future. "She is not yet ready to be Niko's teacher."

Akira smiles. "You're right. She is not ready to be Niko's anything."

I let her think what she will and climb into the SUV.

Akira glances at me in the rear-view mirror as she drives, "I spoke to your mother yesterday. She would like to come for a visit."

I stiffen. "When?"

"She did not say."

My mother had said nothing of the sort when we spoke last week. To be fair, she usually spends most of her time chatting with Niko anyway. The two are close.

"Keep me updated. Whenever she arrives, I will clear my schedule so I can meet her at the airport."

"She is proud of all you are doing," Akira says, slowing down for a red light.

Mother was the only one who voiced support when I announced I was moving to America to be closer to Niko and to build the foundation. Her quiet but rebellious nature got passed down to me.

My phone buzzes.

Ashanti: Thanks for your help yesterday, Ryo. We were able to meet the studio exec you recommended.

I tilt my head back in the seat and close my eyes.

Ashanti's call seemed to destroy the fragile camaraderie that had formed between me and Dejonae during lunch at Miko San. What I overheard between Dejonae and her sister last night only confirms this.

I don't want any misunderstandings.

Her words echo in my brain and I breathe in slowly, forcing the thought aside. This is the kind of obsession that can destroy a man. I refuse to stumble down a thorny path for a woman who is smart enough to avoid taking a step in my direction.

No matter how enchanting Dejonae is.

No matter how much Niko loves her.

No matter how much she takes over my thoughts.

The car slows in front of Niko's school. I peer through the

window. My heart soars when I see my daughter surrounded by her friends.

Usually, Niko is sitting under a tree, looking bored and alone. It broke my heart every time, which was why I found it hard to pick her up after school.

However, since Alistair invited us to the farmhouse and Niko made new connections, there has not been a day when she was alone.

Today, I recognize three of the faces around her.

Micheal, the older boy with the dark hair and somber personality.

Bailey, the energetic younger brother with the glasses.

And Beth, Max and Dawn Stinton's bright and well-spoken younger daughter.

Niko has mentioned that Belle's school ends at an earlier time, which is why they do not meet in the evenings.

Akira smiles softly. "She seems happy when she is with them."

"They are good kids." I glance at Akira. "I am glad to hear you acknowledge this without any preconceived notions."

Her ears tinge red. "I did some self-reflection." She pauses. "What matters is Niko's happiness and safety. This has always been my concern. It is my wish for you too."

Niko notices the car. She waves to her friends, who grin and wave back.

I open the door and meet her on the sidewalk. She wraps her arms around me and my heart rocks with love. My daughter is my sunshine. I do not remember my life before her and I have no desire to go back to a time before I knew her either.

I nod to Beth, Micheal and Bailey.

The children wave and smile happily.

"How was school?" I sign to Niko when she is settled with her seatbelt on.

"It was fun." Her eyes burn with more excitement than I have seen in weeks. "I ate lunch with Bailey and Beth." Her smile widens when she signs Beth's name. "She knows a lot about cars."

"Well, her mother is a mechanic." I twist my finger like a wrench.

She grins. "That doesn't mean anything. My mom is a singer," she gestures. "But I can't sing."

"That's not true. You have a beautiful voice."

She rolls her eyes.

Whether she believes me or not, she cannot deny the truth. Niko rarely speaks, but the few times when she has tried, it is always an emotional experience.

If that is not the definition of good music, then I do not know what is.

"I told them about bowling," she signs. "They want to come with us next time."

"Are they learning sign language?" I gesture.

She nods. "They know how to spell my name." Her lips curve into an even bigger grin. "And poop."

My lips twitch. "How mature."

She laughs out loud and the sound is like magic to my ears. Since meeting Dejonae and making her new friends, Niko seems to have come alive. It is beautiful to see.

Akira stops the car in front of the foundation. I help my daughter out of the vehicle and escort her inside.

Dejonae is in the lobby, talking closely with one of the instructors. The moment Niko sees her, my daughter bolts forward.

Dejonae hears her footsteps and turns around. When she spots Niko, she drops to her knees and spreads her arms. The two collide in the center of the lobby like a long lost mother and daughter.

Dejonae lifts her head and those expressive brown eyes lock on me.

Akira stops beside me, her lips tightening again. "Are you certain it is a good idea to let Niko spend so much time with Miss Williams?"

"They have a connection."

"Exactly. And they have only known each other a short time. Imagine how close they will get in the future."

"Niko has always been alone. She deserves to have friends."

"This is more than just friendship." Akira warns, "What will Niko's mother think if she sees how close her daughter has become to another woman?"

"Ashanti will always be Niko's mother," I return gravely.

But, looking at the way Niko stares up at Dejonae, I realize that Akira might be right to feel concerned.

CHAPTER 9
IN THE GUT

DEJONAE

"This skirt is way too short for bowling," I sign to my sister.

"Stop complaining," she gestures. "You look cute."

I glance down at the striped crop top paired with a black leather mini skirt. At least I was allowed to wear sneakers.

Yaya usually takes up a hobby when she comes home for a visit—knitting, skateboarding, video gaming. This time, her mission is to have me bare as much skin as possible when I leave the house.

Which is why I went to work in that ridiculous pink dress this morning.

And why I might flash half of the bowling alley when I play tonight.

The sound of pins clamoring to the ground fills the night. The other lanes are all occupied. Mostly by teenagers and young couples. Pop music blasts from the speakers and the smell of chewing gum and sweat collide in a unique fragrance.

My sister's dark brown eyes start twinkling. She signs, "They're here."

I whirl around and spy Sazuki walking in with Niko. Akira isn't around and I wonder if she's parking the car.

Niko sprints across the bowling alley and hugs me the way she did in the lobby this evening. I exhale contentedly and wrap my arms around her. How can anyone not love this little girl? She's a pure, sweet soul.

I run my hands down her curls. As usual, her hair is pull back in a tight ponytail. I remember what Sazuki said about doing her hair every day and smile.

Niko pulls back. Her eyes jump behind me and linger on my sister.

"Hi. I'm Yaya." Yaya signs out her name.

Niko turns giddy. Her mouth moves in silent communication while her hands speed through a greeting.

"I'm Niko."

"Pretty name," Yaya signs back.

"You're pretty."

"Thank you, so are you."

As they lather each other in compliments, I glance at Sazuki.

He's not looking at Niko.

He's looking at me, a dark flame in his eyes that could drown out the sun.

My heart skips. Seeing him every day is proving to be a bigger challenge than I anticipated. Especially now that there's this awkward tension between us.

"Where's Akira?" I ask, breaking our silent staredown.

"She is not feeling well," he says slowly.

My eyebrows draw together. "How sick is she?"

"I believe it is a monthly ailment." He gives me a pointed look.

"Oh." My cheeks flush with heat. I wonder how close he is to Akira that he would know her period cycle.

Sazuki's gaze travels down my face to my legs, which are on full display thanks to the poor excuse of a skirt.

Prickles of awareness spark all the way up to my neck.

Maybe he's thinking I'm a bad influence on Niko.

Maybe he's regretting this idea.

But when his eyes jump back to mine, I don't see censure.

I see hot, burning desire.

My heart pounds.

I don't *want* to notice Sazuki's interest in me.

He's my boss.

Grumphole supreme.

A cold, sharp, impatient person who can tear someone's heart to shreds with a few well-placed words.

I need to remember that.

Even if he makes my stomach twist into knots when his eyes latch onto my mouth like it's a gourmet meal.

Even if he looks ten times sexier in casual clothes, a jacket, jeans, T-shirt and sneakers, as he does when he's in suits.

Even if his sharp, powerful body steps closer to mine, knifing through the distance between us like he's at war with it.

He's just a distraction.

He's just hot.

He's just…

"You were out of the office for most of today. Did the training sessions keep you so busy?"

I tilt my head up. "Is that an observation or are you scolding me?"

A smile curls his lips.

This time his dimples aren't just a fleeting wink that flash out of view.

They stay.

Two giant craters.

My heart clamors to my throat like it wants a better view. This close, I can smell Sazuki's aftershave, the same rich, minty fragrance that lives in his car.

His presence presses in against me, as tangible as his mile-wide shoulders.

Those stormy brown eyes dip to my mouth again as if he can't help himself, as if he's waiting for a moment to taste it.

Holy crap.

I swallow hard. "Um… did you get my report?"

"I did," he says calmly.

"I met with three of the eight instructors. I also spoke to them about the challenges they'd faced in the past. I compiled their concerns into a spreadsheet. It's something to consider when you and Adam tweak the MTB."

"I know. I forwarded the email to Adam."

"You read it and forwarded it to Adam, but you couldn't reply back?"

"Why would I reply to a report?" He seems genuinely puzzled.

"Because it's polite. Because you're letting me know the email was received. Because I put in a lot of effort and a simple acknowledgement can go a long way."

He takes another step toward me. "You have never worked in an office before, have you?"

"I don't see what that has to do with this conversation."

"In the office," he lowers his head close to mine and points to himself, "I am the boss." He points to me. "And you are the employee. I receive the emails and I choose whether or not I respond to them."

I tilt my face up. My lips are an inch away from his. "Just because you've been doing things that way all your life doesn't mean you've been doing them right."

"Is that an observation or a scolding, Miss Williams?" The dimples wink at me.

I'm burning up. Too hot.

So much for thinking that drawing a line in the sand would bring me any peace. If anything, it only made the tension thicker by acknowledging that there's something between us we shouldn't explore.

Yaya makes a grunting sound.

I break Sazuki's gaze and face my sister. She and Niko are standing behind us. Both of them have their hips tilted to one side, their arms folded and their eyes locked on us.

Face burning, I sign, "Are you guys ready to start?"

"Aren't you going to introduce us?" Yaya gestures.

I force myself to turn to Sazuki. "This is my sister Yaya."

"Nice to meet you," he signs.

Yaya smirks. "You are very handsome."

Sazuki shakes his head. "You are the beautiful one. I believe your future in modeling will be bright."

Yaya melts at his feet.

I roll my eyes.

Why is he acting sweet in front of my sister? Where's the guy who snapped at me to sit down during the conference today? Who kidnapped me on my way to class and manipulated my life just to get me to work with him?

"Will you stay and play with us?" Yaya offers.

I come to life right away. "Mr. Sazuki is busy. He doesn't have time to—"

"Okay."

My eyes widen.

Niko jumps up and down, celebrating silently.

I sign to Yaya, "What are you doing?"

She gives me a mischievous look and gestures to Niko. "Let's get our bowling shoes."

Niko nods.

"We'll be right behind you," Sazuki says.

I whirl on him and fold my arms over my chest. "You weren't invited."

"Your sister just invited me," he points out. "Were you not listening?"

My teeth grit in annoyance.

Sazuki gives me an amused look.

"If you're worried about Niko, we'll watch her like hawks and we'll text you when we're finished with the game. I won't let her leave the building without your permission."

"You sound experienced in alleviating a parent's worry."

"I worked as a babysitter in high school."

"How old were you then? Fifteen?"

"Sixteen."

He scrunches his nose. "A baby watching a baby."

I laugh. "How old were you when I was sixteen? Fifty?"

He looks offended. "I am not that much older than you."

A sick part of me pounces on the opportunity to grind his gears a bit. It's much better than feeling self-conscious and breathless in his company.

"When was the last time you bowled? Did we have smartphones yet or…?" I tease.

His eyes narrow on me, coolly arrogant.

Why is it so fun to get under his skin?

"Would you care for a wager, Miss Williams?"

"I would." I tap my chin. "If I win, you release me from having to work at the foundation for my graduation project."

He frowns. "Choose another wish."

"Why? You have the power to release me early."

He shakes his head.

I frown and think again. "Okay. Then I want you to take us all to that Japanese place for dinner tonight."

"You enjoyed the miso soup?"

"I saw miso soup in my dreams." I sigh longingly. "But for some reason, it feels weird going back there without you." The words slip out before I've thought them through.

It's too late.

Sazuki looks pleased.

I nudge him. "Not that you're going to win, but… what do you want from me?"

"From you?" His eyes dip to my mouth again.

Heart banging against my chest, I lick my lips.

"I will think about it," he says.

Niko and Yaya return to us.

"What's the hold up?" Yaya signs. My sister grabs me by the hand while Niko latches onto Sazuki. They drag us to the counter to get our bowling shoes.

I finish tying up my sneakers and stand beside Yaya. "Let's keep our teams as is. Me and Yaya against Niko and Sazuki."

Niko grins from ear to ear. "I like that," she signs.

Sazuki catches my eyes and nods. "Good luck, Miss Williams. You are going to need it."

Oh, it's on.

Niko is up first because she's the cutest, obviously. The bowling ball looks like it'll drag her straight to the ground, but she handles herself like a pro and lets the ball fly.

I bite back a chuckle when her ball hits the gutter. No matter how competitive I am, I'm not going to laugh in a kid's face.

But Yaya does not share that philosophy.

When Niko hunches her shoulders and plods back to the benches, my sister lets out a boom of laughter. Like everything she does, it's loud and unapologetic. Several of the tables next to us glance over.

Sazuki looks frightened by the loud guffaws.

"Your sister has a contagious laugh," he signs.

Yaya grins. "Just because I'm deaf doesn't mean I have to be quiet."

Sazuki inclines his head to her, thinks about it and then nods. "Fair point."

Yaya's up next.

For all her teasing, my sister's bowling ball finds the gutter even earlier than Niko's did.

The father daughter duo laugh and high-five.

Yaya stomps back to the bench, her eyebrows knitted. "It's been a while," she signs.

I shake my head. "Get it together. Don't embarrass me out here."

She snorts. "You are way too into this."

"Tonight's dinner is at stake."

"Did you make a deal with your sexy boss?" Yaya signs.

I frown. "Don't call him sexy."

Her hands flutter. "It's what he is."

Sazuki clears his throat. "I am right here, you know."

Yaya just winks at him.

I squeeze my eyes shut in absolute horror.

Thankfully, Sazuki is next.

He knocks down all the pins. A perfect strike.

I slow clap. "Not too bad, Sazuki."

"I told you, I never lose. There will be many more of those in tonight's game."

I roll my eyes. "You're so conceited."

"It is not conceit if it is true," he corrects me with a mischievous smirk.

Damn him.

But I'm smiling when I retrieve my bowling ball from the shoot. Sazuki hasn't mentioned what he wants from me if he wins, but at this point, it doesn't even matter. Given Niko and Yaya's terrible bowling skills, this game will come down to him versus me.

And I refuse to let him win.

I test the weight of the ball in my hands, swinging it back and forth. Then, slowly, I approach the lane and calculate my strike. When I'm certain of my strategy, I bend over, quicken my steps and let the ball fly. A perfect strike.

"Yes!" I throw my hands up and jump in celebration.

Yaya's on her feet, dancing around.

Niko is grinning even though these points aren't for her team.

Sazuki is the only one wearing a scowl. There's a hot, searing glint in his eyes. It darkens when he looks beyond me to the teenagers playing in the next lane. I glance that way too and notice the boys pointing at me.

In horror, I realize all the bending over and running caused my skirt to hitch up. I duck my head and pull the hem of my skirt down as I run back to my seat.

Yaya stops me and gives me a big hug. "That's how you do it," she signs.

Niko's eyes are sparkling like twin suns. "You were so cool, Deej."

"Thanks," I mumble. My chest is burning with awkwardness. I refuse to look at Sazuki.

We play another round.

Yaya and Niko each take a turn and score very few points.

As promised, Sazuki hits another strike.

When it's my turn, I shuffle toward the bowling balls. I can feel the teenage boys eyeing me from the next lane and it makes my heart pound.

I told Yaya this skirt was too short.

My fingers are so sweaty that I'm scared the bowling ball will crush my toes. How do I bend down without giving those boys something to snicker at? I tuck my knees together and begin a slow descent into a crouch when I *feel* Sazuki's presence behind me.

I'm in trouble.

There's no way I should be able to know he's close to me just by the way the air around me changes.

I straighten and turn slightly. "What are you doing?"

"Hold still," he rumbles. He's right behind me, his bicep almost kissing my arm. In one smooth motion, he yanks his jacket off.

I almost pluck a one-dollar bill from my wallet and throw it at him. *Please don't stop taking things off.*

My mouth turns dry. He looks determined, dangerous, and way too delicious with his face pinched in concentration. I watch as he pinches the jacket by the sleeves.

"You keep trying to test me, Miss Williams," he growls.

"Huh?" I sound like an idiot.

But can anyone blame me?

His voice is deep and soul-sucking. So close to my neck, it sends a hot breath dancing over my skin.

Sazuki slides the jacket sleeves along my waist. My body comes alive while the thick material glides across my crop top. His fingers barely skim my skin in the sliver of space between where my skirt and the shirt meet. He draws me close in a smooth motion, crushing me against his rock-hard body in order to tie the jacket sleeves at my stomach.

"The rest of your skirt is missing," he snarls against my neck. "You should demand your money back."

"I—"

He steps away before my brain starts glitching. I turn fully around, the jacket flailing behind me like a coat.

Heat is racing down my spine. My heart is pounding like a crazed drum.

And I need a paper bag to breathe in.

I don't know what to do. What to say.

My mind is blank.

I wish I could call it embarrassment or anger.

I just… it would be a lie.

I dig my fingers into the bowling ball to stop them from tingling.

Deep breaths.

Sazuki gestures. "Now that I have your attention, feel free to throw the game."

The spell breaks.

I scowl at him.

So much for being a gentleman. Was he just trying to rattle me?

"Watch and learn, old man."

He scrunches his nose in distaste.

Good. I want him as annoyed as I feel.

Approaching the lane with more confidence, I fling the bowling ball.

It goes straight into the gutter.

Sazuki's eyes burn into me and a slow, mocking smile spreads across his face, revealing his shameless evil.

My lips curl back in a sneer.

If it's the last thing I do tonight, I'm going to make sure that he regrets messing with me.

* * *

Sazuki wins the game.

Which proves that Fate is against me.

The only thing that makes losing just a tad digestible is Niko's excitement.

"I won," she signs. If she smiles any harder, she just might explode. "I won!"

"Congratulations." Yaya clasps her hands together and rocks them on either side of her head.

Niko hugs her dad around the neck. He lifts her up and spins her around.

I steel myself against any sweet feelings that are creeping up to me. Sazuki made a point to tell me he was divorced, so it's not like it's *wrong* to feel the tug I do towards him and Niko.

It's just not wise.

"Come on," Sazuki says, holding out his hand for Niko. "Let's get you a prize from the concession stand."

Yaya pins me with her puppy dog eyes. "Sorry we lost."

"Whose fault is that?" I tease.

She elbows me in the side.

Minutes later, our group stops in front of the concession stand. The boy behind the counter looks slightly petrified. I wonder what shocks him more, that we're a mix of black and Asian people or that everyone keeps signing to each other.

"Take a look, Niko," Sazuki says. "Choose any toy you want."

Niko points to a balloon.

"You sure?" Sazuki signs. "I thought you would want the teddy bear."

"It'll last longer," I agree.

Yaya gestures, "Ignore them, Niko. Get what will make you happy."

"How much for the balloon?" Sazuki speaks out loud. He signs along, making sure that Niko isn't left out of the conversation.

Sweat breaks out on the kid's neck. He digs his fingers into the counter, leans over it and in a loud voice, enunciates every word. "Fiiiiive! Dolllars! Sir!"

"You don't need to shout," I say, grimacing.

"Oh, sorry. I didn't mean to offend."

Sazuki sets a five dollar bill on the counter.

The blushing clerk hands over Niko's balloon. It bobs happily toward the ceiling.

"Let me tie that for you," Yaya signs. Kneeling in front of Niko, she grabs the string and secures it around her tiny wrist.

"Thank you." Niko signs.

Yaya beams.

"Dad," Niko gestures and the balloon bobs its head, "what's *your* prize?"

"My prize?" His knowing smirk falls over me like melted chocolate, dripping down my spine and clogging my throat before I can so much as breathe. "Miss Williams has it," Sazuki says.

Slowly, Niko's eyes turn to me.

Yaya's too.

Air gets trapped in my lungs.

Finally, I crack out a laugh. "Me? I have your prize? When did I say that?"

"Don't go back on your agreement, Miss Williams." He arches a brow. "I'm looking forward to my reward."

The way his tongue rolls over the word 'reward' sounds absolutely obscene. I search desperately for a witty comeback. Nothing comes to mind. *I'm blank.*

I lick my lips, my body vibrating like a guitar string as I imagine all the things Sazuki could ask for.

"Are you Ryotaro Sazuki?"

The question comes from a couple who'd been lining up behind us.

Sazuki's eyes drift away from me and land on the strangers.

"You are!" A middle aged man and his wife giggle like teenagers. "I didn't think it was you. I actually told my wife she was crazy! No way would a Sazuki be playing bowling like this. I thought you were some other Asian."

I cringe.

Sazuki doesn't bat an eyelash. "Can I help you?"

"We're huge fans. Huge. We think your last album was impeccably done. Do you know when you'll be releasing another?"

"I have no plans to do so right now." Sazuki's voice is hard. He takes a step back.

They take one forward. "What are you doing in America? I thought all the Sazukis lived in Japan?"

Sazuki's jaw clenches.

"Marge will never believe this. Can we take a picture?"

Sazuki holds up a hand. "Excuse me. I would not like to take a picture now."

"Why not?" The man turns red in the cheeks.

I grit my teeth at their pushiness. "Didn't you hear him? He doesn't want to take a picture. Get out of his face."

Sazuki holds a hand in front of my torso and gives me a pointed look. *Be calm.*

I scowl in return. *How can I?*

"Is this your girlfriend?" The old man surveys me curiously. Then his eyes jump to Niko. "Are you two..." The old man points. "Is this your..."

I step in front of Niko. Since Sazuki doesn't want me to go off on these pushy fans, then the only other option is retreat. Because if I don't leave, someone's going to get seriously hurt.

And it won't be me.

"Excuse me, Mr. Sazuki. We'll wait for you outside." I shade Niko with my body, making sure they can't gawk at her like she's some kind of exhibit.

Sazuki dips his head gratefully.

I gesture to Yaya. "Let's go."

She takes Niko's other side and, together, we fast-walk away from the fans.

Outside the bowling alley, a strong wind blows. Barely any stars poke through the dark, velvet sky.

I look down at Niko. "Are you okay?"

"I'm used to it." She shrugs and signs, "Dad doesn't want me to get photographed. He says it's safer that way."

"It is," Yaya signs. "There are some crazy people out here."

Niko bounces her balloon, seeming unconcerned. Since she grew up with Akira watching over her every minute of the day, she's probably used to being protected and yanked out of sketchy situations.

Although I don't think signing autographs is anything scary, I know Sazuki enough to say he wouldn't want Niko getting too much public attention.

"Does that happen often?" Yaya signs to me.

"What?"

"Sazuki getting mobbed by fans."

I think about that day he came to my school. "It's not that bad. It usually only happens around music students. The rest of the world doesn't know enough about him to attack."

She purses her lips the same way I do when I'm thinking. "I didn't realize he was so famous."

"You haven't seen famous yet," I sign. "You should stick around when he's on campus. They treat him like a god."

She studies me. "You're protective of him."

"It's not about him. I get annoyed when I see people acting entitled. He doesn't owe them a signature. He doesn't owe them a conversation. And he doesn't owe them access to his family."

I glance down, expecting to see Niko by my side.

All I see is a crack in the sidewalk.

Where did she go?

My eyes widen and my body jumps into instant panic mode, complete with internal alarm bells and a frantic leap into 'worst-case scenario' imageries.

"Niko?" I look to my left.

The sidewalk stretches on into darkness for miles. I dig my fingers into my purse, struggling to breathe as my brain overloads with anxiety.

"Niko?" To my right, there are brightly lit shops and a few people strolling leisurely.

Yaya sees my freaked out face and starts looking around too. Then she slaps my back and points.

Niko.

She's darting into the street, chasing her balloon.

Relief pours through my veins when I see that she's not vanished into thin air like a ghost. But that relief quickly turns into ice when I notice a car roaring down the street at warp speed.

My heart starts pounding harder when I realize that Niko isn't paying attention and can't hear it.

I don't think.

I just move.

Pumping my arms, I race straight into the path of the oncoming car. Niko grabs her balloon by the string just as the car starts flashing its signals. Her head twists around. She sees the car and her mouth falls open in shock.

I push my body to the limits, my heart exploding.

The driver slams his hand on the horn, blasting the air with his outrage. He's not slowing down fast enough.

My arms close around Niko's body, twisting her so she lands on top of me when I fling us out of the car's way.

My shoulder slams into the ground. Hard.

I hear a thud as my head ricochets against tarmac.

Pain rattles my knees and back, but it's nothing compared to the joy I feel when I look at Niko.

She's okay.

My arms tighten around her when I see the tears gathering in her eyes.

"It's okay." I smooth my uninjured hand down her head. "You're okay."

A door slams.

The driver sprints around the car. "Are you crazy? Why the hell would you let your kid dart into the road like that!"

"Niko!" Sazuki's voice cuts through the night. Moments later, he's beside us. I have no idea how he got here so fast. He must have teleported.

Niko makes a sound of distress. She wraps her arms around her father's shoulders and hugs him tight. Her body is trembling like she'd been dunked in ice.

Sazuki's eyes meet mine and he leans over, a hand extended to me. I'm about to take it when Yaya runs to my side. She digs her fingers around my waist and helps me to my feet.

I hiss in pain.

She's watching me closely and sees the anguish that skips over my expression.

"Are you okay?" the driver asks, looking at me. "You don't need to go to the hospital, right? I'm not paying out no insurance fees."

"You should drive more carefully," Sazuki scolds him in a voice that sounds like death come alive.

"It's not his fault," I mutter. "It's mine. I should have kept a better eye on Niko."

Sazuki's gaze returns to me and tightens in alarm.

Niko looks equally shaken. "You're bleeding," she signs.

"It's okay." I shake my head. The skin on my thigh is burning. It serves me right for wearing a mini skirt while pretending to be Superman. "I'm okay."

"No, you're not," Yaya signs.

"I'll take her to the hospital," Sazuki says to my sister.

"No need. Really, Sazuki."

He gives me a scolding look. "You're hurt."

His tone would rub me the wrong way if I didn't hear the worry running right beneath it.

Yaya chews on her bottom lip. She signs, "You could have died."

The driver's eyes bug. He starts backing away. "Y-you heard her. It was her fault the kid went darting into the street. Not mine!"

After saying his piece, he jumps into the car and takes off.

Sazuki's eyes zip to the license plate before he returns the weight of his intensity to me. "Let's get out of the middle of the road before another car comes."

"Good idea," I whisper.

Yaya guides my arm around her shoulder and leads me to the sidewalk.

The moment Sazuki sets Niko down, she flings herself at me. Tears sail down her tawny brown cheeks.

"It's okay." I soothe her arm. "I'm fine. Really. I'm just a little banged up."

Niko is still shaking and looking guilty.

I grin over at her and whisper, "You know what would make me feel better?"

With her face upturned and her eyes full of hope, she's wringing out my heart like my mother would twist a dish rag.

"If we could all go for ice cream."

"Ice cream?" Sazuki hisses. "You need to go to a hospital, Dejonae."

I frown at the bossy tone. "I told you. I'm fine."

"Your knees are bleeding."

I fight back a hiss of pain and start dusting off my knees. Yaya sees what I'm doing, dives into her purse and hands me a wet wipe. I clean off quickly and show Sazuki my legs.

"See, doctor? No need for surgery." Using my hands this time, I sign, "Can we please get ice cream now?"

He scowls at me.

I drag Niko by my side and look up at him, batting my eyelashes. Together, Niko and I push out our bottom lips and give our best 'puppy dog' faces. Yaya smirks when she sees what I'm doing and joins us.

Sazuki gives in reluctantly. Niko celebrates by hopping up and down. I smile at her, glad to see the smile return to her face.

"I'll drive," Sazuki says.

Yaya and Niko hold hands and skip toward the parking lot.

Sazuki falls into step beside me. "What happened?"

"Niko's balloon slipped off and she went into the road for it," I say, trying hard not to limp. If I show any signs of pain, I know

Sazuki will cut this ice cream venture short and Niko will be heartbroken again.

"I'll talk to her," Sazuki says darkly. "Niko should know better."

"It's not her fault."

"You could have both gotten hurt tonight."

"Yes, but we didn't." I look at his clenching jaw. "I'd hate it if she blamed herself for what happened tonight."

He looks like he's gearing up to argue with me.

I speak first. "This road doesn't have much traffic and I'm sure she looked both ways before she crossed. In her mind, she probably did her best to be responsible and someone got hurt." I lower my voice. "There will be many times when being deaf puts her life in danger, but I never want her to think that being deaf makes her a burden or a liability. Especially not to me."

He stops walking.

I turn to him.

Large hands rise and cup my cheeks. He brushes sand from my face softly.

My heart starts leaping inside my chest, pounding like a war drum gone berserk. I lift my head, looking up at Sazuki.

He moves in.

I'm uncontrollably aware of how close his lips are.

"This does not change anything. I will still demand my pound of flesh," he says dryly.

My eyes narrow.

Breathless awe turns to striking hate.

His lips twitch at my reactions and I know he's laughing at me. I stomp ahead and catch up with Niko and Yaya. It's my fault for assuming that Ryotaro Sazuki has a heart.

CHAPTER 10
A QUIET CHORD

SAZUKI

"You do realize that my background is in martial arts? I am not a spy, Ryotaro."

I adjust my ear buds and respond to Akira, "I will take this to mean you have not found the owner of the car yet."

"You gave me a partial license plate number," she hisses.

I thought I had memorized it all. Perhaps Dejonae was right. I am getting old.

Akira sighs on the other end of the line. "Why am I looking for the driver of that car anyway?"

I glance at Niko in the backseat. She is drilling a hole into the screen behind my chair, watching every movement of my lips.

"I will tell you later."

After hanging up with Akira, I pull the car to the side. Niko scoots to the front seat and gives me a kiss on the cheek.

"Remember what we spoke about, Niko," I sign.

She nods soberly.

After last night's scare, I treated everyone to ice cream as per Dejonae's request. But when we got home, I sat Niko down and gave her a firm talking to about being more aware of her environment. I believe she will not be running into the street after balloons again.

Checking that my daughter gets into the school building safely, I then drive to Dejonae's university and send her a text.

Sazuki: Where are you?
Dejonae: Why are you asking?
Sazuki: Are you already in class?
Dejonae: I'm walking there now. Why?

I peer through the windshield and see her limping down the path. Her head is down and tucked toward her cell phone. I climb out of the car and the sound of the door slamming prompts her to lift her head. The moment she sees me, she freezes in place.

Though I did not expect her to be welcoming, I am not prepared for the dismay that crosses her pretty face.

Does she dislike me so much?

I march toward her. The wind picks up, grabbing fistfuls of her honey-tinged curls and throwing them over her gold-dusted cheeks. Today, she is wearing another dress. This one is sleeveless and clings to her shapely form.

My eyes thirstily soak in her curves before I drag my gaze back to her face. Her mouth is pursed as I approach. The pressure of my gaze increases when her tongue darts out to nervously lick her lips.

My entire being longs to capture that mouth of hers until I know exactly what her tongue feels like against my own.

But I inhale a deep breath and wrestle those thoughts away.

"What are you doing here?" Dejonae hisses.

Again, I get the feeling that she is not pleased to see me.

"Is there somewhere private we can go?"

Her eyes widen and a tinge of alarm lights in them before she wipes it clean. "P-private? Why do you need to speak to me in private? What's so urgent that it can't wait until I go to work?"

I pin my lips together, saying nothing.

"Is this about yesterday? Is Niko okay? Did she get hurt?"

"Niko is fine. Thanks to you."

Her eyes dart away. "Don't thank me."

"You saved her."

"She never would have been put in that situation if I had been more attentive." Squaring her shoulders, Dejonae looks me right in the eyes. "I'm sorry that I put her in danger."

This woman.

I recall the moment I walked out of the bowling alley and saw Dejonae fling herself in front of an oncoming truck to protect my child. She saved my daughter.

I owe her my life.

Stretching my hand forward, I curl a finger under Dejonae's chin. "I do not want your apology."

Lightning flares between us, lured closer by the hopeful look in Dejonae's enchanting brown eyes.

In that moment, I realize how trapped I am in her.

It feels as though someone put me under a spell. The deepest hypnosis.

And I have no wish to wake up.

The sound of footsteps causes Dejonae to stiffen. Shooting a terrified look over my shoulder, she grabs my hand and drags me around the side of the building. Plastering her body against mine, she flattens us both into the wall.

"Why are we hiding?"

"Sh." She places a finger to her lips and buries her head in my chest. A protective surge, that had only been activated for my mother and my daughter, awakens in my chest.

This odd sensation is beyond me. Terrifying, really. I am always steady, always certain of my next move. Yet here I am, feeling like I have lost my mind, as a woman who can't even reach my chest has me backed up against the wall. I have never felt so out of control in my life.

"Is she gone?" Dejonae whispers.

She is so small. So soft. So fragile.

A fresh-faced beauty with the power to bring any man to his knees.

Her fingers go slack on my shoulder when she sees me staring at her. Her mouth falls open slightly.

I bite back a groan.

That mouth.

Capable of trading insults and whispering my name.

Brown lips so ripe for the taking.

What would she taste like? Brown sugar? Gold rum? Something more addictive?

Her eyelashes flutter up and down, filling all my senses with desire. I settle my hand around her waist to press her closer.

Can she feel the way my heart is beating against my chest?

Does she feel this connection too?

I brush my nose in her hair, inhaling the scent of coconut oil and some other, fruity product.

"Uh, I think she's gone." Dejonae steps back.

"Who was that?" I ask darkly.

"Taylor." Her voice holds a hint of disgust. "If she saw us together, it would be game over."

"Game over?"

"She thinks I'm your drug dealer." Dejonae rolls her eyes in a way that Niko will probably learn to do when she is older. "Or that I have something over you. Whatever. She's annoying and I'd rather not deal with her right now."

"Mm." I spot a bench nestled in the shadows of the building. Given how secluded it is, I can see it being used by campus couples, sneaking away for a moment together.

This will do.

"Sit." I jut my chin at the bench.

Dejonae narrows her eyes at me. "Why?"

"Must everything be a fight with you?"

"If you're the one hurling instructions? Yes." She tilts her head sassily.

I smile for a beat, but quickly coach my face into a scolding look. "The sooner you sit, the faster I will be gone."

She remains standing.

I walk a few paces away. "Perhaps I should attend your class with you. Mr. Howel has been eagerly awaiting a collaboration."

Dejonae lunges for my hand and holds on. "I'll sit."

I smile while my face is turned away. By the time I spin around, she is already seated on the bench. Her brown eyes dart between mine, apprehensive and searching.

"You do not need to be so nervous," I say.

"You're being quiet and secretive."

"I am always quiet."

"Yes, but this is different. I can feel you… planning something." She juts her chin at me. "What's in the bag?"

"I know what I want as reward," I say, not answering her question.

"What?"

"May I lift your dress?"

She sucks in a shaky breath. If she had not been seated, her knees might have given out.

I slide the strap of my bag down my shoulder and open the flap to reveal the first aid kit inside. Her eyes widen. I crouch to one knee, letting my trousers sink into the ground. Moving like this causes my cell phone to bunch in my pocket. I pull it out and hand it to Dejonae to keep her hands occupied.

Next, I set the box on the bench beside her. The kit makes a soft click as I unsnap the lid and reveal the medicine I brought from home.

"You probably did not care for your wound yesterday," I say in a lightly scolding voice.

"I…"

My eyes dart up and I hit her with a stern gaze. "You should have let me take you to the hospital."

"That would have been too much of a fuss," she mumbles.

I stare at her for a long while before looking down at her dress. "Is that the only reason?"

"I… didn't want Niko to feel like what she'd done was a big deal."

"But it was a big deal," I murmur. My fingers slide along the smooth edge of her hem. The fabric is cotton and soft to the touch.

"She's a child. She's bound to make mistakes. It's called 'growing up'."

"Other children can make mistakes and walk away from them. Niko is different. She cannot." I begin to roll up Dejonae's dress.

Heat burns the back of my neck. Undressing her feels too intimate. Too much like the dreams I have had lately. I am breathing hard by the time I roll her skirt halfway to her knees. When I glance up, she looks almost *shaken*, her face flushed and her eyes glinting.

I keep talking to keep us both distracted. "Brushing issues under the rug and smothering Niko in love might be your way of doing things. But it is my job to prepare her for the dangers of the world."

"You don't think the world will teach her that lesson by itself?" she argues.

Gone is the dewy-eyed girl who makes me forget about our age difference, our cultural differences and the fact that she is, currently, my employee. In its place is the Dejonae who will fight passionately for what she believes in.

Why do I find her more irresistible when her eyes turn sharp and her voice turns vehement?

I successfully roll her skirt above her knee. There are several bruises on her foot and a long scrape on her right leg. As I observe, my hand brushes her upper thigh unintentionally and we both suck in a sharp breath.

Her eyes get hazy. She bites down into her bottom lip and I watch her teeth skim the center.

Focus, Ryotaro.

I am not here to fall under Miss Dejonae's spell. Between the two of us, I am older. I am her boss. And it is up to me to keep my senses intact.

My voice is firm when I say, "Niko's inability to hear makes her susceptible to danger. Would you rather she learn lessons the hard way or the easy way?"

"You think your way is the easy way?" She arches a brow.

I take out the antibacterial ointment and unscrew the wand at the top. "I think she should walk into the world with her eyes wide open."

"I'm not saying you shouldn't prepare her. But there's a limit to how much you can do. I've watched my sister navigate in places that have no idea how to accommodate her. I've watched her stand tall against obstacles my parents could not even imagine." Her eyes flicker with pain.

I stop smearing the medicine immediately. "Does it hurt?"

"It's okay. I can bear it." She digs her fingers under the bench.

Rather than offer her assurances, I present another argument to distract her. "Do you propose then that I simply tell Niko nothing? Coddle her to the point of paralyzing her? Give her the false impression that there will always be someone to help? Always be someone to take care of her? This is not the truth."

"As long as you're alive, it is the truth. She should know that there's a place she can come back to that will always feel safe. That won't pressure her or hold her mistakes against her. Somewhere she can run and hide when it feels like her back is against the wall."

"That has not been my experience."

"Even if it hasn't been your experience, it doesn't have to be hers."

She stares frankly at me, her eyes revealing everything she feels. She's as transparent as a book. As bold as she is unguarded.

Without warning, Dejonae swoops down. Her nose stops directly on top of mine.

"Why do you keep looking at me like that?" she mutters.

I feel my throat bob.

With her this close, I'm once again reminded of how idiotic I am to think that I can resist her.

Her presence means something.

Her words.
Her challenges.
Her smile.

The needy feeling in my chest eclipses my good sense. It drags me toward her lips as if I am a comet on a trajectory to earth.

And when she bends toward me too, her full lips parting, easing ever closer to mine, I—

My phone rings.

Dejonae's eyes drop to the screen and her entire body stiffens.

I look down too.

Niko's Mother.

The sudden pang in my chest takes me by surprise.

"I will answer it later," I say.

"You should answer it now. It might be important." Her voice is dry. Her face, pointedly blank. My fingers are still on the band-aid I was about to place on her. She plucks it from me and applies it herself.

"Is there anywhere else that needs attention?" I ask almost desperately.

"No." She rolls her dress back down and pins her legs together.

I feel her reorienting, clearing aside all the interest that had risen to the surface just a moment before. Gone is the prickly awareness that refuses to be denied whenever we share the same space and breathe the same air.

Now, there's an icy distance. A clear and abject rejection.

"Mr. Sazuki, I have class now. If you don't need anything else…"

I stagger to my feet slowly. My gut churns.

Dejonae does not spare me a second glance. Fingers twisting her purse strap, she hurries past me and turns the bend. I see her fast-walking up the path that leads to her music lecture hall.

My phone keeps ringing.

I suck in a deep breath and put it to my ear. "Ashanti."

"Why didn't you call me, Ryo?"

"Call you? For what?" I ask, rubbing the bridge of my nose.

"You know I spoke to Niko last night."

I did. They speak every night.

"And you know Niko told me about what happened at the bowling alley," Ashanti adds. "So then, you know I'd be extremely concerned and want to discuss why some stranger almost got my baby killed."

"Dejonae put her life on the line to save Niko."

"A sacrifice she wouldn't have made if she hadn't been involved in the first place!"

Annoyed and trying my hardest not to be, I keep my voice still. "Ashanti, you were not there last night. I am sure Niko told you that *she* was the one who ran into the road, knowing that she shouldn't. If Dejonae had not acted as fast as she did…"

"Ryo, our daughter has *never* tried anything so impulsive. Where did she learn to do something like that?"

"She is a child."

"Exactly. She's susceptible to bad influences."

"Ashanti, what do you wish to hear from me?"

"I don't want my child around someone so careless, Ryo."

"You do not know Dejonae. You do not have a right to judge her," I say through gritted teeth.

"I don't have a right? I am Niko's mother!"

"Yes, but you are not *here*."

A long beat of silence passes.

"Well, maybe I should be."

"Ashanti—"

The call ends abruptly.

She is gone.

* * *

UNSETTLED by the morning's events, I throw myself into meetings with the admin team. That keeps me occupied until Dejonae stomps into the foundation after her class. She does not take a seat at her desk. Instead, she pulls some files from the center, tucks it under her arm and plods to the elevator.

I do not chase her.

Until I sort through what I feel for her and what it will mean if I pursue those feelings, I will give her space.

My computer pings with a new alert.

An email update from Adam.

I browse through the data and start to click away when I remember Dejonae's words.

'Why don't you reply? A simple acknowledgement can go a long way.'

Clearing my throat, I tap the reply button.

Thank you, Adam. Received.

"Can something that small really make a difference?" I muse. With a shrug, I move on to another file.

My phone rings.

The moment I pick up, Adam's voice blasts in my ear, "Sneeze twice if you need me to call the police."

I sit in stunned silence.

"Come on, Sazuki. Have you been taken hostage or what?"

"You must have a lot of time to waste today," I say, clicking to a data spreadsheet.

"You replied to an email."

"And?" I mutter.

"You never reply to emails."

"That alone warranted a call?"

"I spoke to Nova about it. She agreed that if someone randomly changes their bad habits, they're probably about to die."

I chuckle. "Change does not always mean death."

"No, but a drastic change out of nowhere? That has a deeper cause. People tend to only realize what's important when it's too late."

His words strike me. I take a moment to absorb them.

"Since I have you on the line, Sazuki, there's another matter I wanted to discuss. It's about the MTB's batteries."

We go back and forth about the details, battling the pros and cons of rechargeable batteries versus removable batteries.

"We will use the removable batteries then," I say finally.

"Done." Adam coughs. "Speaking of, I'm ready for Dejonae to come and check out the tweaks I made to the MTB. Since it's inspired by her input, I think she deserves to see it first."

"I will send her an email."

"An email? Isn't she working with you?"

My eyes slide to the glass windows. Through the blinds, I see that Dejonae's desk is still empty.

"I will let her know."

There's a knock on the door.

Akira pokes her head through.

I hang up with Adam and face her. "Did you get the information on the license plate number?"

"I did." She slides a folder over to me. "*Now* will you tell me what this is about?"

"Niko was almost run over. I would like to find the driver who was so careless that he did not slow down when he saw a little girl in his path."

Akira's eyes widen. "When did this happen?"

"Last night." I flip through the pages.

"Last night?" she murmurs. "Was it during your appointment with Miss Williams?"

"It was."

Her lips go taut.

"Before you say anything both you and I will regret," I murmur, keeping my eyes on the file, "the reason Niko is unharmed is because Dejonae rushed into the street and pushed her out of the car's way."

Akira says nothing for a long moment.

I glance up and find her studying me.

She frowns. "You have gone soft for her."

"Is it that obvious?"

"Will you really not deny it?" she asks breathlessly.

What would be the point?

"I will admit that Miss Williams and Niko seem to have a sincere connection. Of course, you may find it heart-warming. Any father would think favorably of the girl who his daughter adores. It does not mean you have feelings for her."

"What else could it mean?" I glance up impatiently.

"Loneliness." She waves a hand. "You are accomplished, wealthy and handsome. People who lack in all three of those categories have someone and you do not. It is only natural that you feel the loss."

I narrow my eyes.

"Gratitude," Akira continues. "She saved Niko's life. You can gift her a house. A car. Send a fruit basket to her family. The Sazuki family repays all debts. Once you fulfil your obligations to her, you will not be so attached."

"You think I do not know my own heart?" I snap.

"I think," she says slowly, "that you were moved, yes. But feelings waver. There is no need to give her your heart."

"Who says I gave it to her?" I challenge.

Akira looks blankly at me.

"I do not believe I had a choice in the matter, Akira." My eyes skitter to Dejonae's desk again.

"Ryotaro," Akira urgently approaches my desk, "you have been down this road before. The last time, it did not end well."

"Ashanti and I did not divorce because she was a foreigner. Nor because of my family."

"Do you really believe that?" Akira's eyes dart between mine. "If you had secured the approval of the family, would they not have rallied around you? Would they not have done everything to make her feel at home and welcome? Would they not have encouraged her to come back? They did not. They rejoiced when she left. They hid it well, but they reveled in your heartbreak."

"Are you provoking me deliberately?"

"I would not speak out of turn if it were not important."

She is right. This is the longest scolding Akira has ever given me.

"I only want to point out the truth. Something which you seem determined to ignore. Miss Williams is not only foreign and dark-skinned, but she is much younger than you, Ryotaro. The differences between what you value, what you believe, and what you want in life simply cannot match hers because she has experienced so little. If you look beyond her beauty and her affinity for Niko, you would be able to recognize that."

My eyes linger on Akira's tightened brows. "Whether I choose to pursue her or not, it will be my decision."

"You misunderstand." Akira lowers her head. "I am not saying you cannot pursue her. If you choose to… experience the American way, you have all freedom to do so. As I mentioned, you are accomplished and wealthy. You are also a man. It is natural to feel loneliness." She shifts in discomfort. "You are not the first Sazuki that I have worked beside. I have seen how the lures of the world can draw a young man to… experiment."

My heart rebels. "Miss Williams is not an experiment to me."

Akira purses her lips.

"If I, indeed, saw her as something to experience, I would not be so hesitant. It is precisely because my interest in her is deepening that it requires my careful consideration."

"Then consider this, Ryotaro, and this is the final thing I will say about the matter."

I nod.

"You went against the family to wed Niko's mother and shattered your grandparent's hearts. This time, you have Niko watching you. What if you take her new friend and turn her into something more? And what if that relationship does not work out? Then you have not only failed twice, but this time, the heart you will shatter is your child's. Are you willing to risk that?"

Satisfied that she has delivered her final blow, Akira jerks her chin down once and stalks out of my office.

***

I work outside of the foundation because Dejonae's desk is too big of a distraction for me.

At evening's end, I pick Niko up from school.

She seems eager to discuss her day, gesturing excitedly about her invitation to the farmhouse, Bailey's joke at recess that he shared via sign language, and Beth gifting her a 'Hand Me That Wrench' T-shirt.

Her hands will cramp later tonight from all the signing.

I cut up an apple to tide her over until dinner. She shoves an entire slice into her mouth and continues gesturing.

"Dad, when can I go to the farmhouse again?"

"Maybe after your mock exams," I allow. Opening the fridge with my shoulder, I take out a pile of leftover food dishes.

I am thinking of making rice balls and corn soup. Our fridge is always filled with *tsukemono* thanks to Akira's ability to pickle everything that can possibly be pickled. It will pair well with the meal.

"I can't wait to tell mom." Slowly, Niko's smile fades to intense concentration. She signs, "Did mom talk to you?"

"Talk to me about what?" I ask, checking on the rice cooker. When I glance up again, Niko is waiting for me.

She signs, "Deej."

I swallow thickly.

My daughter gestures, "I told her about what happened after bowling. She got upset."

"Your mother isn't upset with you," I sign. "She is upset with me."

"Why? You didn't do anything wrong."

I rub the back of my neck. This is tricky territory. The one thing Ashanti and I promised to do after our divorce was never drag Niko into the middle of our fights. I do not wish to expose Niko to the truth, but she is too smart not to notice.

"Sometimes," I sign hesitantly, "when adults are scared, they react with anger. Because that is an easier emotion to handle than feeling vulnerable."

Her eyebrows knit together. She signs, "That's dumb. Even when you stop being angry, you'll still be scared."

"That is true, but…" I speak out loud, "Your mother loves you very much. At the thought of losing you, her heart probably stopped." I hit my chest.

Niko's thoughtful look remains. She signs, "I don't think mom likes Deej."

The rice spatula clamors out of my hands. "Did she say that?"

Niko makes the motion for 'feelings'. "I felt it."

Her observational skills have always been higher than other kids her age. Which is why I did not excuse her for running into the road. She made a deliberate choice that could have cost her and Dejonae greatly.

I try to calm her fears. "Your mother hasn't met Dejonae yet. She might feel differently if she gets to know her."

Niko points in my direction.

"Me?"

"How do you feel about Dejonae?" she signs.

I look away, my gaze drifting past Niko to the windows and the star-studded city skyline.

Niko's fluttering hands drag my attention back to her.

"Do you like her, dad?" she signs.

Akira's warning about breaking Niko's heart ricochets in my head. I answer carefully, "If I said yes, what would that mean to you?"

She scrunches her nose and twists her lips. "That's not fair. I asked you first."

My eyes flash with affection. I bend over and pinch her cheek. "You have a lot to say tonight. Why don't you wash your hands and come help me with the rice balls?"

"I've got homework!" Niko signs. Popping out of the chair, she hurries to her room. Then her head ducks around the corner. She gives me a thumbs up. "I think it would be nice."

"What would be nice?" I try to keep my expression neutral.

"You and Deej," she gestures. "When Deej is around, I feel like mom is here."

Shocked, I can only stare at her.

Niko grins again and hurries to her room. Her bedroom door slams shut, punctuating her exit.

I sink against the counter and distractedly wipe my hands against my apron. By comparing Dejonae to her mother, Niko just gave her approval.

The rice cooker beeps.

I pick up the rice spatula from the floor, rinse it in the sink and scoop the rice into a bowl. With my thoughts percolating heavily, I am not sure how I manage to prepare dinner without over-salting the corn soup.

Niko eats while watching television with the captions on and I retire to my room early.

Taking out my phone, I scroll to Dejonae's number.

My hands shake slightly.

It has been a while since I have expressed interest in anyone. With Ashanti, it was easy. She had clearly been interested in me. Although we were different in some areas, I did not have to worry about her being younger than me or working in my foundation.

Come on, Sazuki.

I gather my courage and call Dejonae.

The line rings.

Once.

Twice.

"Hello?" Her voice is soft. Hesitant.

My heart beats a frantic rhythm against my ribs.

"Miss Williams," I pause. Lick my lips. "Dejonae…"

"Do you need something?" Confusion seeps into her tone.

"I…" My body turns to steel, tension racing through me like a live current.

Why is it so easy for me to play for a live audience, command boardrooms, and build a music hall from the ground up, and yet asking a woman out makes me feel as though I am jumping out of a plane.

"If this is about me leaving work early today, I sincerely had a group project this time. I wasn't lying."

"No, that is not why I called."

"Then?"

I say in a firm voice, "A reporter will be visiting the office tomorrow. I won't have time to do the interview."

"Okay. No problem. I can do it."

My eyebrows jump at her confidence.

"Can I talk about the MTB?"

"We are starting to leak more information about the MTB, but it is not ready for mass release yet. You may hint at it if it comes up." I clear my throat. This is not the direction I expected the conversation to go, but perhaps it is best. What I have to say to Dejonae is best delivered in person anyway.

"Understood."

"This is the foundation's very first interview with the public," I remind her.

"It'll go well. Trust me."

"I do," I say.

She goes quiet.

"I do trust you, Dejonae," I whisper.

"Thank you. I won't let you down."

The silence goes on for so long that it becomes awkward.

Yet I cannot seem to hang up the phone.

"Is that it?"

"Yes." I release a quick breath.

Later.

I will tell Dejonae how I feel about her when the time is right.

CHAPTER 11
HEAD-BANGING IDEAS

DEJONAE

T<small>HE REPORTER WAITING</small> for me in the cafeteria is slim and pretty with tan skin, big brown eyes and a red-lipped smile. Her skirt and jacket are a bright yellow and the blouse underneath is black.

She looks like a fashionable bumblebee.

"Are you Dejonae Williams?" Her eyes widen when I draw closer. She blinks a couple times as if I might be a ghost.

"Yes, that's me." I extend my hand.

She takes it and laughs in shock. "I expected you to be older."

"Sorry to disappoint." I let my laughter ring.

"I'm Beverly Thompkins, reporter for the Financial State Magazine."

"Dejonae Williams. I'm one of the instructors here at The Sazuki Foundation."

She plucks a little notebook out of her purse and gives me a mischievous grin. "Oh, I heard you were much more than that."

My heart smacks against my ribs. "You, uh… what?"

Did she hear about Sazuki walking me to class? Or that I went bowling with him and his daughter? Or that I think about him all the time to the point that it's slowly becoming an obsession?

"Aren't you higher in rank than all the other instructors? I was told you work closely with Sazuki."

"Oh. Right." I belt out a nervous laugh.

She chuckles along, but her sharp eyes are studying me closely. "What did you think I meant?"

"Exactly that," I point to her. "Exactly."

With a prim grin, she takes something else out of her purse. It's a recording device. "Do you mind if I record us?"

"As long as you don't mind if I do the same." I set my phone on the desk next to her recorder. On the screen, there's a running clock and a glowing red button.

Her eyes glint with amusement. "You've done this before?"

"My sister is a model. One of the first things she learned about giving interviews is the importance of having your own evidence."

Beverly laughs. "Is your sister someone I would recognize by name?"

"Not yet. She's still building her empire for now." I put my arm on the back of the neighboring chair. "Before we begin, would you like to order something to drink?"

Beverly raises a hand. I glance behind me to see who she's smiling at and notice one of the baristas approaching our table. She's holding two trays of steaming hot coffees.

"I ordered for you. I hope you don't mind."

"Not at all," I say, sitting back down.

Beverly blows steam from the top of her cup. Wrapping manicured fingers around the base, she looks over at me. "Why don't we start with what the purpose of the foundation is?"

"At its simplest, we want to help every deaf child in the city experience the magic of music." I lift my coffee and lounge back in my chair.

"How do you plan to do that when the children can't hear?"

"Music isn't just heard. It's felt. When a song comes on, one that touches your heart, it's not just about the rhythm or the lyrics. There's something about it that *moves* you. Even children with disabilities can experience music. That experience might be different compared to someone who can hear it, but it's just as powerful."

Her lips arch up, but there's a hint of boredom in her eyes. "You're clearly passionate about your work, Miss Williams, but I think what people really want to know is who's the man behind the money."

"Excuse me?"

She leans her elbow against the table. "Sazuki put his own fortune into this foundation."

I blink rapidly. "He believes in the good it can do."

"Billionaires don't simply create spaces like this for the brownie points. It's usually because of a personal connection." She glances around. "Or a political one."

I drum my fingers on the table. "I can tell you about the mission of The Sazuki Foundation. I can tell you about our progress. I can even tell you that, over the past few days, we've had our first group of kids come in and learn music. Just yesterday, a little girl touched my hand and signed, *'I can feel it'*. For the first time, she was able to understand what those rhythmic vibrations meant and how to repeat them in a musical pattern. But more than that, she learned that being deaf is not a curse. It's a gift—one that puts her in touch with a loving and supportive community. If that's not what your story is about, then maybe we should cut this interview short."

I start to rise.

She shoots out a hand. "Miss Williams, sit. Please. I didn't mean any offense." Her smile has a hint of contrition behind it. "You have to understand. The Sazukis have kept a low profile for decades. Despite being the world's biggest album sellers, they never leave Japan, never tour and never give interviews. I'm this," she pinches her fingers together, "close to one of the biggest stories of my life. It wouldn't be natural if I wasn't curious, right?"

I nod. "Maybe."

She smirks. "You're very protective of your boss."

"And you're very good at spinning a story. What in that entire speech made you feel I was protective of one person when, in fact, I'm very protective of the deaf community."

Her eyes turn sharp although her lips remain frozen in a smile. "I can see why he put you in charge."

"Should we carry on with the interview or have you gotten everything you need, Miss Beverly?"

"Let's continue."

We stick to the pre-arranged questions and then I give her a tour.

Purple Hair AKA Sheila Cottingham is in the music room with seven-year-old Ricky. She whips her head around when we enter and gives me a dark look. A look that quickly changes when she sees I'm not alone.

"Sheila, this is Miss Beverly Thompkins. She's here for an interview."

"Ah." Sheila's smile is so brittle that I'm afraid it won't last for long.

"Impressive room." Beverly takes a picture.

"It's completely soundproof." I gesture to the foam boards. "As you can see, great care was put into the design."

"Why does it need to be soundproof when the students are deaf? It's not like they'll be able to hear anything." She chuckles.

Both Purple Hair and I whirl around and pin Beverly with a dark stare.

"The soundproof foam is to keep the music and vibrations from bleeding out into the other rooms. Just because the students can't *hear* doesn't mean they won't be disturbed."

"I see," Beverly says with a smirk.

Sheila gives me a *can you believe her* look.

I shake my head.

"Let me show you the concert hall." I make a sweeping gesture to the door.

Jordan is jogging down the stairs on our way up.

Oh no. Please don't talk to me.

His eyes latch onto me and he slides into my path. "Deej."

Beverly stops abruptly.

I slant him a sharp look. "Not now, Jordan," I say beneath my breath.

"You haven't been answering my texts."

"I said not now."

"Then when?" He whirls around when I try to usher Beverly past him. Eyes beseeching, he says, "They sent me out for training I didn't need and I didn't see you for days. You keep saying we're going to talk, but it's like you're avoiding me."

Beverly arches an eyebrow. Intrigue glitters in her eyes as she glances between us. "Who is this?"

"This is the foundation's in-house translator."

"French? Mandarin?"

I scrunch my nose. "What are you talking about?"

"You said he was a translator."

"I translate ASL." Jordan lifts his chin proudly. "It makes it easier for the students to have someone who can quickly communicate what they're trying to say or translate what the admin or a guest is talking about."

"That seems like a lot of trouble to go through. Don't most of the students and teachers already know ASL?"

"It's not a lot of trouble," I correct her right away. "It's a way to make communication easy on all fronts. The easier communication is, the better the environment for the students and everyone involved."

"Hm." She nods with a glib smile.

Jordan arches an eyebrow in her direction.

I shrug. It's clear this woman had very little interest in covering the story. Her empathic skills are severely lacking. If she hadn't met me, she probably would have bulldozed her way into getting a story about Sazuki and his mysterious family. Now that there's no hope of getting a single crumb about Sazuki, I feel a clear disconnect.

"This stage," I gesture to the wooden floor in the concert hall, "is made completely of sound boards. At their first concert, the kids will be able to feel the vibrations of the music. Mr. Sazuki is also working closely with a renowned engineer to create a device for deaf music students. It'll convey vibrations with more clarity than anything else on the market."

"Mr. Sazuki sure is keeping busy." She glances past me to the exits. "Do you think he's back by now?"

"Mr. Sazuki will be in meetings all day, which is why he asked me to accommodate you."

What is this woman's problem?

My impatience is climbing, but I refuse to let her see my snappy side. Sazuki trusted me with the task. It's one thing to share my knowledge of vibrations with the instructors and another thing entirely to be the first official spokesperson of the foundation.

I can't mess this up.

"Do you have any questions about the concert hall's construction or the measures taken to make the venue more accessible to deaf students?" I look hopefully at her, but deep down inside, I don't expect any excitement.

She shakes her head. "No, not really."

Well then.

"Could you point me to the bathroom?" she asks.

"It's that way."

"Thanks." She offers a bright smile. "When I come back, I'd like to take a few more pictures for the article and then I'll be out of your hair for the day."

"No problem."

Her heels click against the stage as she walks off. I cringe, wishing I'd insisted that she take off her shoes. When I asked her to do so earlier, she politely declined and I swallowed my insistence in deference to her.

It's for Sazuki and the foundation, Dejonae.

I suck in a deep breath. No matter how ignorant she is, Beverly is the one who'll be shining a light on the good things that we're doing here. Keeping her happy matters.

The interview is almost over anyway.

My phone rings.

I set it to my ear, surprised when Holland Alistair's wife starts talking.

"Hi, is this Dejonae?" Kenya's pretty voice croons.

"Yep. This is she."

"I got your number from Hadyn. I hope you don't mind."

"I don't." I tilt my head. "A while back, he mentioned that he was planning something for Vanya. I'm guessing you're calling about that."

"You're a mind reader." She laughs cheerfully. "Yes, this is a little something he planned for Vanya. He asked me to steal her away from the house and bring her to the farmhouse. Once we're there, we're planning on having chai latte and girl chat."

"And I'll bring the chai?"

"According to Hadyn, Vanya adores your chai just slightly more than she does him."

"Slightly?" I snort.

"Okay, a lot. But he's a man with an ego to protect."

I burst out laughing.

Having to deal with Beverly's ignorance was chipping away at my hope in humanity, but Kenya's sunny personality is starting to bring a little light in.

"I'm just kidding. Vanya loves that man more than life itself. But Hadyn hinted that she's not feeling well these days."

"Does he know what's wrong?"

"I think he has a suspicion, but he chose not to share it with us to protect Vanya's privacy. I respect that. And it really doesn't matter to me what's wrong. All that matters is she knows we're there for her."

"I'm in. Did you say it was tonight?" I check my watch.

"Yes, tonight. By the way, Hadyn doesn't want Vanya to find out that he set this whole thing up. Let's pretend us stealing her was totally spontaneous and not related to her concerned husband at all."

"Got it."

"Perfect!"

"Do I need to bring blenders and ingredients?"

"No need," she assures me. "Hadyn's handling all of that. He said he'd have food catered and everything. The only thing his black card couldn't provide was your fancy chai latte." I can hear her smiling through the phone. "You know, I'm really curious about what Vanya finds so addictive about those."

I smirk. "You'll find out tonight."

"I can't wait."

When we hang up, I check the time again. "Where's Beverly? Did she run away?"

Reluctantly, I set out to the nearest bathroom and push the door to enter. Beverly's voice carries through to me and I freeze with the door cracked open.

"I'm telling you, Voss, there's no story here. This girl won't give me an ounce of info on Sazuki."

I lean closer to the door so I can hear better.

"I know. It's like I'm wasting my time."

My eyes widen. Does she think my time isn't being wasted too?

"You know Chief and Sazuki are golf buddies. Maybe that's why she pushed me to get this fluff piece. As if I don't have better things to deal with than a story about…" The next word that comes out of her mouth makes my head spin.

Did she just…

Her laughter after saying such a degrading slur makes something crash in my head. Before I can talk myself out of it, the rage inside me takes control. I stomp the door down with my foot and it bangs against the wall.

Beverly lets out a bleating scream, almost like a cornered goat. Her eyes swing toward me and she gives a nervous little chuckle.

"Miss Williams… were you… did you… um…"

I storm over to her. "What did you say about my kids?"

She backs up. "Are you crazy?"

"How dare you call yourself a reporter and speak about children like that?"

"… you…" She struggles to speak.

"Those kids may be missing one of their senses, but they have more common sense and integrity than someone like you will ever have. You should be ashamed of yourself."

"How dare you talk to me that way?"

"How else am I supposed to talk to scum?" I roar. "You think you're brave to say that word about someone else's child? No. It just makes *you* seem childish and ignorant. Should I let the world know what a piece of crap you really are?"

I see her hand coming at me and I block it, but she's quick. With her other hand, Beverly grabs my hair.

I shriek and grab her back.

She drives me backward.

I slam into a bathroom stall almost ripping it off its hinges.

My back hits the door.

I go temporarily insane.

Hitting, biting and scratching are all on the table as we tussle, tearing at each other like rabid wolves.

"Oh my gosh!" I hear a new voice.

Beverly and I stop at the same time.

When I turn, I see Sheila gaping at us from the bathroom doorway. "Are you insane?" she screams.

I start to feel hope when I think she's jumping on my side.

But I should know better.

Her eyes flit to the reporter. She hurries over and smacks at my knuckles until I release Beverly's hair.

"What the hell is wrong with you?" Sheila barks.

"She—"

"This is a place of music and arts, Miss Williams. Don't bring your ghetto here."

Her words are a smack to the face. My jaw drops.

Beverly puts on a show. Her eyes get teary and she pats her

cheek. "I was just washing my hands and she suddenly attacked me."

"I'm so sorry." Sheila pats down Beverly's hair which is sticking up all over her head. "Let me get you some ice."

While Sheila leaves with Beverly leaning heavily on her like a war veteran, I seethe in rage.

"Wait!"

The two women stop and look back at me.

With dark, burning eyes, I march closer to Beverly and raise a hand.

She flinches.

I don't hit her. I open her palm and drop a clump of hair in it. "You'll want this back."

She grits her teeth at me.

"Really, Williams?" Sheila shakes her head darkly and carries Beverly out of the bathroom.

I limp to the mirror and peer in. There's a scratch on my neck from where Beverly clipped me with her talons. It's not bleeding, but it's throbbing slightly. My hair's a tangled mess of curls and frizz. One side of my shirt is hanging off my shoulder. It wasn't meant to withstand a grown woman tugging on it like a leash.

On the other hand, I'm sure I gave Beverly a bald spot.

The grin I aim at my reflection is dark but satisfied.

Worth it.

I clean myself up as best as I can, scraping my hair into a tight ponytail and reapplying lip gloss. Then I go around the bathroom picking up the clumps of hair and making sure we didn't break the door in.

When I'm satisfied that we didn't leave extra work for the cleaners, I return to the main hallway.

My heart is still racing with adrenaline. I could go another round, but the evil Beverly has probably hopped on her broomstick and disappeared by now. I hope she learned her lesson.

And I hope she never disrespects the deaf community again.

Urgent footsteps clamor toward me. It's Sheila. She's marching like a drill sergeant ready to give the order to the firing squad.

"Before you ask, I didn't throw the first punch. She did. And I had a very good reason for—"

"Do you know what you've done?" Sheila hisses, cutting me off. Her purple hair swishes in front of her face with the force of her head bob.

Uneasy, I lean back. "What?"

"That reporter just uploaded *this* to her social media account and tagged our foundation." Sheila shoves her phone in my face.

I go cross-eyed for a second.

And then the photo becomes clear.

I gasp.

It's a picture of Beverly holding the clump of hair I gave her. Beneath the picture, it says, '*A mentally unstable instructor is working @SazukiFoundation. She grabbed my hair. People like her should not be taking care of disabled students*'.

The world drops away until there's just blurry chaos.

This.

Bastard.

* * *

I sit petulantly in the chair outside of Sazuki's office. Right after Sheila showed me the post, I got a call from Sazuki.

"*I can explain,*" I said.

"*Go home. Immediately.*"

"*But—*"

"*I do not want to see you when I get back.*"

My eyes dart to the clock on the wall.

I twiddle my thumbs.

Sazuki sounded pissed over the phone. Is he going to kick me out of the foundation? Will I not be able to graduate?

The elevator door rips apart.

Sazuki storms in, strong and formidable. One hand is in his

pocket. Akira is right behind him. She's taking urgent steps, her loose pant leg flapping. She slants me an angry look.

I don't pay her any mind.

My entire body is turned toward Sazuki.

His jaw clenches. His eyes turn into onyx jewels when he sees me.

I stand so fast my chair almost crashes into the wall. "Mr. Sazuki."

"I told you to go home."

"Give me a chance to explain what happened."

"Akira," Sazuki growls.

The bodyguard stands in front of me, blocking my way. She looks delighted to do so.

I stand on my tiptoes to see past her shoulder. Sazuki doesn't look back. I see him dragging his tie down his chest just as the door clicks shut.

"Do you need me to escort you to the elevator, Miss Williams?"

"No," I snarl.

My heart is pounding when I grab my purse and bag. The entire admin team gives me weird looks as I pass them.

The moment the elevator doors slide closed behind me, I press the back of my hand against my mouth. Tears are stinging my eyes. My chest swells with emotion.

I've seen Sazuki angry. Belligerent. Enraged.

I've seen him steely with silence.

And I've seen him annoyed.

But that look wasn't just anger.

It was more.

Disappointment.

I didn't think I cared about what he thought of me, but his expression left an imprint. It's a weight I feel keenly when I get to the lobby and the instructors, who'd been huddled around whispering, stare at me.

My throat burns, but I keep my head held high as I walk out. When I'm outside, the sun caresses the top of my head. A gentle wind touches my face, whispering that it's okay. That I did the right thing.

But it doesn't help.

My heart is burning and the tears refuse to be held back.

I keep seeing Sazuki's eyes. So cold. So stoic.

If he'd kneed me in the gut, it would hurt less.

I make a fist and pound it against my chest. What did I expect? That he would run to me when he saw the scrapes on my arms? That he would set me in a chair and kneel in front of me and dress my wounds the way he did at school? Did I expect him to fold me into his embrace and sway with me from side to side?

What the hell was I hoping for? And why are tears running down my face in the middle of the sidewalk?

I sniff and tilt my head back, trying to ease the droplets back into my tear ducts.

It doesn't work.

I need to talk to someone.

Yaya is out with her Hearing Is Overrated friends, the deaf club that she attended in high school. I don't want to drag her away from her time with them.

It's too early for our girl's night, but someone should be at the farmhouse, right?

On the ride over, I calm myself down. I know I acted impulsively, but it wasn't like I meant to hurt anyone.

Maybe when Sazuki isn't so angry, he'll believe me.

* * *

"Are you okay?" Sunny asks, setting a cup of tea in front of me.

I accept it with a grateful smile. Or at least I try to. My lips aren't working the way they should and I'm pretty sure I look like a feral cat right now.

"You showed up early. Hadyn hasn't even dropped by with the decorations and snacks."

"I thought… maybe I could help with cleaning or something."

"Cleaning?" Her pretty eyebrows hike. "You came over here to… clean my house?"

I squirm guiltily.

Sunny sets a brown hand on top of mine. Her expression is full of worry.

I bite down on my bottom lip, trying hard to control the weeping that wants to burst out of me. Instead of thinking about Sazuki and his cold shoulder, I focus on Sunny's face. She's a tall and slender woman with shiny black hair that goes all the way down her back.

With her reddish-brown complexion, pointy nose and exotic eyes, I bet she could find work in modeling. If not, she can probably open a Belizean fry jack food truck and help her mom share their culture with the rest of the city.

"I can see that you're trying hard not to cry," Sunny says gently.

"I hate that I'm getting emotional. I swear I'm not always like this."

"I know we just met and you probably don't want to share with me, but I promise that what you say won't go any further than here." She gestures to the door. "Darrel went to get our boys and take them to the library. Kenya's still at her publishing house and Dawn is a workaholic. I'll probably have to send Max to drag her away from fixing a car."

I chuckle because I did get that impression from Dawn that day. As small, delicate and classically beautiful as she was, she wore a pair of overalls stained with oil and talked about car gaskets and internal wiring all day.

"What's going on?"

"It's nothing big," I whisper. My voice is suddenly tight. Probably because I'm using every ounce of will I have to keep my emotions in check.

"Sweetheart, if I pretended to believe you, then I wouldn't be a very good friend." She winks. "And that's what we are. The moment you step through those farmhouse doors, you're a friend.

So don't be shy." She folds her arms over her chest. "Lay it on me."

I tell her about the interview and overhearing Beverly in the bathroom. I skip the details about the fight and jump straight to Sazuki. "I didn't want him to see the post without hearing from me. But he'd already been aware of it. He just… he cut me off and didn't want to talk about it. I saw him in the office again and…" My bottom lip trembles.

She slides a tissue box over. "Was he rude to you?"

"He was just… cold. We haven't seen eye-to-eye on a lot of things. It started that night at the gala and it's only continued from there."

Sunny bobs her head. "I remember the look on your face when you stumbled off the stage. If looks could kill, it would have been his funeral that night."

"A lot has happened since then. I met his daughter, who's absolutely incredible. He told me his vision for the foundation and it's something I want to be a part of. I thought we were coming to some kind of understanding and it all just…" I make a 'poof' gesture. "Disappeared."

"I see."

I scrunch my nose. "What do you see?"

"Tell me, Deej." Sunny clamps her hands together and leans forward. "What is making you cry right now? That you angered a reporter?"

"No. I would fight her again." I scowl.

"That you might have caused damage to the foundation?"

"Of course that bothers me."

"More than the fact that Sazuki didn't take your side?"

My eyes lurch to hers.

The tears refuse to stay in their place. One comes slipping down my cheek.

"You care about his opinion of you. You want that opinion to be good. You want him to believe you even when all the evidence is stacked against you. But he didn't." Her words are soft and gentle. "Isn't that what hurts you more than anything else?"

"No." I swipe away a tear.

She pats my back. "No?"

"Yes," I admit. Another tear falls. "But caring about Sazuki's opinion of me would mean that I care about him."

"Maybe you do."

"I can't."

"Why not?"

"Because he hates me now." I sniff. "He gave me a big job and I disappointed him. Even worse, I smeared the entire foundation. Everything he believed about me being young, impulsive and immature was proven true."

"Is it true?"

"Am I young? Yeah. Am I impulsive, not usually." I frown. "The thing is, he didn't even ask me about my side. He took that reporter's caption and ran with it. You should have seen the way he looked at me. I mean, he could barely make eye contact. If he'd just talked to me, I would have been able to tell him the truth."

"You feel betrayed."

"I feel like my head is about to explode," I say with a tearful chuckle. "I can't remember the last time I cried like this."

She smiles sweetly at me. "Without realizing it, you had expectations of him. He might be disappointed in you and maybe you deserve it, but you're disappointed in him too. And that's something you should probably explore."

"Disappointment? I'd rather not."

"Not the disappointment." She chuckles. "Where it comes from. Why did you expect so much of Sazuki even though you know how cold and ruthless he is? Why did you expect him to take your side against all odds? Why does your heart break because he didn't?"

"Because I'm an idiot. Obviously. A monster never changes his spots."

"Do you really think he's a monster?" she prods.

I give her a dark look. "I thought your husband was the therapist?"

"I might have picked up a thing or two." She lifts one shoulder in a casual shrug.

"You think… you think I *like* Sazuki? After everything he's done?"

"You're the one who needs to answer that. Not me." Sunny sips her tea.

I sit back and let the silence soak through me, working past the pain in my heart to the root of it. The truth must be wearing knuckle rings because when it punches me in the face, I see stars.

"Oh crap."

Sunny arches a brow knowingly.

I give her a frightened look. "I think I have feelings for Sazuki."

CHAPTER 12
OFFICE TAKEOVER

SAZUKI

"You only formed this board for appearance's sake, Sazuki, but we still have a bit of sway here. I think you need to be very careful about dismissing our concerns." Robert Cardinal's threat is accompanied by a chorus of tight-lipped nods from the other men around the table.

I glance at each of them in turn.

They are all influential in their own right. Chosen by design—some because of their sway with official ASL organizations in the US and others with their ties to local politics.

A project as massive as The Sazuki Music Foundation could not have been accomplished alone. Especially when my responsibilities to my family in Japan and those to my daughter kept me occupied for most of the process.

Adam is the only member around the table who is not wearing a disdainful frown.

"Whether Miss Williams assaulted the reporter or not isn't the real issue. The problem is that the foundation got dragged into it. Our response to this matter will either gain the trust of the people we're trying to serve or it'll drive them away," Adam says.

"I have been working closely with the PR team to monitor the public's response. We will put out an official apology soon."

"An apology? That's it?" Robert shakes his head. "According to an eyewitness, Miss Williams was *seen* assaulting the reporter. At minimum, that woman should be fired. The fact that she has not been arrested yet is baffling to me."

I grit my teeth. "As Adam said, this is not about Miss Williams. Our focus should be on ensuring the foundation escapes the scandal unscathed."

"What do you mean this isn't about Miss Williams?" Robert's eyebrows tighten above his stormy eyes. "You're going to leave an emotionally unstable college student around impressionable and vulnerable children? After this ridiculous scuffle? Does that sound like a good idea to you?"

"Mr. Cardinal—"

He lifts a hand curtly. "I have been supporting you one hundred percent in your endeavor, Sazuki. I might not have put a dime into the foundation, but it was through *my* connections and *my* efforts that you were able to network successfully." He lurches to his feet and closes the button of his suit jacket. "Just as I paved the way for you, I can block you out. Resolve this quickly. That is all I have to say."

Robert stomps to the exits. The other board members follow suit, avoiding my eyes and keeping their heads down.

A heavy, crushing silence descends when they are gone.

I sink into the chair at the head of the table and pinch the bridge of my nose. The sound of a chair skittering back prompts me to look up.

Adam rises slowly. "You look awful. Did you get any sleep yesterday?"

I shake my head. I asked Akira to watch over Niko and could only squeeze in a quick phone call before she went to school this morning.

My heart still aches. It was my first time since moving to America that I did not see my child off to school.

"What did Dejonae say?" Adam asks.

"I have not spoken to her."

His eyebrows jump. "You've gone to all these lengths to protect her and you haven't even taken the time to hear what she has to say?"

"Later." I push wearily against the table and clamor to my feet.

"Sazuki," empathy rings in Adam's voice, "I understand that you're trying your hardest to protect both Dejonae and the foundation, but you might not be able to do both."

I stare calmly at him.

"It's going to be a fight, and you know it. Don't think the board is going to roll over and play dead. They can't stop you from the inside, but they can bring enough pressure from the outside to keep the foundation from succeeding."

I absorb his assessment. "I know."

"You will have to choose," Adam says gravely.

I clamp my lips together.

His eyes are assessing. "You've spent *years* building this foundation and you're so close to the finish line. Now isn't the time to lose focus."

"What do you suggest then?"

He glances away. "Do what you have to do to save your legacy."

"Adam."

"She's young. She can bounce back."

I walk determinedly over to him. "If I cannot protect both her and the foundation, then I do not deserve to have either of them."

He does not look surprised. "I knew you'd say that."

"If it were Nova," I arch a brow, "you would say the same."

"That's different."

"I do not see how."

"Nova would never put the business in jeopardy. She wouldn't put me in a position that I would have to choose."

"Then how are you so sure that you would choose her?" I ask pointedly.

He tilts his head, opens his mouth and then closes it. Perhaps admitting the reasons might unlock the feelings he has kept so well hidden.

A glance at my watch makes me wince.

"I have a meeting at the foundation."

"I'm on your side, Sazuki," Adam says as I leave. "Even if I think your way is risky, I'll do what I can. I don't want to see Dejonae suffer any more from this than she has to."

I stop in my tracks. "I do require a favor."

He pushes up his sleeves. "What do you need me to do? I can do anything except fight." One corner of his lips curls up. "Not that you'd need that kind of assistance. You have your scary cousin Akira."

"It is not a fight I need." I turn slightly. "And it is not you I need either."

"Huh?"

"Lend me Nova."

His eyes bug.

"My team has never handled a scandal of this scale before. Nova has spent the latter half of her career handling your public persona. I want her to do the same for us."

"I'll talk to her. I don't think she'll have a problem."

I dip my chin.

His chest swells on a deep sigh. "I hope you know what you're doing, Sazuki."

We share the same wish.

As it stands, I feel as though I am entering a dark and dangerous cave while blindfolded. But I will not let Dejonae leave the foundation under these circumstances. Somehow, I will find a way to protect everything that is precious to me.

* * *

My receptionist gives me a frightened look when I step out of the elevator and head to my office. I take note of it, but I keep walking.

When I turn the bend, I see what prompted her nervous look. Dejonae is seated around her desk.

Skin bright. Lips pursed. Head raised.

As defiant as ever.

She skitters to her feet when I stride across the room. Her brown eyes are full of determination. "Sazuki."

"I told you to stay home," I growl. The sight of her makes my heart clench. I cannot afford to waver.

"I'm here to turn in my resignation."

I freeze.

My nostrils flare.

"I have a meeting." I stride past her and push my office door open.

I know she is going to follow me in.

Her sneakers are quiet on the carpet.

She is not wearing a fancy dress or lipstick today. Instead, she is wearing her staple of a cropped T-shirt, jeans, and tennis shoes. Her honey-tinged curls are in a tight ponytail at the back of her head.

My eyes linger on her. I soak in the glossiness of her dark mocha-toned skin and the hint of gold that naturally lives above her cheekbones. Her stance is strong, but she is already beginning to chew on her bottom lip.

Keeping my eyes on her, I walk closer. Her lashes flutter rapidly. She keeps her feet rooted in place and yet her entire body eases back, away from me.

I step past her, shut the door and lock it.

The loud *click* sends a skitter of tension through the air.

Keeping my back to her, I say firmly, "Did you think of the cost before you acted?"

Her breath becomes louder. It hits the air in rapid beats.

"If you weighed every option and still decided to take the one you did yesterday, I would have a better explanation for the board members. For the people who had to stay up all night with me, monitoring the responses to that damaging post."

I turn to face her.

Her eyes are so large they seem to take up half her face. Her lush mouth softens, falling partly open.

"On the day I announced you as manager, the instructors gathered in my office. They demanded to know why I chose you when all of them are older, more experienced and have more degrees."

The boldness leaks out of her eyes. She no longer faces me as an opponent, but clasps her hands together and stares a hole into the ground.

I assess her trembling fingers. "I told them I would stand by my decision to put you in that place. Because of you, Niko reclaimed the joy of learning the piano. I wanted the creativity, patience, and care that you showed her to become the standard. But now, not only the instructors, but everyone is doubting my words. They suspect me of making the wrong decision. Of being swayed by your youth or your beauty or something even more untoward."

She pulls her lips into her mouth. Her nail scrapes against her thumb.

I take three steps toward her. "But I do not care what they believe about me or the decision I made. I care about who you really are."

My phone chirps.

It is a reminder about the meeting.

I set a timer and show her the clock. "You have eight minutes." I fold my arms over my chest. "Before I have to leave, you need to give me a reason to trust you again, no matter what anyone else says."

She looks up at me with her big, heartbroken brown eyes. And I steel myself against the lashing urge to wrap my arms around her.

"I came in here with a speech," her words are low, as if they are scraping against her heart, "I have an iron-clad defense, but the more you look at me like that, the more it feels like it won't matter."

"You have seven minutes and twenty-eight seconds."

"I have a question first." She licks her lips and looks up at me hesitantly. "Are you asking as Niko's father, as the head of the foundation or as… something else?"

"I am whatever I need to be to hear the truth from you." I glance at my watch. "You have six minutes and forty seconds."

She licks her lips.

"I want you to tell me as straightforwardly as possible. So even the children who attend class can understand. I don't want fancy words and I don't want excuses. Be honest, the way you are when you are displeased with me."

Her thick lashes drop, hiding her eyes from view. Her throat bobs as she swallows.

"You have six minutes and twenty seconds left."

"Can you stop that?" Her eyes dart up. A flare of frustration tightens her mouth. "I need more time to explain myself."

"Then start by explaining what you did wrong yesterday."

Her shoulders tense. She laces her fingers together. "I fought with a reporter."

I gaze past the blinds and into the rest of the office. "Phyllis Wu. Head of our IT Department. Her son has a rare genetic heart condition that requires him to carry around a machine. She was scheduled to go with him to the doctor when the foundation's website began to receive so many complaints that it crashed. She refused to leave and insisted on fixing the website because no one else could handle the matter."

Dejonae sinks into a chair. Her face creases in distress.

"Evangeline Warren. She is five years old. She recently lost her hearing but before that, she loved music. Her mother is working two jobs to support the family after her husband left her and returned to his country. Evangeline was set to join the foundation in our second phase. Her mother cried over the phone when she asked how much the fee was and we said it was free. But yesterday, Evangeline's mother called and said she would no longer allow her daughter to attend the foundation. She would rather

Evangeline never learn music than to put her in a dangerous place."

Dejonae digs her fingers into the arm of the chair.

"People are petitioning for the foundation to be shut down. They say it must be a front for money laundering because deaf children do not need to learn music. They are asking for the government to get involved." I keep my expression blank.

Silence falls like a toxic rain.

I move toward her. "The day I first showed you the music room, you told me that accessibility is always an after-thought. Do you remember that?"

She nods.

"This means the accessibility we *do* have, we have only because it was fought for." I press my hand against the arm of the chair and hunker over her. "Knowing that, how could you be so irresponsible?"

Her eyes shift swiftly to mine. Pride and remorse are at war inside her. It causes her bottom lip to tremble.

I straighten and keep my voice level. "Do you still think this is a small issue? That you were wronged? Misunderstood? That it should only concern you and the reporter? If you made a mistake and handed in your resignation as punishment, do you think you will be the only one to suffer the consequences?" I shake my head. "While you were writing that letter, did you think about the people who are being punished alongside you? All of the instructors' efforts, the team that pulled an all-nighter, the children whose parents are wary of sending them here—if you run away, do you think it solves their problems?"

Her head twists around so she is facing the window.

"You have three minutes left."

She slowly turns back to me.

I look down, clenching my jaw. "I told you before. I don't care about what people think of me and my reasons for choosing you. I care about who you really are. Were you always someone who would run in the face of pressure?"

"Someone needs to take the flak for this." She gives me a long look. "We both know that people aren't going to go easy on you if I stay. And I don't think you really want another complication right now."

I square my shoulders. "I don't care what you think, but I'm certain about one thing. The Sazuki Foundation is going to change the way that deaf students interact with music. I recruited you because you can help us reach that goal."

She scrubs a finger over her dark forehead.

I reach out to touch her shoulder and pull back before I make contact. "People will find reasons to hate you, pity you and look down on you because of your age and inexperience. And others might coddle you, go easy on you and take your side because of your looks, your race or your gender. But I won't do either of those things. The Sazuki Foundation is my legacy. Once you contribute to that legacy, it doesn't matter if you're a man or a woman. If you're black or white. If you're ugly or beautiful. We're on the same side."

There's a knock on the door.

"Sazuki," Akira's voice seeps through, "why is this locked?" The door knob rattles. "Traffic is terrible. If you plan to get to the meeting on time, we have to leave now."

I check my watch.

Two seconds.

One.

The alarm chimes.

"Your eight minutes are up. If you have no answer for me, you can leave the resignation letter on the desk. I will speak to your school so this does not affect your graduation project."

I take a step toward the door.

A warm hand slips into mine, grabbing my fingers.

My heart trips over itself.

I stare ahead, frozen.

"I'm not going to lie just to please you. And I'm not going to apologize for something I feel no remorse about."

My eyebrows hike.

Is she trying to raise my blood pressure?

"Any reason I give for fighting with the reporter won't solve the effects that it's having on everyone. But I don't know what else to do. I don't want to let the kids down. I don't want to be a burden to anyone, not to the admin team, not to the instructors or the parents. I want to work with you until The Sazuki Foundation touches the world—"

Akira knocks on the door again. "Sazuki, we need to leave now."

She removes her hand.

I barely restrain the urge to take it back again. "I know you have a good reason for fighting with her. Whatever she did, it must have warranted your response."

Dejonae gasps loudly.

I walk to the door because I really cannot miss this next appointment.

My fingers twist the lock.

I start to turn the knob.

"Sazuki."

I stop. She has my heart by the throat. I could not move even if a hurricane tried to sweep me away.

"If you knew," her voice is hesitant, "why were you so cold to me yesterday?"

"Because I was afraid." I grip the door harder.

Akira knocks again. Her voice sounds heavy and urgent. "Sazuki, you're really going to be late."

"Afraid of what?" Dejonae whispers.

"Afraid I would be too soft on you."

I feel her shock, but I do not turn around to witness it. Quickly opening the door, I stride to Akira. "Let's go."

She takes one look at my face and nods.

*** * *

Hours later, I shake hands with the editor-in-chief. She smiles when I confirm the exclusive interview, her eyes lighting up with dollar signs.

I return to the car.

At first, Akira says nothing.

Eventually, she glances at me in the rear-view mirror. "Will you really try to resolve it with money?"

"There is little that it cannot solve," I sigh wearily. My eyes are beginning to throb.

I close them. Unfortunately, the sun is too bright and it still bothers me.

"Do you believe that they will uphold their end of the agreement?"

"The money will not be paid out until I see their amendment article. At this point, we have to trust each other."

She frowns. "What about the reporter? Did you speak to her?"

"The reporter was on medical leave."

Akira huffs. "Medical leave? I saw the security footage of them leaving the bathroom. There was barely a scratch on her."

"Are you taking Dejonae's side, Akira?" My lips arch up.

Akira sputters and gasps from the front seat. "This is not about sides. I simply have no time for those who exaggerate their injuries."

"An article will be released tomorrow."

"That reporter has already done so much damage to the foundation with one little caption and a picture. If she decides to go against her chief and writes something damning about us in her article…"

I sink my head back. "We will cross that bridge when we get to it."

What feels like minutes later, someone shakes my shoulders. I startle awake.

"Ryotaro," Akira whispers.

"Did I doze off?"

"Almost immediately." A line creases her forehead. "I'm

waking you against my better judgement. You should get more sleep."

"There is no time. Now that I have sorted things out with the magazine, the foundation has to put out a statement."

She nods.

I climb out of the car and notice another black SUV drive past. I recognize the model as Nova's. The engine stalls and then falls quiet. Nova climbs out and approaches us. As usual, she is dressed sharply. Her hair is in braids and her lips are stern.

She gives me her usual, no-nonsense nod. "Sazuki. Akira."

"Nova. We appreciate your help."

"Adam said things were desperate."

I gesture to the elevator. "Let's discuss in my office."

When we arrive upstairs, I am stunned to see Dejonae sitting at her desk outside of my office.

Her eyes drift to mine.

She looks sober and withdrawn.

I hold her gaze.

Nova stops short and glances between us.

I clear my throat. "Nova, this is Dejonae Williams."

"The one at the heart of this whole debacle, right?" Nova arches an eyebrow. "You don't look like the type to be starting fights in bathroom stalls."

"I didn't start it."

Nova purses her lips.

"I usually clean up my own messes." Dejonae lifts her chin. "But I'm willing to follow the script if it helps the foundation."

Nova motions her head at my office and then walks inside as if it belongs to her.

Dejonae narrows her eyes. "Who's she?"

"Adam's…"—I stumble over my words. Nova is more than a mere secretary, business partner or advisor—"everything."

"Ah." She still seems confused.

When it comes to Nova and Adam's relationship, so am I.

Drawing near, I place my hand to the small of her back. "You stayed."

"I don't run away." She blinks rapidly. "Also, I didn't have the courage to walk past the admin team again."

My lips twitch.

Nova takes a seat in the sofa and gestures for us to do the same. Since I am asking her for a favor, I make no comment about her pushiness and let her do what she wants.

Dejonae and I sit in the love seat. Her thigh presses into mine. The warmth of it makes my body turn hot in an instant.

"Tell me everything that happened yesterday." Nova's eyes narrow. "Leave nothing out. Even if it seems like a minor detail."

"I met Beverly at the café downstairs," Dejonae says, pinning her hands together and setting them in her lap. "At first, she appeared friendly."

"Was there anything strange about her interview with you?"

"She kept asking about Sazuki's private life."

I arch an eyebrow. The editor-in-chief hadn't said anything about that.

"When I shut that type of conversation down, Beverly seemed a lot less enthused, but I decided not to hold it against her. We went on a tour of the music rooms and the concert hall. Then she went to the bathroom."

"And this is where the incident happened, correct?" Nova's face is pure concentration. It feels as though I am watching a police interrogation.

"Yes. It happened in the bathroom." Dejonae's eyes flicker to me. "I heard Beverly on the phone. She was talking to a friend about how annoyed she was to be doing a story on the foundation. She called the kids here… a derogatory word."

My muscles coil with tension.

"Which one?" Nova prompts.

When Dejonae tells us, my blood boils.

I clamp down my emotions before I turn to face her. "Is that when the fight started?"

"If you're asking if *I'm* the one who initiated the first physical attack, I wasn't. I marched into the room and told her off, yes. But I didn't put my hands on her. She's the one who screamed at me and grabbed my hair first."

Nova drums her fingers on the arm of the chair. "The problem is we have no evidence of that."

"Even if we did," I add, "attacking the reporter publicly would not help the foundation."

"What did the security cameras catch?" Nova asks.

"The only feed they have is one that points to the bathroom doors. It shows the reporter and Miss Cottingham leaving together. The reporter looked distressed and disheveled."

The calm in my tone is not mirrored in my emotions. I understand why Dejonae did not apologize for what she did. I went after the man who almost ran my daughter over and had no apologies about it, making sure he understood the folly of his ways.

Dejonae is not the type to sit things out in the face of injustice. She might not have my resources, but she certainly has my grit.

I want to pat her shoulders, but I cannot risk looking as though I approve of her methods. Especially since they cost the foundation so much.

"If only we had a way to rattle the reporter's cage," Nova says. "A bargaining chip."

Dejonae jumps in her seat. "Holy crap."

I raise a hand to steady her but, she settles down on her own. When she takes her seat, she is sitting closer to me than before.

"I have evidence." Taking out her phone, Dejonae plays a voice recording. "I learned from my sister to always record interviews. Especially if you're being recorded too. I didn't take off the recording until I got home."

My eyes gleam. "Good work."

She smirks, making her lips look so delectable it causes a physical pang inside me. For the hundredth time, I want to lean down and nibble on her mouth.

Almost as badly as I want Nova to wave her PR wand and fix this nightmare of a scandal.

"Dejonae, forward that recording to me. I'll speak to the reporter and make sure she understands the ramifications of what happens if this recording gets out." Nova pulls out her phone and taps furiously. "Sazuki, you said you'd worked out a deal with the magazine, right?"

"Yes, Beverly is to post an article refuting all the gossip and writing a glowing review about the foundation and its instructors."

"That won't be enough. We need to change the narrative. Bury this under positive PR." Nova rubs her chin. Then her eyes latch onto me. "How do you feel about doing a performance?"

"I do not perform anymore," I say sternly.

"Not for an audience. That would take too much time and we need something fast." Nova waves the thought away. "Something low-key here at The Sazuki Foundation. We'll use your fame to get people to click on our post and then we'll ask the parents' permission to share videos of the students learning music. You would be the lure. The kids would be the hook. We need people to see why the foundation's mission is important to get them on our side again."

"I think it's a good idea," Dejonae says.

"If you think so, then I will do it." I nod.

"Just because I said so?"

"You have evidence against Miss Beverly that would clear your name. If you released that recording, everyone would know that you were not the villain in the scenario." I give her an understanding look. "But you are choosing to be quiet about it even if it is against your nature. You are making a sacrifice for the good of the foundation. If you can do so, I can do the same."

"Are you saying you learned something from me, Mr. Sazuki?" She nudges me in the shoulder. "Be careful. You might actually start to seem human."

"What did you think I was before? A beast?"

Her eyes crinkle. "No comment."

There it is again.

That spark of electricity. It dances in the silence between us.

Nova slides a suspicious glance at me. "Since you've already handled the magazine editor, I will handle the reporter. Look forward to a glowing review in the next magazine issue. Sazuki, I will need a recording of the performances by tomorrow so I can release it along with the article. We need to move fast so this doesn't get any more out of hand."

I rise when she does. "Nova."

"Yes?"

I glance down at Dejonae. "Do I have to play alone?"

She follows the line of my gaze. "No, I don't think you have to. In fact, playing along with an instructor might show just how... close of a bond you all have here at The Sazuki Foundation."

I start to walk her out.

"No need to see me out, Sazuki." She gives me a curt nod. "Look forward to my update."

"I will." I dip my head.

She leaves, stalking down the hallway like a woman on a mission.

Dejonae purses her lips as she stares in Nova's direction. "I like her. She's a boss lady."

"She, technically, works for Adam, but yes... she is quite boss-like."

Dejonae scrunches her nose. "Be careful, Sazuki. Your age is showing."

"You're quite confident, aren't you? Making jokes after causing such a stir." I reclaim the seat beside her because I am not yet ready to leave her presence.

"I'm starting to see the light at the end of the tunnel. Besides, you already rejected my resignation. I don't need to hold my breath anymore."

I chuckle, but it is broken up by a yawn.

She gives me an alarmed look. "You worked all night, didn't you?"

"I did."

"I'm sorry."

"If you're sorry, then don't move," I grumble.

"What?"

Without explanation, I lean down and rest my head on her shoulder. She makes an audible sound of surprise. Her shoulders are small and a little bony, but I get comfortable.

Dejonae holds herself completely still. I open my eyes to check that she's breathing.

She is.

Satisfied, I close my eyes again.

It feels good.

My heart settles. My anxiety calms.

I needed this.

Needed to be close to her.

This scandal unraveled what was left of my resistance. I do not wish to run from the truth any longer. No matter what anyone says about our age, our cultural differences or any obstacles that may come our way, I want to be the one protecting her and finding rest in her as well.

Sleep comes for me quickly, but I fight it as best as I can. "Dejonae?"

"Hm?"

"Do the performance with me," I mumble. My eyelids are heavy. Sleep is winning the fight.

"What? Why?"

"Because I do not want anyone else beside me," I mutter.

I do not hear her response. My exhaustion catches up with me and I fall fast asleep.

CHAPTER 13
IMPERFECT HARMONY

DEJONAE

DEEP BREATHS.

In. Out. In. Out. In—

Crap.

I cringe when I hear the tell-tale sound of fabric getting ripped apart. I guess sucking in my stomach won't get me back into this dress.

I exhale and the snapping sounds get louder. Releasing the zipper I was wrestling with, I drop my arms and sink my head against the bathroom door.

My nerves are in a tangle. They have been ever since yesterday in Sazuki's office.

I don't want anyone else beside me.

That confusing bastard.

After saying something like that, he fell against my shoulder and conked out. What did he mean by it? Was he serious? Was he teasing me?

"Stay calm, Dejonae," I murmur.

I *need* to get it together for tonight's recording. We've had no time to prepare our song and I'm freaking out.

He's the piano *legend*, Ryotaro Sazuki.

And I'm… a music student with three-quarters of a degree.

The last time Sazuki heard me play, his bodyguards surrounded me and he kicked me off the stage. It left a bad taste in my mouth.

And now the *world* is going to see me play the piano with him?

A knock on the door shatters my thoughts.

I ease it aside and see Yaya grinning at me. That smile fades quickly when she notices the fraying seams of my dress.

"You said you had a little black dress," she signs.

"I do." I jut my hands at the scrap of fabric.

"This dress is begging you to put it out of its misery," she gestures.

"Is it that bad?"

"When did you buy this? In middle school?"

"I'll have you know that I bought it for my high school graduation."

She rolls her eyes. Clamping her lips together, she signs, "Borrow one of my dresses."

"Your dresses aren't my style," I complain.

"Do you have a better option?" Yaya signs.

"Deej," dad yells from downstairs, "you've got a package!"

I sign, "Dad is calling."

Yaya shifts directions and follows me down the stairs.

As usual, we make a ton of noise as we race each other. Yaya wins by cheating and bouncing me out of the way. I shoot her a dirty look and approach my dad who's still standing at the door. He's studying the person outside intently.

Dad has never met a stranger and is known to trade jokes with the pizza guy—no matter how impatient the poor kid is to leave, so the fact that he's not saying anything is weird.

The moment dad steps aside, my eyes bug.

"Akira?"

Sazuki's bodyguard is standing on my parents' front porch with eyes that could kill. As usual, her hair is in a ponytail, her skin is pale, and her lips are blood red. The clash of red, white and black gives her a cold, ethereal aura.

"Do you know her?" dad asks me.

"She works with Mr. Sazuki."

A hesitant smile spreads over his face. "Hi, there. I'm Dejonae's dad."

Akira dips her head but doesn't speak to him. She hands a package over. "This is for you."

I accept the box. "How did you know I was at my parents' tonight?"

"Your sister posted on her social media." Akira glances past me to the living room where Yaya is watching everything with curious eyes.

Well… that's not creepy at all.

Akira turns to leave.

"Wait." I shove the box at my dad. It bounces against his stomach before he can get a good grip on it.

I step onto the porch and close the door. From the corner of my eye, I notice the curtain shifting. Dad and Yaya are probably spying on us.

I edge Akira over to the corner.

She bristles.

"Akira," I lick my lips, ignoring her obvious irritation, "I wanted to ask you something."

She taps her foot.

"Has Sazuki ever… played a duet with anyone before?"

"Yes."

My heart drops like a stone in the ocean. "Who?"

"Niko."

I glance up quickly. "Just Niko? No one else?"

"No." She looks at me with cold eyes. "Why is this important?"

"No reason." I turn toward the door, my mind churning.

Sazuki asking me to play piano means something. It has to.

My heart skips a beat.

"Miss Williams," Akira calls.

I stop rigidly.

"Mr. Sazuki is not like your peers. He is established in his own right and he bears the responsibility of the foundation as well as his familial duties."

"What are you trying to say?" I ask pointedly.

"Whether he chooses you or not," her eyes darken, "you will never be his priority. There will always be something or someone more important than you and this is a truth you will have to live with."

Annoyance flares in my heart, but I say nothing.

Akira stands tall. "If you cannot handle this, it might be better to find someone of your own age who can grow with you, who bears less responsibility and has no commitment besides making you happy and following you around. If you seek this in Ryotaro, you will be harshly disappointed."

"Mr. Sazuki and I are just a boss and employee."

Her eyes remain on mine. "We both know that your relationship has ceased to be so simple." Akira takes a step toward me. "Which is why I feel it is my duty, my highest obligation, to ask you to stop now. Before Niko is involved. Before Sazuki must face his family again. Before this," she gestures to me, "gets any further."

"Further than what?"

"Do not play coy, Miss Williams. If you close the door, he will not walk through it. He will respect your choice. So make the best choice for yourself and for him."

"I think you're crossing the line here, Akira. If Sazuki and I ever change our boss-employee relationship to something else, that will be between him and me. We don't need your intervention. Second, I may be young, but I'm stubborn and I don't run away from something because of the difficulties I might face. In fact, those difficulties excite me. Maybe that's why the thought of finding someone my age, someone who can 'follow me around' as you said, bores me to death. So thank you for clarifying that I really might be into older men."

Her bottom lip gets firm. "I have nothing more to say about that matter."

"Great. Neither do I."

She moves down the stairs and then turns back. "Sazuki will send a car to pick you up and take you to the foundation this evening."

"A car? Why? I can get there on my own."

Akira just gives me a wary look and stalks back to her SUV. I watch her, stunned by the visit and the conversation. *Why does she seem so concerned about me and Sazuki getting together? Did Sazuki say something to her that sent her into defense mode?*

The moment I step back inside the house, Yaya pounces on me. Excitement glitters in her eyes when she signs, "What was that about?"

"Nothing. We were just discussing work," I lie.

She narrows her eyes because she knows me better than anyone.

Dad gestures, "Are all your co-workers so scary?"

"No, just her." I pick up the box and take it to the living room.

The front door opens while I'm pulling out the tissue paper. Mom, who works as a teacher at the local middle school, enters. Dad pops up immediately and takes her bag from her.

"I'm sorry, my love." He gives her a kiss. "I didn't hear your car or I would have come out to help you."

"It's okay." Mom smiles brightly. "Hi, girls."

Yaya waves.

Mom sees the box and stops in the middle of the living room. "Who sent a present? Dejonae's birthday isn't until next year."

"She got a gift from her boss," Yaya signs. With a wicked grin, my sister picks up the card that came with the box. It says simply 'From Sazuki'.

"It's not a gift." I snatch the card from her. "Sazuki is a control freak. He probably doesn't want me looking shabby in the recording."

"I don't know." Dad scrubs his chin. "A man won't go around

buying clothes for just any woman. And he certainly wouldn't buy clothes for an employee." Dad stabs a dark hand in his chest. "Imagine me gifting something like this to the women in the office. Your mother would have me sleeping on the couch."

"No, I would have you out of the house immediately," she says with a wry grin. Sinking into the sofa beside him, mom signs, "Do you think your boss had no ulterior motives in sending this?"

"I... don't know."

"Do you want it to mean something?" Yaya signs.

I think about Akira's warning.

Having an age gap romance is one thing, but Akira was right. Sazuki has giant responsibilities on his shoulders—he's a father, a son, a businessman.

An ex-husband.

I broke up with Jordan because he cheated, but I'd known that he still had thoughts about his first love. Will Sazuki put me in the same position?

Dad peers closely at my face. "Dejonae?"

"It's almost time for the performance. I need to get ready." I pick up the box and make a mad dash for the stairs.

"But we haven't seen what he bought you," mom yells.

"I'll try it on and show you later." My feet thud as I race up the stairs and lock myself in the bathroom.

With thick breaths, I unwrap Sazuki's gift.

It's a dress.

A wave of butterflies crashes through my stomach.

What are you trying to say to me, Sazuki?

And what should I say in return?

"Oh. My. Goodness." Mom covers her mouth with one hand when I descend the stairs.

Dad's eyes bulge. "Dejonae."

Yaya lifts her chin proudly, her arm on my elbow as she escorts me down.

I already saw her open-mouthed and awestruck reaction to me in the dress. I wanted to show her and my parents together, but it couldn't be helped. Yaya's a magician with makeup and I needed her skills.

And boy... does my sister have skills.

After getting caught in her whirlwind of beautification, my eyebrows are primped, my lips painted, and my nose dusted with gold.

I almost topple when I get to the last step, but my sister's grip on me is firm and I end up regaining my balance. This is my first time wearing heels since high school. These heels are Yaya's, which means they're at least three-inches higher than anything I would buy.

But from the looks on my parents' faces, pairing the shoes with Sazuki's dress was the right move.

"You look magical," mom says, getting teary-eyed.

Dad grins. "Do a little spin."

I sign, "Are you crazy? I'll fall flat on my face."

Yaya snorts as I totter to the mirror.

Honestly, I do look hot.

The dress Sazuki picked out for me looks like a black gemstone that got turned into threads. The top has black sleeves that glitter like they've been handsewn with crystal.

An onyx skirt starts at my waist and ripples down to the floor, shimmering like a sea of stars. There's a part to the side that flashes my legs whenever I walk, adding a sense of sultriness to an otherwise modest gown.

This is not *just* a little black dress.

It is *the* little black dress.

Fragile as a rare flower.

Delicately woven.

Way more expensive than anything I've ever worn in my life.

"We need to take a picture," dad says, sounding choked up. He looks around for his phone.

I press my lips together in mortification. "Dad, I'm not going to junior prom."

"Hold still," Yaya signs. She comes up to me and adjust the teardrop necklace so it's sitting in the center of my collar bone. Next, she brushes a tendril of my hair away from my face.

My hairstyle is a half-up, half-down swoop with two curls at the front.

"Perfect," Yaya signs.

I squeeze her hand in gratitude.

Dad takes photos.

And then mom takes photos of me and dad.

And then Yaya jumps in.

By the time we're finished with our mini-family photoshoot, the car Sazuki sent is waiting outside.

"Go have fun," Mom says, looking at me as if she's my fairy godmother watching me get whisked to the ball.

"I swear, it's like you people forgot that I've already been to prom," I mumble.

"Stop grumbling and enjoy yourself," Yaya signs.

I wave goodbye to them and step into the night.

* * *

I GET an odd feeling when I see the bouquet of roses on the backseat. Thinking it's not for me, I don't touch it except to slide it across just in case the person it's really for arrives.

But they don't.

The driver takes me straight to the foundation.

My eyebrows crinkle when I notice someone is outside waiting for me. I recognize him as one of the suits in Sazuki's bodyguard ring. It's kind of hard not to pinpoint a face like his with its long scar. That and the buzz cut give him away.

Did Sazuki hire the bodyguards to keep the videographers in

check? It feels a little over the top. It's not like they're crazed fans who are going to mob him the moment he steps on stage.

The suit gestures for me to walk inside.

My heart trips over itself.

"Wait," I say, holding up a hand.

The giant keeps moving. After a step, he glances over and sees I'm not with him. His eyes get bigger and he hurries back to me.

"Are you okay?" he signs.

My eyes nearly pop out of my face. "Are you deaf?"

"Partially." He touches his right ear. "All of my hearing is gone in this ear."

A sudden thought hits me. "Are all of Sazuki's guards deaf?"

"That would be foolish." His sudden smile is charming. "No. I am only one of two. But he gave me a job when I had no other option."

Sazuki's been looking out for the deaf community all over the place.

My palms get sweaty. As fluttery and beautiful as I feel in this dress, I'm starting to realize what kind of man I've fallen for. He's powerful enough to give hope to someone who had lost it all and ruthless enough to hide that golden heart from the world.

Maybe I shouldn't go into that building.

Maybe I shouldn't be wearing this dress.

Maybe I shouldn't look forward to seeing the way those ice-brown eyes will react when he *sees* me in this dress.

The suit gestures for me to walk ahead of him.

I inhale a deep breath. Tonight isn't about me. It's about helping the foundation and fixing the mess I made because of my impulsiveness. Even if I crash and burn playing next to Sazuki tonight, it won't be because I gave less than my best.

I'm going to play my heart out.

No.

Matter.

What.

* * *

PRICKLY ROMANCE

I GASP when I enter the concert hall. There are giant lights set up on thin poles, their heads bent toward the stage. A semi-circle of unmanned cameras are all pointed at the grand piano.

But that's not what surprises me.

Rose petals are scattered around the piano, creating the illusion of a vibrant red sea.

My heart picks up speed when I see the lavish decorations.

Do not assume this is for you, Dejonae. Don't you dare embarrass yourself.

This is a production for The Sazuki Music Foundation. Nothing more.

"You're here," Sazuki says.

My heart explodes. I've never seen a man look more regal in a tux. His expression is quietly intense, lined in concentration, like an eagle about to swoop in on a mouse. His hair is brushed back to reveal more of his chiseled cheekbones and square jaw.

I can't breathe.

What is oxygen?

What is reality?

Am I dead or alive right now?

Sazuki's lips curl up. The way he gazes at me as I stumble closer sets my entire body on fire. He watches me steadily, eyes darkening with desire and unapologetic heat.

Sazuki meets me halfway to the stage. "You look beautiful," he says softly.

"T-thanks. Y-y-you too."

Since when did I stutter?

Sazuki holds out his hand. I take it nervously. His hands are so much bigger than mine. It feels like I'm being swallowed by his fingers.

Desperate to fill the electric silence between us, I ask, "Where are the camera operators?"

"They left."

My eyebrows arch. "Shouldn't they be *here*? You know, while we're recording?"

"Thankfully, our performance is stationary, so they do not need to be present to film." He lifts a remote. "The cameras will begin recording when I press this button."

"Oh." I don't know why Sazuki wanted privacy tonight. Is it because he didn't want to give a performance to even the cameramen? Or is there another reason?

He lifts my hand. "You are shaking."

"The last time I performed was at the Belle's Beauty gala."

His eyes go dim. "The night we met."

"It didn't exactly give me a thirst for performing again."

"I am sorry about what I said that night."

"Wow," I joke shakily. "An actual apology?"

"A sincere one." He steps closer to me. The scent of mint and something uniquely him fills my nose and makes me feel like I'm floating.

Crap. I have no idea how I'm going to get through a performance without melting out of my shoes.

"Come." He leads me to the piano.

I recognize it immediately. "It's the same one?"

"Your fingers belong on these keys." His eyes bore into me. It seems as if he's saying something much deeper.

I approach the piano and slide my finger over the top. It's glossy and smooth. "It looks a little different. Are you sure you didn't just put a fancy logo on a regular grand piano?"

I feel more than I see Sazuki approach me. Then one large hand settles on top of the piano. His chest presses in close to my back. His body is a giant wall, half-caging me against the lip of the instrument.

I'm afraid to look at him.

I know if I do, he'll see how much he affects me.

"No one can counterfeit a masterpiece," he murmurs in my ear.

I'm too aware of how close he is, his body against mine, almost touching me but not quite.

I force myself to step away. "Thank you for the dress."

His eyes make another heated sweep over me and I realize it

was a mistake to bring more attention to my body. If I get any hotter, I might have to start stripping and that won't end well.

"Did you see the flowers?"

"Those were for me?"

He narrows his eyes. "Who did you think they were for?"

"I thought we were going to pick someone else up. You know, like Uber Pool."

His dimples flash.

My throat tightens on impact.

"The roses were for you, Dejonae," he says with an unexpected tenderness.

"Oh."

"Oh?" His eyes sparkle like the stars.

I can't do this anymore. "How about we get started? I don't know how many takes we'll need before we figure out how to harmonize with each other."

"We will not need more than one take," he says confidently.

"You think you're that good?" I tilt my head back to look at him.

"I think whatever music we create together will be perfect."

Okay.

A grouchy, reserved Sazuki, I can handle.

A dimple-flashing Sazuki, I can barely survive.

But this?

He's going to lay me out on the floor before we play the first note.

I fight to maintain my composure. "You're teasing me."

"I am being honest."

"You're being strange. If this is your way of apologizing for the Belle's Beauty gala, there's no need. It happened a long time ago and I understand why you were upset." I try to sound stern. "There's nothing left to discuss, Mr. Sazuki."

"Ryotaro."

I freeze, hardly believing my ears.

"Call me Ryotaro," he instructs in a low, husky voice.

"Definitely not doing that," I mumble, hurrying around the piano.

I take my seat. When Sazuki sits beside me, he gives me a small, affectionate smile that stalls my brain. It takes me a second to remember where I am and what I'm doing.

"Uh... am I playing the melody?" I point to the sheet music.

"You can play the higher keys. I will play the bass."

My stomach clenches again. Why am I so nervous? Because of the event or because I'm sitting so close to him?

"Miss Williams." In his thick accent, my last name sounds like something different. Something special.

I look over at him.

"It will be okay."

"I'll take your word for it." My throat is too dry to swallow. "I'm ready."

He nods once and presses the button to start recording.

I play the opening notes of Faure's *Pavane*. It's a hauntingly beautiful melody, but I'm not focused on it. Sazuki is distracting me and I can't help peering at him from the corner of my eye.

Everything, from the tall, upright way he sits, to the tilt of his head, to the way his big hands spread over the piano keys, hints at strict classical training.

I try to sit straight too, but I don't have the same princely air and my hands are much smaller when they expand over the piano keys.

Focus, Dejonae. You have a job to do.

I settle down, letting my fingers tickle the top of the keys. We're sharing the same bench, his thigh pressing lightly into mine. I'm both keenly aware of him and comforted by his closeness.

The notes ring out in the concert hall, filling the air with something—not heavy but anticipatory. Like someone holding their breath as they wait for their lover to appear.

Sazuki plays the lower notes and a shiver runs down my spine at the way his melody answers mine. Rather than mirroring me, he's playing the harmony. His notes dance just below mine in an expert cadence.

The music swells, moving steadily toward the climax.

When I look over at him, I see sweat dotting his forehead. He's bent over the keys, giving himself passionately to the music.

Then he glances at me.

And the world stops.

My hand gets heavy, holding down the chord.

But Sazuki doesn't let that stop him.

He plays a melody around my sustained chord, filling the air with a light, tinkling energy.

I lift my hands and the chord ends. Throwing myself back into the song, I keep my eyes on him this time and marvel at his exquisite skill. Sazuki's hands create poetry out of thin air and vibrations.

The music isn't coming from the piano.

It's like it's *inside* him.

Every brush of his fingers, every stretch of his hand, is creating a story. A movie.

A confession.

It strikes me then.

Because I hear him.

I feel it.

In a way that only music can communicate.

His dimples pop out and he nods once, letting me know I'm right. Letting me know it isn't in my head.

I stare at him as I play. A part of me feels this moment isn't real. That I'm going to roll out of my bed at any moment and realize that it was all in my head. It was all a dream.

Sazuki plays the final chord and steps on the suspension pedal for a second, letting the last note ring out in the silence.

I raise my hand slightly off the piano. Sazuki says nothing. He only takes out the remote again and cuts off the recording.

As the silence settles, I lurch to my feet, stumbling in my heels.

"Dejonae," Sazuki says.

I turn around slowly.

He's standing at the piano under the spotlights, looking at me with eyes that belong in the sky next to a full moon.

"*Kimi no koto ga suki desu.*"

I close my eyes. It's my first time hearing him speak Japanese. It's the most beautiful thing I've ever heard.

"I tried to fight my feelings," Sazuki says, "but I have no desire to do so anymore."

My brain implodes when he walks right up against me. His fingers brush my chin. His eyes drop to my lips.

I can't breathe.

I can't think.

My heart is leaping, pounding, a powerful drum that refuses to stay quiet. It knows. A deep, primal part of me knows that this is a moment in my life that is about to change everything.

Because this is Sazuki.

Passionate.

Driven.

Larger than life.

I'm in the presence of a love that's just as overwhelming as the man who offers it.

My heart beats faster and faster. I've had guys send me notes in school. Or send a message with their friends. Or text me at random asking if I wanted to 'hang'.

But I've never had someone go out of their way to make me feel special.

Sazuki isn't like the boys I'm used to because he *isn't* a boy.

He's a man.

A man with the world on his shoulders.

I breathe hard. "What about Niko?"

"Niko favors you just as much as I do."

I tilt my neck back to stare into his eyes. It's a stark reminder of just how *tall* he is. My neck is going to break at this point.

"What about the foundation?"

"Nothing at the foundation will change because of us."

"Everyone will think I got out of that scandal because we're… because you…"

"Because we are now dating."

My legs shake and lightning zaps from my stomach all the way down to my toes. "Are we dating now?"

"Do you know how much I spent on those roses?"

I burst out laughing.

His dimples wink at me.

And then they quickly disappear when he closes the distance between us. In the blink of an eye, he tilts my head and kisses me.

The push of his mouth to mine turns my world inside out.

My blood implodes.

My heart stops.

I step back, my hand flailing in an effort to remain upright. Discordant notes claw through the air. It's coming from my fingers that somehow found the piano keys and played a frantic note.

Sazuki eases back and looks down at me, a question in his darkening eyes. Just beneath the heat and the intensifying hunger is genuine concern for me. For my comfort. For whatever I need.

"Don't stop," I whisper.

He folds me into his arms, holding me steady this time. The ground falls away. So does the roof. And the chairs. The cameras. The lights.

It's only me and him.

There's not a single inch of resistance in me when his lips press softly to mine again. I mold myself to his broad chest, inhaling his mouth, his scent, his regal charm.

It's soft enough to break me.

Then the kiss changes.

From sweetly exploring to charged thunder. It's more gladiatorial than when we clash in real life and yet so much sweeter too—lips tangling, warring.

I'm sure I'm going insane.

But I don't want it to stop.

His hold on me tightens, his gravity dragging me into him. A blackhole of pleasure.

I'm gone.

Deceased.

Tiny bits of flesh and desire and violent explosions.

My body flattens against the keyboard when he closes in, his arms sliding against the back of my neck as he tilts me for a better angle.

And then he goes deeper.

Fingers.

Tongue.

Fireworks.

Any hint of resistance is wrenched aside, leaving nothing but a need that's been building between us for so long. Throbbing. Pulsing. Demanding. Now that it has an outlet, it becomes an unrelenting wave. Devouring everything in its path. And wanting more.

So much more.

He's obscene.

And I lap it up, allow him to sweep his tongue across every corner of my mouth until he knows more about me than I do.

I dig my fingers into his shoulders, holding on for dear life as Ryotaro Sazuki batters me with his lips of pure honey and war.

There are so many reasons why we shouldn't be together, why our bodies shouldn't touch, why this shouldn't feel so right.

But in the moment, none of those reasons matter.

Because I've never had a chance to feel love like this.

And even if it might hurt like hell when it's over…

I want to put my fingers to this dangerous, forbidden piano and play until the song ends.

CHAPTER 14
GREEDY HEARTS

SAZUKI

"I can't believe you're just going to throw away that many roses..."

As she speaks, Dejonae slips her fingers into mine. The slide of her hand against my palm fills me with a heat that rivals the sun.

I never want to let go of this hand.

"How much did you pay for those?" she insists.

I open my mouth.

She turns her face away. "Stop. Don't tell me. It'll make my heart hurt."

I chuckle.

She chews on her bottom lip worriedly.

My eyes linger there.

That mouth—brown and full and ripe for the looting.

On the stage, I could not stop myself from tasting her. She was sweeter than I expected. Softer still. I do not know how many minutes passed while I kissed her. Time, as a concept, seemed distant. Like we had transformed to a plane outside of it.

It was only one of my men walking in on us that pried my

mouth away from hers. A necessary interruption. I was enjoying myself so much that I could have easily devoured her for hours.

A sudden silence in the car snaps me back to focus. I notice Dejonae smirking at me.

"Are you going to keep doing that? Zoning out on my lips when I talk to you?"

"Your mouth is distracting," I admit.

She smiles prettily. I find her lack of pretention appealing. Dejonae knows she is a beautiful woman and accepts all of my compliments with a mixture of grace and confidence.

I rub my thumb over her mouth. Her lips are slightly swollen, fuller from the way I'd bitten them.

"Does it hurt?"

"Nope. But you did rub all my gloss off." She grazes my lips with her thumb. "It's a good thing I don't normally wear lipstick or your lips would be brown by now."

"I do not have a problem with that."

"I do." She narrows her eyes. "I don't want to leave any clues for people at work to find out about us."

Heat spreads through my veins. "Are you saying you are open to being affectionate at work?" An image of Dejonae on my desk, her nails raking down my back as I quiet her with a kiss explodes in my mind.

"No, that's not happening either."

My eyebrows cinch together.

"People at the foundation can't find out about us."

"We are not doing anything wrong."

"You're my boss."

"Technically, you are interning."

Her expression turns scolding. "Same thing."

"That is not a good reason."

"You're older than me."

"We're both adults."

"We can't expect people to understand. They're going to think that you're… my sugar daddy."

"Me? A…" It is so ridiculous I cannot even bear to repeat it. "You and I both know this is not the case, so why should we care whether others understand or not? As long as we know the truth, this is all that matters."

"I'm not ready for the scrutiny yet. Telling people about us would make things awkward for me. And Sheila… ugh. Sheila would give me the stink eye of death." She shakes her head. "We don't need my co-workers in our business." I think of Taylor and add, "My classmates either. We can't let them find out."

"I do not have a problem with keeping our relationship quiet if it is what you truly wish. But I do have a problem if we are keeping it quiet in order to please others. There is no need for us to inconvenience ourselves to make them more comfortable."

She tilts her head. Her lips pucker. "This feels like a fight."

I think about it. "Is it?"

"It's a disagreement. So, technically, yes."

"Then let us fight."

"Wrong answer. From now on, you're supposed to let me win all the arguments."

"I do not think I can do this." I rub my chin and in a dry voice, I tease her, "Letting you win might be too much for me to handle."

"Sazuki."

"Ryotaro," I correct her.

"I told you I'm not saying that."

"Why not?"

"Because…"

"Because?"

"It's too intimate."

I bear down on her, drawn to her body with a strength I cannot resist.

My lips cover hers.

She wraps an arm around the back of my neck. Her lips grasp mine passionately, so impatient, so willing, so filled with dark need.

I could plunder her right here in the backseat.

She would not push my hand away if I slid it beneath her skirt. But I have decided to restrain myself.

I want her to know that I am not with her for her body or her youth. Dejonae seems to be influenced by other people's opinions, so I am determined to ease all her doubts. She is not a way to 'experiment' as Akira once insinuated.

She means more to me. There is a *rightness* to being with her. A sense of a missing piece slipping into place.

Her thick eyelashes remain closed even when I pull back. I swipe my tongue across my top lip, testing whether her mouth is, indeed, pure sugar.

"Oh Lord, if this is a dream, do *not* wake me up," she mumbles.

I smile.

Dejonae Williams is *anmitsu*.

Savory, satisfying, and addictive.

My hands cup her cheeks.

I have not allowed myself to want someone in so long.

Yet, I long for her.

Everything about her.

Everything that she is willing to give.

And even that which she would rather keep hidden.

She is my light in a dark, chaotic world.

"If it bothers you so much, I can have the rose petals boxed up and delivered to your apartment."

She scrunches her nose. "In a few days, those will be dead roses and then bugs will crawl in and eat them."

"Hm." I muse.

The glinting silver lights of the city splashes across her face. She looks up at me suspiciously. "What?"

"You are un-romantic."

She swats my arm.

I smirk down at her.

"I am *very* romantic, okay? But I'm also rational. You spent a fortune so that I could walk on roses. Which is nice. I'm not saying it wasn't. But it was excessive."

I bring her knuckles to my lips and kiss it. "If you wish, I will refrain from further 'excessive' displays."

"Aw, you're letting me win?"

"If…" I add sternly.

She sighs and eases back. "I knew there was a catch."

"If you agree to tell others that you are taken."

"Sazuki."

"Ryotaro."

She gives me a dark look.

"I am not asking you to tell them that *we* are dating," I gesture between us, "only that you are involved with someone."

The angry stare softens a smidge.

"I do not trust that men will leave you alone if you pretend to be single." My fingers clench. "Especially your ex."

She laughs and, if I was not so irritated by the thought of her previous lover, I would kiss her again. Her laughter is big and magnetic. There's warmth in it, the kind that invites a man to get comfortable.

"You didn't seem like the jealous type," she says with a grin.

"This is not jealousy. This is common sense. When a man sees a beautiful woman, he will pursue her. Even saying you have a boyfriend may not be enough of a deterrent. If anyone continues to bother you," my voice darkens, "I would like to be informed."

"So you can go and beat them up?" She sounds amused.

"It depends."

When her eyes meet mine, my heart quivers. I have stumbled into very dangerous territory. Miss Williams has the power to turn me in any direction she wishes and I would follow her willingly.

"If Jordan ever gets on my nerves again, I'll tell him that I have a boyfriend," she promises.

"The boys at your college as well."

She chuckles and settles back into my arms.

"Do we have an agreement?" I mumble.

"I'll think about it." She smiles when I glare at her. Her hand caresses my chest, soothing me as if I am a wild animal. "I'm not ashamed of you, if that's what you're afraid of by the way. I'm just being cautious. People have already seen you at my college. They'd put two and two together."

"Me showing up at your college and us dating is a big leap."

"You showed up and walked me all the way to class. It's not that big of a leap."

I squint at the passing city. "Touché."

"I wish I could say 'screw them' and focus on my own life, but I'm not that brave. You're the owner of the foundation and I'm lower than an actual employee. People like us don't get together." She sighs. "I want the foundation to do well, especially after this scandal with the reporter. If I cause *another* stir, it's not going to help us get where we need to go."

I rub her shoulder. "I see the wisdom in that."

For a moment, the car falls silent.

Dejonae clears her throat. "Can we… talk about your ex?"

Surprised, I look down at her.

Her voice is carefully poised. "Niko told me that she's a singer currently working on a cruise, but that's all I know."

"You can ask me anything."

"Are you serious?" She sits up.

"I am an open book."

"Your last name is Sazuki. You are the very definition of a closed book."

"My family chooses to live a quiet life, away from the cameras and the pressures of being a celebrity. This is a lifestyle choice, not a personality. We are private, not secretive."

"Can I really ask you anything?"

"There is nothing in my past that I regret nor is there anything in my past marriage that would hold me back from giving you what you deserve. You do not have to be afraid of asking."

She gives me her full attention. "How long were you married for?"

"Three years."

"Why did you get a divorce?"

"On paper? Irreconcilable differences."

"And in reality?"

"Ashanti came to Japan along with a singing troupe. Her goal was always to travel the world and perform. After we met and got pregnant, I asked her to marry me. She said yes, but it was not a yes to the life she wanted. Soon, our differences became spikes that we inflicted on each other." I pause and reflect on that time. "This was my fault. We did not know much about each other when we married."

"Were you really that different?"

"Our values, our way of life, it was all different. She thrived in going to new places and meeting new people. I do not like going out and I keep to myself. Meeting others is tiring. I could not be the kind of man she needed."

"And your family? How did they react to her?"

"Not… well."

"Did they treat her badly?"

"They did not acknowledge her at all."

"Because she was black?" Her entire body is tense.

I run my hand down her arm and she relaxes a bit. "This may have played a part in it, but any foreigner would have been met with dismissive treatment. My family views all foreigners in a negative light. Especially Western women."

"Why?"

I arch a brow. "Are you sure you want to know?"

"Of course I want to know. If I didn't, I wouldn't have asked," she says sassily.

My lips twitch. "The western world is known for its instability. 'Hook up' culture, weak families, multiple divorces, and single-parent homes. Family is very important to us. It affects everything, even our business."

"If family was so important, then they should have welcomed Niko's mother with open arms. She was your wife and the mother of your child. She deserved that respect at least."

Such passion.

I stare at her, soak her in, and wonder if I can survive loving a woman like her.

"What?"

"We are discussing my ex-wife."

"So?"

"So, had I not divorced Ashanti, we would not have met."

She purses her lips. "It's the principle that bothers me. People should be treated fairly and with respect."

I kiss her forehead tenderly. "You are right. My family chose to shut her out because of their ignorance. The elders made assumptions about Ashanti before she had ever been introduced to them. Because of the way we had gotten pregnant before marriage, they assumed she was overtly sexual and unreliable. Because she wanted to sing, they thought she was after the family's fortune and glory."

"So you just… let her face all that pushback on her own?" Dejonae's voice carries a hint of accusation.

"I distanced myself from my family and warned them that I would not see them if they continued to treat Ashanti this way."

"What happened?"

"They cut me out."

She gasps. "They kicked you out just because of that?"

"Without their support, I had to scramble to make my own money. That is when I forced myself to perform on stage."

Her eyes glint. "When you said you made that album for a friend…"

"I was desperate to make my marriage work, to prove my family wrong, to make a name for myself so that I could provide for them and keep my wife and child together. But seeing me go on tour while she was forced to stay at home alone was a prison for Ashanti. She did not know the language and had made few friends in Japan. It was not an ideal situation."

"You were doing what was best for them," Dejonae defends me.

I want to kiss her again, but I keep my hands to myself . "She was broken and I did not see. It was not her fault."

"But—"

"I did not give Ashanti what she needed. Reassurance, love, understanding. I believed that I was meeting her needs when, in reality, I was only pushing her away. When she asked for a divorce, the distance between us had already been growing for a while. I did not fight for her to stay."

"You loved her." It is a statement, not a question.

"I did. She gave Niko to me. I will never regret the way we met or the way we ended because it gave me my child."

"Do you still have feelings for her?"

I wrap my arms around Dejonae. "No."

"How do you know?"

"Because when I end something, it is truly over. I do not allow room for regrets."

Dejonae burrows in closer. "Did you ever date a black woman before her?"

"No. And I never seriously considered marriage to anyone before I met her either." I rub my chin. "Suddenly, she was pregnant and we became a couple. What mattered was the family we were going to create, not the color of her skin."

"Were you always so open-minded or…?"

"Perhaps because of my mother. She was the only one who would visit our home when the family turned their backs. I believe Ashanti managed to stay so long in Japan because of my mother's welcome."

As I confess it all to Dejonae, my heart feels strange. Heavy. What happened with Ashanti tore the both of us, but it left more damage on her. Now that I am starting again, I feel a sense of caution. I never want to inflict the same wounds on Dejonae.

I play with one of her curls. "My first marriage taught me that being a father and being a man are not the same as being a husband. I had to hurt someone to learn that lesson, but I am not the type to make the same mistake twice. Thankfully, Ashanti found someone who could be the man I couldn't be for her and they are happily traveling the world together."

"I'm glad for her. After everything she's been through, she deserves that."

I press a kiss to her temple and murmur, "And what do I deserve?"

"A beautiful college student." She laughs.

"That is more than I deserve." I encircle her waist and drive her as close to me as the seatbelt will allow. Tucking my lips to the side of her throat, I whisper, "Everything that happened in my life led me to you."

"You really are more romantic than you look."

I smile against her dark skin. "Only in private."

She pouts. "So no PDA for us? Darn it."

I laugh softly. "Is it my turn to ask about your past relationships?"

"That's on a need-to-know basis."

"Very unfair."

"Life isn't fair.

I kiss her ear and chuckle.

It does not matter who Dejonae was with before me. From now on, she will be by my side. Nothing and no one can change that.

The car slows.

Our driver glances back at us with blank eyes. "We are here."

I nod my thanks.

"I'll see you at work Monday," Dejonae says, reaching for the door.

"Monday?" The distaste in my voice is palpable. "Tomorrow is Saturday."

"I have to study. Thanks to *someone*, my weekdays are always hectic and I'm too exhausted to crack open a textbook when I go home."

"I can help you study."

"Yeah, slow down, buddy." She places a hand on my chest to

stop me from coming closer. "I'm smart enough to know how that ends."

"How?" I whisper.

She kisses me softly. "Like that."

"Mm. That is not so bad."

"For you, maybe. But for my grades…"

"Is it Howel? I can talk to him."

She rolls her eyes. "I want to graduate because of my own efforts. Not because my boyfriend threw his money and fame around."

My disappointment melts.

I glance down and train my lips not to smile.

Boyfriend.

I'm far too old to get excited at such a word and yet, with Dejonae, I feel like a teenager with his first crush.

"Fine. You can have Saturday," I allow. "Sunday is mine."

"Oh?" Her eyebrows hike. "You're not asking?"

"I will kidnap you away if I have to." I give her a look of challenge.

"I believe you." She laughs.

"Where would you like to go on our first date?"

"How about we stay home on Sunday?"

I frown. "I may not like to go out, but I will take you wherever you want to go."

"I'm not saying that because of your preferences. I'd really like to hang out with you and Niko. A day indoors, sharing a meal and spending time with you both sounds like the perfect day to me."

I am not a creature of impulse. Yet I cannot help unbuckling my seatbelt, lunging across the car and kissing her furiously.

I am greedy for her, obsessed with every flutter of her lips.

I do not even recognize myself anymore.

The porch light on her parents' house comes on.

Dejonae notices and pulls back from me. "I should go inside before they send a search party."

"Tell your parents I said goodnight."

She leaves the car laughing loudly. "I am *not* doing that."

I smile and watch her walk all the way inside before driving off.

* * *

As Dejonae requested, I leave her alone on Saturday, only exchanging a few texts back and forth.

On Sunday morning, I sit Niko down in the living room and inform her that we will be having a visitor.

"Who is it?" she signs sleepily.

"Dejonae."

Her eyes brighten. "Really?"

"There is something else I have to tell you." I hesitate. "Dejonae and I are dating now."

Eyes going wide, Niko launches over and hugs me. She signs, "What took you so long, daddy?"

I chuckle and run my hand down her hair.

Niko moves her hands excitedly. "When will she be here?"

I check my watch. "In about an hour."

Niko whirls around and hurries to her bedroom to get ready. While she is gone, I call Ashanti. I promised her that I would inform her if my relationship with Dejonae changed. Since that is now the case, I wish to honor my word.

However, her phone goes to voicemail. I send her a text.

Ashanti, I need to speak with you. Call me when you have the time.

Footsteps patter down the hallway. Niko runs into view, her arms burdened with natural hair oils, creams and gels. Smiling at her obvious excitement, I brush her hair, secure it in a ponytail and send her out to watch TV. After I finish getting dressed, I start the meal and then join her in the sofa.

Neither of us are paying the television any mind. We continuously look at the door like twin addicts.

At last, Dejonae knocks on the door, right on time. Niko glances up when she feels the shift in my energy. Together, we scramble to the door. My daughter wears her eagerness on her sleeve while I keep my expression plain.

Dejonae smiles at Niko first and my daughter makes a sound of glee. In a blink, she attacks Dejonae with a tight hug. The two embrace and then Dejonae glances up at me.

I smile in welcome.

She smiles back and the feeling of rightness settles over me again.

Niko signs, "We got you your own slippers." She hands over a pair of music-themed slides that came as a three-pair set. Niko has been trying and failing to get me to wear the ghastly things around the house. "Dad and I have one too."

"I got you something too," Dejonae says. She hands over a tin of cookies. "I hope you like them."

Niko squeezes the tin to herself, her eyes alight with pleasure.

"Chocolate chip cookies are her favorite," I explain.

"Lucky guess." Dejonae's eyes linger on me.

Niko grabs her hand and drags her off. Probably to show Dejonae her collection of mangas. Dejonae looks over her shoulder with a wry smile and a shrug. I watch her until they both disappear into Niko's room.

I do not mind my daughter stealing my girlfriend away, as long as I get to steal her back later tonight.

Heading to the kitchen, I check on the roast. It is almost ready. I stir the soup on the stove and then set it to simmer.

Giggles erupt from Niko's room.

Curious, I tiptoe up the stairs and peek in.

Dejonae has Niko sitting between her legs. Niko is flipping through the pages of a comic book, while Dejonae is spraying her hair with water and smoothing down the edges.

I lean against the door, enjoying the sight of them together.

Niko realizes I am there first. She always seems to sense when I am around.

Dejonae glances up.

Her eyebrows hike and she gestures to Niko's hair. "Niko asked me to put in a new style."

"It is beautiful," I sign. Dejonae created little twists at the front, secured them with neon pink rubber bands and then crisscrossed them in an intricate design. The back of Niko's hair is divided into two plaits that fall down her shoulders.

"The food smells great." Dejonae's lips arch. "I didn't know you could cook."

"I only know a few dishes. Do you cook?"

"Sometimes. I only know a few dishes too."

"Then together, we can double our knowledge."

Her eyes brighten and she laughs. "True."

I did not realize how much I missed her until I hear that musical laughter. It is sweeter to me than any note of the piano.

My eyes linger on her body as Dejonae rises to her full height and brushes off the curls that had shed from doing Niko's hair. She is wearing a long green dress. The fabric clings to her curves. The slit up the side offers a brief flash of her slender legs.

My self-restraint falters.

I do not think I will be able to keep my hands off her tonight.

"Should we take a picture?" Dejonae asks.

Niko nods.

My girls smush their cheeks together. Dejonae lifts her hand and takes the shot.

Niko gestures to me. I draw closer to the two of them. Slipping one arm around Niko's waist and another around Dejonae's, I pull them close.

"You're too tall," Dejonae says. "You take the shot." She hands the phone to me.

Niko moves closer to Dejonae so I can fit us all in the screen.

I capture the moment.

"Silly faces now!" Dejonae sticks out her tongue.

Niko bares her teeth.

I narrow my eyes.

Dejonae takes the phone and swipes through the photos. When

she gets to my silly shot, she glances up in censure. "Sazuki, what kind of silly face is that?"

"It's subtle."

Her lips part. "Are you kidding? You look like you were posing for a fashion campaign. You even *smized*. The point was to look silly."

"What is 'smize'?" Niko gestures.

"It's from *America's Next Top Model*. Tyra Banks." Dejonae makes a disgruntled sound when she sees our confusion. "You've never seen the show?"

"We do not watch much Western television," I fill in.

"Unacceptable. We're going to binge every season," she promises Niko.

My daughter smiles as if Dejonae just offered her the world.

I escort them downstairs for the meal. It is more lively than any meal we have ever had around the table. There is laughter, conversation and teasing. The way Dejonae communicates with Niko is confident. No hint of awkwardness. No hesitation.

In the past, when we ate meals with others, the conversation was often stilted. Even when all parties understood ASL, the delicate balance of eating, signing, and talking could not be achieved.

From the way Dejonae carries herself, I can immediately tell that her family dinners are full of life. Her excitement to get to know both me and Niko better—not only the deep parts of us, but the tiny ticks and quirks that make us unique—is genuine. She enjoys the conversation and does not seem tired by having to sign along with her words.

Her sensitivity and kindness move me almost as much as her beauty.

After the meal, we retreat to the living room. I want to sit close to Dejonae, but my daughter steals her away again to do puzzles. I watch from a distance, sipping on tea.

Dejonae glances at me with a heated look. "If all you're going to do is stare, you might as well come and help."

"You seem to have it well in hand," I say.

"Is he always like that?" she signs to Niko.

"Boring?" Niko gestures. "Yes."

Dejonae looks back at me and shakes her head, eyes narrowed.

I lean forward and slide one of her curls behind her ear. In a dark whisper, I defend myself, "I become a lot more exciting after bedtime."

She bites her lower lip.

My body instantly hardens in response, riveted by the sight of her full bottom lip surrendering to her teeth.

I smile wolfishly and steal a kiss when Niko is not watching.

Dejonae's eyes pop open and she pushes me away, her gaze darting pointedly to my daughter.

I tilt my head in response.

One taste of her is not enough. I need more.

But Niko looks at us and Dejonae withdraws from me.

"What a complicated puzzle," Dejonae says, her voice high-pitched and shaking. "I think I might have to stay all night to put this together."

I pull my lips in to choke back my laughter.

After a few minutes, I get up to prepare snacks for the hard-working ladies. Dejonae's competitive spirit has been awakened and she does not even notice when I leave.

But Niko's footsteps follow me into the kitchen.

"Do you need something?" I sign.

My daughter gives me a secret smile.

I know she is here to speak to me about Dejonae. Though I have spoken to Niko about our relationship, the fact that Dejonae is spending the day with us is evidence that she is someone important to me. It is our first time having a guest over.

"Do you want me to go to sleep early?" Niko signs.

"And spoil the fun Dejonae is having with that puzzle?" I touch the top of her head, careful not to spoil the fancy hairstyle.

Niko smiles to herself. And then the smile dims. "Have you told mom?"

"Not yet." I sign. "Later."

"I'm worried."

"There is nothing to worry about." I kneel in front of my daughter and hold her shoulders. "Even if we are not together, your mother and I have one thing in common." I touch her nose. "How much we love you."

She signs, "Fine. And try not to be so boring, dad. Next time, take Deej out on a proper date."

"Troublemaker." I tap her nose.

She blinks candidly and signs, "I'm going to get ready for bed." Her expression turns serious. "Don't mess this up."

My smile breaks free. I give my daughter a big hug.

"I love you so much," I say into her ear.

Although she can't hear me, Niko squeezes me back as if she understands.

We return to the living room, hand-in-hand. Dejonae is staring at the puzzle, her tongue sticking out slightly and her back bent over the puzzle box. When she glances up, it's with surprise.

"What's going on?" Dejonae asks, glancing between both our faces.

"Niko is going to bed now."

"Already?" She checks her watch. Then her eyebrows arch. "I didn't realize it was that late." Dejonae stands gracefully to her feet. Her skirt sways around her ankles and a little more of her dark leg flashes at me. "I'll help you take out those rubber bands."

Niko places a protective hand over her head.

Dejonae steps closer to my daughter. "Okay, you can keep it in. But you're going to have to secure your bonnet with bobby pins. If those twists get frizzy, it's not going to look as good." Her expression shifts and she looks up at me. "She *does* have a bonnet, right?"

"Of course. I am not an uncultured man."

Dejonae laughs softly. She takes my daughter's hand and looks up at me. "I'll help put Niko to bed and then join you. Is that okay?"

I dip my chin.

Dejonae walks away with my daughter. I start to follow them when my phone rings.

It's Akira.

My voice is a pleased rumble. "If you are calling to ask if I have seen the magazine article. I have."

The pre-print edition was forwarded to me yesterday. There was a small paragraph of clarification about the social media post, but the rest of the article was glowing praise for The Sazuki Foundation. Miss Beverly is, indeed, a good writer. I understand now why she has so many followers online.

"I am not calling about that," Akira says. "It is about your mother."

My smile freezes.

"She is coming tomorrow."

I inhale sharply but, when I speak, I keep my voice casual. "When will she be arriving at the airport? I will arrange to pick her up."

Rather than be dismayed, I will take the opportunity to bring Dejonae into our family. The meeting of the parents might as well happen now. I have no doubt in my mind that Dejonae is a part of my future. The sooner I can meet her parents and she can meet mine, the better.

"She is not arriving alone, Ryotaro."

"Is father coming to America with her?" I cannot hide my surprise. My father hates planes, traveling, and Western ideals with a passion."

"No. She will not be accompanied by uncle." Akira pauses. "She will be coming with your ex-wife."

CHAPTER 15
SECRETS IN THE LIBRARY

DEJONAE

"That's it? There was no sexy time after you put Niko to bed?"

I shake my head as I push the basket of baked potato chips over to Vanya. "None. It was so weird. He seemed kind of… I don't know… distant."

"What exactly did you *do* all night?" Yaya gestures. "You texted me that you got home after midnight."

"We watched a movie and then he called Akira to stay with Niko while he drove me to my apartment."

Vanya's eyebrows crash together. She looks gorgeous as usual in a thigh-baring red rumper. Big, chunky white sunglasses hold her hair away from her face.

We're sitting in an outdoor courtyard, a large red umbrella blocking out the sun. The gardens surrounding us are well-tended, flowers blooming in a colorful array.

"I thought we'd cuddle, kiss or *something* in the couch. But he was so distracted. It felt like he didn't realize I was there."

"Did you talk to him about it?" Yaya signs.

"No." I snort. That would be emotionally mature of me.

"What did you do then?" Yaya gestures.

"I refused to hold his hand in the car and didn't hug him back when he said goodnight."

Vanya gasps. "You threw a tantrum?"

"I wanted him to explain what was wrong, but he was quiet the entire way. It was like a switch went off. He didn't even notice that I was upset."

Vanya swirls her glass of orange juice around. Her nails are painted bright orange with diamonds in the center. "Do you think he felt awkward when it was just the two of you?"

My sister signs and I interpret out loud for Vanya, "You haven't seen them together yet, have you? Sazuki and Dejonae are many things, but awkward isn't one of them."

I push my straw around my drink as a contemplative silence fills the table. Yaya is leaving soon, which is why I reached out to Vanya today, hoping she'd be willing to meet. My sister almost fainted when Vanya came gliding out of her car to meet us. But now that we're talking about my relationship, the hero worship has faded.

Vanya leans forward. "What if you talked to Sazuki about how you felt? I'm sure there's an explanation."

"When did this become about me?" I gesture between them. "Yaya, you're supposed to be getting modeling tips from a celebrity."

"I'm not worthy," Yaya signs. "Plus your love life is juicier."

Vanya's eyes light up after I translate what my sister said.

"I don't mind talking about modeling, but she's not wrong. This is juicy stuff."

"I wish I had juicier details." I pout.

"Let's just stop for a moment and take this in. Ryotaro Sazuki, from the legendary Sazuki family, a man who doesn't talk to anyone or anything unless he has to, is letting you into his life. Even more than that, he's letting you into his daughter's life. The fact that such an extremely private man trusts you is a big deal. Maybe he was quiet because he enjoys being quiet with you."

I'm glad to see Vanya getting excited again. Her eyes are clearer too. It seems like Hadyn's plan worked. After our chai intervention a while back, Vanya's bouncing back to her old self.

I just wish my love life wasn't the topic at hand.

"He's been quiet with me before. I've been working for his foundation for a while now. I've seen him in all kinds of situations. I know how his angry quiet feels. I know how his thoughtful quiet feels. This was different. He was worried about something and rather than talk to me about it, he retreated."

"How has it been at work?" Yaya asks.

"He's been out all morning. We texted, but I haven't seen him since last night."

Vanya tilts her head. "You think he might be putting distance between you because of your age gap?"

Yaya taps her hands on the table and points to Vanya in agreement.

"If my age was a problem, he wouldn't have asked me to be with him in the first place."

"You're several years younger than him. Maybe he doesn't want to push you too hard. This is technically the beginning of your relationship. Plus you said he only married his first wife because she got pregnant and that didn't work out. It's possible he's going slow with you because he wants to protect you."

"Protect me from what?"

"I don't know. I'm not Sazuki."

"Or maybe he doesn't think you're mature enough," Yaya signs.

Her words hit me hard.

Is that it?

Sazuki has feelings for me. I'm sure of that. The way he watches me, like he wants nothing more than to kiss me until our clothes come off, isn't just in my head.

But being sexually attracted to someone and building a relationship with someone are two different things.

Sazuki doesn't trust me with his thoughts yet.

And maybe that's a trust I haven't earned, but it still hurts.

I wish I knew what was going on with him.

* * *

After lunch, I return to work.

Sheila is in the lobby like an emotional vulture circling around my bloody carcass. I sling her a dark look of warning when she approaches me, but she doesn't heed it.

Stopping right in front of me so there's no room to step aside, she frowns. "Nice article this morning."

"What are you talking about?"

"Beverly, the reporter you punched in the face?"

When the heck did I punch anyone in the face?

"She had nothing but good things to say about The Sazuki Foundation. She even made sure to clarify that the post she made was just a misunderstanding. I wonder how much they had to pay to shut her up."

"You don't know what you're talking about." I try to step past her.

Sheila follows me. "Obviously, Sazuki is trying to protect you. I wonder why."

"The video editing company asked for the parent release forms." I fold my arms over my chest and face her. "If you have nothing to do, you can photocopy the documents and send it over."

Her top lip curls up in a sneer. "Do it yourself." She stalks past me, making sure to knock into my shoulder as she goes. Her purple hair swishes back and forth like a My Little Pony tail. Should I just grab on and yank?

No more fighting, Deej. You barely got out of the last one with your job intact.

Gritting my teeth, I head upstairs to the admin team. They all stare at me like I'm a pariah. The PR crisis has been averted, but it will take a while for me to earn back their respect after Beverly's allegations. Everyone thinks I'm an impulsive, hot-headed idiot who nearly shut the foundation down.

"I'll, uh, I'll photocopy the forms myself," I say awkwardly when no one gets up to help me with the task.

My heart pinches, but I force myself not to look as defeated as I feel. Sazuki knows the truth about what happened in that bathroom.

I do too.

It doesn't matter what anyone else thinks of me.

After finishing with the photocopy machine, I scan the release forms for the PR company. Just after pressing 'send', I hear the elevator doors and the steady thud of footsteps.

My heart knows even before he turns the bend.

Sazuki.

The sight of him, in a simple white button down and pinstripe trousers, takes my breath away. He looks fit enough to be a medieval pirate. But instead of pillaging the sea for gold, he goes around stealing hearts.

I watch him as he draws closer.

His eyes are distant.

Although he's looking forward, he's not really seeing me or the office or anything else. I can tell that there's something weighing on his mind.

I drop my gaze to the computer when he notices me. Pulling up a file, I scroll through it and make a point not to look at him even though my heart is pumping fast.

Sazuki makes a beeline for my desk, his steps strong and sure. His scent wafts over me, making my heart waver.

His voice is a deep, secret thrum when he says, "Miss Williams."

"Mr. Sazuki," I return coldly.

"Can I see you in my office?"

I stop abruptly. Lips pursed, I look up. "Is this regarding work matters?"

An eyebrow hikes in surprise.

"If not then," I scowl at my watch, "I have to double-check the edited footage of the kids' performance this morning. Nova asked me to handle it personally and I can't let her down."

He steps back when I gather my binders and stalk away from the desk. I can feel his gaze burning into me.

My chest contracts on a sigh.

Was that the most mature way to handle things?

Probably not.

But what could I say? *Hey, boss. I thought we'd be getting hot and heavy in your couch while your daughter was sleeping last night. The fact that you didn't touch me and you seemed checked out made me feel some type of way. Can you tell me what's going on so I don't jump to every bad conclusion in the world?*

I'd sound like a crazy person.

Even worse, I'd sound like a *weak* person.

The last thing I want to appear as is naive and clingy. Akira already warned me that Sazuki will have other priorities besides me. Maybe this is how being low on the priority pole looks.

Besides, I really do have a lot of work today. Beverly published a glowing article, but we still have to make sure there are no lasting negative effects on the foundation. This is my responsibility.

Sazuki is in a video conference when I return to my desk. A part of me is relieved. I feared he would corner me when I left to go to school. I don't think I could have resisted if he offered to drive me to campus.

In the bus, I feel my phone buzz.

Sazuki: Did you leave? I wanted to take you to school.

I ignore the text.

Whether he's blocking me out because he thinks I'm immature or because he wants to protect me, I don't care anymore. I'm determined to get over myself. There will be way bigger obstacles in our path later. Something as small as him being distracted during a date shouldn't be a big deal, right?

This time, at least, I'm going to trust him.

Sazuki: When is your first class?

I stare at my phone and then I type back.

Dejonae: I'll be finished soon. We can talk after.

I focus on the lecturer droning on about science. Why a music student needs to take a science class is beyond me, but I'm here to fulfil my credit requirements.

Movement at the end of the row catches my eye. I glance to the side and drop my pencil when I see Sazuki walking confidently toward me. He falls smoothly into the chair beside mine. His shoulders are so broad, they're crowding me.

The temptation to turn to him and start firing questions is great, but I pull my hands into my lap and stare straight ahead.

This lecturer doesn't care about late or absent students, but he doesn't tolerate anyone disrupting his class. And he isn't afraid to call students out either.

"What are you doing here?" I whisper.

"You were ignoring me."

"No, I wasn't." *I totally was.*

"Since you were determined to ignore me," he gestures to himself, "I am here. Determined to follow you until your anger is sated."

My lips twitch.

Keep it professional, Deej.

"Following me around? Isn't that stalking?"

"I don't have time to stalk anyone."

"Then why are you here? In my class? Next to me?"

"Because you are not just anyone." His eyes capture mine. "You are my girlfriend."

My lips stretch with a smile, but I squelch it quickly before he thinks it's that easy to console me. "I told you I didn't want people at school to find out about us."

"They will not. I was discreet on my way here." His eyes remain on me. "I am also aware that you do not share this class with any of your fellow music majors who are more likely to know and understand who I am."

I narrow my eyes playfully. "Fine. I'll allow it. *Today.*"

He smiles.

Straightening my shoulders, I try to focus on the lecture, but it's practically impossible. Sazuki is rubbing his thumb over the back of my knuckles. Our legs are pressing against each other, from thigh to ankles.

He's a grumpy, pushy, mysterious jerkhead sometimes, but he's here. And he's unbelievably gorgeous. And I'm so tired of giving him the cold shoulder.

My eyes dart to the clock.

The lecturer is still talking.

When will this class end?

I try to shove my thoughts back in order and away from the hunk next to me, but I fail. By the time the class is over, I have no idea what the lesson was about.

"Come on." I tug on Sazuki's arm.

He points behind him when I take him to the back exit. "Why are we not going that way?"

"You didn't bring your bodyguards this time, right?" I arch a brow.

"They are more like a public appearance protection team."

"Either way, I can't protect you if we get mobbed. Better to avoid the main path than take any chances."

His long legs eat up the steps as we run away. "In such a situation, I would be the one protecting you."

"Is now really the time to argue with me?" I lead him into the hall and look both ways.

He stops me by tugging on my hand. "Why were you upset with me this morning?"

"I..."

A group of students turn the corner and walk past us. They give us funny stares. Dressed up in his white shirt and trousers, Sazuki looks like a lecturer or a special guest. In contrast, I'm wearing jeans, a T-shirt and sneakers. Not only do I look younger than him, but I look a lot less put-together.

They're probably thinking the worst.

I drop my hand and step back.

Sazuki frowns at me and takes my hand again.

I hiss, "Sazuki."

He links our fingers and holds on tight so I can't get away no matter how hard I tug.

"You were about to say something," he insists.

I duck my head. "Not here."

"Where then?"

My gaze strays to the students who are beginning to flood the hallway. "The library. Let's go to the library."

We dash into the building, taking the less crowded path. The librarians all stare in fascination when Sazuki walks in. It's usually quiet in the library, but it gets so silent I could hear a pin drop.

I dig my fingers into Sazuki's arm when we walk down the aisle of bookshelves. All the girls we stalk past are starting to take notice of him, their heads popping out of books and their greedy eyes lingering.

I struggle to push my possessiveness away. The pit of fury in my stomach is something I'll have to get used to if I plan to stay with a man as arresting as Sazuki.

But it's not a lesson I have to learn today.

I drag him into the reference section. The smell of dusty books fills the air. Sunshine pours through a few small windows near the roof.

"Okay." I drop his hand. "We can talk here."

He glances around. "Is this a secret room?"

"It might as well be. Most people don't use the library for reference anymore. All the information we need is readily available on the internet." I gesture to the small booth at the back of the room. "When I wanted to catch up on a nap after class, I usually came here. No one disturbed me."

"You must have worked very hard to get where you are now." He turns, showing off his strong profile. I thirstily absorb the angle of his jaw to the slope of his throat and the pale skin disappearing beneath the collar of his shirt.

My voice is raw with a hunger that has nothing to do with food. "I did what I had to do. As everyone does."

He shakes his head. "You choose the strangest things to be humble about."

I stare frankly back at him.

The air carries a hint of *something*.

Something electric.

Something powerful.

Something overwhelming.

I want more of that feeling. I want it on my skin. Deeper than that. In my heart, firing up my veins like a cord snapping into a power grid.

Oh no.

I'm becoming obsessed and it hasn't been that long since we started dating. How much more of myself am I going to lose to him? How much of myself am I going to discover?

Why does that both scare and invigorate me?

I feel him move closer. It's like a hot, stretching thread that tightens and tightens as the distance between us disappears. One second, I'm standing by the table with my backpack on. The next, his arms close around me and snatch me against his body.

Anticipation bubbles in me with a violent force, but I can't help teasing him. "Is this how mature adults solve their arguments, Mr. Sazuki? I only brought you here to talk."

He whirls me around and pins me against the bookshelf. The smell of stories, weathered pages, and sunshine tangles with the scent of leaking desire.

His touch on my back presses harder. "If you only wished to talk, you should not have looked at me like that."

I feel the smoke coming off my body.

I'm in flames. Singed.

But it doesn't matter. Not when his mouth caresses mine and the last remnants of my anger and dejection fade away.

The kiss is firm and demanding. It's like he's digging deep inside me, reaching for the parts of me that I haven't given to anyone else, and branding them with his name.

My heart squeezes and squeezes until it threatens to *pop*.

Mercy.

I scrape my fingers over his shoulder and across his back, fighting for purchase. Fighting to stay upright against the onslaught of hot pleasure. But it keeps battering me. Wave after wave. Like a volcano that's already erupted, lava rushing down the mountain and devouring everything in its path.

Uncontainable.

Insatiable.

I grab for his hair, my fingers tingling, my knees buckling, my body disintegrating into hot ash as he spears me with his lips and tongue.

Something rattles behind me.

The bookshelf.

A book hurtles toward my head.

I gasp and duck, but Sazuki moves fast. He slips the book back into place, pressing me deeper into the bookshelf until I can feel every part of him like an imprint on my body. His hand leaves the book and traces down my shoulder, deliciously rough, the tip of his fingers hardened by years of playing the piano.

I'm being hypnotized.

He leans down again, back to being gentle, and grazes his mouth across my lips. A low whimper escapes my throat and he growls in response, the sound rattling every bone in my mouth.

The savory kiss ends abruptly when he pulls back.

His chest brushes against mine.

I can feel the skitter of his heartbeat.

Hard against soft.

A flower trapped against a beast.

I whisper his name, begging for more. For relief. For everything that I dare not speak aloud.

"Please," I whisper.

I would be ashamed if I wasn't so needy for him. For his taste. For his body.

I arch against him. "I'll be quiet."

He looks down at me with a tortured expression.

Then he steps back.

The loss of his body against mine leaves me feeling bereft and cold. I wilt against the bookshelf, my fingers catching on the spines of old books. Why is he stopping?

I know he doesn't want to.

I can see it.

So hard, so ready. When we were kissing, I could practically feel him charging at me through my clothes.

He curses in Japanese. I don't know what he said. I don't understand the language, but I understand the tension of his shoulders, the hardness of his jaw, and the glint of frustration in his brown eyes.

"What's wrong?"

"Nothing." He walks over to me again, kissing me with a hint of impatience. He traces a line of hungry-rough kisses down my jaw and throat. There is no hint of the regal Japanese emperor now. He's shed his cloak of elegance, revealing the fairy tale beast underneath.

There's something absolutely feral about the way he touches me. His hands slide under my T-shirt, but it's messy this time. Like his mind isn't fully here and he's trying hard to escape into me. Trying hard to keep me with him.

The wild flutter of my pulse nearly sends me into cardiac arrest. I want to keep going, but the energy is off. I grip the back of his neck. Rising on my tiptoes, I press my lips to his in a sealing kiss.

He closes his eyes, his sharp nose brushing against mine.

My heart roaring, I ease back.

He looks down at me with eyes that smolder like twin storms in an endless universe. I brush my hand over his cheeks and sculpted jawline. My heart knows something isn't right and I lean into it rather than shy away.

"Did something happen?" I search his eyes. Watch the way they cloud over defensively before he sighs and the walls go down.

Sazuki takes my hand and leads me away from the bookshelves. He sits in the booth and pulls me into his lap. I wrap my arms around his neck, watching him intently. Holding my breath. Waiting.

The fan above spins in a steady circle, pushing breeze into the hot pocket of the library. My leg dangles over his, the toe of my sneakers barely scraping the wooden floor.

Sazuki's throat bobs. A line etches between his thick eyebrows. Beneath the surface, desire cools and is replaced with a foreboding feeling. A boot is dangling above my head and any minute now, it'll descend, crushing me like a cockroach.

I slide my fingers over the back of his neck as he sighs. "Sazuki."

"I wrestled with whether I should tell you this or not." His eyes meet mine. I'm shocked to see the turmoil. Maybe it's because we're close now or maybe he's letting me see the real him, but I never expected that he would wear his emotions so close to the surface.

His fingers grasp mine intently. "I do not want you to misunderstand or feel anxiety in any way."

"You're making me anxious right now," I warn him. "Spit it out."

He glances aside. "Yesterday, while you were putting Niko to bed, I received a call from Akira. She informed me that my mother and Ashanti were coming to visit."

Twin bombs.

Boom.

Boom.

I almost totter off his lap. Sazuki gathers me close, his eyes boring into mine. "Dejonae."

"When are they coming?"

His Adam's apple bobs. "They are here."

My soul cracks in half. "Why didn't you tell me the moment you found out?"

"I did not want to upset you."

The cool, crisp feel of his hand on my back turns to ice in an instant. I feel the blood drain from my face and wonder if I can handle this.

I knew there would be challenges. Before I started this, I knew he had an ex-wife. Not just that. He has a good relationship with her. For Niko's sake, I respected that. Applauded it even.

But Ashanti hasn't been around lately, and it was easier to pretend she didn't exist. Even if I knew she was a part of Sazuki's family and always would be, she was nothing but a phantom. Haunting just the edges of my reality, but never floating close enough to do any real damage.

Now she's here.

I didn't expect to have to face her so soon.

Sazuki and I have been dating for such a short time. We're not ready for a big obstacle.

I'm not ready.

"Dejonae." Sazuki takes my wrists and draws my attention back to him. "I went to the airport this morning. I met with them." He clears his throat. "My mother insisted on having Ashanti stay at the house."

This time, it's not an explosion that rocks my heart.

It's a sharp and poisonous arrow.

He and his ex-wife are staying under the same roof?

Walking past each other's bedrooms.

Putting Niko to sleep together.

Making dinner together.

Playing games together.

I start imagining a beautiful black woman leaving the bathroom in the morning, foggy smoke curling around her. A towel slung low over her body, exposing most of her chest and legs. I see her casting sultry eyes at Sazuki, the very eyes he fell in love with in Japan so many years ago.

My nostrils flare.

I push at him, trying to jump out of his lap.

He holds me. "Let me finish."

"No, you've said enough." I fight with him, my heart pumping. The weight of what I've agreed to, the man I've decided to open my heart to, is starting to sink in.

If it was just a matter of Sazuki being older than me, I could survive it. Age does not determine a good man. Some teenagers are mature enough to take care of a family. And some old men still have the emotional maturity of a fetus.

I can even live with us coming from two different cultures. My parents are open and accepting. And Sazuki mentioned his mom was more open-minded than anyone in his family.

I'll learn from him.

He can learn from me.

We can work through what those differences mean and how they affect our lives together.

I can accept almost anything.

But having his first love parading around in front of him…

I think of Jordan and the pain I felt when I saw those messages in his phone. If he had cheated on me with a random woman he'd met in a bar, it might have hurt less.

But he didn't.

He was still emotionally entangled with his first love. There was a pocket of his heart that belonged to her even though he claimed to love me and, when she sauntered back into his line of sight, he realized that he didn't love me enough to turn her away.

"Dejonae, look at me."

My stomach heaves.

"I can't," I croak.

Sazuki settles his fingers on my chin. "I told my mother that she could have the house, but Ashanti would stay in the guesthouse at the back of the property."

His hand flattens on my back with a possessive heat, drawing me closer to his chest, to the warmth of his body.

I breathe hard, struggling to believe him and the effort he's making when my last experience taught me that I shouldn't ever believe a man who'd been reunited with an old lover.

He tilts my head down and presses a desperate kiss on my forehead. The softness of his lips belies the firmness of his hand. Then he kisses my nose with the same intense focus, as if each kiss is a stamp of his initials. Finally, slowly, he kisses my mouth.

I kiss him back, even if my heart is still aching.

Sazuki scrubs a thumb over my cheek. "My heart is with you." His voice is dark and grave. His eyes are heated. "You do not have anything to fear."

I want to believe him. With all my heart and soul, I do.

But men staying away from their exes?

That hasn't been my experience.

CHAPTER 16
THE SURPRISE GETAWAY

SAZUKI

THE LIFE I left behind is so far removed from the life I lead here in America that it is shocking to see my mother flitting around my kitchen preparing breakfast.

Sunshine pours through the windows, lighting up the canned pickles and *natto*—fermented soybean paste—that she brought along with her.

My mother hears my footsteps and whirls around. Her eyes are bright despite the early hour. She wears her hair short and fluffy and favors using makeup, even if she plans to spend the day at home.

Today, her eyebrows are painted on perfectly and her lips are a purple-red color. Faint wrinkles curve like happy smiles beneath her eyes and bracket her mouth.

She is not the type to fuss too much about sunscreen or wearing hats. My mother believes in aging organically. She visited a clinic only once—and it was to receive double eyelid surgery when she was sixteen.

I cover my mouth to hide a yawn and croak out a 'good morning' in Japanese.

My mother stops short. Her eyes narrow on me. "Why do you speak so formally?"

"Why did you bring half of sobo's cupboard?" I gesture to the cans that are taking over my kitchen. "Did you have room to fit clothes into your suitcase?"

"You are trying to change the subject." She hefts the pot spoon that had been stirring the miso soup at me. Drops of the soup plop at her feet, but she does not seem to notice. "You leave for America and suddenly, you forget we are family?"

"I have not forgotten."

My mother whirls around, her colorful blouse fluttering behind her. She lowers the flame and uses chop sticks to flip the fish over. The smell of frying fish skin makes my stomach gurgle.

"Tell Niko to join us. I have already invited Ashanti as well."

I stop and study her stern face. Not even the lines of age and exhaustion have softened her. "Mother, what are you thinking?"

"Me? I am thinking that Niko must eat a hearty breakfast to do well in school." She sets the fish on a plate. "These American cereals. So full of sugar. They are not good for her."

"Why did you bring Ashanti with you?"

"I told you. We met by accident," she says, stepping past me and moving the plate to the table.

"Why is your story so hard to believe?"

Her eyes sharpen. "Are you calling me a liar?"

"Of course not." I trail her back to the stove where she slips on gloves and pulls the miso soup from the open flame. "Let me." I reach for the soup, but she hurls it away. "If you want to be of help, serve the rice."

I take out three bowls.

Then I hesitate.

Slowly, I take out a fourth bowl for Ashanti.

My mother gives me an approving nod when I return with four bowls. "Sazuki blood runs through Niko's veins. Because of this, Niko's mother will forever be joined to our family, whether we want to acknowledge it or not. It would be extremely improper of me to ignore her."

"The rest of the family had no problem doing so."

Her mouth tightens. "They have their reasons."

"The elders barely wish to acknowledge Niko because of her half-American blood. They have not once called or asked about her welfare. She does not even remember her life in Japan."

"She was too young."

"And that is a mercy."

"Are you upset that I am here?" My mother finds my eyes. "Do you think I believe the same as the elders?"

"I do not know what you are planning."

"Perhaps I simply miss my son." She glances around. "Now where do you keep your chopsticks?"

"Mother." I take her hand to stop her from flitting. This is important. I need her full attention.

My mother shakes me off. She wipes her hands on the apron and arches a brow at me. "Ryotaro, we do not have time."

"I am dating someone," I say.

The words rattle in the air, floating around as if they cannot find a home.

My mother is a strong, formidable woman. She does not curb her words nor does she hide her thoughts. So it is unsettling to see her hesitate, her eyes shifting, her body language full of discomfort.

Frowning, I lean forward and say, "Her name is Dejonae and she is important to me. Niko has already met her. The two of them are close."

"You do not need to tell me this." She shakes her head. "I am not foolish enough to believe you have remained single since moving to America. There is much temptation here in the West." She shakes me off and steps lightly to the counter, fiddling around with the pickles. "Did I bring enough side dishes?" she murmurs to herself.

"Mother—"

Niko flies into the kitchen and heads straight for her grandmother. The two collide in a joyous hug.

My mother's delight is all over her face. She brought two giant suitcases from Japan—one was filled with seasonings, fermented soybean paste and pickles. The other was filled with expensive gifts and toys for Niko. Although they do not talk often, my mother dotes on her. She learned a bit of ASL and speaks exclusively in English so that Niko can understand her.

"How did you sleep, my princess?" she coos, tilting Niko's dark face with her wrinkled hands. "Look at you. Did you grow overnight?"

Niko shakes her head.

I pat my daughter on the shoulder. When she turns to look at me, I sign, "Wash your hands and then we'll eat."

She nods her understanding and darts away.

There's a knock on the back door.

My mother gasps. "Ryotaro, did you lock the door?"

"Of course I locked the door," I murmur. "I lock every door before I go to sleep."

"Why should you lock the back one? Now Ashanti has to knock like a stranger." My mother swats my shoulder. "Go and let her in. Go."

"Mother—"

My mother flings her chin in Ashanti's direction.

I sigh heavily. Mother's story about meeting Ashanti coincidentally in the airport is too convenient. Either way, it does not matter. I refuse to allow their machinations to bear fruit.

That is not only for my sake.

But for the company's.

Yesterday, when Dejonae was angry with me, I could not focus on my meetings. Emails went unanswered. Phone calls went to voicemail. All I could see was her cold expression when she refused to join me in my office.

Dejonae has become a distraction to me.

If she is pleased, I am pleased.

If she is angry, it is all I think about.

To keep the foundation from sure ruin, Dejonae's happiness must be preserved.

I walk to the door and admit Ashanti. She offers a brilliant smile and a 'hey', before lurching forward and hugging me. Her body presses against mine. The scent of her perfume drags me back to the past.

For a moment, I feel as though I am in Japan, returning home after a concert.

Then I blink.

I remember that we are divorced.

Remember the pain in her eyes when she walked away.

And remember Dejonae.

I wrestled with telling Dejonae about Ashanti's arrival yesterday. In the end, she was too in-tuned to my emotions and sniffed out that I was hiding something from her. The look she gave me when I told her Ashanti was back in our lives is one I will never forget. Her eyes had widened with horror, fear, and dismay.

Though I did my best to assure her, words are far too fragile.

I refuse to give Dejonae a reason to mistrust me.

Prying Ashanti's hands from around my neck, I slant her a dark look. "Ashanti, we are no longer together. Kindly refrain yourself in the future."

"Sorry." She glances down. "I got excited for a minute. It's been a long time since I've come home to you."

My eyebrows cinch. Why is she talking in this manner? Isn't she married to someone else?

I step back. "Wait here. I will bring a pair of indoor slippers for you."

"No need." She smiles and dangles a pair off the tip of her fingers.

I nod and together we walk into the kitchen.

Niko grins when she sees us. She waves to her mother. Ashanti gives her a kiss on the head. Her hair is straight and long today. It flows over her shoulder, hiding her face from view as she rocks Niko back and forth.

"Come. Come." Mother interrupts them. "The food is getting cold."

I move to the chair beside Niko.

My mother hurries to claim it. "You sit over there." She points to the chair beside Ashanti. Before I can protest, she falls into the seat as if we are embroiled in a heated game of 'musical chairs'.

I straighten and give the chair a surveying look.

"Go on, Ryotaro." My mother pushes my arm.

Niko studies me, her intelligent eyes taking in everything. I do not wish to give her a reason to worry, so I bury my misgivings and sit beside Ashanti.

"*Itadakimasu.*" Ashanti presses her hands together. Niko bows her head too.

My mother dips her chin, smiles and repeats the phrase.

I mumble it out, which earns me a dark look from my mother and an amused one from Ashanti.

As we eat, my mother spears pieces of the fish and places them on top of Niko's bowl of rice. My daughter gobbles it all.

"Here, Ryo." Ashanti expertly pins a vegetable between her chopsticks and places it on my bowl of rice. She leans over me. Her dress is low cut and reveals a hint of cleavage.

My eyes dart there before I force them up to her face. I am relieved that the only thing rising in me is confusion.

Ashanti and I have eaten meals together with her husband and Niko present. At those times, she did not serve me, nor did she wear such revealing clothing.

Expression stern, I remove the vegetable from my rice and place it in Niko's. A twitch of disappointment flickers over Ashanti's face, but she hides it well.

"Beth wants me to go to the farmhouse today," Niko signs.

"What did she say?" Mother asks.

"Her friends invited her out today." I tilt my head and think about it. "You have a test on Friday."

"We will study together," she signs.

Ashanti gets Niko's attention. "Sweetheart, you need to focus on eating."

Niko loses the twinkle in her eye.

I glance sharply at Ashanti, despite knowing it is slightly unfair to blame her. Breakfast is always a silent affair. And we have both scolded Niko in the past for signing instead of eating.

However, since our dinner with Dejonae showed us how lively and 'loud' a meal could be, I understand why Niko would want to engage in discussion this morning. I resent the fact that she was shut down.

Seeing that my daughter is dejected, I give my consent. "You can go to the farmhouse if Akira accompanies you."

Niko brightens again like a dying balloon receiving hydrogen.

Ashanti turns to me. "What 'farmhouse' is she talking about?"

"Her friends from school are the children of several wealthy and influential couples in the city. The adults often gather together, allowing the children to meet outside of a school setting."

"Interesting. Are these children deaf too?"

"They are hearing."

Ashanti's eyebrows drop low. "So how do they get along?"

"They make an effort," I say simply.

The conversation becomes stilted. Perhaps it is my tone, my thunderous expression, or my lack of interest that convinces Ashanti to let it go.

After Niko excuses herself from the table, my mother leaves as well. I get up to take a shower when I feel Ashanti's hand on my arm.

I stop and look down at her.

She is staring at the floor. Her fingers curl around my wrist urgently. "Ryotaro, can we talk?"

I wait—silently—for her to continue.

"Why are you treating me so coldly?" Three wrinkles appear above her eyebrows. "When we divorced, we agreed that we would be friends. We agreed never to be like the other divorced couples who are constantly fighting and talking badly about each other."

"I am not fighting with you, Ashanti. I simply do not understand why you are here."

Her eyes dart away. "I missed Niko."

"And what of your husband? Did he agree to let you quit your job on the cruise ship midway?"

She rises to her feet. Her dress sways around her ankles. "Why didn't you tell me you were dating someone?"

I am not surprised that she knows. Perhaps Akira informed both her and my mother.

I take a slow, calming breath before I speak to her. "I tried to. You did not answer your phone."

"Are you serious about her?" Ashanti's voice is quiet. Prying. She pulls her bottom lip into her mouth and chews.

"I am."

She makes a strange sound in her throat, a mixture of surprise and disappointment. "You are not usually so transparent."

"We agreed to let each other know," I say. And also, I want to make it clear to both her and my mother about Dejonae's place in my life. "I have intentions of marriage."

Ashanti's eyebrows flutter. "Marriage. Wow."

I check my watch. "If I have sufficiently answered your question, then—"

"I want to meet her."

Warily, I glance behind me and study Ashanti's face. She tilts her chin up. Her eyes survey mine with a desperate calculation.

This is a trap.

A dirty trick.

A thorny path.

I grind my teeth together. "Why?"

"Why do I want to meet your girlfriend?" Ashanti walks toward me. "Isn't it obvious? She's going to be a part of my daughter's life. If she's involved with Niko, then I deserve to know who she is."

I face her cautiously. Fighting Ashanti on this will only allow her to become more stubborn and more creative in her schemes. Better to introduce Dejonae on my terms, rather than have my mother and my ex-wife spring themselves on her.

"Alright," I say slowly. "I will speak to her. And if she is interested, I will bring her to the house."

"Perfect." Her lips curl up in a victorious smirk. "I look forward to meeting her."

* * *

I keep my eyes on my tablet as Akira drives me to the foundation. When I feel her gaze on my face, I glance up and she quickly looks away.

"Do you have something to say?"

"Did Niko's mother take her to school this morning?"

"She did." I close the tablet.

"And how did Young Niko react?"

"She was happy. Her mother has been away for a long time."

Akira adjusts her fingers on the steering wheel. "How did Miss Williams react?"

"Akira."

"Are you going to say it is none of my concern?"

"You seem uniquely interested in Dejonae's feelings."

"My job is to protect Niko. I left everything behind to do so." Her eyes stray from the road. "I see things becoming very tense in the future. And this would not be good for Niko. She has taken a liking to Miss Williams."

"I won't let anything happen to my daughter. Or to Dejonae."

"Life is very unpredictable," she warns.

"But one thing is constant—my ability to forge my own path. I have learned from my mistakes. This time, I will protect the people I love and keep them close to me."

Akira settles back in her seat, a pensive tilt to her lips.

Just then, my phone rings.

Adam.

I sit up straight. "Did you receive the email?"

The MTB passed our internal checks, but to manufacture a medical device requires FCC compliance. We have been waiting for a message regarding our approval status.

"I have bad news, Sazuki."

My shoulders slump and disappointment surges down my spine, tensing my muscles.

"It got approved!" Adam exclaims.

I jerk up in my seat, my mind buzzing.

"Nova had the factory on stand-by. We're flying over to finalize the contract."

"I'll secure a jet. It will be faster than flying commercial."

"Show off."

I smile and hang up.

Warmth spreads through my chest and the only person I want to share the news with is Dejonae.

I check my watch and realize that Dejonae should be finished with her last class soon.

"Akira, turn the car around."

Twenty minutes later, she parks in front of Dejonae's campus and glances back at me. "We should have contacted your protection team."

"You are worth five of them," I say genuinely.

She looks unimpressed by the compliment.

Eagerly, I leave the car and hurry to the music lecture hall. The doors open and students come flooding into the hallway. I glance past each of their faces, searching for the loveliest one.

One glimpse of her turns me into a pillar.

Dejonae is wearing a white dress with a thin braided belt around the waist. The jean jacket she is wearing over it matches the blue bandana braided across her hair.

A boy is speaking to her, standing a little too close for comfort.

I go tense instantly. My eyes narrow on where he is breathing her air.

Dejonae glances up and notices me. She stops. Her jaw drops. Her eyes widen.

I stalk toward her.

The boy wisely moves aside, putting as much distance between him and Dejonae as possible.

"Sazuki, what are you doing here?" Her eyes dart around.

We are drawing a crowd. One particular girl with blue hair is staring at me as if I am a ghost.

"Let's get to the car quickly," Akira warns in a low voice.

"Miss Williams," I gesture to the path, "I would like a word."

Dejonae's eyes dart back and forth. Is she thinking of fighting me? I take a step forward, my body alight with adrenaline.

Her stubbornness drives me stark, raving mad and it is the most invigorating feeling.

"Dejonae." I call her by her first name when she still does not move.

She flings me a panicked look.

Relax. I arch an eyebrow. "It is in regards to Mr. Howel's collaboration request."

Relief flits across her face. She gives a serious nod. "Mr. Howel, right. He mentioned that."

I keep my expression firm and professional. Dejonae asked me not to expose our relationship to her classmates. I will honor every wish she has spoken aloud and even those she has only whispered quietly in her heart.

But if I see any hormonal college boys sniffing around her again, I will not be so quick to hide our connection.

The back of my hand brushes hers as we walk to the car. It is all I can do not to take her hand in mine.

The moment she is settled in the backseat, I drag her to me and plant a deep kiss on her mouth. She draws back when Akira gets into the car and gives me a playful punch on the chest.

"You just do whatever you want, don't you?" Her words are sharp, but her eyes are twinkling. I interpret that she is not too mad at me.

"I thought I covered that well," I muse.

"Akira," Dejonae says, "does he have time to be goofing off like this?"

"Miss Williams, since he met you, Ryotaro's actions no longer make sense to me. I have given up on understanding him."

On the ride to the airport, I explain where we are going and why. Dejonae seems excited by the adventure and the experience is ten times more thrilling because she is with me.

We meet Nova and Adam in the private air strip.

Nova gives Dejonae a curt nod. "You look nice."

"Thanks. You too." Dejonae motions to Nova's outfit. Adam's assistant traded her staple of work jackets and pantsuits for a looser skirt and a blouse. Adam has not been able to take his eyes off her since we arrived.

"You're right," Dejonae whispers in my ear when we settle into our seats on the plane. "She is his everything."

I smile down at her. "I understand how that feels."

Her eyelashes flutter.

She glances away.

I lift her chin, trying not to get distracted by her lips. They are a vivid red today, as tempting as a freshly-plucked apple against the dark brown of her skin.

"Is something wrong?"

"Yaya went back home today." Her mouth pulls down at the corners. "I'm trying not to let it get me down. She goes back and forth all the time. But it never gets easier saying goodbye to her."

"Would you like me to turn the plane around? Nova and Adam can sign the contract on their own."

"No." She shakes her head. "Yaya didn't just move to another city for modeling. She moved to be independent. As long as we're around, we're going to coddle her. She wanted to live on her own. I won't take that from her."

I roll a finger around one of her curls. "I understand. When Niko had to return to America to live with her mother, my heart broke each time."

She sits up and looks at me. "You're right. It is kind of like that."

With her face upturned, my eyes slide to her mouth. It is not the time to kiss her, yet I am absolutely distracted by the prospect.

"Why did you paint your lips red today?" I ask.

She pushes out her bottom lip. "Yaya picked out my outfit. She said I shouldn't wear T-shirts and jeans anymore."

"Why not?"

"Because I'm dating you."

"I prefer you in T-shirts and jeans."

"Is that your way of saying I don't look good when I'm dressed up?" The cutting look she slants me says *'watch your words carefully'*.

"You look beautiful either way." I caress her shoulder. "But you do not have to wear anything special to be desirable to me."

She smiles. Her eyes drift away from mine. "Do you always rent private jets?"

"It is not 'rented' exactly. It belongs to my family. I use it on my trips back and forth to Japan."

Her smirk blooms into an impressed smile. She glances around the plane.

The main cabin has comfortable leather seats. Each section has two seats facing inward to create an intimate cluster. The sections to the back contain desks for a small dining area and a mini bar.

I do not take much pride in the family wealth, but her gawking is quite adorable.

"Would you like a drink?" I ask her.

She shakes her head and checks her phone. Her gaze turns melancholy. Dejonae must still miss her sister.

I take her hand.

She glances up suddenly.

Without a word, I lead her to the cluster of chairs where Adam and Nova are seated. The two look up from their laptops.

"Would you two like to play a game?" I offer.

"A game?" Adam blinks at me as if I have been abducted by aliens. "*You* want to play a game?"

I find the box of playing cards and return to the table.

Dejonae's troubled look is replaced with a hint of interest. The blood-thirsty need for competition inside her has awakened.

I distract her with round after round. By the time we have landed, laughter has replaced her pensive silence and the smiles she flashes me are full of life.

"Who knew Sazuki was such a sneak?" Adam mumbles to Nova when we disembark.

"Don't be a sore loser, Adam," Dejonae teases.

Nova jumps in to protect him, as she always does. "Adam wasn't familiar with the game. You both could have gone easier on him."

"Don't hate the player. Hate the game." Dejonae winks.

"I demand a rematch," Adam insists. His fair skin is turning red beneath his worn baseball cap. "Next time, we play something I'm good at."

"Which is what?" I tease.

Adam's jaw drops. He stares at me. "Did you just crack a joke, Sazuki?"

"Not bad." Dejonae offers her hand for a high-five.

I bring her hand to my lips and kiss it instead.

"Ew!"

"Please refrain yourselves!"

Protests erupt from both Adam and Nova.

Dejonae smiles, her entire face lighting up with joy. And I realize that the tangled web of my ex-wife, my mother's secret plans, and even my family's coldness should never touch her.

I will protect her from it.

All of it.

So the only thing she sees is the sunshine.

* * *

After finishing with the factory, Adam, Nova, Dejonae and I go for dinner. We stay in the city another hour to visit an escape room.

Adam and Nova beat us to the finish line. Something that causes Dejonae to grumble all the way back to the airport.

"Dejonae, slow down," I tell her. "You will trip and fall to the tarmac."

"I told you the key was under the suitcase," she hurls an angry glare over her shoulder, "but no. You insisted that it was under the chest."

I snicker beneath my breath.

Adorable.

Not that I plan to say that out loud. With the mood Dejonae is in, she might push me down the stairs.

"Don't be too hard on him," Nova says, rubbing the loss in our faces. "Adam and I have worked together for a long time. We practically share the same brain." She gestures to where Adam is walking in behind her. "Not everyone can be this in sync."

Dejonae grits her teeth.

Steam pours from her ears.

The good news is… she is no longer worried about her sister being gone.

At least I accomplished that.

"I demand a re-match!" Dejonae plunks into a seat. "This doesn't end here."

Adam passes me by, pats my shoulder and mumbles, "I never thought I'd find someone more competitive than Nova. Good luck, man."

I nod, accepting his well wishes.

We fasten our seatbelts as the plane takes off. The air pressure changes and the plane smoothly lifts off the tarmac.

Dejonae is still pouting about the loss.

How strange.

Any other person and I would be annoyed at their stubbornness.

On her, I am utterly charmed.

She is a pop of color in my world.

An explosion of energy.

My gaze lingers on her honey-tinged curls, the thick black lashes, and the sunlight glittering against her dark cheeks like threads of gold.

She glances up. "What?"

"Thank you for joining me today. It was an important moment in the foundation's history and it would not have been the same without you."

Her annoyance melts away. She tucks her head into my chest. "You're welcome."

I nuzzle my cheek against her hair and marvel at my own irrationality. I cannot allow too many people to see the soft side that Dejonae brings out in me. My reputation is at stake.

Dejonae yawns. "I think the food and the escape room knocked me out. I'm feeling sleepy."

"Take a rest," I whisper. "I will be here when you wake up."

I work on my tablet while Dejonae curls up against me. Her body is warm and her hair smells like a sweet dream.

It takes an immense amount of concentration to absorb the words in front of me when all I want to do is mark her face with kisses until I know every curve and line by heart.

The temptation is too great to ignore. As the plane descends and the *'Fasten Seat Belt'* light pops on with a chime, I lean over Dejonae.

Her mouth is parted.

Her eyelashes are still.

With her head balanced on my shoulder, her lips are as close to mine as my next breath. I can feel every sigh she makes against my skin, the gentlest caress.

My heart picks up speed.

I could very gently shake her awake.

But I do not want to be a gentleman about it.

I glance around to make sure that Nova and Adam are not looking this way. They are engrossed in their own world, both of their heads tucked in front of a laptop. They have been whispering since Dejonae fell asleep so as not to disturb her.

Satisfied that we are not being watched, I cradle Dejonae's face in my palm. The first kiss is soft, a simple press of my lips to hers, a quiet mixture of oxygen and life.

But it is too tender.

She settles right back against me, unbothered.

I capture her mouth again, sucking on her bottom lip with a sultry, impatient rhythm. She responds to me in her dreams before she opens her eyes.

Our gazes meet.

Dejonae pulls herself closer to me. I shower her soft, perfect lips with nips and caresses until all the lipstick has transferred from her mouth to mine. I tease her with agonizingly slow advances of my tongue until she moans and—

"Sir," the flight attendant clears her throat, "you need to put on your seatbelt."

Dejonae and I break apart. She covers her face with her hands and sinks into her chair while I secure my seatbelt.

Despite fearing that the kiss set the whole plane on fire, we manage to land safely.

I help Dejonae to the tarmac.

She holds my hand and looks up at me.

I smile in response.

Being with her is so easy. So delightful.

I keep finding more things to admire about her.

Her intelligence, her wit, her sharp sense of humor, her competitive spirit, her determination to never accept injustice and her refusal to find me as terrifying as the rest of the world does.

She smiles at me and opens her mouth to speak, but her eyes catch on something in the distance. I glance ahead to see what put that grim expression on her face.

Niko is here at the airport.

And she is accompanied by her mother.

CHAPTER 17
HOUSE OF WONTONS

DEJONAE

I LOOKED Ashanti up long before this. It was late at night. I was just starting to admit my feelings for Sazuki. Yaya was beside me, manning the computer.

At first, I didn't want to look.

What did it matter who she was or what she'd meant to him? Why did I need to open things that were best left closed?

Pandora's box.

But it called to me.

My sister was kind. She offered to close the laptop and turn off the screen. Scrub the search from my laptop's history and then scrub her mind too.

At the time, I told myself that I didn't like Sazuki *that much*. And his past didn't have the power to hurt me yet.

Yaya turned the laptop around.

And there she was.

Ashanti.

She was stunning.

But now, looking at Sazuki's ex-wife in the flesh, I realize that pictures do her no justice.

With long, straight black hair and big, expressive eyes, she could easily earn the role of a sun goddess in a Greek musical production. Her skin is darker than mine, moving shadows and obsidian. The contrast makes the soft pink of her dress stand out against her tall, womanly figure. There's a graceful sway to her hips and a motherly tenderness in the way she touches Niko and signs for her not to run.

I feel numb when I see her. And I wonder if it's my body going into protection mode. As if some part of me senses the tidal wave of *crap* that's about to hit me and every fiber of my being is trying to delay it for one second longer.

Sazuki steps in front of me protectively.

What is he trying to protect me from? I doubt he even knows.

None of us know.

This situation is new.

But it's what I've chosen.

I chose him.

Which means I chose this weird, tangled connection to his ex-wife too.

I come back to myself and step away from Sazuki's protection. Niko's eyes are on me and I don't want her to be confused by adult things.

I kneel. The bottom of my knee scrapes the hard, uncomfortable tarmac, but I keep the discomfort from my face when she wraps her arms around my neck.

I close my eyes and, for a second, everything feels normal again.

Niko hugs me tightly.

I rock her back and forth, inhaling her little girl scent.

My heart quivers.

I don't know how or when, but I fell in love with her long before I fell for her father.

She releases me and points to her hair. It's braided. Long, neat plaits with beads at the ends.

I smile. "You look beautiful."

"Thank you," she signs.

"I wanted her to have a proper hairstyle." Ashanti looks down on me. "The style she had before was a little… unsophisticated." The emphasis on 'unsophisticated' is clear.

The smile on my face turns brittle, but I force myself not to take her words to heart. For one thing, those words might not have been aimed at me. For another, if I take everything she says personally, she'll have all the power to manipulate my emotions.

I hate giving up control.

Especially to people who would love to see me squirm.

Inhaling deeply, I wrap an arm around Niko's shoulders and then slide my hand around Sazuki's waist. Ashanti's face tightens when she sees me sidling up to her ex-husband and her daughter.

Wonderful.

"Who is this?" I look up at Sazuki, smiling innocently even though I know good and well who is standing across from us.

Sazuki studies my eyes for a moment.

I blink up at him frankly, unashamed.

This is his choice.

He chose a college student with a penchant for getting even.

I arch an eyebrow, daring him to call me out. Instead, he gives me a hot look that warns, had it not been for his daughter and his regal decorum keeping him in check, he would have kissed me harder than he did on the plane.

"Let me introduce myself. My name is Ashanti Miller. I'm Niko's mother."

"I'm Dejonae Wiliams, Sazuki's girlfriend."

Her lips tighten. "I've heard a lot about you."

"All good things, right?"

"Mostly." She brushes her dress down with a hint of distaste.

I don't let her little dig get to me.

Niko tugs my hand. "Can you stay with us?" she signs.

"Oh right." An oily smile spreads across Ashanti's face. "Did you ask her about dinner, Sazuki?" Her smugness thickens. "I told him to invite you over during breakfast this morning."

They're having *breakfast* together?

My nostrils flare as an image of Sazuki, his legs entangled with Ashanti's under the table, sipping coffee and feeding each other pancakes, flits through my mind.

If they were having breakfast, then what were they doing *before* breakfast.

More images assault me.

Sazuki's eyes burning. Ashanti digging her fingers into his hair. The tangle of their legs and then their lips…

I struggle not to let my disgust show.

Sazuki's fingers dig into my shoulder as if he wishes to anchor me to his body. It's not enough.

I thought I could do this.

I really did.

But I don't want to be a petty person. This small conversation is just a taste of what interacting with Ashanti will be like. And I don't like myself when I feel small or when I try to make others feel small.

I look up at Sazuki.

He understands without me saying a word. "I will take Dejonae home. I kept her out all day."

Niko pushes out her bottom lip. She signs, "Please."

Why is she so cute?

I have one—and only *one*—weakness.

And I think it's this little girl.

With a sigh, I give in to her. "Okay."

Sazuki looks alarmed. "Are you sure?"

"Yeah."

Adam and Nova descend the stairs and see our little dramatic reunion.

"Hey, Niko." Adam greets the little girl warmly.

She gives him a shy wave.

Nova's eyebrows furrow when she notices Ashanti. "Who's this?"

"I'm Niko's mother." The wind tugs a lock of Ashanti's brown hair. It dances elegantly.

"Niko's... mother?" Nova's eyes stray to me.

Heat burns my cheeks. Given the way Sazuki and I were making out on the plane, it makes sense that she'd have questions about why his ex-wife is suddenly showing up in front of us like we're one big happy family.

Ashanti gives both Adam and Nova bright smiles. "Would you like to join us for dinner?"

The two exchange looks.

A world of ideas seems to pass in that one, silent exchange.

If I were in my right mind, I'd find it funny how into each other they so obviously are.

Adam hasn't taken his eyes off Nova all day. They keep things professional on the surface—no touching or flirting or even prolonged eye contact—but he's always there to give her exactly what she wants, meeting her needs before she expresses them, and caving to her when she has an idea.

Sazuki said that Nova was working for Adam.

But in reality, it feels like Adam is the one who's taking care of Nova.

"We're going to bow out on this one," Adam says finally. His eyes dart to Nova before jumping to me. He raises his eyebrows in a brotherly gesture, as if to say *need an out?*

If even *they* can feel the awkwardness, then maybe I'm not doing a good job of hiding my feelings.

I shake my head. I already promised Niko.

Adam smiles. "We'll head back now. There's still some details to work through with the MTB's programming."

Sazuki lifts a hand. "Don't work too hard."

"You too."

Adam and Nova head in the opposite direction.

Sazuki glances at Ashanti. "Did you drive?"

"We called an Uber." She watches him with soft eyes. "Can we catch a ride with you? Your mom said Akira would drop a car off."

He nods in agreement.

Ashanti smiles.

There's something behind that smile.

Something I don't like at all.

Sazuki turns to me. His eyes do not falter when they meet mine.

I give him a little smile of assurance.

I'm okay.

I'm not going to melt like the Wicked Witch of the West because I share the same vehicle with his ex-wife.

This is going to be awkward.

But it's not going to be life-threatening.

I don't think.

He dips his chin in understanding. I don't know if he's reverted to Silent Sazuki because of the tension or because he genuinely has nothing to say. Thankfully, I have Niko to distract me from the not-so-subtle drama.

We sign nonstop on our way to the car.

Once we get to the giant SUV, Sazuki opens the front door for me.

"Oh, you don't mind if I take the front seat, do you?" Ashanti wiggles in between me and Sazuki. She launches one foot on the runner. "It's so much roomier." She gestures to her legs. "I'm a little tall, you know."

My lips part, but it's not to speak. It's to release a frustrated breath.

How am I supposed to say no to her now? If I do, I'm going to look petty.

"Ashanti," Sazuki starts to intervene.

I hold up a hand. "It's fine. You can take the front seat. Niko and I were talking anyway." I loop my arm around hers. "Us shorties should stick together."

She laughs and signs, "Definitely."

I buckle Niko in, making sure her seatbelt is secure before I do the same. Sazuki's eyes find mine in the rear-view mirror.

"Stop looking. I'm fine," I sign for only his eyes.

He focuses on the road again.

I try hard to concentrate on Niko and her recount of her day at the farmhouse with Beth, Belle, Micheal and Bailey, but Ashanti's laughter from the front seat keeps messing with me.

"I re-printed some of Niko's old photos so you could have your own album at the house. It was so sweet going through those old memories…"

Old memories?

Irritation blooms in my heart.

Do not get upset, Dejonae.

"Oh, Ryo." Ashanti darts a hand out and places it on Sazuki's arm.

My vision turns red.

Ryo? He's 'Ryo'?

Sazuki shakes her off, but it's too late. I can't un-hear the way she called to him in a sweet voice.

"I just remembered. Your mom said you needed more soy sauce. Let me run to the store real quick."

He takes her to a store, but that isn't enough to satisfy Ashanti.

"Ryo, can you come in with me? I don't remember the soy sauce your mother liked."

"Just get any one."

"I'll come with you," I say, starting to undo my seatbelt. "Since I'm meeting your mom for the first time, I should probably bring something nice."

"No need." Ashanti holds out a hand, stopping me from moving.

I glare at her.

She smiles glibly and aims damsel-in-distress eyes at Sazuki. "Can you come with me? Please?"

Sazuki frowns.

"Come on." Ashanti checks her watch. "There's not enough time."

Expression firm, he opens the car door. To my surprise, he doesn't follow Ashanti around the car. He opens my door for me. Swooping in, he leans over me to undo my seatbelt.

His head is right against my chest.

His hair falls into his eyes, making his sharp cheekbones look softer than usual.

A burning hot desire flares in me when he pulls back and his fingers skate over my thighs.

"Come on. I will help you pick something that my mother will like," he says.

My knees are butter but, somehow, I swing them out of the car and join him on the sidewalk.

Sazuki undoes Niko's seatbelt and helps her out of the car too.

Ashanti waits for us on the sidewalk, her lips puckered and her foot tapping on the cement.

"Let's go," Sazuki says, totally unruffled.

His intense energy is making me nervous. It's one thing for *me* to put Ashanti in her place, but it's another thing entirely to *feel* him choose me.

Sazuki isn't big on PDA, but he sticks close to me in the grocery store. His hand comes up to brush my back when I choose the bouquet of flowers. His hips press against mine when I bend over to choose a box of chocolates.

Whenever I look at him, he's staring at me like he wants to devour me.

My gaze turns dark and heavy, answering his need with my own. It's like he's trying his best to communicate, in every way he can, that I shouldn't be shaken. That he's with me. That he sees *only* me.

And I can barely contain myself.

My pinkie locks with his when we get to the cashier. I hold on for a beat and then release him, looking down to smile at Niko as she begs her dad for candy.

Sazuki says no.

I slide the candy into my cart when he isn't looking.

By the time we leave the store, Ashanti is seething in the front seat, Niko and I are happily snacking on our banned chocolates and my spirits are lifted.

Ashanti can try her hardest to knock me off-balance tonight. But Sazuki's got my back and so does Niko.
Those two are the only ones that matter.
I'm not going to let her win.

* * *

"We don't let outdoor shoes inside," Ashanti says, turning back to me as I step through the door. "Most Asian homes don't."

"Actually, not letting shoes inside isn't an Asian thing. It's a global thing. My grandparents don't do it either. Something about not letting outside dirt into the house." I sit on the bench.

Niko slides my matching pair of music-themed slippers over to me. I smile my appreciation and slip into them.

Ashanti's eyes widen when she sees it. "Why do you have the same slippers as Niko?"

"Sazuki and Niko bought it for me when I first came over." I rub Niko's head. "We all have a matching pair."

"Sazuki would never wear…" Ashanti's mumbled words drift to nothing when Sazuki shoves his giant feet into the cheesy, plastic slides with the music note imprinted on the band.

The satisfaction that drowns me when I read the dread on Ashanti's face proves that I have a lot more growing to do as a person.

She recovers quickly and tosses her hair over her shoulder. "I wonder if mother needs help with the filling for the *gyoza*."

"Are we making dinner tonight?" I sign to Niko.

She nods.

"What's gyoza?" I ask aloud.

"Don't you know what gyoza is?" Ashanti sounds alarmed. When I shake my head, she pops a brow and speaks to me like I'm a child. "Gyoza are Japanese dumplings."

"My grandmother makes the *best* dumplings," Niko gestures.

"I'm excited to try it out."

"Niko," Sazuki signs, "go and wash up. Your hands are sticky from that candy I told you not to eat."

Niko gives me a guilty look.

I return it in a flash.

Shoot. We've been found out.

"I'll take you to wash your hands," Ashanti says, wrapping an arm around her daughter's shoulders.

While Niko scampers away, Sazuki folds his arms over his chest and stares at me. "Did you really think you could get away with that?"

"I have no idea what you're talking about," I say innocently.

His eyebrows lower in disbelief.

"We were very quiet."

"Not quiet enough." He holds out a hand to me.

I frown at it. "What?"

"Give me your hand. I'm sure I'll find the evidence."

"I licked it all off."

He shakes the hand that's extended to me.

Rather than give in, I reach down and pretend to wipe my hands on my white skirt. "You'll never take me alive."

His dimples flash.

He grabs my hand and lifts it to his face before I can ruin my dress. To my surprise, Sazuki pops my index finger into his mouth and sucks it.

My heart whips around my chest.

My vision goes white.

I can't see anything at all except the blinding-hot image of Ryotaro Sazuki with my finger in his mouth.

Have mercy.

I'm instantly addicted to the feel of his tongue flicking against my flesh and the way his eyes pinch shut as he makes a soft 'mm' sound.

I jolt like he's a stack of unleashed electricity when he pulls my finger out and presses a soft kiss to it. "Too much sugar isn't good for you."

He's the one who isn't good for me.

Or my sanity.

Or my heart.

Or my body.

"Sazuki," I rasp his name like it's a magic spell.

Sazuki takes my hand and gives it a squeeze. "I am sorry."

"That we aren't alone right now?" I whisper.

The smile he flashes is brief and wolfish. Then it fades. "I am sorry about Ashanti."

I'm still blindsided by what he just did with my finger, so it takes me a minute to catch up with the conversation.

"Um who?"

The dimples make a second appearance.

I can't believe he's mine.

This has to be some crazy dream.

Sazuki taps my forehead. "Ashanti."

Oh right.

Ashanti.

His ex-wife.

Major douche-canoe who's trying to one-up me in The Who Belongs With Sazuki Olympics.

"Is the solution simply to kiss you until you are dazed enough to make it through a meal?"

I blink rapidly. "No, no that's not a good idea."

I'm beginning to *crave* this man.

If he touches me like that again, I won't just be in a daze. I'll be a wet heap of need that'll have to be sopped off the floor with a Swiffer Jet.

And how am I supposed to face his daughter after that?

I force myself to remain on task. "You don't have to apologize. In a way, I kind of get where she's coming from. Niko's *her* daughter and yet this random woman is suddenly in her life. This is weird for all of us."

"You are being gracious."

I scowl. "I didn't finish. Just because I understand doesn't mean I approve. There's a line and I think she's inching over it."

"I do not understand why she is behaving this way." A crease appears between Sazuki's brow.

"Isn't she married?" I ask. "I think you told me that she had a husband who was also a singer?"

"She does."

Weird. The way Ashanti looks at Sazuki is not like a woman who has an entire *husband* at home.

"I will speak to her," Sazuki says quietly.

"It's okay." I run my hands down his lean but muscular arms. "I can handle her."

"It is not just her I am worried about."

Before I can ask what he means, an Asian woman skids into our line of sight. Sazuki straightens and puts a decent amount of space between us.

I smile charmingly and extend the chocolate and flowers I bought from the grocery store. "Mrs. Sazuki, hi. It's so nice to finally meet you. I'm Dejonae Williams."

She gives me a head-to-toe scan. "You are very young."

Her accent is even thicker than Sazuki's. It takes me a moment to sort through what she's saying. The awkward pause makes the tension in the air even worse.

I laugh to break it up. "You look young as well."

Her lips twitch, but she quickly returns to her stern expression. "Have you made dumplings before?"

"No, this will be my first time."

"Come." She motions to me.

Sazuki takes a step forward too.

She stops him with a fierce gaze. "Only women in the kitchen."

"That's an archaic philosophy," I mumble.

Sazuki squeezes my hand and murmurs back, "Try not to say that to her."

I scrunch my nose. "No promises."

I've never been great at holding back when I feel the need to speak up. However, Sazuki's mom is from a different time and a different culture. The last thing I want to do is come off as argumentative when I'm supposed to be making a good impression.

Just can it for one night, Dejonae.

I force a smile and follow Sazuki's mother into the kitchen. Niko isn't there, which makes me feel bereft. She would have been a friendly face in the middle of this cold war.

The ladies lift their eyes and spear me with sharp looks.

I cough. "How can I help?"

"Come. I will show you." She sits me down around the table and proceeds to give me the quickest dumpling tutorial *ever*.

I'm lost and have the burning urge to ask 'what was step one again'? But both Ashanti and Sazuki's mother settle in to make their dumplings and I don't want to look like the clueless one.

I'm surprised by the way silence falls on the kitchen. There's no music and no conversation. I guess everyone is concentrating, but I'm not used to interactions like this.

With my parents and Yaya, there's always someone laughing, talking, teasing and trading stories about their day.

With Vanya and Hadyn, the teasing and joking is multiplied.

Even though I haven't been around Sunny, Kenya, and Dawn for long, the few times I were, I saw how tightly-knit and vocal their group was.

Don't even get me started on their kids.

Those little critters have no filters, especially when they're playing games with each other.

But every family is different.

I square my shoulders, determined to work on my dumplings without asking for help.

"What are you doing?" Sazuki's mom explodes at me. "Do not do it like that." She points to my dumpling. "Too much. Too much. Why are you doing it like that?"

I panic and throw the filling out. "Sorry."

"No, do not put it back here." She frowns at me.

"Dejonae, you have to put just the right amount." Ashanti's

smile is gentle but her tone holds way too much condescension for it to be genuine. "Not too much. Not too little. Just right."

"Just… right…" I concentrate on adding the filling back to my wanton wrapper.

"It's kind of like life," Ashanti says, her voice a buzzing in my ear.

I cringe.

Why did I complain about the silence? Now I wish she'd just shut up.

But she keeps talking in that steady tone. "Not everything that walks in is the right fit. Some things are too big, too small." She plops the perfect amount of filling in, showing off her skills. "It takes a special person to be 'just right'."

I don't respond to her. If I do, I'd probably make an even more damaging first impression on Sazuki's mom.

The wrapper is thin in my hand and keeps breaking.

The filling is raw.

I'm not sure if we should be cooking it or not before we put them into the gyoza wrappers. I don't see Ashanti or Sazuki's mom doing so and figure I'm okay.

When we're done, Sazuki's mom cooks the dumplings in a skillet until they're golden brown.

The smell lures Niko into the kitchen.

"How did yours come out?" she signs.

"I think it came out well," I sign back.

Sazuki soon follows, his nose in the air. "Almost done?"

"Yes." Ashanti laughs and pats his hand. "You always were a sucker for gyoza. Remember when we first got married? That was the first recipe you wanted me to learn."

Sazuki's eyes dart to me.

I look away, a burning feeling in my chest.

She won't get to me. She won't get to me.

"Yes," Sazuki's mom says, "he has liked gyoza since he was a boy. At that time, we used to make enough gyoza for a full meal. He even asked for it on his birthday."

"Oh, I know. When we were in Japan, I wanted to buy him a fancy gift for his birthday, and he told me not to bother. That he'd just eat gyoza and be happy." Ashanti laughs until her eyes squeeze shut. "I got so angry at him because I wanted to do something big and he was asking for so little."

The muscles in my jaw clench and unclench.

It's their past.

Their history.

And it's what resulted in Niko's birth.

I don't want to be jealous of it.

I don't want to be the immature, younger girlfriend who can't take a joke.

But I can't hide how upset I feel.

Sazuki clears his throat. "We are hungry now. I will help you move the trays to the kitchen."

We settle around the table and all the gyoza gets separated into trays. I notice that Ashanti and Niko are eating the tray from Sazuki's mother.

And Sazuki is gobbling Ashanti's dumplings like he's a dying man with his last meal.

My gyoza remains at the end of the table, untouched.

Sazuki slows down long enough to come up for air. He touches my hand. "Are you not hungry?"

"I'm okay." I drum up a smile for him.

Ashanti observes us with her hawk eyes and then she leans forward. "Sazuki, why don't you try this one?"

My eyes whip up.

Ashanti shoves my plate at Sazuki. He fetches one of my dumplings with his chopsticks and chews.

"Now," Ashanti says mischievously, "out of all these plates, which one do you like the most?"

"I like this one!" Niko points to her grandmother's dumplings.

"I like this one." Sazuki juts his chopstick at Ashanti's tray.

My smile remains pinned on my face, but it's only because of my pride. Chaos blows through my mind. Sazuki prefers his ex-wife's plate. Does he miss her cooking too? What if he misses more than that? Her kisses? Her lovemaking? Her face in his bed in the morning?

My pulse picks up steam.

Anger rears its ugly head.

Irrational.

Uncontrollable.

I set my chopsticks down and it hits the table with a *thunk*. Sazuki looks over at me. His eyes scan my face as he accepts the beaming look of doom that I give him.

In a second, it clicks.

He lunges for the untouched tray at the end of the table and sets it in front of him.

"Son, what are you doing?"

Sazuki doesn't answer. He stuffs his face with my gyoza, shoving dumpling after dumpling in his mouth like a human vacuum.

"Is it that good?" Niko signs.

I shrug.

She spears one with her chopsticks. I do too.

As we eat, both of us scrunch our noses.

"I don't like this one," Niko signs.

"Me either." I cough and reach for my water. "There's not enough meat in there. It's too dry."

"I think it's delicious," Sazuki says, his bottom lip trembling.

Ashanti gives him a stunned look.

Sazuki's mother seems equally confused.

As an awkward silence settles on the room, I tilt my head back and burst out laughing. Niko giggles, her eyes darting between me and her father.

Sazuki's eyes widen. He still hasn't swallowed any of the dumplings yet.

Poor thing.

"Spit it out, Sazuki." I get a napkin and gesture to him.

But he refuses.

He swallows my dry dumplings with a giant gulp of water and proceeds to polish off everything in the tray.

Abruptly, he gets up.

His chair scrapes behind him.

Every head launches in his direction.

"I need to go to the bathroom," Sazuki announces.

"Why are you telling us?" His mother frowns.

"Dejonae, come with me."

"Me?"

"Yes." He wipes his mouth with a napkin, drops it forcefully into his plate and leads me down the hallway.

Once the bathroom door is closed, his eyes slide over my face. "I do not know what to say. My mother…" His nostrils flare and he taps his chest. "I want to protect you, but I do not want to disrespect her. It might be better to leave."

"I'm not going to run away. If I plan to stay with you, I might as well get used to these awkward dinners now."

His eyes darken. Sazuki backs me up against the sink and cages me between his arms. His desire smothers me, filling in all the places that his body can't reach.

"I will speak to Ashanti. My mother is one thing. But I will not have her disrespect you."

He's so soft with his family, with his mother and daughter.

I forgot how sharp he could be.

It makes me want to grab his face and suck the life out of it.

"Watch me take care of myself, hm?" I arch a brow.

He nods.

We leave the bathroom together.

Everyone has moved to the living room and they swivel to watch us.

"Niko," I sign, "now that dinner's over, how about we play for your grandmother?"

Niko brightens and nods.

Sazuki's mother looks confused. I wonder if she doesn't understand ASL.

"Niko and her teacher have been working on a song," I explain, walking around to the piano Sazuki keeps in his living room.

Niko takes the bench beside me, her face beaming with excitement.

I press my fingers to the keys.

She does too.

Together, we play Beethoven's *Moonlight Sonata*, capturing the texture and loveliness of the piece.

I sway to the rhythm.

Niko bends her head close to the keys as if drawn by a magnetic frequency. Together, we let the music fill us, leaning more on the feeling even as we accurately play the notes.

When we're done, Niko gives me a hug.

Sazuki winks in approval.

His mother has tear-filled eyes.

I look over at Ashanti and I see the storm cloud over her face. She's starting to realize something that most people overlook.

It's not just blood that binds a family together.

And though I may not have given birth to Niko, I'm here to stay.

CHAPTER 18
THE ORIGINAL FAMILY

SAZUKI

"We need to talk." I gesture to the path leading up to the back deck.

Ashanti stands in the doorway, the light from the garage house throwing her face in shadows. She's wearing a big pink bonnet and a matching robe.

"Give me a minute," she says.

I nod. "I will wait by the pool."

The door swings shut, choking the light until it's gone.

I walk away. Silent. Thoughtful.

My head tilts down to make out the path. The water hose is lying on the cobbled walkway. I kick it with my slippers. I do not wish for Ashanti to trip.

Crickets scream bloody murder from the garden to my right. Moonlight shifts through the inky darkness.

My slippers make a dull sound when I step up to the pool deck and find a seat around the outdoor patio table.

Through the filmy curtains covering the balcony doors, I notice a glowing white light. The sounds of a Japanese late night television show filter to me. My mother is inside watching videos on her tablet. In Japan, she would often fall asleep to the sound of the television.

My fingers drum on the table.

Tension winds around my shoulders.

I hope this conversation can remain calm and quiet. I do not wish to wake my mother or alert her to the fact that I am speaking to Ashanti. Tonight's shenanigans emphasized that my mother has chosen a side.

And it is not mine.

If she finds out I have taken Ashanti to task, she will try to intervene and I will be forced to give in to her.

Ashanti's footsteps patter toward me. Her shadow falls on the bench, a black mark stretching across slaps of varnished wood.

"What is this about, Ryo?" Her voice is subdued.

I jut my chin at the bench across from me.

Ashanti hesitates and then takes her seat. She is still wearing a robe, but I notice the belt isn't cinched as tightly as it was before, allowing her dark skin to peek out from the folds. The bonnet is gone. Her hair is bone-straight around her shoulders. The hint of gloss on her lips and shimmer on her eyes tells me why she took so long to join me on the patio.

"This is unexpected. You're not going to ask me to take a midnight dip with you, right? I can't get my hair wet."

I stare at her in the twilight. "I would like to know the meaning of your behavior tonight."

The smile on her face wilts.

For a second, there is silence.

"What behavior?" She bats her eyelashes slowly. "I thought the evening went well. Dejonae is a delightful girl. Very sprightly. But that's expected for someone her age. And Niko gets along with her. Probably because she has more in common with our daughter than either one of us."

I frown at her.

She squirms. "What?"

"Your ability to throw veiled insults have improved over the years."

"What are you talking about?"

"Dejonae is not Niko's age. She is not a child. You keep insinuating that she is, somehow, immature and inexperienced when that is not the case."

"She's so much younger than you, Ryo."

"That is not a factor for us. And it should not be your concern either."

"How can it not be a factor? That's an entire generation of a difference. I saw her in action today. She's quick with a comeback or a sarcastic word. That's the mark of people her age. It's all about that lip."

I remain silent. Dejonae's 'lip' is exactly why I was first drawn to her. The more time we spend together, the more I enjoy the way her mind works. Her passion and drive are invigorating. She quickly caught the vision of the foundation and adopted our mission as her own. Every day, she arrives at her desk, charged up and ready to dive into a task.

Her charisma is contagious. A fire that cannot be replicated.

And it is making a difference.

I have never seen such unbridled enthusiasm in my employees. The students feel it. The instructors feel it.

Her leadership quality is commendable.

I can order people to work for me.

But Dejonae can inspire them.

I would never wish to stomp out that side of her.

"I do not mind her 'lip' as you say," I respond finally.

"Oh, I'm sure you don't." She motions to my face. "You wear her lipstick well, Ryo."

Heat creeps up my cheeks, but I remain largely unruffled.

Ashanti shakes her head. "Have you spoken to her about what it really means to be a mother? A stepmother? Girls her age are out having fun with guys, hooking up and reveling in their lack of responsibility. They think it's 'cute' to have a kid, until they face the immense responsibility that it takes. Not everyone is cut out to be a mother."

"Dejonae is not the type to shy away from responsibility." I grunt.

This is not the way I wanted the conversation to go. When did this become a defense of my girlfriend?

"Ashanti—"

"You can't be so clueless, Ryo. These days, women aren't taught to be homemakers. It's all about doing what they want for themselves. Why do you think so many 'modern women' are single or divorced? They don't know what it takes to please a man."

I refrain from pointing out that Ashanti also belongs in the 'divorced' category. Does that mean she did not know how to please me?

"She said it from her own mouth." Ashanti flails her arms. "Dejonae had trouble accepting that a wife is supposed to be in the kitchen. She is neither quiet nor submissive. Your family is going to hate her. Do you think she can handle that? Do you think she'll stick around and hold her tongue the way I did?"

"My family's opinions did not matter when I married you and they will not matter now that I have chosen her."

"She's not ready—"

"She is my choice."

Ashanti falls silent.

"You are right to say that she is headstrong, but she also knows when to be silent and when to speak. Dejonae showed an incredible amount of self-restraint tonight. Frankly, it surprised me. I was certain she would say something to you or my mother."

"Say what? I never antagonized her, Ryo. I thought I was being perfectly welcoming."

I fold my arms over my chest. This is a slippery slope. I do not wish to fight with Ashanti. Our relationship must remain respectful and friendly for our daughter's sake.

Niko did not ask to be brought into this world. It is not her fault that her parents rushed into marriage without properly checking that their visions and personalities aligned. I refuse to bring any more anguish and dysfunction into her life by creating an enemy of her mother.

However, Ashanti is making it very hard to remain civil.

I fold my hands together. "We have discussed at length what you perceive as Dejonae's wrongs. Now I would like to address yours."

"Ryo, if you're upset about what happened with the dumplings, that had nothing to do with me. Clearly, it was her first time making gyoza and she had no idea what she was doing. Besides, it's not strange that you preferred my dumplings. I've been cooking for you for years. Some of our best times were in the kitchen as a family."

"Ashanti, why do you keep speaking of the past as if it were perfect?"

Her eyes dart between mine. Her mouth gapes open slightly.

This attempt at playing naive does not fool me. I did not know much about Ashanti when we married. However, I learned much about her during our three years together. She is notoriously skilled at side-stepping serious conversations, especially when those conversations revolve around something she does not want to discuss.

I would often let things go rather than fight.

But this matter is too important for me to throw my hands up and let it pass.

"Ryotaro, I'm genuinely shocked that you're out here *scolding* me, when I was nothing but polite and respectful to your girlfriend. Did you want me to lay down the red carpet and bow before her? I'm not going to do that."

"I never asked you to worship her. I simply ask that you respect her."

"And I did. But you have to understand that this is strange for me."

"Being uncomfortable is one thing," I insist. "But you took it a step further."

"How?" she shrieks.

"I will not make a list, Ashanti." She would only find a way to explain or defend each choice. "What I want to know is why."

"Why what?"

"Why are you behaving this way with Dejonae?"

"What way?" She throws her arm up.

I study her. Does she really not know? "You found every opportunity to make her feel as though she did not belong."

"That's ridiculous!"

Gritting my teeth, I grasp at all the patience I have stored in me. "I have given you the benefit of the doubt because you are Niko's mother. But I will not cater to you at the expense of Dejonae's feelings."

"How exactly have you catered to me?" she demands.

"You showed up at my home without warning and I accepted you in—"

"You accepted me into the garage house," she points out.

"You eat breakfast with us in the morning and I have not complained."

"To be fair, your *mom* is the one who invited me over."

"You ask for time with Niko and I make all the arrangements for you. Even cutting her time at the farmhouse short so you could pick her up early." I give her a stern look. "I do not wish to see either you or Niko hurt. This is why I make the effort for you, but I do not want you to misunderstand my intentions. Dejonae is important to me. She is not leaving my life or Niko's life. Just as I wish to protect Niko, I wish to protect her."

"From what? *Me?*" Ashanti's voice climbs. "Am I the big bad ex-wife in this story, Ryo? How cliché."

"No one is calling you a bad person, Ashanti," I say as patiently as I can.

"That's what you're saying, Ryo." She rises from the table and points an accusing hand. "In your eyes, I'm this… *Evil Queen* trying to get sweet, young, not-a-wrinkle-on-her Snow White to eat the poisoned apple. Well, you know what, screw you. I'm not the villain and I resent you for making me out to be one."

She starts to storm away.

"Why have you not mentioned your husband since your arrival?" I ask pointedly.

Her body becomes as straight as a sword.

"Is there something you need to tell me?"

She turns to face me.

Her eyebrows hover lower. She squirms.

I tap my finger against the table. "Ashanti, why did you suddenly leave your cruise?"

Her nostrils flare. "I missed Niko."

"Is that all?"

She licks her lips. "I got a divorce."

I stiffen in shock.

"It hadn't been working out for a while. We both knew it. But he…" Her voice breaks. "He was the person I chose. I didn't want to fail twice. I tried holding on with all my strength." A tear creeps into her eyes. "He told me pointedly that it was over. He didn't want to keep lying to himself or to me anymore."

"I am sorry," I say gravely.

She taps at her eyes with the pad of her fingers. "The divorce is almost final."

I drag a hand through my hair, uncertain on how I should comfort her. That feeling of helplessness, pain and failure had plagued me after our marriage ended too.

"It is not your fault, Ashanti," I say.

"It is my fault."

"No—"

"Because I shouldn't have left you in the first place."

My breath catches in my throat.

"Ryo," she calls my name in a broken voice, "I was so young when we got together. I hadn't fully developed an identity yet. I still had so many dreams. So many things that I thought were more important than my family. But I was wrong. All the things I thought I wanted are not the things that truly fulfill me. And all the things I thought I needed in a man turned out to be the wrong things."

She sniffs. "I thought I wanted someone who would leave everything he knew to be with me, to make me more comfortable. But I realize I had a man who would turn his back on his family just to protect ours." She laughs self-deprecatingly. "And I thought that being with someone who liked staying in, watching movies, and not going anywhere on the weekends was torture. But I realize that having someone who loves being home with me, just spending time with me without all the other distractions, is priceless."

As the shock wears off, I shake my head. "Ashanti, I do not think you should continue."

"You should know where I stand, Ryo." Her lashes clump together from the tears.

"I do not wish to return to the past."

"But… haven't you seen how in sync we are? Over the past few days, we've made our own routines and connected our lives again."

"The lives we lead are separate and they only interconnect for Niko's sake. That is different than living each day together, exposing each other to the good and the bad parts of ourselves. We can make the first part work, but we have already proven that we cannot live together."

"But—"

"Ashanti," I stand, "I did not want you to leave Japan. I was willing to change for you, but you chose to leave me and I accepted it. Now, time has passed and that desire to be what you wanted, to change myself for you… it left."

She steps closer to me. Her robe sways over her dark feet. "What attracted us to each other hasn't changed."

I step back before she can touch me. My face impassive, I remind her, "What drove us apart has not changed either."

Her expression crumbles with hurt. Inside the deepest chambers of my heart, I feel a prick of guilt. Had I not gotten involved with her, had I walked past her in Japan, had we decided to go our separate ways without sleeping together, would her life be this damaged? Would those tears be in her eyes?

I would not give up Niko for anything but, in this moment, I grieve the life Ashanti could have had, the marriage she could have had, the career she could have had, if we had never met.

"For Niko's sake, I hope we can continue to remain friends," I say.

Ashanti glances down. "Are you rejecting me because of that girl?"

"Even if Dejonae had not been in my life, I would not be interested."

"That's quite," she blinks rapidly, "that's quite decisive."

The gurgle of the water is all that can be heard as Ashanti gets her emotions under control. I watch the pool lights dance against the beach chairs. It's a deep and unnatural blue, almost as if we are both stuck in a dream.

"I, uh,… I guess… goodnight, Ryo." Ashanti turns and plods to the guest house like a listless ghost.

* * *

THE NEXT MORNING, my mother informs me that Ashanti left early.

"She is only going to move out of her old house and finalize the divorce," Mother warns. "She will be coming back."

"Did you know about her divorce? Is that why you were trying to push us back together?"

"A family should be together." She twines two fingers. "Original families are better."

"That is not always true."

"It is true," she says stubbornly. Tracing her hands in the air, she explains, "Father and mother. Down to the child. See? Simple." She rakes her hands through the air, marking invisible lines in multiple directions. "But see this? Father. Step-mother. Step-father. Mother. Child. Confusing." She shakes her head. "Not good."

"I am dating Dejonae now. How unfair would it be to her if I left her for Ashanti?"

"You leave her to go back to the original. She is not the original. She will never be the original."

I realize that fighting my mother on this would be pointless. Abandoning the topic, I get Niko ready for school.

Akira drives us as usual. She asks no questions about the dinner. I assume my mother has already told her everything.

The morning is quiet.

Dejonae greets me at work after her class. She shows no sign of trauma from the night before.

The day passes and bleeds into another.

Two days.

Three.

A week.

Two weeks.

My mother returns to Japan.

I relay Dejonae's greetings myself, not wanting her to suffer any cold words from my mother's lips.

After returning from the airport, I get a call from Adam. We discuss the MTB fervently until I sense a presence at the door of my office.

Dejonae is leaning against the doorway, one jean-clad leg propped over the other. Her lips arch up in wicked invitation.

"I apologize, Adam. Can you repeat that?" I ask.

He speaks, but the words slip out of my head like slime.

Embarrassing.

Almost as bad as the nights in bed with a cell phone plastered to my ear, listening to Dejonae talk about her day, her dreams, her challenges. Helping her work through them with a different perspective. Laughing about things that only we can understand.

These days are almost a little too easy, time slipping away in a brush of the calendar on the wall.

"It's time for the weekly management meeting. Should I hold the elevator... *boss?*"

My lips curl up. "Thank you, Miss Williams."

I abruptly end the call with Adam, shut off my laptop and walk beside her to the elevator. We keep a professional distance. But once the doors slide shut, I obliterate the space between us and press her against the wall.

She smiles. "Careful. There are cameras."

"What are you doing this evening?"

"Me? I planned to go see my parents. Why?"

"Your parents?" I contemplate it for a moment. "I'd like to join you."

"What?" Her jaw drops.

The doors open.

I step away from her and calmly walk out.

Her legs struggle to maintain my stride. I slow down so we can walk in step.

Dejonae gives me a suspicious look. "Why do you want to meet my parents?"

"We have been dating for some time now."

"And?"

"And I have been meaning to meet your parents."

"Mr. Sazuki."

"Morning, sir."

I lift a hand in greeting and stride past my employees.

Dejonae casts them a quick nod before lowering her voice. "That is a big step."

"I would have taken that step a long time ago if I had it my way," I tell her.

She frowns up at me.

I dig my fingers into the door handle to keep from touching her. "After you, Miss Williams."

"Thank you, Mr. Sazuki," she grinds out.

The room is full already. I abhor tardiness and it has trickled into the psyche of all the employees.

"Mr. Sazuki." Miss Cottingham rises when I enter.

I wave her back to her seat.

She and Dejonae exchange frosty looks.

They have developed a functional working relationship, but the scandal with the reporter left its mark.

Dejonae takes her seat around the table. The harsh look she floats my way informs me that the conversation is not over.

I wipe my chin to keep my smile away. This is not the time and place to expose how amusing I find her.

After settling in my chair, I start the meeting. We discuss the MTBs, which the instructors have been training with for a few weeks now. We then discuss the group classes and our ability to handle an influx of students.

Since the article's release, we have been receiving requests not only from parents, but from churches, schools and community centers who wish to participate in the program.

While the admin give their presentations on how they are choosing students, I find my eyes straying to Dejonae. She is listening intently to the discussion but, when she feels me watching her, her eyes falter.

I have iron concentration... unless she is in the room.

Her eyes narrow at me.

I glance down to hide my smile.

The room falls quiet.

"Mr. Sazuki, did you have something to say?"

I straighten immediately. "No. Carry on."

The presenter gives me a strange look before proceeding.

Dejonae laughs behind her hand. I give her a sharp look, but she does not quiver as others would. Her eyes continue to tease me.

When it is her turn to speak, she gets up and gives her speech with confidence.

"So far, students have made immense progress and that's largely due to the instructors and to the early adoption of the MTB. We're seeing a better grasp of concepts such as rhythm and timing.

But one of the hardest things we're dealing with right now is belief."

I set my chin on my fist, riveted.

"When someone is told from a young age that they *can't* do something, it gets difficult to change that mentality when they're older. What we're seeing is students making progress and doing well, but not believing that they are. It's causing a high turnover rate."

Her eyes dart to me. I give her a small, encouraging smile.

She returns it with a faint smile of her own. Her voice carries steadily through the room.

"I think students who are wavering in confidence should have some kind of affirmative project."

"What kind of project?" I ask.

"It could be a small five minute performance for their families or their schools. A concert at a hospital. Somewhere they *see* the impact their music is making."

"That's a waste of time and resources," Miss Cottingham interjects. "We can't go around worrying about every student who lacks confidence. That's not our job. Our job is to teach them music."

"We can put all the information in their heads and strap more and more MTBs to their bodies to help them, but it won't change anything if they don't believe they can do it."

Mumbles of agreement echo through the room.

But Dejonae is not done.

She plants a hand on her hip. "If our job was only to teach music, then why did most of you leave your previous positions to come and work here? Wasn't it to inspire? Wasn't it to encourage the belief that music belongs to the deaf community too?"

Pride swells in me, causing my chest to inflate.

Dejonae has never backed down from a challenge, whether it is a simple game or a challenge of her authority. Even if her responsibilities are on a smaller scale compared to mine, there is much I am learning from her conflict management skills.

The meeting reaches a smooth conclusion with a few instructions from me and clarifications from the other members.

I text Dejonae to stay behind.

Everyone files toward the door while she remains seated, pretending to fiddle around with her bag.

I push my chair back and walk to the door. After the last person leaves, I secure it shut and turn to her with a heavy look.

"If you had something to say, you could have said it in your office."

"My office has too many windows and I do not trust the blinds." I gesture to the bright overhead lights, the quiet air conditioning unit and the exposed brick walls of the conference room. "Look. No windows."

"I knew you would do this eventually." She tosses her head.

I advance on her. "Do what?"

"Abuse your power."

I drop my arms over her chair, caging her in. "What do you have against me seeing your parents?"

She rolls her eyes. "I don't *know*. Maybe the fact that you're older and you have a daughter and it's kind of a lot to take in."

"You have not mentioned me at all?"

"This is our dirty little secret, remember?" She fiddles with one of my shirt buttons.

I narrow my eyes.

I am tired of keeping us a secret. If I had my way, I would announce it dryly and succinctly, as I do everything that is important to me.

"Dejonae," I say softly, straightening up and leaning against the table, "do you doubt me when I say that I am devoted to you?"

"Of course not." Her eyes dart away.

I press my lips together.

Jealousy is a natural thing. I still seethe when I see her ex-boyfriend hovering around her.

But I let him be.

Because I trust her.

And I trust that I treat her so well, she would not even think to leave me.

Does she not trust me the same?

A warm hand falls on my thigh, turning me to liquid silver. "Are you upset?"

"It is fine. I will not mention meeting your parents again."

How strange.

Disappointment. Yearning.

All feelings I thought had died along with my first marriage.

And yet, Dejonae has my heart in a chokehold. When am I going to stop falling for her? When will I reach the end of this obsession? Why is it so much harder to remain balanced and distant when it comes to her?

Her lips quirk up. "You're cute when you sulk."

"A grown man does not sulk."

She shakes her head. "Did you know your dimples flash when you pout?"

Intent on proving my point, I pounce across the table and kiss her so passionately that her chair goes flying backwards.

We bounce into the wall.

Dejonae gasps. "What was that?"

"Proof that I am not angry. Or petulant. Or any other emotion that you wish to tease me about. I respect you and I will follow what you want. There should be no confusion about that."

She smiles and jumps out of the chair, wrapping her arms, legs and mouth around me. I grab her tighter, sipping from her lips as if she is rare, premium *sake*. A liquor I could easily get drunk on.

My fingers skate across her jeans and cup the back pockets. I kiss her ferociously, desperate for every stroke of her lips.

Her limbs turn languid, fingers sliding off my hand and melting against my shoulders as if she has lost all bones. Her low moan slides against my neck and invites me to do my absolute worst.

Do not worry, kitten. I will.

I carry her to the desk, setting her on the edge of it and keeping her thighs spread. Her mouth is pure danger against mine, unleashed desire, the hottest flames.

I press into her, finding the center of her with my trousers. She bucks her hips, every whimper skittering out of her bruised lips telling me that I am not the only one who wishes to take things to the next level.

My thirst for Dejonae has been burning me up inside. Every night when I have to roll out of bed for a cold shower, every glimpse of her dark lips in the middle of a meeting, every brush of her hand and sound of her laughter drives me to the brink.

I slip my hand under her T-shirt.

Delirious.

Desperate.

I need more of her skin. More of her body.

She kisses me urgently, her hands skating through my hair. Every flicker of her tongue, every taste of her lips, every nip of her teeth propels me forward.

When did I lose my rational mind? When did I become this beast?

I only know that Dejonae's mouth holds the key to every pleasure I wish to unlock. Plump and brown and divine. It feels like the deepest levels of intimacy just to press her mouth to mine.

She has never failed to kiss me back with a passion that meets or exceeds my own. Even now, her fingers tangling and tugging on my hair, she is part beast herself.

Only a soft knock on the door and a quiet *'is someone in here?'* forces me to pull back.

My eyes land on Dejonae. She is stunning in the harsh artificial lights, eyes dazed, curls messy, and breath thin.

I enjoy touching her.

But the pain of ripping myself away without being fulfilled is beginning to affect me. I am holding on to my restraint by a thin thread. Every bone in my body wishes to tear her apart without mercy.

Another knock sounds.

Dejonae hides her head in my chest.

Panting hard, she blinks at me. I feel her fingers playing with my shirt and glance down to see her looking stunned.

"When did I start to unbutton you?" she murmurs, flapping my shirt.

Winding a honey-tinged curl around my finger, I smooth it back into place.

"Ignore them. They will go away." I press my forehead against hers, breathing hard. "And you can continue."

A slow, knowing smile spreads over her face. "I'd kind of prefer to continue on something softer." She pats the table. "Preferably a mattress."

My head squeezes.

A wild, hot, mutinous adrenaline surges straight to my pants.

"Tonight?" I croak.

Sacrilege, my body roars.

Tonight is too long.

I want her right *now*.

There is another knock. *"Hello?"*

"We are having a meeting!" I snap.

Outside the room, it goes quiet.

Dejonae laughs softly.

I do not.

"Tonight?" I ask her again, waiting for confirmation.

She nods.

My eyes burn into her. I cannot wait to fill her so roughly that she forgets her own name.

Which is not the best thought to have circling through my brain when she says, "Yes, tonight I'd like you to meet my parents."

CHAPTER 19
BOILING TO THE TOP

DEJONAE

"Don't be nervous," I breathe out and shake my hands at my sides.

Sazuki gives me an amused look. He shifts the gift he brought for my parents to his other hand. "You should take your own advice."

I glare at him. "My parents are loving, welcoming people. They're going to accept you."

"Then why are you sweating?" Sazuki removes his handkerchief from his suit pocket and dots at my face.

"Don't." I swat his hand. "You're going to mess up my makeup."

"I did not."

"Yes, you did." I grab his hand and inspect the handkerchief in the porch's golden glow. There's brown foundation smeared across the pristine white cloth. "Look at that." My hands flutter around my face. "Do I look awful?"

"You look beautiful," he says, his voice deep and rumbly.

My skin tingles.

For a second, the nerves flee, replaced with a deep and throbbing desire to touch him.

But it skitters away when I remember where we are.

And why we're here.

I suck in a deep breath and pound my fist against the door.

"Coming!" my mother yells.

I have a mini-heart attack.

"You were not this nervous to meet my mother," he points out.

"Because you already married a black woman once. Ashanti took the brunt of all this—" I gesture to the door—"for me."

His lips twitch. "I do not know why I feel slightly insulted."

"I didn't mean it *like that*. It's just that my parents haven't really… I mean they're not *racist* or anything, but you're a lot of… unexpected things."

"Japanese? Older? A divorcee with a child?"

"All of the above." I glance behind me at the street. "Is it too late to bolt?"

The door swings open, cutting off my escape plan.

My mother and father stand together in the doorway. Mom is wearing her favorite apron over a flowered dress. Her hair is done up in a swoop and pearl earrings glitter from her ears.

She looks like a million bucks.

Dad is spiffy too in an ironed, button-down shirt, black slacks and his 'church' shoes, black loafers that are so shiny I can see my reflection like I'm looking at glass.

I don't understand why they're dressed like this.

I don't understand why they're smiling like that.

I don't understand *anything*.

"Come in. Come in." Mom gestures with a thin, graceful hand.

I shoot her a *what's going on* look when I pass her by. Sazuki is right behind me, towering over me with his broad shoulders and sexily stern face.

He and my parents should switch their expressions. I thought Sazuki would be the nervously grinning one and my parents would be the calm, serious ones.

What is going on?

"Mom, dad." I clear my throat. "This is my, um," my heart pounds, "my boyfriend, Mr. Sazuki."

"You don't actually call him Mr. Sazuki, do you?" Dad scrunches his nose.

I blink rapidly.

"No, she does not." Sazuki sticks out a hand. "Nice to meet you, sir."

"And you." Dad gives his hand a good shake.

"Mrs. Williams, I can see where Dejonae and Yaya get their beauty."

My eyes nearly bug. Who is this charming Sazuki? And when did he learn to kiss butt like that?

Mom laughs. "Oh, how sweet."

"Are you calling me ugly?" Dad smacks his belly and gives Sazuki a hard glare.

"No, sir." Unruffled, Sazuki motions to him. "I'm saying you're a very lucky man to have chosen such a beautiful woman as your wife."

Dad booms out a laugh. "I know, son. I thank God every day."

Son?

Am I in the Twilight Zone?

Dad and mom usher Sazuki around the table where they've prepared a feast. I only gave them a couple hours notice, so I'm surprised by the three different casseroles and glazed chicken that they managed to whip up.

"Did you forget something?" I call to them from the living room.

Mom drags her face out of Sazuki's personal space long enough to ask, "What, dear?"

"Me?" I wave. "Hello. I'm your biological daughter."

Dad booms out a laugh. "She got her comedic timing from me."

Sazuki smiles.

I scrunch my nose and drift over to them. "Yaya couldn't make it?" I ask, sitting around the table.

"She had a photoshoot."

My shoulders slump. I'm happy for her, but I wish she could be here.

Sazuki pats my thigh. "We can visit her next week if you would like."

My heart inflates with excitement. I miss my sister more than I could ever express.

Mom and dad exchange looks.

Dad clears his throat. "So Sazuki, how old are you? What are your goals in life? Where do you see yourself in ten years? And what do you like about my daughter?"

"Dad," I groan.

"It's a viable question, baby girl."

I bury my face in my hands.

Sazuki carefully and methodically answers every question. After working with him for so long, I've observed just how much attention he pays to details. Tiny things that most people wouldn't fret over are important to him. It's what makes him so successful.

"Your daughter and I are similar in all the ways that count. We both value family. We both have a passion for music and the deaf community. And we both fight for what we believe in, although we do so using different methods."

I take his hand beneath the table and squeeze.

Dad leans forward. "So the age thing…" He gestures between us. "It isn't a factor for you?"

"Her age is not a deterrent for me. We teach each other." He strokes my knuckles with his thumb. "I have changed in many ways since meeting Dejonae. She inspires me to not only be a better man, but a better leader and a better mentor."

Mom clutches her heart. "That's so sweet."

Dad arches an eyebrow, still unconvinced. "Why do you have so much interest in the deaf community?"

"My daughter is deaf."

Dad freezes.

Mom goes still.

I was hoping this wouldn't come up yet.

"A daughter?" Mom gasps.

"Yes."

I hold my breath as silence falls.

Then dad booms out a laugh. "How old is she? When can we meet her? Does she like brownies? My wife can whip up a mean double chocolate brownie."

Sazuki looks momentarily stunned. Throughout the interrogation, he's remained unbothered by my parent's prodding, but for the first time, he seems a little emotional.

He blinks rapidly and stutters, "Yes. Yes, she likes brownies."

"I remember what it was like for me when I first learned that my baby was deaf. I felt like I'd done something wrong," mom says. "Like God was punishing me for a mistake I'd made in the past. I didn't realize that having a child like Yaya would be one of the biggest blessings in my life."

"Again, what am I? Chopped liver?" I mutter to break the tension.

Mom smiles. Then her eyes switch to Sazuki and linger. "I think the work you're doing at the foundation is incredibly important. And I also want to say, as one parent to another, that I appreciate," her voice breaks and dad has to rub her back in encouragement, "how…" mom gathers herself to finish, "…much you've had to endure because you refused to let the world count your child out before she'd even begun." A tear leaks down her cheek and she sops it up with a handkerchief. "I think it's amazing that you're making a difference, not only in your daughter's life but in all the kids like her. And I think someone that kind and caring will certainly treat my daughter well."

Dad tips his head back as if that'll reverse the tears.

Sazuki pushes his chair out, stands and bows deeply to my parents.

They both look shocked.

Sazuki stays bowed for five seconds and when he rises, his eyes are a little red. "Thank you for your trust in me. I will not let you down."

Dad chuckles nervously. "A-alright. Let's eat."

Dinner is a loud, boisterous affair. Sazuki talks much more than usual, not that dad gives him a choice. The interrogation continues when dad pulls him to the living room to show off the baby albums.

I help mom in the kitchen.

Sazuki glances at me from the sofa, his eyes softening as if to say *do you need me?*

I shake my head.

He nods and returns his attention to dad.

"He doesn't say much." Mom rinses a dish. "I don't think we've ever had a quiet one in our family."

"His throat is probably on fire. Tonight is the most I've ever heard him talk."

Mom smiles tenderly. "He's very attentive to you."

"Is he?"

"He has these little moments where he'll do a quick side glance, as if he's checking that you're okay and you don't need anything. When you pushed out your chair to go to the bathroom, he pushed out his chair too to make room for you. They're tiny things, but they paint a picture."

"He treats me well."

She nods and sets the plates in the drainer.

"I… didn't expect you and dad to be so open."

"Open?"

"To him." I face her. "Did Yaya tell you about him beforehand?"

"She did not."

"Then why aren't you…"

"What? Throwing a tantrum? Screaming about how he's too old for you? That you're too young to be a mother to a child you didn't create? That his family might not treat you well because of your dark skin?"

"All of that."

"Of course we're concerned. Especially about that last part." She pins her lips together. "But the world is going to rage against you for those differences at every turn. We don't want to join them." She finishes with the dishes and sets the dish cloth to dry over the faucet. Her sweet brown eyes stare into mine. "We raised you well enough to make the right choice."

"Your mother is right."

I jump when I hear my dad's voice. He left Sazuki in the living room with the albums and is standing in the kitchen.

My bottom lip trembles when he walks around and gives me a hug. "I've lived my life showing you girls how a husband is supposed to treat his wife by the way I treat your mother. I've given you all the tools you need to choose someone who'll treat you the same way. If this is the guy you picked, then I'm going to trust—not in you, but in everything I've taught you about what you deserve."

My eyes get misty. "Dad."

"Group hug!" Mom yells to Sazuki. "Young man, get over here!"

Sazuki makes a sound of soft confusion.

Mom urges him over. I don't see him, since I'm wedged against dad's side, but I smell his minty fragrance and feel his arms wrap around me.

Mom joins our family huddle and we hug for a few seconds.

"Alright," dad breaks the hug, "let's get straight into the dessert. While we're eating, I'll show you all of Dejonae's awkward and embarrassing childhood pictures."

"Dad!" I shriek.

"I would really like to see that, sir," Sazuki says dryly. *The traitor.*

"You're not showing him those albums." I groan.

"Yes, I am. Do you know how long I've waited for this day?" Dad cackles like an evil henchman and dances out of the kitchen while I chase after him.

* * *

S<small>AZUKI DRIVES</small> me home and walks me up to my apartment.

Our hands are linked.

The silence between us is easy and welcome. We don't need to say a lot to feel content. That's something I've learned from him. To be calm in the silences.

"Thank you for coming with me tonight," I say, stopping in front of my front door.

"Your parents are lovely. It was an honor."

"They like you."

"And they love you." His eyes are dark and intense. "Very much. It is clear how close you all are. Your father wants you to move back in."

"I know." My smile is wry. "One of the hardest decisions I made was to move out, but I wanted to see the world and have my own independence. I couldn't do that under their roof. They would have smothered me with love."

"A painful way to go."

I laugh. "Your jokes are getting better."

"Your father's wit must have rubbed off on me." His lips arch up at the corners.

I fiddle with my keys, glance down, glance up again.

The silence turns heated.

Tension crackles between us.

"Is Niko waiting for you?" I ask.

"I already kissed her goodnight before leaving."

"And do you, um, have to go back?" The ridges of the key dig into my finger.

Rather than answer, he lifts his phone and dials a number.

I watch with heated breath as he speaks without taking his eyes off me, "Akira, I will not be home until morning."

"I figured." Akira's voice sounds muffled, but the words are clear.

Sazuki ends the call and arches an eyebrow.

"Until morning?" I raise my chin, fighting not to look as nervous as I feel. "Is it going to take all night?"

"I have waited a long time for you, kitten. I do not plan to rush."

My heart swells with longing and hot anticipation. I barely manage to open the door before Sazuki drags me inside as if he owns the place and pushes me against the wall. His eyes drill into me, filled with an untameable heat.

I feel the burn sweep up my skin like I'm standing in the middle of a giant oven.

"Aren't you," I swallow, "going to close the door?"

Still watching me, he calmly kicks the door shut.

I try to breathe. My throat is clogged.

I feel undone. Turned inside out.

And he hasn't even touched me yet.

But that gaze…

It's always been intense.

Always been searing.

But tonight, I feel it dig under my skin, singeing me, warning me that I will never be the same after he's done with me.

Sazuki's arms slide around my waist, dragging me into him. The motion is smooth, but I still gasp when we collide.

He puts a hand to my chin and tilts my head back. With excruciating tenderness, he plants a kiss on my upturned face. The heat of his lips on my forehead makes me suck in a breath. I hold that breath as he kisses my cheeks.

And then finally, his mouth falls on mine.

I release my breath, my nerves, my sanity.

I kiss him back, unleashing the need deep inside me.

I want to trust you.

Sazuki savors my mouth, kissing me with such gentleness that my heart stops beating.

A quiet, simmering heat bubbles to the surface. It takes over every part of me, whipping into a blaze that begs to be set free.

I clutch at his fancy button-up shirt, my fingers trembling, my knees melting, my body tightening as his kiss deepens.

The concentration required to get him out of his shirt is stripped away from me when he pushes me harder against the wall, effectively flattening me against him.

The feel of his desire makes my head spin, but his kiss shows no sense of time or urgency. It goes on forever, attacking my mouth with the vigor of a boa constrictor taking its time to coil around its prey. Only… this mouse enjoys falling into the spell.

"Sazuki," I moan.

He snarls in a way that conveys exactly what he wants from me, *patience*.

But I have none.

I slide my hands around him. Untucking his shirt from his pants, I delight in the freedom to roam his back muscles. His body is lean and warm. Smooth skin beneath my palm.

He makes a deep sound in the back of his throat and I'm almost swept away in a wave of passion.

The kiss gets harder. Each insistent stroke ignites my senses, ripping apart every last ounce of restraint I have. I'm practically burning with desire. It's too hot. Too violent. How did we manage to deny it for so long?

My hands roam lower, fishing at his belt.

He grunts and thrusts against me. My hands are immediately captured and pinned over my head in a quick but gentle maneuver. His fingers trace a symbol over the undersides of my wrists as his mouth brands me with more torturously languid kisses.

I should have known Sazuki would drag it out.

He always has to be in control. Always has to do things his way. Always has to make it count.

"Relax," he whispers.

"Let's move this along," I whisper back.

He drops his chin to my ear and nuzzles the lobe. "The more you fight, kitten, the more you will beg."

His words send a thrill through me.

Sazuki seems to revel in my impatience. His kiss drips like honey to my neck, sweet and sticky and addictive.

I shudder in helplessness drowned by flaming need.

It's so intense that it rockets me to a new level of desperation. One I never knew existed.

But I never run from a challenge.

Since my upper half is currently pinned against the wall, I lift one leg and wrap it around Sazuki's waist. His obsessive sipping of my pulse stops abruptly when I rub against him.

"I don't think you want to play that game with me," he growls.

"I've never played a game I can't win." I meet his eyes.

When he descends again, it's like a tsunami slamming against the coast. He attacks my mouth until it throbs in submission, licking, nipping, bruising—a chaotic blend of wicked delight.

His tongue takes command and wipes every thought clean from my mind, so I don't even realize that I'm airborne. When I come back to myself, Sazuki's arms are around my waist, lifting me so my legs dangle off the floor.

I press against his hard chest, noting the dark glint in his liquid black eyes. If I saw smoke escaping from his gaze, I would believe it. His smolder is hot enough to melt my clothes straight off.

"Bedroom," he rumbles, his heart drumming against mine.

My fingers tremble when I point.

Sazuki's crackling gaze and savage half-smirk is a gunshot warning. Some dark, dangerous part of me comes alive in response.

He sweeps me into the bedroom that's way too small for a man as big and charismatic as him. He doesn't bother turning on the lights and makes his way to my bed in three confident steps.

Shoot. I didn't clean my bedroom this morning. Clothes are still on the bed from where I dragged them out of my closet as I bemoaned what to wear to my parents tonight. The dresser is filled with all the natural hair products I emptied to get my hair moisturized and curly.

I feel Sazuki's weight against me and his fingers under my chin. "Come back to me, kitten."

My entire body tingles at the pet name.

I have no idea where it came from. He's never called me that before.

Anyone else, and I wouldn't let them. But the way Sazuki's deep voice rasps out the word makes it sound exciting and sexy.

For a moment, we stare at each other.

Not a sound breaks the silence.

It's just me and him.

And the pulsing desire that's mounting over my back and pawing at my stomach.

His mouth descends on mine.

Slowly. Torturously. A punishment.

He kisses every thought out of my mind until nothing else matters.

Soon, his mouth rips away, leaving me reeling with want, and slides across my neck and shoulders. I grip him, wondering why his shoulders are rippling. It's not until he throws a handful of clothes off the bed that I realize he's cleaning up.

I stiffen.

His hands cup my hips. "You are overthinking."

"If I'd known it would be tonight, I would have cleaned up and bought candles or something."

"Next time, you bring the candles. I will bring the roses."

My lips arch up.

His hands slide down my body with a possessive heat. "Do you know how badly I have wanted you?"

Molten desire surges through me, molding me to his hands, to the friction of his palm through my jeans.

I want his touch on my skin so badly. But I don't have to express it. Sazuki unbuttons my pants with his long, slender hands. He drags it off in three jerks, stopping to kiss every inch of skin that it exposes.

My teeth bite down in a tortured hiss. He succeeds in

undressing me and yet the kisses don't stop. Never ending, his lips coat every inch of me, determinedly marking all my pleasure points as if he came with one intention and one intention only—to learn my body in explicit detail.

I'm quivering, panting, spinning out of control by the time he's conquered every inch there is to conquer.

The lights that blind my eyes are far too violent.

I shake with it.

So does he.

He's so beautiful, muscles tensing and eyes wild and hot.

Screw it. I don't mind losing this game.

As long as he puts me out of my misery.

As long as I get to feel every inch of him too.

"Please," I beg.

There's a darkness in his eyes.

Sweat on his forehead.

The strain of holding on to his restraint is bulging to the surface. He's about to snap. About to give out completely.

I lift my fingers to his lips, grazing their wetness, teasing his stubble. He kisses the tips of my fingers, breathing out my name like a prayer.

My pulse quickens. "Why are you hesitating?"

He looks at me with eyes that are more beast than man, darker than the blackest night and wilder than a mystical creature set free to wreak havoc.

"I do not wish to hurt you, but I do not think I can be gentle," he growls.

My body jolts with a desire so sharp I wonder if I'm bleeding into the sheets.

Ryotaro Sazuki—perpetually unruffled, unbothered, and unfeeling—crippling beneath his need for me makes me feel like I'm unraveling in a vast and endless universe of stars.

"I won't break," I whisper. "I can take it."

His eyes pierce mine, glimmering with a fire that could wipe out an entire city.

"Then hold on."

It is his final warning before he sinks into me and shows me what it means to be *ravaged*.

* * *

It is morning when we collapse into bed for the last time, not to dive into each other, but to settle into a tangle of legs and sheets and fall asleep.

A faint chirping sound pierces my dreams.

I try to ignore it, but my thoughts are already churning.

Someone is beside me.

I feel his warmth. The heaviness of his breath on my forehead. The scrape of his stubble on my flesh.

Sazuki.

Images of last night zip through my subconscious mind. My fingers digging into the sheets. Sazuki grunting in Japanese, words I didn't understand delivered in a tone that I had no choice but to obey. Pain and pleasure colliding in a fit of sweet insanity.

No matter what I imagined being with Sazuki would be like—and there were many nights when I dreamed of it—what happened last night blew my fantasies out of the water.

Is he made of some kind of magic?

I saw so many stars it's a miracle I'm not a blind mess.

The chirping sound peals again, shaking me from that place in-between sleep and consciousness.

I glance up and observe Sazuki lying next to me. Pale skin stretched over lean, toned muscles. Broad shoulders bruised from my lips. Long legs covered only in a pair of boxers. His hair is hanging over his eyes, making him look boyish. But I dare not assume that innocence is real. He is all man. A surreal bundle of pleasure wrapped in the face of an Asian prince.

My phone chirps again. I reach for it.

Sazuki curls me into his body to keep me from rolling away. He captures my hand and pins it against his chest.

I wiggle against him, but that only brings me closer. And now my hair is all in my face. Thanks to his grabby hands, my curls are a rocking, steaming mess. Sweat slicks the sheets and makes cuddling hot and uncomfortable.

Even in his sleep, he won't let me go.

"Sazuki," I whisper.

"Mm." He tucks his chin against my head, fitting me into him like a puzzle piece.

"My phone."

"Not yet," he rumbles.

I smile at his hoarse voice. He was very... vocal last night and it's no surprise that he hasn't yet recovered.

My body turns languid again.

"Sazuki."

His eyes remain closed.

"I need to use the bathroom."

He releases me a smidge. I wiggle from under his arms, grab the button-down shirt that somehow landed on the dresser and put it on.

The shirt smells like him. I take a deep whiff, loving the fragrance. It feels like I'm getting a big hug from him.

After using the bathroom, I tiptoe back into the bedroom and watch the sun dance over Sazuki's back.

No, not Sazuki.

Ryotaro.

I grin secretly to myself.

I wonder how he'll react when he hears me using his first name. I'm used to calling him Sazuki, but after last night, it doesn't really make sense to keep being distant when we were, quite literally, the closest we have ever been.

Leaning against the dresser with one leg raised and resting on the bottom drawer, I check my phone.

My heart stops when I see the text messages.

Hi, Dejonae. This is Ashanti.

Can I see you downstairs?

I read and reread the message.

She's downstairs?

At my apartment?

Another message comes in.

I'll come up if you prefer.

My eyes jump to the bed where Sazuki is still sleeping. The air smells like every wicked thing he did to me last night. The sheets bear the evidence of our frantic desire for one another.

I don't want Ashanti anywhere near this. Just the memory of her, conjured up in these text messages, makes me feel dirty. Like I took something that doesn't belong to me.

I shake my head.

Be strong, Dejonae.

I text her back and let her know that I'll be down. Rather than brush my teeth and fix myself up, I head outside wearing Ryotaro's shirt.

Ashanti is in the foyer. She turns with a sweep of her long black hair and fancy pumps. Her dress is full of polka dots and shimmers down to the floor.

She really is beautiful.

Which makes me feel petty, like I should hate her more because she's so attractive.

Her eyes slide down my attire. "I thought I saw Sazuki's car in the parking lot."

"How do you know where I live? In fact, how did you get my number?"

"Akira. That's the answer to both those questions." She smiles.

"What do you want?" I fold my arms over my chest and keep my tone chilly.

"I saw a café nearby, but I don't think you're dressed appropriately for that. Did you just get out of bed?"

Her tone rubs me the wrong way. "I don't think that's any of your business."

"Dejonae," her grin is sharp even if it's pretty, "put your weapon down. You and I have many things in common. We both enjoy music, we both love Niko and we both fell for the same man."

"It's not like we're signing up to be the next sister-wives, Ashanti. You and I don't need to have anything in common and you don't need to be here either. Please leave."

"He has great stamina, doesn't he?"

My entire body stops cold. I turn slowly around.

"*Kimochi ii.*" She points a soft smile at the window as if she's imagining something. Her eyes hold a distant wistfulness.

A slap to the face would have been less shocking. I suck in a sharp breath, grasping at thin air as my hands curl into fists.

"Do you know what it means?" Her heels click against the tile in a steady rhythm. Lowering her voice to an intimate hush, she mimics Sazuki's breathless panting. "It... feels... so... good."

My eyelashes flutter. I'm shaking with rage, with embarrassment, and with hurt. It's like she walked into my most sacred memory and tarnished it.

"If you'd like more translations, I can help with that." She rubs her chin. "Ryo doesn't talk a lot, but he gets strangely mouthy during—"

"*What* do you want?"

The smile finally leaves her face to reveal the true cruelty beneath. She tilts her head. "I came to inform you that I will always be right there, in every memory, at every event, and in every sacred moment between you and Ryotaro. I'm not going anywhere."

A sharp, fiery arrow plunges into my heart. I let it coat my words in venom. "You're sick."

She laughs.

"Does your husband know how obsessed you are with your ex?"

Ashanti gives me an *oh, aren't you cute* look.

"Didn't Sazuki tell you? I got a divorce."

Her words rock my entire world. "A divorce?"

"You know," she moves in closer, "at first I was going to play up the evil ex-wife role. Really throw all the ways you and Sazuki don't work in your face, but I think you already know that, deep down, you're nothing but a nice little detour for him. Every man wants a younger woman to bring a bit of excitement to his life. But it doesn't mean anything more than that. One day, he's going to tire of you as all men do of their toys."

"You drove all the way here thinking you'd accomplished something, didn't you? But in the end, you look petty, foolish and desperate." I fold my arms over my chest. "Thank you for your advice, but I should go. My boyfriend is in bed probably wondering where I am."

Her eyes twitch, but she hides it well. "Oh, this isn't advice. This is a warning." She leans forward. "I'm coming back for my family."

"What makes you think you can take them from me?" I grind out.

"I'm not going to take them." She flutters her eyelashes. "You're going to give them to me."

She's insane.

"Why would I do that?"

"Because you love Niko. That much I saw from the night you played piano together. You love my little girl like you pushed her out the womb yourself." Her laughter is tight. "And what Niko needs isn't for her parents to be fighting, cold and distant from each other. She doesn't need a tiny, inconsequential college student mucking up the family tree. She needs her mommy and daddy together because *that* will give her the future, the life, that she deserves."

My heart slams against my ribs.

"I trust you'll make the right decision, Miss Williams." Ashanti plucks a pair of sunshades out of her purse and slides them over her face. "Oh, remember. My offer for those translations is still valid."

CHAPTER 20
AFTER THE FALLING

SAZUKI

I AWAKEN TO AN EMPTY BED. The sun taunts me, dancing over the space where Dejonae should be.

I am a private man to my blood.

Yet, it bothers me to find myself alone.

Rolling to a sitting position, I glance at the open door leading into the hallway. I have a faint recollection of Dejonae slipping out of my arms, claiming she needed to use the bathroom.

Has she not returned yet?

I run a hand through my hair and imagine Dejonae skipping through her morning routine, trying to pretty herself up for me.

Unnecessary.

I have not met a more beautiful woman than her.

"Dejonae," I call, hoping she appears.

She does not.

I contemplate my next move with an air of disbelief. How did I stray so far off the path? How did she consume me to the point of insanity? I did not set out to fall in love with anyone. Especially not a woman who, on the surface, is my opposite in every way.

Yet here I am, waiting, head turned to the door like a dog restless before his owner comes home.

Enough.

I should find Dejonae and make her breakfast.

She must be sore and hungry.

I find my trousers on the floor. Zipping up my pants, I swipe my phone from the nightstand.

There is a message from Niko.

Where are you, dad?

The text forces me to remember my duties. I am not just a man, but also a father. It is time to return home.

My eyes skate around the room.

I skip over Dejonae's panties. Her jeans. Her bra.

Where is my shirt?

The front door opens.

I glance up in surprise. Did Dejonae leave while I was asleep?

I hurry to the living room. Dejonae has her back turned as she closes the door. She is wearing my shirt.

The sight of her in my clothing bewitches me. If I had the time, I would invade her again, run my hands through her frizzy hair and discover what she tastes like in the morning.

But the thought is quickly cast aside when she faces me, looking scattered and dazed. The expression sets me on edge instantly.

"Is something wrong?"

She jolts at the sound of my voice. Her eyes are strained. "You're up?"

I draw closer to her. "I was preparing to leave, but I will need my shirt."

She nods absently and walks past me. "I'll change."

The bathroom door opens and closes softly.

I frown at the heavy silence.

The air seems cold, bereft.

Is Dejonae feeling shy after the night we spent together? Or is it something more?

"Here." She appears in front of me and holds out my shirt.

I wrap my arms around her instead. Holding her close, I breathe in the scent of *us*, a musky essence baked into her skin and hair.

My heart senses that something is off.

But perhaps now is not the best time to pry it out of her. I am worried about Niko and conscious of the time. My duties for the day are demanding my attention. I have a meeting with the president of the local school for the deaf. I need to prepare for an inspection of the MTBs that are set to arrive soon.

Even knowing that I must leave, I cannot let her go.

Dejonae's arms remain lax at her sides. She does not hug me back.

I kiss her on the forehead. Once. Twice.

Reluctantly, I pull away and walk to the door though every molecule in my body wishes to stay.

Unacceptable.

I will have to marry her soon so that there is no need to part in the morning.

"I met Ashanti downstairs," Dejonae says abruptly.

A sense of doom rattles through me.

This conversation will not end well.

I look into Dejonae's wide, pretty brown eyes and all I can think about is how to defend myself.

"She wants to get back together with you." Something flickers in her expression. "Did you know that?"

I hesitate. "I did."

"You did." Her eyes narrow.

The silence fills the space between us, creating a gulf that I am desperate to scale.

"Why did you go down to meet her alone?"

"She asked to see me."

"You should have told me."

"That's not really the issue, Sazuki," she snaps.

My shoulders tense on impact.

I stare at her.

"She told me she'd gotten divorced." Dejonae's eyes lift to mine. Fury whips through her gaze. "That you already knew about it."

"I did know."

"And you kept it to yourself?" she accuses.

"It is not important."

"Not important?" Her voice rises. "Your ex-wife is leaving her husband. She came here to declare *ownership* over you and you thought that wasn't worth a mention?"

"Ashanti is simply confused."

"So now you're taking up for her?"

"Dejonae." My voice bristles with impatience.

"You didn't want to tell me that night when you found out she was coming to the city. You hid the fact that you'd been having breakfast with her in the mornings. And now you hide that she's getting divorced."

"My mother was the one who invited her to breakfast and that was weeks ago. Why are you bringing it up now?"

"Just because I didn't mention it doesn't mean it didn't hurt," she spits.

I blink in shock. "Dejonae, do not let her get into your head. I am not interested in going back to Ashanti. I told her that very clearly the last time we spoke."

"How are you so sure you don't want her back?"

"You should know the answer to that question better than anyone."

"That's not a straight answer, Sazuki."

My fingers curl into fists. I have done everything I can to assure Dejonae of my intentions. Why would she allow Ashanti to poison her mind?

Dejonae marches forward. "Ashanti plans to stay in the city. She wants to start over with you. She's pursuing you like a dog with a bone. How can either of us know what's going to happen in the future?"

My face goes blank. Perhaps the only option here is to let her fume.

She shakes her head. "More importantly, how can we work through this awkward, tangled mess if you keep holding everything close to the chest and leaving me to be the last to find out!"

My phone vibrates in my pocket.

It must be Niko.

"Do you know how humiliating that is for me? I'm dating you, but I know less about your life than she does!"

"There is no need to yell," I grind out.

Her eyes bug. "Is that all you can say to me? Did you not hear a *word* I just said?"

"Dejonae," my chest heaves on a sigh, "this is not the best time." I check my watch. "I need to leave, and you need time to cool off. We will discuss it later."

"No." Her expression turns stony.

My heart stops beating. "What do you mean 'no'?"

"I don't want to talk to you anymore."

My lips tighten. "Do not say things you don't mean."

"Do I look like I'm kidding?" She blasts me with an angry scowl.

"Be mature about this."

"So now I'm being immature? Me? I'm the one who's been open with you. I could have hid the fact that Ashanti and I met, but I told you immediately. I've been smiling and holding myself back because she's Niko's mother. She was someone you used to love. Now you dare to look at me and call *me* immature?"

"This matter is simple, Dejonae. I want you. I have wanted you from the start. But Ashanti is Niko's mother. I cannot simply *erase* her from my life. She will always be a part of it. This is something you will have to get used to."

Her eyelashes flutter. A look of utter betrayal crosses her face. "You're telling me to shut up and be the nice little mistress, is that it? No matter what, I will always be less important to you."

"That is not what I said. Why are you twisting my words?" Heat flushes my neck and the tips of my ears.

Her eyebrows hunker low over her stormy brown eyes. She tightens her mouth, looking off into the distance.

In a calmer voice, she says, "Knowing that, *expecting* that your ex will always be hovering around you with plenty of opportunities to make your heart waver, we should have been stronger. We should have been a unit. But we're not. We have two different ways of communicating and it's not working for me."

"What does that mean?" Pure panic tears at my throat.

Her eyes dart to the floor. "Let's just take some time to think."

"Think about what?" Desperation makes my voice rise. "I do not need to think. I am certain of what I want."

Her eyes get hazy. "But I'm not."

My chest knots tightly.

"Sazuki, I don't want to be hurt again."

My phone starts vibrating in my pocket. I ignore it.

"What do you want, Dejonae?"

"I want you to be certain of what *you* want."

"I am. How else should I express that to you?"

"I don't know."

Her answer rips a groan of frustration from my lips. "I am doing my best. I can't change that she is Niko's mother. I can't change that she lives here in the city. I can't erase my past. *What* do you want from me?"

"Like I said, let's take a pause and try to figure that out."

"Dejonae…"

"Your phone has been ringing for a while. Niko is probably waiting." Her expression is resigned. "Go."

It is my first time getting kicked out of anywhere.

I linger, unsure if it is pride or panic that keeps me in place.

"Leave," Dejonae hurls at me in a broken voice, "now."

When I walk away from her apartment, it feels as though I am getting buried alive.

* * *

With our relationship in limbo, my mood sours.

At work, I lack patience.

At home, I retreat into my shell.

The foundation is my own personal hell. It is where I am forced to see Dejonae every day. To look at her dark skin, her quiet frowns, her pensive brows and *not* touch her.

Every time I see her, it scrapes salt in the wound.

But her behavior toward me remains civil and detached.

Is she so unaffected by the distance?

It bothers me to think that I am the shaken one. I am determined not to give in first. Instead, I satisfy myself with watching her from afar like a crazed stalker, peering at her through the blinds in my office, calling more and more meetings and making random visits to the music rooms under the guise of checking on the students.

I pin my hands behind my back and stride through the brightly-lit hallway. The sound of a piano draws me nearer.

Miss Cottingham is sitting on a piano bench next to a small child. The MTB is hooked around the child's head and wrapped around his back. He picks through the music scale and smiles when he is rewarded with applause.

Miss Cottingham notices me standing there and she jerks forward. "Mr. Sazuki."

I motion for her to be seated.

Continuing down the hallway, I stop in front of Dejonae's door and take a deep breath before I open it.

She is standing next to a piano, wearing her signature T-shirt and jeans. Her curls are pulled back into a small ponytail, exposing the finer details of her face. Gloss shimmers on her lips, filling me with a raging urge that threatens to eat me alive.

I remember when that mouth softened under mine. I remember grazing her soft, perfect lips with gentle bites and slow, torturous thrusts of my tongue—

Enough, Sazuki. Or you will not be able to keep your distance.

Dejonae's fingers tap out a rhythm as her student plays hesitantly. The child stops and slumps her shoulders.

"You're doing great," Dejonae signs. "Let's try it again. Slowly."

The music starts once more.

I thirstily trace the slope of her eyebrows, the curls falling against her dark cheeks and the shape of her temptingly lush mouth.

Our last night together was unexpected but satisfying. Heated. The kind of collision that should have marked a new wave of happiness.

She was mine for such a short time. Or maybe the separation feels far too long. An eternity.

Her eyes are drawn to mine. When she sees me, her expression tightens.

"Can I help you?" Dejonae signs.

I shake my head.

She juts her chin down once and faces her student again, giving me her back. I feel the rejection like a gunshot to the chest.

But my pride rears its ugly head, refusing to back down.

Dejonae's eyes no longer glitter at me. Her sweet, light laughter no longer fills my ears. Our relationship is broken. The longer we pause, the more irreparable it becomes.

All I have left is my position as her boss.

I cannot jeopardize that lone connection.

I retreat and make my way to the rest of the music rooms. After my inspection, I pass Dejonae's door a second time, but she is not there.

"She left early," a voice says.

My muscles tense. "Jordan."

"She said she wasn't feeling well."

My eyes widen. Is she sick? Does she need to go to the hospital?

"She looked fine," Jordan says. "I don't think it was that serious."

I scowl at him. I do not want to receive these updates from her ex.

When I turn to walk away, Jordan stops me with a hand on my shoulder. Stunned, I glance down at where his pale fingers are wrapped around my suit jacket.

"Remove your hand if you do not want to lose it," I growl.

He pries his fingers off one by one. "I know you and Dejonae are dating."

I give him a warning look.

"Most of the office has no idea, but I was with Dejonae for a long time. She's always tough and determined, but it's obvious when she likes someone. She gets soft with them. She can't hide it."

I face him fully. Tilting my chin up, I snarl, "What is your point?"

"Dejonae was talking to someone in the office before she suddenly declared that she wasn't feeling well. Lady's tall, long black hair, pretty. Says she's your ex-wife."

Frustration tugs on my heart so sharply that my entire body jolts with it. "How long ago?"

"About five minutes."

Jordan blocks me when I try to sprint away.

"Look, Mr. Sazuki, I haven't said anything to you or to Deej about your relationship. I lost to you. I accepted that the moment I saw Dejonae smiling at you during that last meeting. I thought you made her happy and I was willing to keep fading into the background so that smile would stay on her face. But now?" He shakes his head slowly. "You're hurting her the same way I did. Deej doesn't deserve that."

"Who are *you* to lecture me?" I fume.

"I'm the guy who couldn't let her go but couldn't choose her either. I messed her up. I know that. I'm an idiot for letting her get away. But I'll be damned if I sit back and watch someone break her heart the same way. Twice. Deej deserves better than both of us."

"You have no idea what you are talking about." I push him out of my way and rush outside. The sun is blinding. Pedestrians stalk past, determined to get to their next destination. A car honks as it speeds by.

I do not see Dejonae anywhere.

Running past the foundation, I turn the curve and keep looking for her.

She is nowhere to be found.

With shaking hands, I call her.

The number goes straight to voicemail.

Gripping the phone tightly, I return to the foundation and take the elevator. The man slumping in the reflection of metal and stainless steel does not look like me. My hair is a mess from how often I've scrubbed my hands through it. My shirt is peppered with sweat. My eyes hold a sheen of panic.

What did Ashanti say to make Dejonae retreat? Why can't my ex-wife stay out of my personal life?

I storm into my office and find Ashanti sitting in the wingback chairs facing my desk. She rises slowly, a bright smile on her face.

"What are you doing here?" I huff, marching past her.

"You've really done it." Her eyes jump around my office. "The foundation you'd been talking about for years is finally here. And it's impressive. Who was your architect? That lobby is just... amazing."

"Ashanti," I growl.

"Did I come at a bad time?"

"If this is not about Niko, then I don't want to hear it."

"It *is* about Niko." Ashanti smoothes her dress. "She wants to know why Dejonae isn't coming around anymore."

I freeze. My eyes slowly swerve to my ex-wife. "She discussed that with *you*?"

"Well, she certainly can't discuss it with *you*." Ashanti gestures to my face. "What with you wearing that 'I hate everyone' scowl all the time. Niko is a very sensitive girl, Ryo. She knows there's something going on."

Because of you.

I want to blame her, but I can't get the accusation to stick. The problems Dejonae and I have would have sprung up eventually.

But if it hadn't been for Ashanti's interference, would the consequences have been so severe?

I round the desk and fall into my chair. "Dejonae and I are fine."

"That's not what she told me downstairs."

My fingers tense.

"We had a lovely chat," Ashanti throws one leg over the other and rests her elbow against it. "She went out of her way to assure me that you two were no longer together."

"She said that?"

"Not in so many words, but a woman knows."

My nostrils flare. "I will speak to Niko."

"And tell her what?" Ashanti shakes her head. "There's no need to confuse her, Ryo. See, this is why I didn't bring Rob around her too often. Relationships are so fragile. I didn't want her to get attached to people who would drop her after a break up." Ashanti leans back and dusts her hands. "I already told her that Dejonae won't be a part of her life anymore."

"Why would you say that?" My voice lashes out like a whip. "You had no right to do that."

She visibly startles and then licks her lips. "That is best for her."

"Ashanti," I rise to my full height, "I have put in effort to be respectful of you. And you are right, the best case scenario would have been for us to stay together and be a family for Niko. But we chose a different path. It is too late to turn back now. Niko will still have two parents who love her, even if they are not together."

"If you know us being together is the best scenario, then why don't we try again, Ryo?" She jumps to her feet and stalks toward the desk. Placing her fist on the surface, she leans forward. "How do we know that it's truly over for us, if we don't at least *attempt* to repair what was broken? Imagine how happy Niko would be to have her mom and dad back together again? Shouldn't we at least try for her sake?"

I clench my jaw, staring her down.

Ashanti takes my silence for agreement and smiles. She wraps dark fingers around her purse. "Call me when you're ready to talk. I'm willing to try couple's therapy, talking with your mom, whatever. As parents, we should do everything we can for Niko's sake."

When she is gone, I slump in my chair, staring at the ceiling and turning her request over in my head.

Did Dejonae really agree to the idea of me and Ashanti getting back together?

I thought we were on a break.

But if she thinks like that then...

It means we are truly over.

AKIRA OPENS the car door for me and steps aside. "Miss Williams is not with you again today."

"She requested her vacation time. I granted it."

"Interns do not have vacation time," Akira points out.

I remain silent.

She closes the door and drives to Niko's school.

It has been several days since my last conversation with Ashanti. She has not mentioned getting back together again explicitly, but she mentions the marriage therapy books she's read and the therapists she has been researching.

It makes every meeting strained and frustrating for me.

Akira clears her throat. "Did you eat today?"

I flip my tablet open and focus on my work.

"I saw the lunch I brought you in the trash yesterday." Her concerned eyes bore into me through the rear-view mirror. "You cannot keep skipping meals. You look as though you are wasting away."

I do not respond.

"Even your mother says you look pale."

"How would she know?" I swipe across the tablet.

"On your last video call, your cheeks were gaunt. She is thinking of flying back to America just to feed you."

I glance up. "Tell her not to waste her time. I am fine."

"Why do you lie, Ryotaro?"

"What would you have me say, Akira?" I fire back.

She keeps her mouth shut.

I sigh heavily and stare at the passing buildings. Should I curl into a ball and cry? Beg for Dejonae to come back to me when she does not trust me? Throw my responsibilities to my daughter away for my own happiness?

As long as Ashanti is in my life, Dejonae will never be at peace.

And as long as Niko is alive, I will always be connected to Ashanti.

We are at a stalemate.

There is nothing more I can do except work.

Unfortunately, Dejonae's absence has left a sinking crater where my passion for work should be.

The car slows in front of the middle school. Niko is sitting on a bench along with Beth, Bailey and Micheal. The children look rather subdued, despite all the colorful banners behind them advertising tonight's talent show.

Beth rubs Niko on the back. She says something to my daughter before they hug. Niko strides to the car. I help her get settled in and fix her seatbelt.

She stops me with a hand to my wrist. Her eyes hold a hint of anger.

"I can do it," she signs.

Stunned, I ease back and attach my own seatbelt.

Akira meets my eyes.

I arch an eyebrow in question.

She shrugs and shakes her head.

"Niko," I turn to her, "are you nervous about the show tonight?"

She shakes her head 'no'.

I set my tablet aside. "Will your friends be performing too?"

"Beth is going to change a tire."

"Oh, that's... well, that's something." I clear my throat. As expected for the daughter of Dawn Stinton. "What of the boys?"

She shrugs.

I tap my finger on my leg. Niko turns away from me, her eyes on the city passing by. I do not understand her attitude. We were fine before I sent her to sleep over at her mother's apartment.

"Is it hard on you?" I sign.

She sees me gesturing in the reflection of the window and faces me.

I repeat the gesture so she can see it.

Her brows furrow. She turns up her hands and moves them back and forth. "What?"

"Moving between your mom's house and mine all the time, is it tiring?"

For a long time, Niko had been with her mother while I flew back and forth from Japan to see her. Then, after Ashanti's remarriage, Niko came to stay with me in Japan before we both relocated to America permanently. She did not have to live in two different houses so often.

"It must be difficult to get used to," I say.

"No," she signs.

Then she returns her attention to the window.

I failed to engage her.

Again.

Akira drops us off at our home. Niko bows to Akira and then shoots out of the car. I watch her backpack bounce before she disappears inside.

"She seems upset," Akira notes.

"Do you think she is nervous about performing tonight? It is her first time playing the piano in front of others at her school. She has finally made friends and spends more time interacting with them than locking herself in her room reading mangas. Perhaps she is afraid she might lose them if she does not do well."

"This sounds viable," Akira agrees.

I leave an envelope on the passenger side. "The ticket you requested."

"I will need twenty more. The men from the security company would like to attend as well."

"Tell them I only received three tickets. The school will not have enough space for them all. But we will take a video of her."

"I will tell them." She dips her chin.

My vision is blurry when I climb out of the car. I push past the wave of dizziness. Perhaps I should heed Akira's warning and eat something even if I am not hungry.

After making a sandwich for both myself and Niko, I take the food into her room. Niko is sitting on her bed, her attention on her tablet. The frustrated look returns to her eyes when she sees me.

"I brought a snack," I say, lifting the plate.

She gestures, "I'm not hungry."

"Niko," I set both plates on the dresser, "is something wrong? Did something happen at school today?"

She shakes her head.

"Did something happen at your mother's house yesterday?"

She frowns.

A slow realization dawns. "Is this because your mother spoke to you about Dejonae?"

Niko folds her little legs beneath her and stares at me. Her mouth moves while she signs, "Why is Dejonae not coming over anymore?"

"Because..." I glance around, at a loss for words, "she is busy."

"Mom said you and Dejonae aren't speaking."

My jaw clenches. Why would Ashanti tell Niko that? Even if it is true, it is not her place to inform my daughter of my relationship troubles.

I reach out and smooth a hand over her shoulder. "Niko…"

"Why did you fight with her?" She gestures roughly.

"It is an adult matter. You don't need to worry about it."

Her hands sail through the air. "I want to see Dejonae. I want her there tonight. She helped me practice. I promised her that I would give her a ticket."

"Even if we get a ticket to her, I don't know if she will want to come," I say honestly.

Niko's eyes fill with tears. "You don't want me to be happy. You are always trying to get rid of my moms."

Her words cut me off at the knees.

Sharp knives burrow straight into my chest.

My daughter flings herself into bed, hiding her face from me as she cries.

My heart breaks.

I let my hand hover over Niko's back. And then I pull her gently by the shoulders and give her a hug.

Niko's tears soak my shirt. Her sobs are low and mournful.

It is almost painful to hear.

"I will fix it," I promise her. "I will get Dejonae there."

She looks up to read my lips.

A small, hopeful smile blooms.

I squeeze her back to me.

I was wrong to think that I was the only one being affected by Dejonae's absence. As desperately as I was falling for her, my daughter was falling too.

CHAPTER 21
THE STOLEN WINE GLASS

DEJONAE

"What are you doing?" Vanya gives me a panicked look. "Hurry up, Deej. What if we miss the kids' performance?"

"Relax, babe." Hadyn checks his watch. "We still got a couple minutes."

"Wow. Now that you've told me to relax, I feel so much better." Hadyn laughs and rocks Baby Ollie in his arms.

Despite her heavy sarcasm, Vanya breaks out into a smile too.

Baby Ollie coos her happiness. She truly looks like the daughter of a fashion icon tonight, her little arms and legs are shrouded in shrills and lace.

I wouldn't be surprised if Baby Ollie had her own social media account with a horde of loyal followers eager to see her next outfit.

"You guys go ahead," I squeak out. It's obvious that Vanya wants to hurry inside and I want to do the opposite.

Vanya turns sharply. Her brown eyes study me in the dusk.

I glance away, pretending to take great interest in my surroundings. The school parking lot is flooded with luxury SUVs. Small photo booths are set up along the back. Photographers are mounting their lights and colorful backgrounds, preparing for an influx of rich parents high off their children's awkward first performances.

"Dejonae?" Vanya calls.

I want to move. I really do.

But it's like my feet are stuck on the cement.

Hadyn and Vanya exchange a wordless look.

Anger boils inside my chest when I watch them.

Adam and Nova and Vanya and Hadyn have shown the ability to communicate without words. So why *the hell* is it so hard for me and Sazuki to get on the same page?

Hadyn clears his throat. "I'll find the others and save you both a seat."

"Thanks, babe." Vanya waves him away and then trots toward me. "Honey, if you clutch that bouquet any tighter, you're going to give Niko a pile of stems."

I relax my fingers, but my heart is still beating fast.

"Are you nervous about seeing Sazuki?" Vanya asks, rubbing my shoulder.

I shake my head.

Somehow, I've managed to survive working at the foundation and seeing him every day. It killed me inside, but I held out for so long because I thought he would come to me immediately.

But he didn't.

I didn't think he'd let our break stretch out for this long, and now everything is a mess.

"Is it because *she's* inside?" Vanya whispers.

My eyes dart to her.

"Niko told Beth that her mom was here. Beth told Dawn and… well, you know how the farmhouse grapevine works."

I inhale a shuddering breath. "I'm okay. Niko asked me to show up. I'm doing this for her."

"Then you better get inside," Vanya says gently.

I follow her into the school auditorium. Fancy, cushioned chairs face the stage. Speakers hang from the walls like we're in a movie theatre. Private schools really are a different breed. *My* public school auditorium did not have air conditioning, surround-sound speakers, and velvet seats.

Sunny and Darrel Hastings are sitting at the front of the room. They turn and spot us wedging into our seats at the back. Sunny shoots me a beaming smile and waves. Her movement catches Dawn and Max Stinton's attention. The couple notice me and Vanya. They nod and smile in acknowledgement.

"Why aren't we sitting with them?" I ask Vanya.

She takes Baby Ollie from Hadyn and adjust the frills around her wrist. Eyes sparkling with love, she focuses on her child even as she speaks to me, "Up front is for the parents."

"Ah." I sweep my gaze over the room again and freeze when I see a familiar head of black hair.

I would recognize Sazuki from the back if I were in a crowd of millions. His hair is longer than usual, brushing his broad shoulders. He turns slightly to the side, showing off his impeccable profile—strong forehead, sharp nose, chiseled jaw line.

My heart rams against my ribs.

Stupid tears start piling in my eyes.

Ridiculous.

I miss him so much, but I'm not going to cry at the sight of him.

Don't be a child, Dejonae.

Sazuki dips his head closer to the woman sitting beside him. The sensation of a thousand sharp needles stabbing my skin hits me. I wish I could go numb, but there's no relief from the pain. No shelter. No life raft to save me from drowning in my own stupidity.

Ashanti tilts her face up to Sazuki. Whatever he says makes her laugh.

My stomach clenches.

I press a hand over my mouth, fighting back the urge to run right out of the auditorium.

"Deej?" Vanya calls.

"Deej, you okay?" Hadyn asks.

Groaning, I fight to keep my composure. "I'll, uh, I'll go find Niko and give these to her."

Vanya says something else to me, but I don't hear her over the rushing of my own heart.

Sazuki and Ashanti are together again as parents. Is that the reason he hasn't bothered to fight for me? To chase me? Did Ashanti get her way? Has he just not found the right time to tell me he chose to be a family for Niko?

My heart sinks fast.

I want to throw my hands high and yell 'screw this!'

But I promised Niko that I'd stay for her performance and I never break my word.

The crowd backstage is thick with parents, teachers and children preparing for the show. Bright lights illuminate the kids' wide grins and heavily made-up faces. Two little girls in tutus hurry past me.

I stop in place and glance around, looking for Niko.

"Dejonae?" Kenya appears in front of me, wearing a curly afro, jeans and a fancy blouse. "Hey."

"Hi." I glance behind her and see Alistair walking in holding Belle's hand. Their adorable little girl is also wearing a tutu. "Is Belle dancing tonight?"

"Yeah, the older girls asked her to be in their performance." Kenya blinks steadily at me. "Who are you looking for?"

"Niko."

"She's over there!" Belle points. Excitedly, the adorable ballerina breaks away from her parents and joins Niko, Beth, Bailey and Micheal, who seem to have formed something of a 'cool kid' table at the center of the room.

Sunny and Darrel's boys are dressed in karate uniforms, hinting of what their performance will be.

"I'll deliver this prop to her teacher," Alistair says. I focus on him and realize he's wearing a pair of sparkly pink fairy wings on his back.

My eyelashes bounce as I struggle to make sense of the tall, intimidating man wearing a fairy costume.

"Don't say a word," Alistair warns me.

Kenya's mouth trembles. She bursts out laughing when her husband walks away. "Poor thing. He had to wear that the entire drive. He can't say no to Belle."

My smile turns pained. "Good fathers will do anything for their kids. I understand."

"Are you okay, Dejonae?" Kenya touches my arm.

"I'm fine." My voice cracks. "I'll deliver these to Niko and then head back outside."

Kenya nods, her concerned eyes watching me long after I walk away.

Niko sees me approaching and a giant grin spreads over her face. She leaves her friends and flies toward me. I have to lean back before I get slapped in the face with her tablet as she throws her arms around me for a hug.

"Hi, baby." I rub her back and sink my head into her neck. My heart rearranges in my chest.

I'm not her mother.

I know that.

But I would honestly die for this little girl.

And I am.

Because being separated from Sazuki feels like I'm dying slowly.

Still, if it means that she has her biological mother in her life and she gets to see her father and mother connecting again then... maybe...

I fight the tears because I really can't finish the thought.

"Is this the tablet you use to talk to your friends?" I ease her hand back and divert her attention to the device before she senses how torn up I am inside.

Niko nods and shows me the tablet.

There's a half-written sentence on it, which tells me I interrupted her in the middle of a conversation. I notice a side tab with pre-written responses too. It must make things easier for her when she's talking with her friends.

Smoothly, she clips the tablet under her arm and uses her hands to sign with me. "I'm nervous."

"Don't be," I sign. "You're going to do great."

Beth approaches us. She waves at me, remembering me from the last time I visited the farmhouse. Her hazel eyes brim with intelligence and she moves gracefully.

"Hi, Miss Dejonae."

"Hey, Beth."

Beth taps Niko's shoulder to get her attention. "Pictures," she gestures. With her mouth, she explains, "Belle's mom wants to take pictures."

From the slight frown, I can tell that Beth isn't into all that fuss.

Bailey runs up to her. "Come on, guys. It's almost time for Belle's dance."

Niko wanders off with her flowers and her friends. I watch her get absorbed into the fray, perfectly content. Perfectly safe.

She *belongs*.

It hurts even as it heals.

Niko might have needed me before she met them, but she's surrounded by so much love and care now.

Maybe I don't need to be in her life anymore.

Maybe it'll be okay if I just disappear.

* * *

I SLIP AWAY the moment Niko's piano performance is over.

She did amazing.

Somehow, Adam engineered the MTB to look like a pink, girly headband. The pack that delivers vibrational frequency to her ribs was under her clothes, so no one in the audience would know that she had any device on.

I was absolutely bursting with pride and completely in the moment…

Until I saw Sazuki and Ashanti hugging.

After that, the night was ruined for me. I hurled an excuse at Vanya, bustled out of the auditorium and hurried home.

Now, I'm sitting in my pajamas, trying to get drunk on wine and popcorn while my sister scolds me from a video call.

"You should have stayed," Yaya signs on the screen. "And grabbed her hair."

"Do you think my life is a reality show?"

"You're friends with a bunch of real-life billionaires," Yaya gestures. Her eyes widen to emphasize the point. "You're not living in reality."

I grip my wine glass. "It's over. I'm going to find a way to graduate without having to work with him. Even if it means quitting school and starting all over, I'm not going to torture myself watching him be happy with her. I can't do it."

"Tell him that."

"I can't," I croak. My mind flips back to Ashanti's speech in the apartment and her smug words when I ran into her at the foundation.

Niko's so much happier seeing her mom and dad trying again.

"Niko deserves to have her parents together. And I'm not a home wrecker."

She flings me an angry look. Her hands flail. "He's divorced. He wrecked his own home. Not you."

"But now he can build it back. I shouldn't get in the way of that."

There's a knock on the door.

My shoulders slump.

I have no energy to get up.

The knock sounds again.

I groan and squeeze my eyes shut.

"What?" Yaya gestures.

"Someone's here."

"Maybe it's Sazuki," she signs.

I refuse to allow that thought to give me hope. "I doubt it. I'll check who it is and call you back."

She blows me a kiss and signs off.

I drag myself to the door. "Who is it?"

"It's me," Vanya's voice echoes.

Stunned, I unlock the door. "Vanya?"

"Hey, Dejonae."

I stop short.

Sunny's eyes sparkle at me beneath her thick lashes. She spots my glass. "Ooh, wine."

My jaw drops when she takes the glass from me and sidles her way into my tiny, one-bedroom apartment.

"You got a head start," Kenya says, waving a bottle around. She walks in like I invited her.

"Cute place." Dawn moves past me, her eyes whipping around.

Vanya is the last to enter.

I meet her eyes and hiss, "What's going on? Why is everyone here?"

"We couldn't think of a better place to go for Girl's Night."

"Girl's Night?" I frown.

"You're familiar with the concept, right?" Vanya tilts her head.

"Of course I know what Girl's Night is. But… why is it here? And didn't your kid's talent show end just a few hours ago?"

"Two hours to be exact. The kids got ice cream and a sugar rush." Sunny folds herself into my sofa. "So naturally, we shoved them on their dads and ran away."

"And the 'Mom of The Year' award goes to…"

Kenya guffaws.

Sunny cackles even louder.

Ugh.

I want to wallow in self-pity, but I genuinely like them.

"We're here to raid your house for snacks," Dawn says.

"I don't buy it." I stalk to the middle of my living room. "This feels like an intervention."

"And your feelings are totally valid," Kenya quips with an innocent tone.

I scowl at her.

She smiles. "Seriously, do you have snacks? I didn't eat much of the ice cream."

"In the kitchen." I gesture that way.

"I brought wine." Vanya offers the bottle to me. "I thought of making you chai, but I'm not that delusional. You are the undisputed chai queen. I'm not worthy enough to touch your blender."

"I found Oreos!" Dawn cries gleefully.

The other women pump their fists.

Slowly, my living room is overtaken by four gorgeous mothers who all seem to have no objections to home invasion.

"Vanya, put that chair down this *instant*," Dawn yells, pointing a finger as the model carries furniture from the kitchen to the living room.

"You guys realize I gave birth months ago, right?"

"It doesn't matter. Hadyn will kill us if we have you lifting a finger," Sunny says, popping to her feet.

"Deej only has this tiny sofa. We can't all sit in it," Vanya defends herself.

"I got it." Sunny takes over from Vanya. She drags the chair over to me. "Sit here, sweetie."

"Thanks."

"Kenya, pass the Oreos," Dawn yells. "You're not a squirrel storing up for the winter. Put some back."

"*Never.*" Kenya shoves two in her mouth.

I laugh and tuck my leg under me.

"Did you enjoy the performances, Deej?" Sunny asks, eyeing me carefully.

"Sure…"

"She left after Niko's piano piece," Vanya tattles.

I give her the stink eye.

She shrugs. "It's the truth."

"Uh, I wish I could have run away too. I came to watch Belle stick her leg out a few times, pirouette once and then skate off the stage. My baby was up there for less than two minutes, but I had to sit through hours of a kid hawking on a trombone and two screechy violin acts."

"Beth's tire-changing performance was nice though," Vanya points out. "I'm still trying to figure out how they fit an actual car through the door."

All the ladies murmur in agreement.

"And Niko's song was just..." Dawn sighs happily. "It was beautiful. She impressed me so much."

"How does she do that without being able to hear?" Sunny asks me.

"Learning the piano as a deaf person doesn't necessarily require hearing. Seeing the keys is enough to get started and after that, your body memorizes the placement of the fingers. It's actually really healthy and therapeutic to play the piano, no matter who you are."

Dawn bobs her head, impressed.

Vanya smiles. "It sounds like you've rattled that speech off before."

"I've had to mention it a time or two at the foundation."

"Speaking of the foundation," Sunny begins.

I tilt my head and face the ceiling. "I knew this was coming."

"What's going on with you and Sazuki?" Kenya asks.

Four pairs of eyes drill into me.

"I... we..." My throat closes up. All the happiness I'd felt being in their company drains into a painful knot in my chest. "We broke up."

Gasps ripple through the room.

"Are you kidding? Why would he make an idiotic decision like that? I thought he was a smart guy!" Vanya shrieks.

Dawn approaches me. Her hand falls on the top of my head. "Are you okay?"

I was before she comforted me.

But now the waterworks are turning back on.

"I haven't been sleeping well lately. Every time I close my eyes, I can... I can see him. Smell him. *Feel* him. The pain," I hit my chest, "is like someone died for me. I thought I could handle it, but I feel so lost."

"Sweetie." Vanya abandons her chair and pounces on me.

Soon, all the women are embracing me. The smell of cocoa butter, natural hair products and sisterhood fills my nose and unleashes the tears I'd been fighting back.

I brush the tears away. "I'm sorry."

"Don't apologize for feeling what you feel," Sunny coaches me. "You just let that wave ride right on through."

"I always thought of myself as strong," I confess to them. "I never thought I'd be the kind of girl who'd let a man devastate her. I'm confident, I'm smart, I'm in control. I can find another one."

"But you loved him," Dawn says simply.

I glance up, stunned.

"When you love someone, you let your walls down. You become soft. You become vulnerable. That's why it hurts. When someone gets you to take your armor off and they impale you, you don't just feel hurt. You feel stupid."

"I can't even hate him. That's the worst part." I straighten and the women give me a little breathing room.

"Before I met Sazuki, I thought all I wanted to be was a songwriter. But since working at the foundation, I've found my real dream. I want to keep helping the deaf community. I want to bring music to the people who can't hear it."

"That's so inspiring," Sunny says.

"But you know the worst part?" I glance at each of them. "Doing the work that I love feels meaningless now. Even though I found my purpose, it feels like... like I lost something too."

Sunny rubs my back. "Did the break up happen because of what we discussed that night at the farmhouse?"

"What did you discuss?" Dawn asks.

"Oh…" Sunny looks to me for permission.

I nod.

She explains, "Dejonae slammed a reporter's head into a bathroom stall and Sazuki didn't take her side."

"You what?" Vanya hurls back.

"Straight into the door? Like MMA style?" Dawn asks, looking excited.

"Which reporter?" Kenya strokes her chin. "Not that annoying one on the local news channel, right?"

Astonished, I pin Sunny with a dark frown. "Why'd you say it like that?"

"It's true, isn't it?" she fires back.

"I have so many questions," Vanya says in a daze.

"I will not be answering any of them," I insist. "Sazuki and I didn't break up because of the reporter incident."

"Does it have anything to do with the woman who was in the seat beside him?" Sunny asks quietly.

Dawn's brown eyes scour my face.

The room falls silent again.

"Her name is Ashanti. She's his ex-wife. They divorced when Niko was three, but they're still really involved in each other's lives. As you can see from the show tonight, he sat beside her, laughed with her, took pictures of Niko with her. They're trying to be a family again."

Vanya chews on her bottom lip.

Kenya glances down.

Sunny is the first to break the silence. "But wait a minute, that seat wasn't for her."

Dawn straightens. "She's right. Sazuki came to the talent show alone."

"Ashanti must have been running late," I mumble. Shards of glass are rolling around in my gut. I don't really want to discuss Ashanti and Sazuki's second stab at a romance.

"No." Sunny's voice rises. "Darrel was chatting with him, so I wasn't really paying attention. But I'm sure I heard him say that

Niko called to invite you to the talent show and he was saving a seat for you."

Dawn jumps in. "When his ex-wife—I didn't know she was his ex at the time—but when she arrived, she took the seat, assuming it was for her. Sazuki didn't ask her to sit there. He looked kind of annoyed, actually."

"Doesn't that mean he still has feelings for you?" Vanya points out.

A sprout of hope rises from the ashes, but I stomp it down. "It doesn't matter. Ashanti will always be in his life, hovering around, waiting for her chance to slip in and get back with him."

"A relationship is two-sided," Dawn points out. "If he doesn't open the door, she won't have a chance to come in."

"I want to trust him, but my faith in men resisting their exes is low." My fingers tremble and I tuck them into my lap. "Things are so complicated. I want to protect myself. I'm afraid that I'll give him everything and, one day, he'll still choose the person that he walked away from. I can't get over that."

"I'll be honest with you, Dejonae," Sunny says. "I sat beside Sazuki today and, honestly, he looks about as broken as you do."

Dawn agrees. "You can tell he's exhausted. Max gets just like that when he's overdoing it at work."

Vanya looks down at me. "It seems like both of you have made the same decision. And you're both running from it."

"What are you talking about? What decision?"

"The decision to choose each other."

Kenya nods along. "The important thing is whether or not the man loves you. If it's clear that he loves you, then I say go for it."

"But Ashanti—"

"If he wanted his ex wife, they would be together," Sunny says.

Her words ricochet through me.

Vanya narrows her eyes. "Isn't his misery a confirmation that the person he's in love with isn't his ex-wife at least? If he wanted her, she wouldn't have to try so hard and neither would he. She's there. Niko's there. All he'd have to do is walk into that picture-perfect reality. But he hasn't. Instead, he's hoping you'll sit beside him instead of her."

"What if he doesn't keep choosing me?" I croak, frightened out of my mind. "What if he gets up one day and doesn't make that choice?"

Sunny speaks up, "My mom always told me that 'love is a choice'. If he stops choosing you, then that wouldn't be love."

"I think we've all had our share of nicks and bruises from past relationships," Dawn glances at the other women who all nod, "but the one thing Max has taught me about love, is that you can't kill it. No matter how hard you try."

As if on cue, all of their phones start ringing.

"The guys want to know why we abandoned them," Kenya mumbles.

"You should head back." I drum up a smile. "I'll think about what you said tonight."

"And remember, you can always stop by the farmhouse. You're not just Vanya's friend." Sunny squeezes my hand. "You're our friend too."

"You're going to make me cry," I tease, pretending to wipe at my eye.

The women all give me hugs as they file out.

Vanya gives me the biggest one.

"Thank you," I say, my voice muffled in her neck.

"Of course. You and the girls were there for me during a hard time too."

"What hard time?" I ask.

Her eyes shift to the side. "We can talk about it later."

I nod and close the door behind them.

In the silence, I get ready for bed and fall into the comforters that still smell like Sazuki, mint, and *us* no matter how much I've washed them. It's one of the reasons why I haven't been able to fall asleep lately.

Can I trust him? is the question that's been running through my mind every night.

But after the girl chat, the question has changed a bit.
Do I want to live in a world where I don't at least try?

* * *

Groaning, I roll to a sitting position and stare at the sun as it makes its way through my bedroom.

Another new day.

I check my phone.

The group chat is exploding with pictures of all the kids at the talent show, and all the couples hugging each other. I scroll for pictures of Sazuki and find one where he's alone with Niko.

My fingers caress his face.

My heart pangs.

Ugh.

It's going to be another long day.

I plod to school and find my seat in Mr. Howel's class.

Taylor sashays past me, one hand on her school bag and the other twirling her blue hair. "It's been a while since Sazuki picked you up after school, Darlene. Are you and daddy fighting?"

I wrap my headphones over my ears and ignore her.

If she keeps talking, I'm going to smack her in the mouth and then I'll lose my scholarship. As satisfying as the thought is, I've learned my lesson after tussling with the reporter. My actions have consequences far beyond me.

Plus, she isn't worth threatening my entire future.

Taylor laughs and trots away.

I glare into her back when she's not looking. The moment graduation's over, I'm going to find her in a dark alley and let her have it.

Until then…

I flip through my music theory book, the words blurring.

Mr. Howel enters the classroom. His eyes go straight to me. "Miss Williams, I'm still waiting on Sazuki to call me back."

So am I, dude.

I give him a tight-lipped smile and hunker low in my seat.

Thankfully, Howel gets the hint and drops the subject.

I barely make it through class. The moment it's over, I'm the first to head through the doors. I don't want to hear another stupid comment from Taylor's ignorant mouth.

The sun is hot on my skin, but inside I feel cold.

Everywhere I look, I see memories of Sazuki.

Him bounding up the stairs in his black jacket like a dream come to life.

Him and his bodyguards surrounding me on the path to the quad.

Even that black SUV reminds me of…

A woman pops out of the truck and I gasp. "Akira?"

"Miss Williams, if you have some time, I would like to speak to you."

"Uh… about what?"

Akira pins her lips together. She looks particularly pale today with her slashing red lipstick and trim black pantsuit.

"Is there anywhere we can talk?"

"We can go to a café on campus." I offer.

She nods and I lead her there. The café isn't too crowded. There are a few students on their laptops, working quietly and sipping on their coffees.

Akira and I snag a free table.

She sits straight as a pin, her shoulders tense and her eyebrows knitted.

I wait for her to say something.

She doesn't.

The silence makes me squirm. I don't know how much more of this I can take.

"So… is this about The Sazuki Foundation?"

"It is about Ryotaro."

I jolt a little. Feeling off-kilter, I drag my hands off the table and set them in my lap to hide their trembling from her eyes.

Akira hesitates, her lips pursed, then she seems to come to a decision because she leans forward. Speaking in low, urgent tones, she says, "When Ryotaro got married, his family was largely against it. They threatened to kick him out. They turned their back on him. Through it all, he remained strong. He took responsibility for the woman he had slept with and the baby they had made. He was determined to do everything he could to make life better for them."

I suck in a rasping breath, hating that I'm interested in Ashanti and Sazuki's story despite the sharp pain that it brings.

"After the divorce, Ryotaro adjusted to the new normal. He willingly shared custody with his daughter, although his heart broke to have her so far away. He flew back and forth on many exhausting trips. He began to plan how he would move to America to spend more time with her. Through it all, he remained determined. He bore the setbacks with a relentless fire."

I'm cupping my chin at this point. I don't know if Akira was a storyteller back in Japan, but the way she's weaving the threads together has me by the throat.

"No fear would stop him. No threats of being cut out of the family ancestry. No doubt about moving to a foreign country where he knew few people and had even fewer friends. Nothing has ever stopped Ryotaro Sazuki in his tracks… until you."

I can't name the feeling that slices me open at that moment. I swallow hard, digging my fingers into the table.

Akira's eyes are as black as marbles. They hammer into me with a powerful force. "He is working, he is moving, he is breathing, but he is crumbling beneath it all, Miss Williams."

"And you're saying that's my fault?"

"I am saying," her voice cracks and she takes a moment to compose herself, "that I have watched over Ryotaro and his family since Niko's birth. His mother sent me to America not only to protect her granddaughter, but to protect her son. Ryotaro is breaking down. We cannot remain uninvolved." She leans forward. "I do not know why you and Ryotaro are no longer together, but if there is *any* part of you that still cares for him, I ask

—humbly—that you either tell him so or put him out of his misery. I cannot watch from the sidelines while he lives in pain."

I lick my suddenly dry lips.

"Please, Miss Williams."

To my ever living surprise, Akira dips her head and bows to me.

CHAPTER 22
BILLIONAIRES DON'T INTERVENE

SAZUKI

I saw Dejonae leave the talent show right after Niko's performance.

It was just a glimpse of her soft cheek and a flash of brown eyes, but the mere impression of her sent my heart into overdrive.

I did not realize I was standing and staring at her until Ashanti tugged on my arm and, sheepishly, warned me to sit because I was blocking the view of other parents.

After the talent show, Ashanti suggested we go out for a 'family dinner', and I was relieved when Niko insisted on joining her friends at the farmhouse for ice cream.

Niko's excitement after performing live and receiving the audience's adoration made her forget her earlier anger with me.

She's still in a happy mood when I make her breakfast the next morning.

"Dad," she signs, "can Beth come over today? She wants to learn piano."

"You're going to teach Beth the piano?" I arch both eyebrows.

Niko nods happily.

I smile at her and nod. "Tell her to let her parents call me. We will arrange it."

Niko pumps her fist.

While we are enjoying our miso soup, there is a knock on the door.

Ashanti breezes past me, her arms laden with grocery bags. "Sazuki, you made miso soup *again?*" Her laughter claws at me. "You're in America now. You can mix it up with a little bacon and eggs."

"Bacon is unhealthy," I say.

"But it's delicious." She sets the groceries on the counter and kisses Niko's head. "Hi, baby."

Niko waves.

I close the door and step wearily into the kitchen. "Ashanti, can I speak to you?"

"You sure can," she says brightly, unpacking a box of sugary cereal, milk, and dairy products from her bags.

"In private."

Niko's perceptive gaze darts between the two of us.

Ashanti's smile falters for a second, but it quickly bounces back. She motions to the groceries. "Let me just put these up first."

I do not wish to argue with her in front of Niko, so I wait until she is finished with the task and then gesture to my office.

"Niko," I sign, "do your homework in the meantime."

"Dad, it's Saturday," she gestures, rolling her eyes.

I frown at her. "Do you plan to do your homework the night before it is due?"

She sighs but dutifully gets up and plods to her room.

Ashanti smirks at me. "She's so cute. You know, I posted her video online. Everyone was impressed. A lot of parents of deaf children wanted to know how they could learn music too. I pointed them all to your foundation. You're going to have a crowd of people wanting to sign up when you officially open."

"Mm." I make a non-committal sound in my throat.

"When are you going to open officially?" Ashanti prods.

"Soon."

Adam and I are satisfied with the MTB's performance. Niko is not the only music student who is seeing a marked improvement in their lessons. Ninety percent of the students have said that they prefer playing music with the MTB than without it. The teachers have also expressed their approval of the device.

With the rest of the MTBs stockpiled in our warehouse and the demand for instructors nearly crashing our website, I believe it is time to enter our last phase—officially opening the foundation to the public.

There is only one important thing I need to do before then.

"Well, don't talk my ear off, Ryo." Her laughter is nervous. Her eyes dart between mine as if she is trying to gauge what I am thinking.

I keep my face blank. "Please, sit."

Her cheeks cave in. "Is something wrong?"

I motion to the chairs again.

She hesitantly sinks into one. I take the other.

"Ashanti," I fold my hands together, "do you know what *oyakoko* means?"

She shakes her head, her eyes wide.

While living in Japan, Ashanti had studied the language in order to communicate well with my mother and to move about on her own. I am not surprised, though, that she has not retained memory of the language.

"It means filial piety."

"Right. It's taking care of your parents even in their old age. It's a law or something, right?"

"It stems from Confucian philosophy. It is one of the values that was ingrained in me when I was a young boy. I did not have a choice. Just as I was born a Sazuki and so I was born into music, I was also born into this way of thinking."

"Okay…" Her eyebrows clench as she tries to guess where I am going.

"It is my wish to grow Niko in this way as well."

"You don't want her to throw us into nursing homes? Is that what you're saying?" The weak smile on her lips tells me she wants to diffuse the tension with jokes.

I do not smile. "I want her to respect you and to take care of you. This is the expectation I hold and the values that I have imparted to her. She has a duty to her family, of which you are a part of by blood. This cannot and will never change, just as I cannot change the line of my ancestors. I will always be a Sazuki. And Niko will always belong to you."

"What about us?" Her voice turns quiet and vulnerable. "Does your family duty extend to me too?"

I take a moment to choose my words. When I speak, it is firmly but carefully. "You will always hold an important part in my life. You can rest assured in this. I will always care for and respect you. Not only for your sake, but for Niko's." I hold her gaze to ensure that she is listening. "But we cannot function as anything more than friends and co-parents."

"Ryo—"

"Ashanti," I stop her before she can argue, "my stance has not changed since that talk by the pool. I would prefer for us to maintain the current agreement."

"Which is what?" She shoots to her feet. Her eyes are thunderous.

"That we remain separated. That we work together for Niko's sake."

She strides to the door in a frustrated march. Stopping a few paces before the exit, she fists her hands.

Her anger stumps me. I wait quietly, giving her the chance to gather her thoughts.

There is silence.

A muffled sigh.

And then she speaks.

"I never had a father. No one in my neighborhood did. I would see sitcoms with the dad sitting at the table, being there for the kids, providing for the home and it felt like a fairy tale to me. It felt so unreal to have a dad, much less one that *cared*."

She turns to look at me. "Then I met you and that fairy tale had come true. You didn't know me well but you took me into your home. You stood up to your parents for me. You promised to take care of our child and always be there for her. You promised to care for me too."

Ashanti breathes out. "I didn't know how to deal with having someone who wanted to take responsibility for me. It wasn't perfect, but if I'd been a little more mature, I would have realized that no marriage is. You were trying. You cared for us. You wanted to be a better man for us and I didn't appreciate that."

"It was not meant to be."

"No, but it was. There was a time when you loved me, Ryo. Call it sexual love or love out of convenience, but you did."

"I did."

"Then how are you so sure that you won't love me again?"

I stare right into her distraught brown eyes. "Because I am truly, genuinely, and deeply in love with someone else. I can no longer give you the parts of me that you are asking for because they do not belong to me anymore. They belong to her."

Ashanti's face crumples in pain.

I shift my gaze away. To give her privacy to hurt. But also to get my own stubborn pride under control. How is it that I can so easily express my feelings to anyone but the person they are meant for?

I hear Ashanti take a deep breath. When I glance at her again, her bottom lip is trembling, but she is otherwise composed.

"I don't think I'll be able to stay for breakfast. Um," her nostrils flare as she inhales, "I guess I won't be able to drop in like this in the future?"

"For now, I believe it would be best to stick to the appointed custody agreement."

She clears her throat, looks me dead in the eye and says, "I hope she knows how lucky she is to have you, Ryo."

From the foolish way I have been acting, I am not sure Dejonae would agree with the sentiment.

It is now time to correct that.

* * *

THE DOORBELL RINGS.

Niko immediately hops up from the couch. She had been monitoring the outdoor camera since I gave my agreement to have her friends over.

I refrain from giving an instruction to 'slow down'. She is already halfway to the door and I doubt she would listen even if I could sign to her.

Niko throws the door open. She and Beth collide in a tangle of arms, legs and smiles.

The boys are behind her.

Bailey seems eager to jump into the huddle.

Micheal glances away, looking uninterested.

Niko insisted on inviting Belle too. Though she is much younger, Niko claimed that she did not want to leave the little girl out.

My daughter has a bleeding heart.

I do not know who she inherited that from.

As the kids race past me to go and play in Niko's room, I notice that it is only the fathers on my doorstep.

"Did the women have another secret meeting?" I ask, noting Alistair's aggravated expression.

"No," he says brusquely.

"They sent us on another mission," Darrel, the therapist and the quietest of the men, speaks. His eyes are as green as matcha powder and it is strangely unnerving to be on the receiving end of his gaze.

"Let's make this quick," Max Stinton says. He glances at his watch.

"I agree," Hadyn agrees. He is Vanya's husband, if I recall correctly.

As she is the model who receives more attention in the spotlight, much of the American news refers to him as Vanya Beckford's husband. Although he is a rich heir and influential in his own right, Hadyn does not seem to mind.

My eyes whip back to Hadyn and I frown. "Did you bring your infant?"

"Oh, no. I'm here for the intervention."

Did he break into a language other than English? "Intervention? I do not understand."

"Our wives think that you need help," Alistair grumbles.

"Help with what?"

"'Getting your head out of your butt-crack'." Hadyn lifts a hand. "Those were Vanya's exact words."

I would be offended if I still was not so confused.

"They had wine, group hugs, and all kinds of talks about feelings," Max Stinton growls. "But we can skip all the emotional bull and get to the heart of this. The bottom line is that Dejonae wants to trust you and needs some kind of assurance that you love her and *will* only love her for the rest of your life."

"So let's come up with a plan to show her that and then go home," Alistair finishes.

"I do not need your help," I say stubbornly.

"Look, Sazuki, I don't know how they did things in Japan, but you don't get to wiggle your way out of this pep talk, no matter where you're from," Hadyn warns. "Trust me."

"How I handle my relationship is not your concern." I scowl at their insolence.

"Dejonae is Vanya's friend, which means it is *exactly* our concern."

I squint at Hadyn.

The way they are all staring at me, one would think Dejonae was their biological sister.

Darrel speaks calmly, "You're right to mistrust our intentions.

And you're also right to say that we shouldn't involve ourselves in your relationship."

"If you know this, then why are you still standing here?"

"It's obvious we wouldn't be here if we didn't care."

Alistair clears his throat. "Or at least, if our wives didn't care."

"We are not here to threaten you," Darrel says. "Just to offer a warning. According to Sunny, Dejonae is so torn up about you that she is going to drop out of school and take a year off."

I stiffen.

Drop out of school?

Should I release her from the foundation and let her finish her graduation project without my involvement?

I remain tight-lipped.

Darrel and Alistair exchange glances.

Hadyn shakes his head as if to say *he's not worth it.*

Darrel looks disappointed by my stubbornness.

Collectively, they start to walk away.

What are you doing, Sazuki? Do you want to lose Dejonae forever?

I call them back. "What do you suggest?"

Hadyn spins first.

Max Stinton stares at me with cold, assessing eyes.

Darrel is the one that speaks. "Move on what your heart is saying."

"You might be a private man who keeps things close to the chest but, in this scenario, it doesn't hurt to go big and public," Hadyn adds.

My jaw clenches. "I know what I will do."

"Our work here is done," Alistair says. He checks his watch. "Not bad. You're as smart as you look, Sazuki."

Hadyn claps my back.

Darrel nods.

Stinton does the same.

The men leave my house as abruptly as they'd arrived.

I watch them get into their fancy cars and drive off. In a normal circumstance, I would have chased them away for daring to intervene in my private matters.

But they are Dejonae's people.

Her family.

Even if they share no blood.

And now, I finally have an idea—a way to remind Dejonae that she is my family too.

CHAPTER 23
RED STRING OF FATE

DEJONAE

THE BANQUET HALL is packed with dignitaries, kids, parents, and reporters. I step inside, holding my breath at the vast display of wealth and elegance. Velvet curtains, golden accents, red tapestry. Everywhere I look delights my eyes.

"How much do you think an event like this costs?" Yaya signs.

I shrug.

"Oh well. At least I have an excuse to show this off." She slips her hands into the folds of her shimmery blue dress and waves the skirt back and forth.

My sister looks *gorgeous* with her hair in faux locs again and scooped up at the crown of her head. Diamond earrings sparkle in her ears and she's finished it off with dramatic black gloves.

The dress she's wearing is a Kimberly Barret original—the brand that she's an ambassador for.

When Yaya could finally tell us the details about her contract, we were beyond ecstatic for her.

Beautiful music sails through the air.

It's coming from the stage.

Mom's eyes glisten as she fixes her gaze on the children playing the piano. "Oh, they're doing so well."

"What are those headbands they're wearing?" Yaya gestures.

I glance at Timmy and Grace, two of our younger students at the foundation.

No, not 'our'.

Not anymore.

I have a draft of my resignation letter saved in my email and I'll send it as soon as my performance tonight is over.

"That's the MTB," I inform them.

"Ah." Despite her nodding, mom still seems confused.

"I'll explain later." I wipe my sweaty palms against my regular, department store dress. I'm nervous and half of me wants to just run through the door.

But I stay.

My performance tonight was scheduled long in advance. Since I honor my word, I plan to perform. I'll give it my best as an ode to the foundation and the direction that I found for my life.

Dad shakes his hands in the sign for 'applause' and watches the students get off the piano bench.

"They were incredible. Look at the smiles on their faces." Dad gets teary-eyed. "Wow."

"Dad, we just got here. Can you save the crying until they're all done?" Yaya signs teasingly.

I smile at my father. He's looking neat and spiffy in a black tux with a bow tie. He and mom make a beautiful pair.

Sheila mounts the stage, doing her work as the host. A vision of hotness trails her, walking up to the stage like a famous model or actor about to receive an award.

Sazuki.

He's carrying two bouquets, wearing a small, warm smile on his lips. He hands the children their flowers individually and signs 'congratulations' to them.

Holy crap.

I'm going to implode with the force of the asteroid that decimated the dinosaurs.

Why can't I breathe?

I knew Sazuki would be here, but I didn't expect how much he would affect me. He's so gorgeous that it makes my heart quiver.

All the memories of our time together working, dating, and loving each other bangs around in my head. He looks untouchable up there. Like someone who would never, ever fit in my world.

I stop and stare so hard that my dad has to poke me in the side to get my attention.

"Sweetheart, you okay?"

"Yeah." I blink rapidly. "I'll go prepare for my performance."

"Break a leg," Yaya signs.

I smile shakily.

Sazuki and Sheila walk off the stage. His tuxedo is a classic navy blue with black lapels. The way his trousers taper down to his ankles and reveals his expensive black loafers is subtle and sophisticated.

I want to run to him so badly that I physically tremble with the need.

I've completely lost my mind.

His eyes burn like twin coals when he searches the crowd on his way down the stairs. I avert my gaze before I get a frantic mental picture of the life we could have had if we weren't both so stubborn.

Ryotaro Sazuki is stunning, princely, and painfully forbidden.

Drawn by a feeling I can't name, I glance at Sazuki again and find him standing frozen at the bottom of the stairs. His vivid brown eyes spear right through me.

My lips part. Heat burns my cheeks.

Sheila, who was coming off the stage behind him, taps his shoulder and says something, probably along the lines of 'why are you blocking the stairs?' Sazuki goes back into motion and I release a breath.

I can't tell what his expression meant.

Is he mad? Happy? Annoyed?

"There you are," one of the admin from the office grabs me. "We were about to call you."

"Sorry I'm late."

She waves away the excuse. "You're up after this performance. Come with me."

She leads me backstage. It's similar to the chaos of Niko's school performance except it's much quieter. Parents and teachers are chatting with the kids via sign language. Despite the quiet, there's a similar level of excitement in the air.

I sit in the corner and tuck my chin against my chest. What feels like a second later, someone motions to me.

I rise nervously.

Just get up there and perform like no one's watching.

My heels feel unstable as I take short steps through the wings. The lights are harsh on my face.

Weird.

It's not until you're in the spotlight that you feel the heat.

I ignore everyone and take my seat around the piano. This is my second live performance since the Belle's Beauty gala when I met Sazuki.

I'm playing the same song.

Will he notice? Will he understand?

I push those thoughts from my mind and focus on the notes. The song is poignant. Tender. Fraught with love.

My head bows over the piano and I play with my eyes closed, focusing on nothing but the music and conveying the feeling to the audience.

A disturbance to my right pulls me out of the zone.

I glance up and notice a line of beefy Asian security guards climbing up the stairs and heading right for me.

My fingers freeze on the piano.

Not again.

Akira is at the head of the line. She and the others form a circle, their backs to me.

I hear the murmurs and gasps of the onlookers, but I'm too

busy trying not to hyperventilate.

Especially when Sazuki enters the circle.

I lift my head to look at him, hardly believing my eyes.

"What are you doing?" I whisper.

"Going after what I want," he says.

Shock climbs up my throat, fighting for dominance against the heat that's surging through my veins.

"In front of everyone?"

"Technically, it is just us here."

"Sazuki…" I can't believe he'd disrupt the foundation's opening night for *me*.

Our eyes lock.

Mine fill with tears.

His brim with quiet determination.

The bouncers standing around us don't make a single move. From beyond the circle, I hear a voice that sounds suspiciously like Vanya's encouraging everyone to get a drink.

Sazuki kneels in front of me.

"I'm not ready to get married," I blurt.

His eyes twinkle at me. His dimples pop out in full force.

"Give me your hand," he says.

I wince and offer it to him.

"Have you heard of the Legend of the Red String?" Sazuki asks, holding up a thin red thread.

"Um, no," I squeak.

I'm feeling lightheaded.

If he doesn't hurry this along, I'm going to pass out in his arms.

"According to the myth, everyone has an invisible red string tied to their little finger. This string will lead you to the one with whom you will make history."

He places the string around my finger and ties it gently.

My breath stalls.

I bend over, unable to keep upright.

Is this really happening?

Sazuki stares up at me. His hair is brushed back in a dashing style. Light bounces against his sleek black mane before meeting a violent end as it cuts against his sharp jawline.

"My thread ends with you." He lifts his hand and I notice that the tie is already bound around his pinky finger. "It was tangled and stretched before, but it led me to you. It will always end with you. This is my promise."

With a relieved sob, I fling myself at him, wrapping my arms around his neck. He almost falls on his back, but he manages to grip the piano bench and stay upright.

"That was so nice," I sob. "I didn't expect you to be so romantic."

He rubs my back and it's warm. I melt into him, reveling in the *rightness* of having him close to me.

But I push him away quickly.

"As much as I love this, people are here for the foundation. Not for us."

"Indeed." He winks. "They are here for us too."

"What?"

"Let us finish the song. Together."

To my surprise, Sazuki sits on the bench beside me.

The bouncers fall away, disappearing into the wings.

Someone shuts off the lights.

A spotlight appears on us.

"Miss Williams," Sazuki says, gesturing to the piano.

I focus on him, ignoring the flashes of the cameras, the murmur of the crowd, and the excited squeals of Kenya, Vanya, Sunny and Dawn, who have somehow migrated closer to the stage.

Together, Sazuki and I play.

In tandem.

Our hearts beating as one.

And our eyes focused on each other.

When it ends, the room is silent.

I look out and see my mom and dad, wiping tears from their eyes.

Yaya is holding Niko's hand. Both of them are beaming at me.

The applause starts slowly.

Then it gains speed until it fills up the entire room.

Sazuki and I take a bow, our hands still joined.

When we walk down the stage together, Niko rushes up to us.

She gives me a hug and signs, "I missed you."

"I missed you too."

A stunned Sheila takes the stage. "Um… well, that was an interesting performance."

I wrap my free arm around Niko, my heart swelling with love and my eyes turning misty. If I hadn't met Niko, then I probably wouldn't have given Sazuki a minute of my time.

I press a kiss to her forehead.

The reporters take pictures as we walk away.

I lean in to whisper, "Are you okay with them snapping photos of us?"

"Their cameras will be confiscated when they leave," he whispers back.

I look up at him and grin, falling a little harder in love with him than I thought was possible.

His eyes turn heated. "Keep watching me like that, Miss Williams, and you will not make it through the rest of the night in that dress."

"Hey," I cover Niko's ears, "children are present."

He gives me a wicked grin.

We get to the back of the room and my parents converge on us.

Dad shakes Sazuki's hand.

Yaya signs, "I knew you were up to something when you insisted I bring mom and dad to the gala."

"Thank you for joining us tonight," he tells her.

Mom signs, "Your daughter is beautiful."

Sazuki smiles down at Niko's head.

The little girl grins in return.

Unfortunately, the family time doesn't last long. Someone calls Sazuki away and I'm yanked along thanks to the string on my finger.

After about five minutes of networking, I'm tapped out.

"Sazuki," I lift our hands, "I love the metaphors and everything. Really. I do. But can we keep the whole 'joined together forever' thing at a figurative level now?"

He shakes his head. "You will be stuck to me all night. It is your punishment for trying to quit the foundation and drop out of school."

"Drop out of school?" My jaw slackens. "Who told you that?"

His eyebrows arch.

"I was going to quit the foundation and start teaching deaf students privately, but I wasn't going to drop out of school. Are you kidding? Do you know how hard I've worked?" I chuckle. "At the start of your little scheme to get my help, I had the dean draft up an agreement that I would perform in the end-of-year showcase if my internship fell through. I planned on reminding him of that agreement."

"Solid plan." He looks impressed. "You are very smart, Miss Williams."

I swat at him.

He takes something out of his pocket and wraps it around my wrist.

I gasp when I see the red bracelet.

"There." He clasps it for me. "That way, we will always be connected."

"Mr. Sazuki!" Someone pulls him away to make the closing remarks.

I watch him cut through the crowd and take the mike to give a long list of thank yous, first to his family, to Adam and then finally to all the instructors.

His eyes meet mine as he says, "I could not have done this without you."

My smile stretches across my face.

"I love you," I sign.

He steps back and motions, "Always."

EPILOGUE

SAZUKI

THREE MONTHS LATER

"Must we attend Adam's birthday party?" I frown.

"He would be very hurt if he knew you were complaining about going," Dejonae says from my bathroom.

"The invitation was for appearances' sake. He knows me well enough not to expect me to go." I study the MTB update reports on my tablet. The reception was stronger than I anticipated. We might need to manufacture our next batch overseas to keep the cost low.

"What do you have against Adam's birthday party?"

I huff. "I am tapped out, Dejonae. We attended your family's intimate graduation dinner. After that, Vanya and Hadyn threw you a 'graduation bash'. Now, Adam requires my company? I cannot. I am partied out."

"This is the last party I'll drag you to for the next week, okay?"

Dejonae patters into view, looking like an angel descended from heaven with her smooth dark skin, sparkling eyes and sultry smile. Two different gowns are held up in front of her. "Now stop complaining and tell me which looks better on me. Yaya wanted me to try one of the dresses she's advertising for."

"You'd look stunning in both," I say firmly.

A text arrives.

It is from Akira, letting me know that Niko got to Max and Dawn Stinton's place safely. She and Beth have arranged for another piano lesson, but as is the case in this group, the boys and Belle refuse to be left out.

Now, my daughter has an academy of her own.

I text a quick reply.

Dejonae stomps toward me. "You didn't even look up."

"I don't need to." I glance over her. "You will always be the most beautiful woman in the world to me."

She rolls her eyes, but a pleased smile spreads across her face.

I set my tablet aside and give her the attention she deserves. "Very well." I wrap my hands around her waist and drive her into me. "Let me see. I like the black one."

"Sazuki, you're wrinkling the gowns," she scolds when I hug her.

I finesse the hangars from her hands and drape her clothes gently on the bed. Returning my arms to her waist, I press my face against her chest.

She is soft and smells like a fragrant flower field.

I slide my palms against her thighs, delighting in the feel of silk and flesh.

"Mm-mm." She tries to resist me. "We don't have time for this."

"Time for what?" I cannot concentrate on her face. Dejonae is wearing a sexy little slip with lace along the top and thin straps. Dark brown skin supple enough to bite tempts me.

"Don't give me that look, Sazuki."

"What look?" I moan, tugging her on top of my lap.

She straddles my waist, her dress riding high and exposing her lace undergarments. The friction of her body against my pants rips a groan from me.

How can I have her walking around my bedroom in this strip of clothing and *not* touch her?

She pops a soft, teasing kiss on my lips, plants her hands on my chest and pushes out of my arms.

I groan again, but she has no mercy.

"Go to Adam's party with me and we can continue this later."

"If I don't?" I ask.

She arches a brow. "Do you want to test me?"

I do not.

Dejonae's negotiation skills are quite sharp, as proven by the salary she demanded when I offered her a permanent position at the foundation.

She disappears into the bathroom. I am forced to cool my passion by pacing the bedroom and doing a few push ups.

"By the way," Dejonae's voice echoes from the bathroom, "Ashanti said to tell you she'd be back for a quick visit this weekend."

"Ah." I make a note on my tablet.

After I clarified our relationship, Ashanti returned to her singing job on the cruise ship. Since then, she has kept her distance from me.

However, she and Dejonae made a small truce for Niko's sake. The two speak on occasion when it pertains to our daughter.

I doubt we will be having a big family dinner any time soon, but at least there seems to be no obvious animosity.

Or perhaps, Dejonae is showing more restraint than I have given her credit for.

Either way, I am determined to ease her mind by assuring her that my heart belongs to her only. My hope is that, when we *do* have to interact with Ashanti, she will be so confident in my love for her that nothing Ashanti does or says can upset her.

"We have that conference next week, but since Ashanti will be here, I'll ask Sheila to attend instead of me," Dejonae says.

"Sheila?" My head lurches up. "You convinced her to stay?"

After Sheila discovered that Dejonae and I were together, she threatened to leave the foundation. No one could get her to change her mind.

"I did," Dejonae says from the bathroom. "She thought that, because of our bad blood, I'd take my anger out on her."

"You could have done that many months ago."

"Yes, but now I'm openly dating the boss and on everyone's good side."

She has a point.

I found out Dejonae had been receiving harsh treatment from the staff. They still held her responsible for the scandal with the reporter. When it was brought to my attention, I scolded Dejonae for not telling me. And then I called a meeting, played the audio in which Miss Beverly used a slur against our students and clarified everything.

"I'll ask Jordan to go with her. Maybe those two can get a little romantic."

"As long as your ex is not getting romantic with... you." My voice slows to a stop when Dejonae walks out of the bathroom in a stunning black crop top with long sleeves, jeans and heels.

"What do you think?" She does a little spin, causing her curls to flail around her. "I wasn't feeling any of the dresses."

"Beautiful." I approach her for a kiss.

She glances at her watch and cringes. "Sazuki, we have to leave now."

I wrap my fingers around her wrists when she tries to dart away. Placing one hand against her back and the other on her cheek, I tilt her head and kiss her deeply.

It is her fault I am so addicted.

She turned a cold, ruthless man who was set in his ways into someone who cannot live without her.

There are consequences for that.

I break off and then kiss her forehead. "*Now* we can leave."

Traffic is light and we arrive on time at Adam's large, country-style cabin nestled in the center of an impressive acreage.

We are the only guests there.

Nova greets us with a strained smile.

Adam is with her as well, drinking beer from a red cup.

"I thought the party would be bigger than this," Dejonae says.

"We thought we'd keep it small. Just members of the MTB team."

"Okay." I agree easily.

I had not been looking forward to mingling with others and wasting time making polite conversation. This is much better.

After an hour of drinking and eating, Nova presents Adam with his birthday gifts. The last one she offers to him is an envelope.

Dejonae leans forward.

I rub her back and look on with interest too, wondering if Nova signed him a check. It seems like her style.

"This is my resignation letter," Nova says, sliding the envelope over to a wide-eyed Adam.

Dejonae clutches my hand and gives me an astonished look.

I stare at her in confusion.

The room falls into tense silence.

What on earth is happening?

"Is this a joke?" Adam croaks.

"I'm sorry," Nova says, her eyes on the ground.

"What the hell is the meaning of this?" Adam's voice trembles.

The party horn that had been halfway to Dejonae's lips falls to her lap.

Dejonae gives me a panicked glance. She signs, "What do we do?"

I shake my head in return.

The silence stretches so thinly that I fear it will snap at any second.

At that moment, the doorbell rings.

Adam and Nova share a charged look.

I motion to Dejonae. Silently, we rise and head to the door. It does not seem like Adam and Nova are in any position to move at the moment.

I expect the person outside to be another guest or a delivery man.

Instead, there is a child around the age of twelve.

"Are you Adam Harrison?" he asks in a thin voice.

"No, sweetie." Dejonae drops to the child's level. "Why are you looking for Adam?"

My eyes dart behind the child to the empty driveway. There are no adults around.

Dejonae notices at the same time and asks, "How did you get here? Where are your parents?"

An uneasy feeling flows through me.

"Adam," I call darkly, sensing that this is a serious matter.

Adam stomps to the door, his eyes narrowed and a vein bulging in his neck. His gaze falls on the little boy. Rather than brighten with recognition, he seems frustrated.

"Look, kid," he says brusquely, "I'm not buying anything."

"I'm not here to sell anything," the child answers.

"What are you here for then, sweetie?" Dejonae asks, her voice kind and sweet.

Nova draws near to the door. She is peeking over Dejonae's shoulders to see what is going on.

"I'm here for him." The child points at Adam.

Adam blanches. "Me?"

The boy nods.

"Why, hun?" Dejonae asks.

"Because," the boy chews on his bottom lip and then blurts, "because he's my dad."

***

Thank you for reading *Prickly Romance*. If you enjoyed this novel, you'll also enjoy Adam and Nova's story.
Grab **BOSSY ROMANCE** at **niaarthurs.com/books**.

Want to spend more time with Sazuki, Dejonae and Niko? Get an exclusive epilogue by signing up to my mailing list at **niaarthurs.com/subscribe**.

BOSSY ROMANCE
EXCERPT

BOSSY ROMANCE
CHAPTER ONE

NOVA

"You should drink something." A bottle of water magically appears in front of me.

"Should you be back here right now? It's almost time for your presentation."

Tan knuckles rap against the table. "No arguing. You've been on your feet for three hours straight and I haven't seen you take a sip of anything. I'm not moving from here until you hydrate, darlin'."

I roll my eyes—privately—before grabbing the water and glancing up at my boss, Adam Harrison.

'Drop-dead gorgeous' is a phrase that's been thrown around to describe him, so I feel comfortable using the term.

Objectively, of course.

Adam is tall, with broad shoulders, big brown eyes, a chiseled jawline, dark hair that's a little curly, and a warm smile that's never far from his face. As usual, he's wearing a tight T-shirt with his pecs straining against the cotton. Jeans and his favorite cowboy boots complete the look.

His vivid brown eyes find mine and linger, waiting until I've finished with the water before he takes it and returns the cap.

He's been working hard lately. I can tell by the dark circles under his eyes. Even looking a little more tired than usual, he's still every bit the hunky country boy-next-door.

Realizing that I'm staring, I avert my gaze and try to get my thoughts back in order.

Adam grabs a napkin and swipes it against my bottom lip. "So messy."

My heart does a little pitter-patter.

I move my head back. "You should be out front."

"In a minute." Adam sits on the edge of the table, his back muscles rolling like well-oiled drums. The light from the stage creeps into the private room, throwing his profile into shadows.

"You okay?" I ask.

"I'm trying to dial back on my excitement. If I go on a tangent, that won't be good for anyone."

"Just do what we practiced. You'll be fine."

"That's a given." He leans toward me and cocks his head to the side. "You're way more intimidating than any of those judges."

He smiles and I...

I don't know what's wrong with me, but I keep getting shocked by how attractive my boss is.

I never used to notice. At least, not in a way that I'd find distracting.

Of course I've always *known* Adam Harrison was gorgeous.

Based on social cues alone, it was pretty cut-and-dry. Women batting their lashes, hands clinging to his biceps, voices turning high-pitched and giggling—there's so much giggling whenever Adam opens his mouth.

Again. Understandable. That Southern drawl of his is more dangerous than a snake charmer.

I know my boss is gorgeous.

I *know*.

But it's been bothering me how that knowledge keeps affecting me more and more.

Applause breaks out from the crowd. I turn my head toward the conference room, slip my feet back into my pumps and rise.

Adam stands with me. "I guess I'm up next."

"Do you have—"

"The presentation notes organized according to your cute little color-coded system? Yes." He reaches into his back pocket and pulls out the index card binders that I like to use. "Right here. In fact, I re-organized them last night to make the flow better."

I narrow my eyes. *Is he getting cheeky?* "I see you didn't need my help."

"I didn't want to bother you."

I look at him for a few seconds. "What do you have planned?"

"Nothing."

He so does.

I sigh because he's the boss and it doesn't really matter. Whatever he announces, I can make it work. "Remember to—"

"I know."

"Do you?"

"I do," he says, his gaze intent on mine.

My chest rises and falls on a shaky breath. I'm nervous for him. Not because I think he'll fail but because I know how much doing well means to him.

Without another word, I jut my chin at the door.

Adam grabs a lanyard from the table, slides it over his head and strides confidently toward the lights of the main room. I stay back a few minutes and then follow in the same direction.

Vision Tech banners are strung all around the conference room, proudly proclaiming the company sponsorship. This is the first round of the competition and the excitement is high.

Long tables hold the most unique and cutting-edge inventions of the year. Holo-boards reveal summaries of the devices as well as the headshots of up-and-coming inventors.

Adam is already at his table. The cameras are pointed at him, sending footage of his face to the giant screen on the stage.

He looks calm and confident in front of the cameras. It's

baffling why he refuses to do a single magazine photoshoot or interview. Not only would it boost exposure for Vision Tech, but he would be an ace at it.

"One of the issues we found when creating the MTB," Adam says, pointing to the headband device that allows deaf music students to 'experience' the vibration of an instrument, "is battery life. The technology of our time still has severe restrictions on energy usage. Sorry to that little bunny, but after a while, energy dies out."

Chuckles break through the room.

A camera flashes.

They're eating this up.

Adam's brown eyes slide over the crowd. "Although we settled on removable batteries, I felt intense dissatisfaction. There had to be another way to improve the energy source. I just had to find it."

The other inventors start bobbing their heads. They're all driven by that primal sense of wanting more, knowing there's a different way, a *better* way to do something, and fighting tirelessly to make that vision in their heads a reality.

Working with Adam forced me to appreciate a person's 'charge into the unknown' spirit. Even if that run-first, figure-it-out-later mentality is why so many inventors are broke.

"That's why I went back to the drawing board and created the world's smallest, self-sustaining, non-nuclear battery."

Oohs break out in the room.

I don't even bat an eyelash.

"What's unique about this battery is that it's powered by movement." Adam lifts the invention to show it off. "And you might say that kinetic batteries have been around for a while, but I would remind you that there's a reason they haven't taken off yet. The amount of kinetic energy a human body alone can create is not enough to power a calculator. Unless you can find a way to harness and multiply that energy."

Another round of 'oohs' break out.

I glance at the judges. They're leaning forward, salivating, eager to pounce from their elevated podiums and get their hands on Adam's invention.

He has them in the palm of his hand.

One of the judges talks into the microphone. "Why does your invention force people to become physically active? Why make the recharging method so inconvenient?"

A crinkle appears above Adam's nose.

He'd been anticipating this question.

"I believe that technology should make our lives better in all ways. Which is why the battery has a mode that functions as normal and one that encourages movement. In other words, if you want to charge it, you don't have to move. However, recharging with movement is the angle we're going to push because that's the part that saves lives."

Applause breaks out.

People are nodding.

Adam's lips curl up. He's trying so hard to be humble, but it's difficult for a man that brilliant to pull it off.

Walking to the left, Adam picks up a water bottle and takes a sip. His eyes find mine in the crowd and he gives me a little smirk.

My heart tightens. I dip my chin in response.

Adam whirls around to face the judges. It's time for his closing statements.

To my surprise, he doesn't say anything more about the batteries. "I thought it was a little boring to only present these batteries to you today." He reaches under the table and lifts a bag.

I immediately tip my chin to the ceiling and sigh in annoyance.

He did not.

"This is a hover-bag." Adam proudly gestures to it. "Powered by the batteries, it hovers above the ground, making transportation a breeze. It can hold up to a hundred pounds of weight and can be stored anywhere." His eyes are glittering in that—well, I call it the 'Mad Hatter' way. "Imagine you're at the airport and you're trying to drag all these heavy bags behind you. With the hover-bag, it's as easy as dragging a basket of flowers."

The crowd seems just as confused as I am.

No one says a word.

Adam grins broadly, glancing around for encouragement before finally pointing his smile at me.

I pull my lips in and shake my head.

He doesn't look disappointed by the restrained reception at all. Clamping his hands together, he announces, "Any questions?"

A bunch of hands go up.

I retreat from the room to prepare for the next segment of the convention. The inventors will enjoy champagne, network, chat and wait for the judges to make their decision.

In the background, I hear Adam droning on about his hover-bag.

Laughter builds in my chest, but I have no idea if it's rooted in amusement or utter despair.

What am I going to do with you, Adam?

"Courtney, Henry," I motion to the two Vision Tech interns, "help me set these tables so catering can bring out the refreshments."

They hurry to follow me and whisper to each other.

"Are all inventors that eccentric?" Henry, a young, college-aged guy who's interning at Vision Tech, mumbles. He wears his hair in a high afro that reminds me of Will Smith in *Fresh Prince.*

I take out my index cards and flip through them, listening keenly to the conversation while I triple check my to-do list.

"That guy wins the competition every year."

"You're kidding."

"Sometimes, his inventions are genius. And sometimes," Courtney shakes her long blond hair out of her face, "they're just stupid."

"Stupid?"

Courtney glances around as if she's scared someone will overhear. "This one time, he invented a spinning knife, fork and spoon. Like… you just press a button and a different utensil pops out."

Henry's eyes widen. "But that's kind of cool though."

"Cool?" Courtney scoffs. "People have been using separate utensils for ages. Inventing another tool to eat with is a total waste of time."

I step in between them to brush out the table cloth. "If it had served a market, then it would have been worth the fuss. The problem is that some of his inventions are commercially viable and others…"

Mentally calculating the surface of the table, I realize that we'll need more room. Thankfully, I'm always prepared for the unexpected.

"Henry, can you bring a few more tables from the storage closet?"

Henry walks off and returns with the tables. He sets it up just in time for the caterers.

I'm too busy running back and forth between the floor crew, the caterers and the management team to keep track of Adam.

It's not until someone taps me on the shoulder that I anticipate coming face-to-face with my boss.

Except it's someone else.

"You're the owner of Vision Tech, right?" A man with greying hair and a pleasant smile motions to me.

"No, I'm not the owner." Although I've been mistaken as such many times.

"The face then? Whenever I see Vision Tech at these things, I'd see you."

"And who exactly is it that's been spying on me?" I arch an eyebrow.

He pulls out a business card. "How impolite of me. Leroy Foster."

I check his card. "Yoon Technologies. You work with renewable energy."

"As well-informed as you are beautiful, I see." He laughs gently. "You're familiar with our work?"

"You've managed to consume most of the commercial market

share in renewable energy and natural resources. I was beginning to think of you as competition."

"There goes my opportunity to wow you with our company slogan."

My lips curl up. "Are you here to scout out our inventors?"

"I heard a rumor that Mr. Harrison's recent invention would have something to do with self-sustaining batteries. I couldn't resist." His eyes twinkle. "Vision Tech throws these conventions just to scoop up the best inventors before the rest of us have a chance. I was determined to get ahead of the game."

My smile blooms a bit more.

Adam walks up to us. His grin is intact, but his eyes are carefully assessing when he sticks a hand out to Leroy. "Hey, man."

"Mr. Harrison," Leroy takes the outstretched hand, "we were just talking about you and your brilliant invention."

"The hover-bag?"

I keep my face intact but, inside, I snort a little.

Leroy's eyes dart to me and back. "Uh, no. The self-sustaining kinetic batteries."

"They're just a little something I threw together," Adam says flippantly.

Leroy gets that shocked look again as if he can't decide if Adam is joking.

He's not.

The man can solve complicated problems before breakfast and then spend all his time coming up with fanciful inventions until midnight.

"Mr. Foster," I gesture to Leroy, "is the CEO of Yoon Technologies, a leader in non-nuclear renewable energy."

"Ah." Adam dips his chin, but he doesn't look that impressed.

Leroy lets out nervous laughter and flashes a business card. "I would love to discuss a research position at our company. I might not be able to match Miss Delaney in beauty, but I can promise you amazing benefits and all the creative freedom you want."

"If you can't even match Miss Delaney's beauty, then why would I want to work with you?" Adam asks.

I furrow my brow and subtly jab him in the stomach.

Adam makes a pained sound and then covers it with a cough.

I smile politely. "Mr. Foster, it's about time for the judges to make their announcement. Why don't I escort you to the front?"

"I'll come with you." Adam sticks close as I lead the way into the atrium.

A few moments later, the MC makes the announcement and the rest of the contestants file in to hear what we all knew—Adam is the winner.

I applaud politely and oversee the doling out of prizes from behind the scenes. The moment the ceremony is over, I call the event company in charge of the after-party.

I'm on that call when Adam finds me again. The conference room is completely empty, the lights shut off and most of the inventions cleared out.

I lift a finger, asking Adam for a moment, and he nods.

"Please make sure no reporters sneak into the after-party. Last year, our latest invention was almost plastered on the front page news. We can't have that again."

"Understood, Ms. Delaney."

"Thank you." I pocket my phone and glance at Adam who has a glass of champagne in each hand.

He extends one of the drinks to me. "Non-alcoholic. I checked."

My fingers wrap around the cold glass and I smile slightly. "Are you donating your prize to the children's home again?"

"Yes." He thinks about it and then adds, "I'll match the prize money. Sister Clarence mentioned they needed a new van to get the kids to school."

I lift my phone and tap out a note.

Adam never keeps his prize money. In fact, he almost acts like it's dirty.

I wish I could share this side of him with the world, but my boss's generosity is another thing he keeps under wraps.

"You didn't seem all that excited about my little surprise," Adam says, noting my expression.

"Vision Tech isn't in the business of creating suitcases."

He laughs. "Hover-bags, Nova. Hover-bags. It's the next big thing."

"Is this one of those situations where I'm expected to humor you or can I be honest and remind you that nobody is asking you to reinvent the wheel."

His eyes glimmer. "People don't know what they want until you give it to them."

"That applies to what they *don't* want too, you know. Sometimes, it takes getting something to realize you don't want that thing at all."

"Pessimist."

"Feel free to lead the marketing campaigns if you're so confident."

He scowls. "You play dirty."

"I'll get you in front of the camera one way or another, Harrison." I take a sip of the champagne. It's bubbly in my throat. "You can't hide who you are forever."

"As long as I have you, I'm not worried about anything."

A strange, strangling sensation fills me.

I glance down. "It's your business, even if I'm running it."

"Nova, I'd prefer to participate in these competitions every year than own the business. You know that."

My smile is strained. I finish off the rest of the champagne. "I saw you talking to the second-place winners. You found our newest engineers?"

"Their robotic arm was brilliant."

I shake my head. "You have a serious thing for robot arms."

"They're cool. What else can I say?"

"I liked them too. I'll offer them positions on Monday and have their lab ready by Wednesday."

"A private lab? You must really like them," Adam says with a grin.

"Medical technology is a booming industry. We need legs in a commercially viable market, especially when our brave and bold leader starts skipping down rabbit holes."

Adam coughs. "Now you're just being mean."

My phone vibrates. I glance down with a smile on my face, but the smile disappears and my entire body goes stiff when I see who's calling.

Lyra.

"Who is it?" Adam asks.

My fingers close over the phone and I turn it so he can't see the screen. "No one. I'll head out now."

"Come with me. I'll take you to the after-party."

"If the contestants see us together—"

"Their first thought will be that I own the company? That's a big leap."

I shake my head delicately. "I'm not going to the after-party."

Adam looks stricken. "Why not? Are you not feeling well?" He moves as if he'll put his hand on my forehead.

I jump back on instinct.

Adam freezes.

My heart pounding, I drum up a polite smile. "There's something I have to take care of. Something... private."

His eyes flash with an emotion I can't name, but he hides it quickly. Flashing me the charming grin that I've seen melt women into literal goo, he nods. "Sure. You worked hard, Nova."

I dip my head and hustle out of the building, calling Lyra back.

She answers with a yawn. "Hey, big *siiiis*. Ready to talk?"

"Where are you?" I ask stiffly.

She gives me directions and I catch a cab to the café.

Lyra is sitting around a booth, eating a burger and a giant plate of fries. She's got her hair closely cropped with the back full of waves. The top is spiky and dyed red and white. Giant hoop earrings with the term 'goochie' in the middle swing along with her head.

"Nova!" She raises a hand and yells so loudly the entire café turns to look. "Girl, over here!"

I cringe a little and slide into the booth across from her.

"Mm." She gives me a head-to-toe scan while sucking on each of her fingers. "Don't you look tidy and *official*. Like those old ladies at the church mama forced us to go to. Remember? The ones with the big hats and the pressed white skirts and the pantyhose… wait a minute. Let me see if you're wearing a pantyhose." She scoots down like a worm and peeps under the table.

I pull my legs back and cross them at the ankles.

"You are!" She bursts out in loud guffaws.

More eyes dart over to us.

Heat flares in my cheeks and I press my fingers together.

"You look like such a *square*, Nova." Lyra grabs three fries at once, dips them into ketchup and pops them into her mouth. When she's done, she wipes her fingers on her cleavage-baring halter top that looks like she fished it out of the trash.

"I sent you all the money I could," I say calmly, holding my head up. "If you're here for—"

"It's not enough."

My eyelashes flutter.

Lyra takes a sip of her soda and talks with her mouth full. "But I ain't worried 'bout that. Can you get me a job?"

"A job?" I choke.

"Yeah. A job at your fancy office. Your boss left the whole thing for you to run, right? I'm sure he won't have a problem."

My nostrils flare, but I keep my tone calm. "What is this about, Lyra? Since when were you interested in engineering?"

"I ain't gotta do that." She speaks with exaggerated head-bobbing. "I can be a secretary or sum'im. Like you."

That feeling I've been having lately—like there's a noose around my neck and it's pulling tight, increases. I take a deep breath and then another. "I'm sorry, Lyra. I can't help you."

"It's because you're ashamed of me, ain't it?" Her eyebrows slash low over stormy brown eyes. "You don't want anyone to know we're sisters." She points an accusing finger. "You think if you talk perfect English and dress like the white folks, they're gonna accept you? Nah, fam. At the end of the day, blood is thicka than anything."

I lift my eyes to the window and think about my to-do-list.

Leroy Foster wants to set up a meeting with Vision Tech to cement future collaborations.

The top-ten winners from the competition today will receive free access to parts and equipment for next year's competition. I need to talk to the manufacturing companies to oversee that process.

Adam has a meeting with the board and, if he plans on pitching the hover-bag, I need to prep the board for that. They rarely welcome his outlandish ideas with open arms…

Lyra taps a long, triangle-shaped nail on the table. "Hello? Are you listening to me?"

I blink slowly and my sister comes back into focus.

Lyra flings herself against the booth. She's slim and athletic. Her skin is pure brown and most of it is on display, including her chest which is jiggling generously. "Are you going to get me the job or not?"

"I can help you get a job at another company. Not Vision Tech."

"Why not?" Lyra whines.

I grab my purse and rise steadily. "I don't know what's going on with you, Lyra, but I've helped you as much as I can. Don't call me again unless it's an emergency."

"Sell-out," she spits under her breath.

Prickles of anger skate up my skin, but I step around the table and catch a cab home.

On the ride, I unbutton my blouse and press my face against the cool glass of the window.

The pulling at my throat keeps getting worse.

The noose is tightening. Tightening. Tightening.

And seeing Jax leaning against my door when I get home twenty minutes later only makes the pressure worse.

"Did we have a date tonight?" I ask him, noticing the flowers and the bottle of wine in his grip.

It's a rhetorical question. I wouldn't have forgotten a date. It would have gone into my calendar and I would have had several reminders on my phone.

Plus, I wouldn't have scheduled a date with Jax on the day of the convention.

"No." Jax saunters toward me, his smile bright against his dark-chocolate face. He's wearing a pressed navy suit, bright red tie and shiny loafers, "But I wanted to surprise you."

Color me surprised.

"Can I come in?" Jax motions to my door.

I think about shooing him away, but I realize I shouldn't be stand-offish. I promised myself that I would be more open to love this time.

There's absolutely nothing wrong with Jax and I've looked. Trust me. If there's anything I can do, it's sniff out the flaws in men. But Jax is a genuinely good guy with a good job and family values. Plus he's tall and handsome. Basically everything I could want in a man.

And it's not like I'm getting any younger.

I let him into my apartment and kick off my heels. He glances around, looking impressed by the open floor plan, the sleek, minimalist furniture, and the sprawling kitchen that I hardly use.

"I'm going to change and be right back," I tell him.

He nods.

I slip into my bedroom and close the door, leaning against it to catch my breath.

Be present in the moment, Nova.

As I take off each of my clothes, I shed thoughts of Lyra, the company and everything else from my mind. One by one, I lay them in the hamper and pull on a fresh T-shirt.

I'm feeling a lot more peaceful when I return to Jax.

He's sitting in the living room, his tie loose and his eyes dewy and brown. I know exactly what he has in mind before he even opens his mouth.

"Wine?" he asks, gesturing to the coffee table. I notice he went ahead and took my wine glasses.

"You know I don't drink, Jax."

"Come on. Just one glass."

Don't overthink this, Nova.

We've been meeting for about six months now, texting each other when we have the time and going out occasionally. It's not like he's a stranger.

Jax hands me a glass and, when our fingers brush, I'm reminded of the moment when Adam handed me champagne.

Shaking my head, I take a sip and relax into the sofa.

"Long day?" Jax asks.

I nod.

He eases closer to me. "Me too. We'll have to take our case to trial. The boss is on my back about it."

I make a sound of consolation.

Jax rubs my shoulder, his thumb caressing the sleeve of my T-shirt. "Today, when I was exhausted and irritated, all I could think about was you. *What's Nova doing tonight? I wonder if she'd be up for dinner.*"

My lips curve up. I drain the rest of the wine.

Jax takes the empty glass from me with a pleased smile as if I'm a child who just took all their medicine. He closes the distance between us and kisses me slowly. At first, the only parts of us that are touching are our lips.

And then his hands rise to my face and he caresses my cheek while his kiss gets rougher.

My heart starts beating fast, but I tell myself I'm enjoying this. This is great. I'm having a wonderful time with a wonderful man.

Jax grazes his fingers under the back of my head, cupping my long braids. I'm starting to feel extremely hot, but it's not in the way I think I'm supposed to—the kind of heat where I want to get out of my clothes or want him out of his.

This is the kind of heat where I want to get out of my own skin, out of my own head. Like I'm being burned, my feet dragged through a fire that I can't see.

As Jax's kisses become less controlled, his hands find the hem of his shirt. He pauses long enough to yank the shirt over his head, but that brief moment of disconnect makes me feel better.

I don't have time to seek out why that is before he's on top of me again, his kiss more intense and his hands dragging off my jeans and panties.

Suddenly, it's all getting very real, very fast.

Jax lowers his head and kisses his way down my thighs. I squirm away, a hand on his shoulder to stop him.

He glances up, his eyes full of eagerness. "Baby, don't worry. I brought protection."

Of course he did.

He came over to my apartment with roses and wine… and condoms.

Because he'd already decided that tonight was the night. He'd invested six months and now it was time to reap the return on his investment.

I don't know why that annoys me.

Jax pushes me into the sofa, his weight smothering me. "Relax, Nova."

The instruction is followed by a kiss to my mouth and a caress of my thigh. His touch is invasive.

Discomfort boils in my gut.

I don't know why Jax groping me makes me want to go take a bath and apologize to…

Apologize to whom?

I gulp in air, but the more I inhale, the harder it is to breathe.

Hands reaching for his naked shoulders, I push Jax off and quickly step into my panties.

He gives me a confused expression, his eyes dazed. "What are you doing?"

"I can't. I'm sorry." I grab my pants and pull those on too. They're stretchy yoga pants, although I don't do yoga at all.

Jax's lips turn firm. Brown eyes narrowing until he's squinting at my TV, he grumbles, "Are you not into me?"

"No, I think you're great, but…" I cover my torso with my hands, trembling.

"They warned me about you," Jax mutters, shaking his head and laughing bitterly. "They told me you had this weird relationship with one of your inventors."

"What are you talking about?"

"Harrison." His eyes lift and he points an accusing gaze on me. "I heard you two are close."

"Close?" I blink rapidly.

"Are you two screwing?"

My heart drops to my toes. The mere suggestion is… it's… insane.

"You know what? Forget this? I don't need this at all." Jax roughly grabs his shirt, his car keys and his flowers. A short second later, my front door slams shut.

Silence.

I stare at the place where the flowers had been and then I ease forward, grab the wine he left behind and drink it straight from the bottle. Minutes later, I throw my guts up in the bathroom. *As if I needed more proof that liquor and I don't mix.*

When I'm finished, I sink against the toilet. My fingers come up to massage my throat. The noose around my neck is starting to ease, not because anything's truly changed but because Jax's words shook something loose from my heart.

I think I might know why I've felt so trapped lately.

And I think I might know a way to be free.

* * *

READY TO ENJOY the rest of Adam and Nova's romance? Visit **niaarthurs.com/books**

ALSO BY NIA ARTHURS

Billionaire Dads Series

Grumpy Romance

Surly Romance

Cocky Romance

Cheeky Romance

Prickly Romance

Bossy Romance

Grudging Hearts Series

Forever Loving You

Forever Craving You

Forever Claiming You

Make It Marriage Series

Be My Always

Be My Darling

Be My Lady (A Make It Marriage Short)

Be My Wife

Be My Hope

Be My Bride

Be My Compass

Be My Reason

Be My Baby

Be My Revenge

DOC EXCLUSIVES

Respect Me: Part I

Respect Me: Part II

Cover Me

Fragile Vows

Value Me

Value Me II

The Love Repair Series

Earn Me

Deserve Me

Choose Me

Trust Me

Show Me

Promise Me

Sign up for the Nia Arthurs mailing list at niaarthurs.com/subscribe

Printed in Great Britain
by Amazon